PRAISE FOR *THE DAMNED*

"A kind of three-way mash-up of horror fiction, war novel and ecclesiastical thriller... works surprisingly well"   *Daily Mail*

"The historical elements are fascinating, as is the author's twist on the werewolf mythos... the brooding, conflicted Tacit is the most compelling element... will leave readers looking forward to the next installment"

Publishers Weekly

"Allegorical and erudite, this imaginative first volume establishes a world, a monolithic villain, and a catapult for Tacit and Isabella, Sandrine and Frost to confront the evil lurking in the volumes to come"   *Kirkus*

"Richardson can definitely write a rattling good tale, with page-turning suspense that never slows down... Poldek Tacit, a violent but oddly honorable version of Graham Greene's 'whisky priest', is a perfect fit in this world gone mad"   *Kingdom Books*

"The atmosphere drips with dark fear of the unknown and, eventually, the unknown's bloody leavings. This is definitely not one for the squeamish"

Bookbag

"Engaging, intense and full of visceral descriptions... a sublime work of dark fiction meets mystery, meets horror that recalls the likes of *Anno Dracula*, *Hellsing* and *Constantine*, with a hint of *Fight Club*"   *Intravenous*

"Morally complex and fast paced, this is a gripping work of dark fiction"

Ginger Nuts of Horror

"A fascinating combination of alternate history, church murder mystery, and horror thriller all wrapped up in a nice dark fiction package"

Jim Riordan, *Read This*, Peabody Institute Library

"Fantastic... the best evocation of the First World War I have yet read. You really can smell the cordite. Better than *Bird Song*. The author's prose is elegant and visceral"   Ed Davey, author of *Foretold by Thunder* and *The Napoleon Complex*

"Werewolves meet WWI history horror mash-up. Great brooding protagonist and razor-sharp historical detail'

Tom Bromley, author of *Dead on Arrival*

TARN RICHARDSON grew up a fan of J. R. R. Tolkien near Taunton in Somerset, in a remote house rumoured to be haunted. He has been a copywriter, written mystery murder dinner party games and worked in digital media for over twenty years. He is the author of The Darkest Hand trilogy, comprising *The Damned*, *The Fallen*, *The Risen* and the eBook prequel *The Hunted*, all published by Duckworth. He lives near Salisbury.

"The Darkest Hand has a remarkably original premise and the individual books are driven by some damn fine characters... Poldek Tacit is an excellent creation. So much back-story and presence... a truly hard-assed priest. The series is an addictive read, with enough blood, battles and violence to satisfy even the most ardent horror fan. Frenetic, gore-soaked, and hugely enjoyable"

David Moody, author of *Autumn* and *Hater*

THE RISEN

TARN RICHARDSON

Duckworth Overlook

First published in 2017 by Duckworth Overlook

30 Calvin Street
London E1 6NW
info@duckworth-publishers.co.uk
www.ducknet.co.uk
For bulk and special sales, please contact sales@duckworth-publishers.co.uk

A catalogue record for this book is available from the British Library

9780715651704

Typeset by Tetragon, London
Printed and bound in Great Britain by Clays Ltd

1 3 5 7 9 10 8 6 4 2

For my parents,
who helped make me a writer.

*The beast that you saw is about to rise from
the bottomless pit and go to destruction.*

REVELATION 17:8

PROLOGUE

A sheet of skin came away in the sailor's hand from the rotting corpse they had pulled out of the sea. Almost immediately, bluebottles settled and began to search the spoiled bleeding husk. A crew member of the small coastal battleship, gunmetal grey and shrouded in smoke between the glistening languid waves, tried to chase the fat greedy things away, but in the heat and stink on the ship's deck, he quickly realised the futility of the exercise. Someone suggested they throw the stinking body back, the smell alone enough to turn their sea-hardened stomachs.

But then the corpse shuddered and a groan rattled out of him.

Against the heat of the deck, his exposed flesh had begun to sear and cook, the smell coming off him like salted pork. Someone cursed, that anything could look like the charred and sodden lump of meat and still live was a miracle.

"Get him inside," the ship's Captain called, a haggard-looking man with too many years at sea behind him. Four sailors took the end of each pole and carried the body into the squalid heat of the interior, coal fumes and oil caught up with the incessant grind of the engines. "Get that off my boat," said the Captain, pointing at the stinking raft of wood upon which the wretched man had been found. Two of the crew took hold of it and flung it overboard, wiping their hands surreptitiously on their greasy uniforms before following the Captain inside.

The crew had set the pallet, and the victim it held, down on a table in the first available cabin they could find, each of the bearers pleased no longer to be carrying such a heavy burden. Ravaged by time and tides, the man plucked from the Adriatic was huge, broad and heavy-set.

Faint amber light lit the worn face of the Captain as he pulled on his cigarette again and squinted at the figure through the scribble of smoke.

About him, sweaty and dirty sailors jostled and pushed for a better view of the body lying still on the table.

"Are you sure he's not dead, Captain?" someone asked.

"He's not dead," the Captain replied, the top button of his jacket open to give a little relief from the heat inside the ship. The bristle on his top lip glistened in the closeness of the chamber. "But how he's not dead, I don't know." He swallowed, and realised then how dry his throat had become, wiping at the salty trails of sweat on his cheeks and neck with the back of a hand. And then something caught his eye and he leaned forward, teasing the man's ravaged clothing aside to reveal a mottled coat of chain mail beneath, its scales like those of a fish, caught in the dull light of the room.

"Who the hell is he?" someone asked. "Who wears stuff like this?"

"An Italian sniper?" another suggested, and the seamen's hands curled into tight fists. They all knew of snipers, the most despised of the enemy they faced, sharpshooters who wore plate mail to protect themselves from enemy fire when entrenched at their posts. But such armour was always crudely forged and constructed from heavy plates of iron. This chain mail had been delicately pieced together and hammered impenetrable ring by ring. No sniper was ever worth such effort in the factories of either the Italian or the Austro-Hungarian war machine.

The Captain searched him further, his interest piqued. Moments later he found a crucifix hooked into the tattered remains of a pocket.

"A crucifix?" the ship's bosun asked, amazed at the find. "Armour? A crucifix? What is he then? A knight?"

"A man of God, eh?" a crewman replied, and he rested his chin in his grimy fingers.

"Maybe that was what saved him? His faith?" said another sailor, through a mouth missing most of its teeth.

The Captain's hand worked deeper into the open folds of his own jacket, coming to rest against his heart. He could feel its slow reassuring beat pulse through his fingers. "Whoever he is, days at sea, weeks maybe, couldn't kill him. Perhaps God was looking down on him kindly? He's one tough bastard, that's for sure. He's seen action, and plenty of it. Look at the scars on him." He waved a hand absently over the bruised and bloodshot skin. The assembly of people in the room nodded in agreement, as if they too had noticed the bullet wounds which riddled his ravaged flesh, some ancient, others inflicted more recently.

"No stranger to trouble," someone said.

"He's seen action, but for which side?" asked the bosun.

"If he's Italian, we should put a bullet in his head and throw him back into the sea," said the ship's chief steward. He signed with his thumb across his throat.

"We'll know when he speaks," replied the Captain, in a more measured tone.

"*If* he ever speaks," someone muttered. "He doesn't look like he is long for this world."

"He must have been in the sea for weeks."

"Ten krone he won't make it till morning," one of the sailors said.

"One tough bastard," another replied, "to have lasted so long, drifting in the Adriatic, clutching hold of nothing but that piece of wood."

"He won't make it," the sailor answered knowingly. "I've seen what being stranded at sea does to a man." He looked about the crowd of faces staring intently at the body, wishing they would look at him instead. "Makes you sick, not just in your flesh but in your head too. Drives a man mad, to be cast away, with nothing but the ocean, the gulls and your own demons for company."

"Perhaps he was mad before he went into the water?" someone croaked. "Perhaps he was already consumed by his own demons?"

"Who wants to take that bet?" asked the sailor.

But the Captain shook his head, turning his eyes on the swarthy man who had made the offer. "After all you've heard and seen, you still want to throw away your earnings?" He looked back at the still body on the stretcher. "No," he said, shaking his head, "a man like this, that's not someone you bet against. This is a man who wants to live. This is a man who *has* to live."

PART ONE

"Yea, I shall return with the tide."

KHALIL GIBRAN, *THE PROPHET*

ONE

JULY, 1917. UZHOK. UKRAINE.

It was snowing ashes.

Great clumps of cinders were falling from a starless black heaven, churning the mud and gravel of the sodden track down which the man ran to a grey glassy paste. The Russian soldiers had lit fires at the front line, twenty miles to the east, fires of revolution to match the fires burning in the squares of St Petersburg, fires of solidarity for their Red comrades in the north. Fires of change.

Each of the infernos had risen to become a monstrous firestorm, over forty feet tall, fed by everything the mutinying soldiers could lay their hands on: blankets, furniture, papers, books, the wooden walkways and ladders from the trenches. Sergeants and Gendarmes ran about the chaos of flame and protest, shrieking and hitting out at the soldiers, trying to herd the masses back to the trenches, break up the mutiny and bring order to proceedings. But the revolutionaries were proving too obdurate to master, too drunk on their violence and the enslaving insanity of brief freedom to obey. It was as if they too had caught the fresh winds of change blowing down from the north of their country and had become unchained.

The fire of revolution had caught in the tinder boxes of Russia, fanned by stark Bolshevik rhetoric and the promise of the end of royal rule. For a nation so long reduced to living on its knees, nothing now could put out the flames which had risen from the underbelly of the Great Bear to scorch the very highest pinnacles of power in the country. The Russian Army was disintegrating quicker than sanity beneath a battery onslaught. The Red Army was at the gates of the Winter Palace in Petrograd, poised to tear down the old ways and replace them with Soviet rule. Czar Nicholas was gone. The Romanovs had fled.

But the man fleeing down the forest road, through the squall of cinders, gave no consideration as to why it was snowing ashes, or for the revolution enacted around him. All he cared about was getting away, escaping from the terrible thing that pursued him and warning the others back at the church to do the same.

He dared to turn around and look as he ran, half slithering across the mire. His hair had matted into feather-like clumps, oily with sweat under the silver moon, his clothes filthy from splashes of mud, as he sprinted down roads ruined by a million soldiers' boots and a war front now writhing in its death throws. A wolf howled somewhere away to his left in the depths of the forest, the trees there blasted and shredded by misplaced artillery fire from the Russians months ago, all stunted and shot back to bare burnt wood and branches.

It wasn't the first time he had run from a foe, but he knew it was the first time he had wept as he had fled, perhaps the first time he had wept since news of his father's death had reached him a month too late. To weep now, great hacking sobs between breathless strides, made him both feel ashamed and embrace entirely the fear which bound him. They had been told that the man he had seen in Uzhok twenty minutes ago was dead and that *he* would never be coming back. But the man who had looked at him through the crowd of people and pierced him instantly with his unflinching glare, finding him as if guided by a hidden unholy sense, there was no question it could be anyone other than the one Poré had warned them of.

His lungs burnt as he ran. His limbs felt as if heavy bands had been tied to them as penance. He wished for all the world to stop and rest, but he knew that he must not. Any pause now and he would have him. Out here, in the wilds of Ukraine, miles from anywhere, weaponless, exhausted, he'd have no chance against *him*. But at the church, with the others, with the wolves and his master and his Kongsberg Colt pistol in his hands, he might stand a chance.

His foot went from under him and he skidded in the mud, turning over and rolling, gashing his hip and elbow. For a moment he lay mindlessly still, staring up at the starless sky, ashes falling on him. Then, as if he had been slapped, he realised the madness of simply lying there, and he spat a curse he had learnt in North Russia, rolling onto his side and forcing himself back onto his Inquisitorial hobnailed boots, limping on in an ungainly weary lope, as if he was wearing callipers.

And then he saw them: the lights of a church ahead, clamour and chatter coming from the ramshackle wooden place. Spirit and resolve flared back and he ran on, finding at once that his twisted left ankle could bear his weight, that his lungs no longer laboured, that he was growing faster and more assured with every step, every step closer to the sanctuary of the church.

In the untended courtyard in front of the stunted three-spired building, the church raven black against the night sky, there was a line of boxes and barrels, piles of revered and holy items, saved from the church that would soon be lit as a pyre. He surged forwards, stealing a glance back into the abyss of dark behind, daring to see if the thing still followed. He saw nothing, but that did nothing to lessen his terror. He had witnessed at first hand the man's tenacity, his refusal ever to stop when pursuing an enemy. All of those who now followed Poré had been told what this man was capable of, how he should be feared.

He blasted through the arched church doors, making the mob of men inside jump and swear, some of them dropping their bundles of sticks and handfuls of straw to reach for their weapons.

"I saw him!" he shouted, his words wrestling against their curses, grabbing hold of his revolver from where he had left it on the edge of the lectern, as if to arm himself would make everything all right. He rushed towards the window, a thin slit of an aperture, his eye to the pistol's sight, the barrel trained to the road up which he had run, bathed in the lustre of moonlight. "It was him!" He surveyed the trail for only a moment before looking back and shouting, "Are we finished? Then for God's sake, burn the place and let's get out of here!"

He blinked the cold sweat from his eyes, wiping them dry with his sleeve, before turning his attention back on the blackness outside and his senses onto its silence, watching, listening for anything to come for them out of the night.

"What is the hurry, Igor?" one of the men cried, throwing down the bundle of sticks he had been carrying and rubbing his hands across his front, brushing at the strands of straw where they had tangled against the weave of his shirt. "What have you seen?"

"Him," said Igor, not daring to take his eyes from the dark or his fierce grip from his revolver. "It was him. Poldek Tacit!"

Someone laughed contemptuously. "Tacit's dead."

"Maybe it was your own ugly reflection you saw?" another spat, and some of the men laughed, but only some. Most knew Igor was not prone to needless panic. And the name he had said was not one to be spoken lightly. He spun on those who were laughing, half threatening them with his gun.

"I know what I saw! It was him. I recognised him from the Inquisition, from when we were Inquisitors like him. He was there, in the town. He saw me. He came after me." Igor scowled and looked hurriedly around the corners of the church, giving the impression he thought Tacit might be hiding somewhere in the shadows. The building was stuffed full of bushels of straw and sticks, as if prepared for a nativity play by an over-zealous Priest.

"Did he follow you?" someone asked.

"I don't know." Igor spun back to the window, his pistol locked tight in his hands, his finger white to the trigger. "I think I gave him the slip, but it was Tacit. He looked different, changed, wounded, but it was him. I'm sure of it."

His words faltered and he hung his head as if finally defeated. He was aware how the old scars from his inquisitional days had begun to ache after all his exertions. In that moment, Igor felt uncommonly old. The lack of action from the others and their apparent doubt infuriated him. "Did you not hear me? Are you finished here? Has Poré collected what he required?" The men nodded, distributing the last of their tinder about the church floor, under pews and around the altar. All treasures from the place, the gold and silver, had been stored outside away from the great pyre about to be lit. "Then let's burn this place, for God's sake, and get out of here!"

A clutch of straw was gathered and flint and steel struck three times before the flying sparks found purchase in the golden strands, slowly beginning to smoulder and then flame. The torch was turned over to encourage the tongues of fire to flourish, sending a weaving braid of smoke up into the shallow rafters above.

The sight of fire cheered Igor, and he exhaled deeply and turned back to rest against the window sill, setting his head onto the hard knuckles of his fist, still clenched around the Colt revolver. Behind him smoke began filling the roof of the church and his nostrils, and for the first time since he had fled from the town he relaxed, slumped over his gun.

As he did so, the shadow of a man moved in front of the window.

TWO

UZHOK. UKRAINE.

Igor saw the silhouette from the corner of his lifting eye, grey movement against the darker shade of night, the twist of a figure in front of the church, the swing of an arm, someone striding towards the main door, just seconds from bursting in.

He swore, throwing himself backwards and firing off three rounds into the thin mottled glass separating him from the blackness outside.

"What the hell is it!" someone cried, moments before the doors were kicked open and an armed man filled the archway. A rifle was in his hands and then lifted up at his eye before it exploded in flame and noise, and Igor spun on the spot and dropped, his pistol falling from his dead sweaty grip and clattering across the floor of the church.

Hands inside the smoking hall went for sidearms like gunslingers in a showdown, whipping them from holsters or belts. But not before the rifle barked again, four more times, and four more of the arsonists sank to the floor. Through the smoke and flames revolvers now sang, shooting at the figure who had ambushed them. But already the silhouette had stepped out of sight, leaving only a yawning black space.

"Was it him?" someone shouted, but the others were jostling for the rear doors of the church, turning over lecterns and stacks of firewood in their rush to escape. For they supposed it was, just as Igor had told them. When they were just feet from the exit, it opened and a revolver barked, its cylinder turning over five times before four more of the raiders groaned, convulsing to the floor. The remaining three men inside the building fired back, but once again their attacker had slipped away.

Panic amongst them exploded like the stacks of dry tinder next to the aged walls of the wooden church, and two of the men threw themselves at the open arched front door, tumbling and rolling out of it, out into the pitch of night, going as fast as they could muster. Twenty feet away, lit only by the mercurial moon, a woman emerged from the darkness, her feet set shoulder width apart in the firm dirt of the path, a pistol drawn up in line with her eyes, scarlet hair plunging over her shoulder and breast.

Isabella.

The revolver barked and the men toppled forward, twisting in the dirt before lying still.

"For pity's sake, I surrender!" cried the last Inquisitor, emerging from the heaving fog of yellow and grey, the altar and rear of the church behind him all alight, an eruption of smoke squeezing through the crackling gaps in the rafters, his hands stretched up. His shoulders and sweat-drenched hair shimmered amber in the scorching heat of the flames licking across the painted nave, turning the beautiful ancient frescos black with soot, before they bubbled and burst into flame. He dropped to his knees in front of the destruction, his head sunk between his shoulders, weeping like a man condemned by an unjust proclamation. "Mercy, I beg of you!"

From one side Sandrine Prideux appeared, rushing forward and kicking him down, frisking him for weapons and kicking him again when she was satisfied he was unarmed. He writhed, winded from the second blow, curling up into a tight groaning ball.

"Get up," called a man, appearing demonic and ruined in the dancing red light from the wild flames.

"Tacit!" he shrieked, trying to draw away from the grappling hands reaching towards him. He caught a glimpse of the looming figure and at once regained a little of his composure. "You're not Tacit…" he whimpered, as part of the building groaned and some of the roof fell in on itself, belching hot ashes and smog.

Henry Frost, his rifle slung over his shoulder, reached down and gathered him from the ground, dragging him away from snatching tongues of fire licking close to where they stood. He threw him down, next to the boxes of artefacts and treasures, the man coughing and spluttering, looking up incredulously at his captor and saviour while trying to find his bearings and with them his senses.

He sat up. As he did, Isabella cracked him hard across the forehead with the side of her revolver, sending him rolling to the ground, weeping. She followed up the blow with her right boot, connecting hard with his chin, snapping him back and into the side of the crates. Its ferocity broke him. He trembled, scrabbling blindly about the cold earth, trying to find purchase and a base upon which to steady himself. A hand took hold of the back of his neck and wrenched him to his knees, pushing him against the wall of boxes, blood in his eyes.

Something rancorous in Isabella's head shrieked and urged her on.

"Don't try to fight me," Isabella growled, pressing her face so close to his that he could smell the borrowed scent of lavender and sweat, her hand tight to his jaw, slick with crimson, glistening in the firelight. "Don't even try to lie." Her voice was as hard as steel. Wickedness had eaten up her beautiful features. Everything about her was insidious and black. "You will tell me everything! You will tell me everything you know and afterwards you will wish you had perished with your traitors in that fire!"

She smashed him three times in the face with the grip of her revolver, so hard that his mouth now resembled a broken bloody maw.

"Isabella!" called Henry, clawing her away. "Enough now! Enough!"

She wrenched her shoulder from Henry's grip and span on him, meeting his gaze with her own fierce glare. There was something unhinged and savage in it, and Henry recognised the look at once. He'd seen it before, in the British Expeditionary Force years ago when he served as a Lieutenant, when German barrages had seemed endless and inescapable, a wild and desperate glare, unfocused eyes, staring into middle space or lurching frantically in their sockets, berserk.

He knew why she acted as she did, even if he could not forgive it. This disintegration of her demeanour had not realised itself suddenly. The change had crept through her like a fever for the last two years, consuming her bit by bit until it overpowered her entirely in its profane dark grip, a malice born from the festering wound of losing the man she loved. Tacit, fallen to his death from the terrible heights of the Carso.

"Enough," Henry said again, his tone firm but conciliatory, and something sharpened in Isabella. She closed her eyes closed for a moment, trying to gather up the frayed ends of her reason. Demons hooted and growled in her and in that moment she felt remote from everything, as if she had fallen into deep water, caught in her own private nightmares.

And then, as quickly as she had vanished from the world, she was hurtling back to it, opening her eyes and staring down at the Inquisitor, his shattered face looking up beseechingly into hers, his eyes spinning and twisting with pain and confusion, wondering what torture was coming next, whether he could chance a lunge and make for the darkness beyond the figures.

"Poré," Isabella began, her eyes not leaving his for an instant, "he was here?"

"No," he stuttered, through bone and blood, his bruised puffed lips like great slugs around his mouth. At once her gun was lifted high and she struck him hard. He rocked back from the blow, collapsing into the crate next to him, his shattered nose spreading across his right cheek.

"Jesus Christ!" hissed Henry, and he wrestled to take the gun from her. Isabella pulled away from him, pointing the revolver at the officer's chest. Sandrine crouched, preparing to pounce, as Henry raised his hands. "Calm!" he called gently. "Isabella, for God's sake, calm!" His hands patted at the air slowly, as if Isabella was a deity he was worshipping.

"Poré," she continued, looking back at the Inquisitor, "we know he was here. Why?"

"To collect the word of the Archangel Michael." He spoke the words in a fevered stream, as if fearing another blow.

"The word of Archangel Michael?"

"The words of our Lord."

"Why did you burn the church? Why have you burnt all the churches you've visited? Six of them now, many along the eastern front, all burnt to the ground?" As she spoke, the church groaned and the main squat wooden spire turned in on itself, vanishing in a great pall of fire and flaming ash.

"To hide… what we have found. So no one else might find the word of Michael and use it against us."

The answers made no sense to Isabella and she addressed her questions to one whose answer she hoped would be clearer.

"Poré, where's he gone?"

"South. To the next church."

"The next one?"

The Inquisitor nodded, shedding blood over the floor and himself as he did so.

"And where is the next one?"

He hesitated, sobbing, and Isabella went to strike him again. He tensed for the blow which never came, instead feeling the cold steel of the revolver's barrel press into his forehead, ruined with blood and torn skin.

"Şurdeşti," he groaned, weeping and pleading for mercy.

"Romania?"

He nodded. "Yes, the Church of the Archangel."

"Another one?" Isabella said. "What are you taking from them? What's so important that no one else can know?"

"I cannot say," he whimpered, hanging his clotted face like a dead weight, so the blood dripped from his broken nose onto his legs.

"Tell me," Isabella pressed, teasing his head up to look at her with the muzzle of her revolver. She peered down the length of the weapon's dark steel into his bloodshot eyes. "Why these churches? What do they have that Poré wants?"

"I don't know," he replied hopelessly, and Isabella gathered herself for another swipe at him. He shuddered, trying to pull away. "The secret words," he said in a rush, spitting teeth and blood. "That is all I know! All any one of us knows! Please, believe me! They left us behind, to finish up here, to burn the church to the ground, to leave no evidence for any other to use."

Next to Isabella, Henry nodded, accepting his version. He looked at Sandrine before leaping at the sound of a gunshot, lashing out to take hold of his love and protect her should another shot be fired in their direction. The captured man fell back against the crate, a great hole torn in his face, his eyes missing, the wooden box behind him showered in a spray of dark crimson and bone.

"What have you done?" cried Henry, reaching forward and wrenching the hot revolver from Isabella's hand. She let him take it.

She shrugged, casting one final disdainful look over the dead figure lying slumped in front of them. "He told us all we needed to know," she replied. "All he knew." She glanced over at the smouldering remains of the church as the walls fell in, leaving nothing more than the burning bones of the building. "Come on," she muttered, like one about to walk to her fate, "let's go."

Henry watched her leave, seeing how she shook the ache of the revolver's recoil from her fingers. Sandrine drew the scowling man into an embrace as Isabella merged into the darkness.

"She is changed," whispered Sandrine. "Ever since Tacit fell, she has been changed. It is me she should blame. I was responsible."

"I knew someone who behaved in such a way," he said at length, tasting smoke and iron in his mouth, remembering Fampoux, recalling Major Pewter.

"A commanding officer?" asked Sandrine.

Henry nodded, dragging his hand across his forehead. He felt sick of his life, trapped in it. "Yes, the smallest of men," and Sandrine knew of whom Henry was speaking, although he never said his name.

In the woods behind them something terrible shifted in the dark trees, something only half alive, drawing the shredded branches behind which he crouched to one side to allow himself to peer more closely at the man and woman embracing, framed by the firelight of the burning church. But primarily he watched the solitary figure of the woman walking away from them, observing her vanish into the trees beyond.

A wolf howled somewhere away in the woods, and the hulking figure knew just how the creature felt.

THREE

POVEGLIA ISLAND. VENICE.

Darkness seemed to boil in the hollows of the graveyard. From the east, a cool meandering pall of sea stink and rot rolled breathlessly onto the land, drawing from the earth a lingering mist, as if a spell had been spoken to raise spirits from the ground.

A bright moon caught in the branches of the great trees around the graveyard, glittering the ground and the men creeping beneath them with soft circles of silver light. None of them had spoken since their boat had drawn alongside the narrow stone quay of the small deserted island-hospital harbour an hour before.

Beyond the boughs of the trees and stunted slabs of gravestones, roughly hewn for purpose rather than out of love or respect for the dead buried beneath them, distant lights from surrounding islands and the Italian mainland could be seen to twinkle white and amber. In the silence of this abandoned lazaretto, long rumoured to be haunted, spirits could still be felt to reach out and grapple the Inquisitors as they passed, the occasional muffled bark of laughter from Venice across the water sounding foreign and mistaken in the hateful dark. In the depths of the graveyard, unseen unblinking eyes watched each of the men with rankling spite.

Without warning, the Inquisitor at the head of the party suddenly stopped and threw down his bundle, thrusting the blade of his shovel into the ground.

"Dig here!" he commanded, setting his boot upon its shoulder and sliding the slice of metal deep into the black earth. Wordlessly, the Inquisitors took their spades and dug with him.

Far off, thunder rumbled suddenly in the heavens.

A crow settled in the branches of one of the trees and looked down at the circle of men, squawking noisily. A chill wind rose from the sea, blowing over the place and summoning up voices from the hollows and tombstones. The mist swayed and then vanished. The spades of the Inquisitors dug deeper into the cloying soil, as their breath grew tighter and the pile of soil, broken roots and grubby bones of buried plague victims grew about them.

"Who would have thought it was easier to find a dead body than a living one?" one of the Inquisitors muttered between shovels, his skin cold and clammy from his exertions.

"*He* might yet be dead," the man beside him replied, and lightning crackled and thunder rolled again.

"Are you sure he's even buried here?" someone asked, and then someone else's blade hit wood, hollow, and at once everyone stopped digging.

"They buried him in a box!" one of the Inquisitors exclaimed breathlessly.

"*If* it's him."

"Clear away the earth," said the head Inquisitor, gesturing over the great hole and the coffin lying in it.

Quickly the Inquisitors found the edge to the casket and worked the last of the earth clear.

"Lift it out," said the Inquisitor, standing at the front of the pit, watching his men work, a fist tight in his hip, his other hand white-knuckled to the handle of the shovel.

The Inquisitors' strong arms strained clumsily against the weight, as if the earth didn't wish to give up one of its dead willingly to those who had come to the island unannounced and unwelcome. A spade was set beneath one end of the casket, levering the coffin free from the cloying ground. Once more the Inquisitors set their hands beneath the box and lifted, this time with less difficulty despite the great weight.

"Set it down there!" commanded the Inquisitor, and his men obeyed at once. Lightning flashed and thunder rolled ever closer in from the Adriatic. Something ancient and cheerless crept silent and unseen out of the trees to watch from just beyond the reach of moonlight. At the quayside, a strange tide drew into the harbour and knocked the Inquisitors' boat firm against its moorings. A single mournful light from high up in the abandoned hospital tower, overlooking the whole island, flickered into life. An owl screamed from its depths, like a spirit drawn back fleetingly into life.

"Open it," nodded the Inquisitor, his face grave.

Without word or pause, the shovel blades were pushed beneath the lid of the casket and it was forced up, breaking its seals and cracking the plain rotting top down its length. An Inquisitor reached forward and pulled the shattered wood aside, the body beneath grinning ghoulishly back, writhing and heaving with a host of slithering glistening worms and insects.

Beneath the body's rotting clothing, something glimmered dully.

"They buried him in his armour!" someone exclaimed.

"Curse anyone who takes another Inquisitor's armour in death!" said the head Inquisitor, stealing forward and dropping down to his knees to look more closely at the skeletal remains.

"Is it him?" someone asked.

He nodded. "We were not misled." He retreated back to his backpack, as the other Inquisitors turned their eyes from the body in the coffin to the shadows all about them and the gathering storm growing closer and ever more fearsome in the heavens. There were voices now in the air, drawn not from the whistling wind but from the graves and melancholy memories caught in the graveyard's hollows.

"This is a hateful place," someone said, in a low growl.

Another laughed cheerlessly. "Why do you think they buried him here? Amongst the plague dead and diseased. A fitting end."

"They must have known who he was? What he had done to the world?"

The head Inquisitor took something red and glistening from his pack. He dropped next to the coffin, pressing it, slick in his fingers, between the skeleton's exposed ribs.

Latin was on the Inquisitor's tongue, a coarse staccato chanting, like an accusatorial spell. There was a rhythm in the lines, a repetition in the words, and while the other Inquisitors recognised what they said, they did not understand the intricacies of the incantation that was being performed. They stood and watched the chief Inquisitor and the shadows and the forked lightning, dropped their hands to the grips of their revolvers and secretly wished themselves away from the graveyard and the island.

The flaccid slick organ, like a bloody airless sack, beat just once in the rib cage and then lay still. Briefly the Inquisitor paused in his recital and studied the cold heart, his eyes narrowing, beginning the lines of the spell over again when he saw that it no longer throbbed. The moment the spell's words were on his lips for a second time, instantly the heart flared back into life, pulsing and flexing like a beached fish trying to return to the ocean from the sand.

And the heart now kept on beating.

Satisfied, he stopped his chanting and he turned his attention to the skull.

Something else slippery and purple was pushed between its jaws, a human tongue, complete with its root, and the Inquisitor started up his dreadful Latin refrain again, but this time the words and their meaning seemed crueller, even more terrible and corrupt. No longer was the chant a call to action; instead it was a command, demanding the corpse to act.

Over and over he spoke the lines, each time his voice growing louder and more compelling. All the time, all about the graveyard, the wind had begun to squall and whirl, shaking leaves from the trees and tumbling debris across the way. Thunder and lightning fought like warring gods in the heavens. It started to pour with rain. The Inquisitors' robes were pulled by unseen forces.

"Enough!" one of them cried. "What are we unleashing here?" only for another to draw his weapon and train its sight on the younger man.

"Quiet," he cautioned, before turning back to look at what his commander was attempting.

In the casket, teeth clacked together and the skull twisted violently, as if invisible strings had pulled it to one side. Moments later, after the concluding lines of the incantation had been spoken for the last time, the head turned its hollowed sockets back to the man who had drawn the phantom from its endless sleep.

"Speak!" the Inquisitor commanded. "Tell me of what I seek! I command thee to tell me!"

From the skull came an ethereal shrieking like an icy wind drawing across a blade. But there were words woven into the scream and every one of the Inquisitors gathered in that haunted place heard them.

"He's alive!" cried the skull.

"Who is alive?" the Inquisitor demanded, his bloody hands turned tight into fists. "Speak his name, servant! Speak his name to me now, Georgi Akeldama!"

"Tacit!" shrieked the revenant, through the slithering pulsing dead tongue clenched firm between its clattering bony jaws. "Poldek Tacit! He's alive!"

FOUR

The Carpathian Mountains. Romania.

Clouds full of thunder swept the night sky, obscuring the moon and slowing the beat of blood in the running wolves. The river they had followed all night since leaving the burning church had plunged into a wood, tangled with young trees and coarse thicket. But the path alongside the river was well worn and broad enough for the long line of grey lumbering beasts to slip effortlessly along, never wavering.

At the head of the procession, the largest and most wicked-looking beast peered back at the clan behind him and felt a gathering pride, even as anger and rage churned inside him. The wolf's eyes, yellow as a hornet's belly, narrowed, and his blood-red jaws, lined with terrible grey-white teeth, prickled, desiring above all else human flesh to satiate the hunger he always felt whenever he wore the pelt.

Gerard-Maurice Poré knew the path would take him, and the wolves who had flocked to his banner, direct as an arrow over the Carpathian

Mountains, onwards towards their next destination, the final church he needed to reach. Away to his left, somewhere in the valleys and foothills, an assault by Russia was beginning to be unleashed upon the entrenched German Army. The rattle of their artillery, the roar of their shells, the march of the army's boots, the vortex of all the trumpets of war seemed like an insanity in his ears, keen and honed as they were to all about him and beyond the path down which he paced. And the maddening sounds drove him to run even harder still, to reach where it was he had to go next, to the Church of the Archangels Michael and Gabriel in Şurdeşti, Romania, to gather the last of the secret words of his Lord, with which he would set in motion all that he had wished for, ever since the voice had come to him, as a young man, broken and cast out. Like a puzzle revealed to him after years of struggle, only recently had the true path been made clear to him.

And now it blazed.

For so long Poré had despised the wolves with whom he travelled and the wicked talents bound up with their curse: their brawn, their anger, their hate, so foreign and loathsome to him. But over the years in their company, from Pleven to the Carso on the Italian/Austro-Hungarian front, from where he had fled and had since been drawing every clan east of the Karst Plateau to his command, he had developed a bitter admiration for them. Their unyielding malice, their unerring resolve.

From the Carso, and the limestone killing field of the Karst Plateau, Poré and his wolves had turned their yellow eyes east to the many clans of wolves who inhabited the high mountains between Austria-Hungary and Slovenia, Triglav, Škrlatica, High Altar, impenetrable, unreachable peaks of the grey barren limestone mountains, huge and limitless, adorned in a mantle of snow the entire length of that jagged spine of rock. It was to this desolate and godforsaken landscape that he had drawn to him the most terrible and depraved of creatures.

The satanic ritual on that black pinnacle of rock with the Carso beside the Soča River, above the field where sixty thousand Italians and Austro-Hungarians lay slaughtered, confirmed what Poré had already long suspected and feared; that the Darkest Hand was real and well advanced in its plans to welcome the Antichrist's return to the world. Long the Darkest Hand had taken root, long it had prospered and grown in the hearts of directionless angry men and women, for whom no solace could any more be found in the world, no ear turned to hear their concerns or fears, no voice of reason to calm them. People weakened by war and poverty, enticed by the false promises of those with serpents' tongues.

It seemed to Poré that, even two years later, he still could taste the bitter blood of the Darkest Hand Priests he and his clan had torn down at their ceremony, the foul taint of witchcraft and devilry about their flesh.

And while Poré had stopped the Darkest Hand's attempt to bring the Seven Princes of Hell into the world to act as the Antichrist's protectors and guides, still the final and greatest of battles yet lay ahead, the one promised to him long ago that he knew was his destiny alone. To stop the Antichrist from returning and thus casting the whole world into a darkness from which it would never be allowed to escape.

He had learnt long ago that arms and might could only ever achieve small victories. In order to influence an entire planet a greater sacrifice was required, a sacrifice to be felt by all, to achieve something impossible to accomplish with words and weapons alone.

And he had not been lazy either. His need was pressing, and every clan he reached he had appealed to, offered every one of the accursed creatures wallowing in their unchained prisons of despair hope, a reason to exist, a war to fight, revenge to taste, every one of their ruinous monstrous kind a place to serve under his standard in return for giving to him their power and their rage. An ever-growing legion of werewolves following in his wake to fight the ever-darkening shades of evil drawing across the world. At least until he could answer his final calling.

This calling, though he had spurned it for years too many to remember, was his conviction now. It was all of him and those who followed him – Hombre Lobo, 'children of the Faith', as they were called by those who knew of their existence, werewolves created by Catholic excommunication and their fiery incantations many decades ago, now cast out by civilisation and hunted by the Inquisition for the nightmares they were – they were bound up with it and him. For centuries they had cowered under the roots of the Earth, hiding from the sun, unleashed at night, maddened by the coming of the moon. Now they were Poré's foot soldiers and guards, along with the Inquisitors who had turned to his cause, commanded and empowered by his might, his army coming to wipe all from the face of the Earth.

No light shone in the forest's depths through which they ran. No moonlight broke through the thick knotted canopy above, but the wolves did not need any light by which to see. They were well used to living in the inky black of the subterranean world. Indeed they preferred the pure black of night to one where silver from the moon hung on boughs and across the ground. Blood and blackness, these were all that they required.

Poré watched the path before him as he ran silent through the forest, his eyes vivid and alive to anything that moved in the wood's eternal dark. He could feel the wolf's power pulsing in him like a charge, his body athletic and lean, taut like a bow. The pelt of Frederick Prideux he wore, taken from the clan in Fampoux near Arras in France, imbued him with a strength and prowess no man, he supposed, could ever possess. When he wore it, he felt something akin to godliness. For all of his life he had been a man of God, made flesh through his words and the guidance of wisdom. He often thought of his sermons spoken at Arras Cathedral, a lifetime ago, the words he had delivered to his congregations, the teaching he implored them to follow. Now, with the pelt about him, the anger and might from it pulsing like a blessing and a curse, he had become a god of a different kind, driven by flesh, manifested in claws and brawn and teeth. And he knew his Lord approved.

He had called out to his Lord and his Lord had answered him, with monstrous devices. And God's own vengeance was destined for all sinners of his world who had fallen under the shadow of the Antichrist.

FIVE

The Vatican. Vatican City.

It started as a frail whimper, somewhere in the buried darkness of the Seers' building. Moments later another joined it from a room deeper inside, a voice spoiled by anguish and fear. Dreadful and harrowing, they entwined and grew like a sonnet of torment.

A third voice started up, a low animalistic moan, then a fourth, the voices gathering into a single cry of agony. From down the halls and private chapels yet more voices joined, and the sound grew louder and more awful.

Something had come to the Seers' edifice. Something had been sensed and felt by those Catholic Sisters who were blessed with the skill of second sight, the ability to snatch brief glimpses of the future, of what it entailed.

And what this vision showed was the ending of days.

The feeling had begun as a sting of regret, of doubt and fear for what might be, the premonition growing and blackening like a cancer amongst them, quickly contorting and mutating in its fury and wickedness, changing from a sad shadow of remorse to something wounding and vile in the Seers' vision. And as each Seer in turn grasped hold of the vision, their cry rose as one, a vast ghastly choir of torture and misery, a combined wail of pain and woe.

It filled every chamber and hallway, coursing like a corrupt wave of filth and degradation throughout the building. It engulfed the place, an invisible ocean of poison pouring through the rooms, flooding halls and chapels, enveloping everything in its wickedness.

The women wailed and cried, dropping onto their knees, their hands clenched to their heads, white bony fingers clawing at their hair and hoods, as if trying to tear the visions from their minds, images of hospital tents filled with rows of beds, every bed occupied with swollen blue bodies, of choking breathless people vomiting blood and curses, of hillsides of graves, of a procession of mourners dressed all in black, heads bound, shuddering in misery and fear of what was to come, if they might be the next to go into the ground after a requiem of agonies, a parade of despair winding out across whole countries, nations and continents, its line stretching around the entire world.

And then, as quickly as the visions and lamentations came, they went, the silence that flooded in behind even more deafening to all inside the building than the clamour of noise before. And with its arrival every clock stopped ticking, every messenger bird fell mute, every breath was held. After the horrors, an uneasy peace had taken hold of the building, a paralysis of confusion and bewilderment, as terrible as the visions of suffering had been. But the Seers took no solace from this peace, for they all understood what the total quiet represented, the silence that would follow, the final act in the approaching Tribulation and End Times, the coming of final judgement upon the world.

The Apocalypse was coming, and it was nigh.

SIX

The Carpathian Mountains. Romania.

Beyond the reach of lantern and camp-fire light, a cold breath of air drew through the heat of the mountainous night. Like a shadowy hand searching dark holes and places, it crept, driven on by some purpose, looking for something amongst the deep culverts and scattered cairns, across the granite escarpments rising to deep-forested crowns, flecked white with snow at the highest reaches.

In the dark, the chill disturbed everything it touched, scattering roosting birds from their nests, sending scavenging night-time creatures to their burrows, stirring the three lazing figures about the smouldering camp fire, drawing them fitfully from their sleep, teased awake from unsettling dreams. Despite the exhaustion from days of travel without rest, the presence of this invisible feeling thing, half floating, half crawling through the scrabble of undergrowth, had been enough to wake them.

And then, as quickly as it came, the spirit was gone, its search seemingly over, vanished into the ether like a shadow before the light. The embrace of night heat, teased by the hot stones roasted all day by the relentless Romanian sun, returned and with it came again the smell of sultry fields, pine forests and dust. And silence. Not a sound. Not even the rustle of mice in the scrub. As if the world had fallen silent and all in it was dead.

Henry watched Isabella, an arm drawn under her head, staring up into the staggering heavens, the Persian-indigo dark holding the glitter dust of stars, her eyes mapping the constellations, her mind... Henry could not begin to comprehend the place into which her mind had contorted itself. He hadn't dared to for so long now. Through the camp's gloom he could see the moist glint of her eyes moving, and though he could not tell what she was thinking, what horrors and regrets she was reliving, he supposed he had an inkling as to how they rankled and twisted inside her. For he too bore his own silent pain, one of missing home in Salisbury, of his life in the army and the subsequent road into which he had stepped and become entrapped. Like a river it now seemed to him, fast-flowing and inescapable. He had stumbled into it and it had taken him away to terrible places and things, and he knew he would never escape it.

Suddenly Isabella rose, pushing back the blankets, stepping silent from the circle of their camp, careful not to wake the companions she supposed were asleep, and vanishing into the trees beyond. For a while he let her go and did not follow, fighting against his own niggling need of sleep. But he found its hold on him now lessened; instead the compulsion to try and speak with Isabella grew, like the promise of cool water offered to a fevered man.

He found her under a shard of moonlight, a single ray which had slipped through the dense canopy above, the light upon her as pale as quince. She heard him and turned, startled, as he stepped into the edge of the clearing close to where she was sitting, her legs slung over the bough of a fallen tree, the moss upon it like a green throw she had unrolled over it. At once Henry froze, holding up his hands as a means of parley, in that instant supposing he should never have come, but when Isabella turned back to look in her lap, retreating again into her private thoughts, he came forward a little more, until he was standing just a little way away from her, one foot on a rotten stump of a tree, gazing into the dark. She was crying, or at least had been until Henry had clumsily interrupted, and he allowed her a moment to compose herself, pretending to admire the view he could not see.

"Do you think it was him, Henry, coming into the clearing?" she asked after a silence which tested all of Henry's determination not to break it, clearing her throat, her words laden with emotion despite her attempt to sound calm and rational. "The cold, that feeling, just before, in the camp. You felt it too, didn't you? You felt it, whatever it was, whether it was nothing or it was…?"

"I don't know," said Henry. "I don't know if it was *him*, or if it was just a draught from the hills. We're high up. The eddies…" His words trailed away as he realised they were banal, just noise, and they listened together to the mountains' silence.

"I feel him," said Isabella, breathing deep into her lungs, drawing her finger across her cheek and dragging ringlets of hair from her face. "I feel him, Henry, all the time, as if he is watching me, watching us." She lifted her head and looked about herself, staring absently into the dark hollows of the surrounding forest. "As if he is observing us. All the time. Even now I can feel him, his eyes on me. Does that make me stupid? Does that make me crazy?"

Her voice had risen to a crescendo, but Henry shook his head calmly and waited for his time to speak.

"No."

He kicked at the stones on the forest floor and listened to the faint bristle of gunfire off in the east, at the far edge of the mountains. Another assault. Another offensive on enemy lines. He had hoped that the war in the east might stagger to a clumsy end after the rumours of Russian revolution, but it seemed to him that the Russian commanders had grown even more determined under the glimmer of peace; their soldiers better prepared for war than ever, better armed, equipped and trained.

"It is not unusual to speak of feeling the presence of loss..." he began, but Isabella talked across him, not listening or interested in what he had to say, just needing to speak, to tell someone what she had carried inside for so long.

"In here." Isabella tapped at her skull, harder than Henry supposed was necessary, as if she needed to feel the bite of her nails in her skin, as if she wished to claw the voices out of her head. "I hear him, in here. Tacit, he often spoke of hearing voices, of words spoken to him by voices he did not appreciate, voices he did not welcome, words only he could hear, words meant only for him, words unkind and depraved. Words that I now hear. Terrible words that I hear all the time." She closed her eyes and breathed deep, as if trying to take hold of herself and her emotion. "I suppose I tried to understand him back then, Tacit I mean. When he spoke of the words, the voices, how they taunted him. At least I wished to understand him. But I never could. But now I do. Now I hear them, feel them, as if I now have become infected." And she turned her eyes onto Henry, and although they were heavy with emotion, there was fight and defiance in her features. "But I understand him now." And she asked him again, "Do you think it was him we felt, in the clearing, earlier?"

"I don't know," replied Henry, taking the question as an invitation to sit on the fallen tree trunk a little away from where Isabella was perched. "I have seen so many strange and marvellous and terrible things over the last few years, that to think of spirits visiting, it does not seem so strange a thing to happen."

And Isabella sobbed, no longer able to hold back her emotion, and said, suddenly, "Henry, I think I have become possessed. There is a poison in me, Henry, a malice, ever since the Carso, ever since," and she hesitated, forcing herself to say the words, words which it terrified her to reveal to another, "ever since Georgi killed me, ever since Tacit drew me back with the power assigned to him, drew me back from that Hell."

She cried and Henry let her, not trying to comfort her or draw her weeping to an end. He recalled the violence at the church in Uzhok, the sudden unexpected flash of anger and brutality shown by Isabella, an event not isolated to that one time, a growing crescendo of anger and savagery which had built since they had left the Carso, the slow degradation and corruption of her character, a cruelty and sadism he had never supposed Isabella could possess. It cheered him to now see her weep and admit the horror she had done. It renewed his faith in her and gave him hope that whatever possessed her, whatever anger had overwhelmed her all those times, might yet be drawn out of her again.

That it had not taken root in her and been buried too deep, as it had in so many people in this war.

He lit a cigarette and sat watching the path of its smoke trailing up into the gap between the trees, tasting bitter liquorice and coffee on his tongue. "I saw many dreadful things on the western front," he began, "of men broken by what they had seen, what they had done, were forced to do, things no man should be made to confront or commit. We think ourselves a robust and stout creature, that we can be prepared for horror in all its guises, trained and sent out with our bombs and our bullets and our commitment to our nations, our leaders. Sent out to face our enemy, an enemy we then discover is so much like ourselves, caught also in these places, these predicaments, these events. These visions." And he dropped his head and his voice. "These visions of Hell made real.

"Perhaps our commanders and seniors think of us as machines? Mechanised? Indefatigable? Perhaps there is a part of us they think can be worn down, hammered iron-hard, plunged into the cooling waters of drill and authority so that our spirit goes cold, worked so long and so furiously that its edge bleeds light and all it knows is how to kill?

"But if so, if we are then just like any machine, then surely like machines we break? My old Sergeant, Sergeant Holmes, he once described men as tools. 'Tools of War' he used to say to me. That sometimes the tools get bent and need fixing and sometimes they break. I suppose he was right?

"But we don't talk of such things, do we? Don't admit that there is a part of us that can be damaged? Damaged permanently. That we, strong men and women, such as ourselves, once bound up by our uniform and our orders and our faith and our pride in our nation and our beliefs, that we are not party to weakness or to showing anything which shows our weakness."

And he shook his head and stared up at the moon, pale as a round slice of cooked veal against the black of the sky.

"God, I am sick, Isabella!" he cried, half weeping the words, the emotion like a charge exploding out of him. And he let the words hang between them for a long while before he said, "I am sick of what we do and how we do it and why we must do it. I am sick that there seems no one else whom we can trust to come to our assistance down this godforsaken path we have chosen. Or is it assigned, I don't know any more? Who can we turn to for help? Who believes us when we tell them? All our allies are dead. Our enemies, multiplying daily!" He curled his hands into fists and waved them against the night sky. "I am not ashamed to admit it. Every day, it is like a penance that we are living, a weight that we must carry. I know what we do is right, and that it must be done, but do you ever wonder why it is that it is us who have found ourselves with this burden? Have we wronged so much in our past that it is *this* fate that has befallen us, that *we* must walk this path until such a time as we complete this commission or it finishes us?

"I spend so much of time wondering, thinking, clawing back over past memories and deeds, wondering if this truly is some curse from God I have drawn down upon myself, some deed that I must do to prove myself to him, to ensure his forgiveness, an opportunity to finally rest. To find peace? Peace, through death."

His eyes were very dark, his words faltering, raw, but Henry snatched tight to them, refusing to be beaten by his emotion.

"I don't mind telling you, Isabella," he said, "that I feel so damned bloody alone!" He looked back in the direction of the camp, to where he supposed Sandrine was sleeping, and allowed his eyes to creep slowly away, drawing hard on his cigarette. "All those who we found, those who fought for us, the Inquisitors, Cincenzo, Kell, Santoro, Accosi, the others in the Vatican, they have all gone, fallen on our road, just like…" He still retained enough of himself and his wits to not say Tacit's name. "It seems as if we are cursed to walk this road, just the three of us, to face horrors that no one should never witness."

"Perhaps Pablo was right to have gone with Poré?" said Isabella. "Perhaps we should have stayed with him also? Ignored our fears, obliged

Poré and his aims, his vision of this ruined world he wishes to create. Perhaps his vision is no worse than the one in which we currently reside, or the one we race towards? After all, he fights the same enemy as us, doesn't he? Perhaps we, you, could have found comfort there among his followers?"

But Henry said, "No." He shook his head, adamantly. "Whatever Poré is planning, we know it cannot be allowed to happen. We trusted him, we believed him, for a little while at least, and we quickly learnt that his ambitions are as dangerous as the Darkest Hand's. His way is not *our* way. It cannot be the way, not for mankind. Not for the good of mankind. Bringing damnation and devastation to the world? Isn't that what he said? Sounds like the ramblings of a madman, if you ask me. No, Poré is dangerous. He needs to be stopped."

"Pablo didn't think so."

"Pablo is his own man. Young and naive, troubled by all that has happened to him. He has his own ambitions. Whatever happened to him on that pinnacle of rock, whatever he did or saw or overcame, however that manifested in him, that is for him to face. It changes nothing. We were agreed and we still are, Poré must be stopped." With that the artillery barrage seemed to intensify beyond the range in which they had their camp. Henry turned his head towards the sound. "And perhaps one day end that."

Something rustled in the woods behind where they were talking, and Henry's hand dropped automatically to the cool leather handle of his revolver. He stared hard into the trees, but whatever had made the noise made no effort to come closer or reveal itself.

SEVEN

The Vatican. Vatican City.

A raw wind swept into the city, an unnatural glacial cold front from off the Tyrrhenian Sea. The chill took the population by surprise, making them shutter windows usually left open to catch the late summer heat and driving people deeper beneath the blankets of their beds. Flowers wilted and fruit withered on the vine at the sudden touch of winter clutched about Rome.

To most in the city this suggested that summer would be snuffed out all too quickly, like the lives of too many young men on the Italian Front three hundred miles away to the north, a conflict for which there seemed no end in sight.

Inside the chapel it was so bitter that the Inquisitors' breath billowed in ragged sheets. Exposed skin prickled and they shivered, drawing their travelling cloaks tighter, still caked in mud from their recent tomb raiding, to try and tease a little warmth into the chilled marrow of their bones.

At the far end of the chapel, where copper candlelight fought vainly with the blackness of the place, a silhouette suddenly moved. At once, the hall seemed to become even colder still and the two Inquisitors shuddered, looking at each other nervously and then immediately back, as if not wishing to reveal their trepidation to their master.

There was the glisten of crimson on the shadowy figure's fingers, white candlelight reflecting in the blood running down his pale hands to his wrists and onto the altar in front of him. A black cloth had been thrown across it, a pentagram of embroidered silver silk worked into it. At its centre was set the statuette of a hideous and twisted figure, the red bronze from which it had been cast also glistening with the blood from a pinkish-looking thing, a small skinless creature like a pig, opened and bloody and set to one side of the altar. Through the sickly light, the Inquisitors knew at once what the slaughtered thing was and swallowed at their revulsion.

"Master," one of them said, clearing his throat to make the hooded figure aware of their presence. But the Priest already knew they had arrived.

"The Seers," he croaked, marking a sign with his bloodied hands in the space in front of the devil's statue, "I hear that they have finally understood just what it is this conflict truly represents, not just to them but to all of mankind." The slash of a cold smile graced his hard gritted face for a moment, before it fell to a scowl and his eyes narrowed further still. "And they tell me that they are blessed with the ability to see glimpses of the future, to predict what is to befall the world? Pah! How is it then that it has taken them so long to realise that the Great Tribulation is nigh? That End Times have come and my ascension is but a short moment away?"

He bowed his head in reverence to the metal figure on the altar and reached across to the cloth lying alongside, wiping his bloody hands clean, the plain fabric discolouring from cream to crimson and pink. "Tell me," he asked, turning to look at the pair of Inquisitors still waiting for him, unmoving at the head of the aisle, "have they always been so blind as to what really lies ahead of us, or is it ever since their head Seer had her eyes taken that they've become so groping with their predictions?"

The Priest chuckled at his attempt at cruel humour, remembering the murder of Sister Malpeghi at the hands of his favoured servant Georgi, her eyes cut from their sockets during the first of the three rituals to bring the remaining Seven Princes of Hell into the world. But again the smile was fleeting as he recalled the moment he was told that the final ritual in the high peaks of the Italian Carso had faltered at the taloned claws and foul jaws of Cardinal Poré and his clan of werewolves. He knew he had been gravely weakened by the demons' failure to come through from Hell and join him. But also that not *all* was lost.

For something had come through, something he desired above all else.

He dropped the towel on top of the black altar and drew forward into the faint radiance of the ambulatory, shambling as if his legs were bound by splints. Perhaps it was a trick of the light, but as he approached the Inquisitors it appeared that the carved face of Jesus upon the cross looking down on the chancel seemed to turn away, as if unable to watch such wickedness gather in this holy place.

"So, you have returned from Poveglia Island?" the Priest began, his face covered by a deep hood out of which dead eyes watched the pair of Inquisitors.

"We have," replied the Inquisitor who had led the mission to that hellish place. Every night since each Inquisitor had been haunted by nightmares filled with leering beseeching faces of the plague victims whose rest had been disturbed, the desecration they had wrought like a stain on their spirits.

"And our dearly departed, was he happy to have his tongue loosened?"

The Inquisitor nodded. "He spoke."

"And what did Georgi say?"

The Inquisitor breathed deep on the frigid air, as if steeling himself for the words he thought he would never bring to his master.

"That Poldek Tacit is alive."

Silence and cold consumed the hooded figure. For a moment the Inquisitors thought that the man behind the hood had been struck both dumb and lame as no movement or sound came from him. But then he turned, slowly, very slowly, as if he had in that moment become ancient, and shuffled with his head bowed towards the chair set in the pulpit's shadow.

"I always knew it to be so," he croaked, reaching out for the seat and lowering himself into it, tucking his trembling hands into the sleeves of his gown as if to hide their murmur. To the Inquisitors he looked shrunken, defeated, and they thought that perhaps the news they had brought with them had in fact been ill. But inside the gown, expectation and passion surged. "I always believed. Of course it would seem only logical that he should still be alive, but man is made of just flesh and bone, brittle and weak. So easy to tear and to break. And to waste away."

"Now that we know he is alive, we will double our efforts to find him," insisted the Inquisitor. "We *will* find him, will send out even more agents to help in the search."

But the Priest replied, "No."

"No?"

There was a book now in the hooded man's hands, drawn from a pocket in his gown, black, but the cover worn to grey in places from where it had been held and read so many times. The Inquisitors could see a five-pointed star and scrawling letters in gleaming silver on its front. Its owner picked his way slowly through its pages, every now and then inserting an index finger into the yawning mouth of the robe's hood before using it to turn to a new one.

He paused, looking hard into one particular page for several moments, before closing the book and clasping it in a claw-like hand, standing and stepping back to the altar and the devilish ceremony he had laid upon it. He stared hard at the beast's wrought figure, saying nothing. Finally, after a long while, during which the Inquisitors were sorely keen to speak, to break the silence, so oppressive it had become, the hooded man himself spoke, as if clear insight had been granted to him from the pages of his black-bound journal and the devilish statuette.

"Tacit," he said, "has chosen to evade us for all this time. If he choses to remain hidden, we have no chance of finding him. He is like a mist in the smoke."

"But my Lord, we command a great army upon whom we can call at a moment's notice," insisted the Inquisitor. "There is no land or nation over which we do not have mastery. Nothing and no one can hide its secrets from us, no government, army or people. Indeed, many world leaders have joined our legion!"

But the Priest shook his head. "No, it is not the man we should be searching for but the thing that *he* himself will be searching for. That is how we will find him."

"And what is that?"

"Isabella." He skewered the Inquisitor with a withering glare. "Sister Isabella, once of the Vatican Chaste, she who died and was brought back into the world through his love and desire for her and the dark power he carries. She of the third ritual. Pride of Life! Find her, and you will find him. And by doing so, the final act ahead of End Times can commence."

And the Priest looked back at the devil's statue, and his cold smile lingered long on his lips.

EIGHT

ŞURDEŞTI. ROMANIA.

Half a mile back from the target of the Russians' shattering barrage, Isabella, Sandrine and Henry could feel the ground shake with the violence of shellfire, the air vibrating in their ears, thundering like clanging bells, as they ran through the undergrowth, praying that a shell or German soldier would not fall on them. They knew this was no inconsequential artillery strike. The Russians were preparing for something, a final roll of the dice, a last assault into Austro-Hungarian lands.

The night air was hot and thick with smoke from the shell bursts which had been slowly obliterating the sweeping vista, a diseased drifting smog, stinking of cordite and ash, creeping like a curse across the entire front line and support trenches behind it.

The three of them had followed the thunderous sounds over the last few days, finding each new day, each new mile, brought them ever closer to the Church of the Archangel, but equally, disturbingly, ever closer to the eastern front, ever closer to the heart of the firestorm being unleashed upon the Germans.

Ever closer to Hell with its fiery polluted air and tormented torn earth.

On the crest of the low hill they had climbed, they could now look down on the warren of trenches stretching into the dark horizon, every section aflame, blazing amber and white beneath the thick trails of smoke and dust. The occasional crackle of gunfire could be heard among the torrent of shells being thrown onto the German defences. The Russian Army's whole weight was being prepared to be pushed against the combined might of the German South Army and the Austro-Hungarian Third and Seventh Army, two million soldiers crashing into one another like crushing waves of metal and flesh.

"Let's go!" called Henry, pushing Sandrine gently from where she was standing looking down on the violence beneath. "I just pray we're not too late ourselves."

The words seemed like a cruel jest when they reached the end of the ravaged wood and the sunken road along which they filed, and their eyes fell on the great flaming torch on the near horizon, the church a sea of flames. Before it, a mass of figures dashed about, shouting and gesticulating, their work completed, the place removed from the earth in a searing flash of blazing heat. Its piercing tall spire, like a spear of flame, rose high into the heavens, a fiery dart thrust into God's heart.

"Too late!" Sandrine cried, drawing back to the cover of the trees from the undulating meadow.

"But not too late to kill some of Poré's men!" cried Isabella. "And perhaps even Poré himself! Come on!" She cocked both her revolvers, racing forward and levelling them at the men, pulling the triggers as she went. Their cheers of celebration from burning the church at once turned to alarm and barked commands.

Henry cried out, looking across at Sandrine and shaking his head, before taking out his own weapons and following the scarlet-haired woman over the field into the mêlée. There had been seven of the arsonists in front of the flaming fire, standing back from the flames, hands on hips admiring their work, or running hither and thither collecting up the last of their belongings before moving on. Two were shot in the head and killed instantly by Isabella. Another was spun by a round in his shoulder, groaning and writhing on the dry earth.

Weapons were retrieved and fired back, bullets zipping and fizzing about Henry and Isabella, as they found cover behind a low stone wall marking the edge of the churchyard and reloaded, retraining their sights on the men seconds later.

"Kill yourself if you must!" hissed Henry, slow simmering fury eating him up. "But please don't involve Sandrine or me!"

"Then don't follow!" Isabella retorted, before levelling her revolver and firing at one of the men aiming at their position.

On the far side of the burning church, beyond where the attack had been launched, a pallid balding man, ravaged like a walking corpse, turned his head to the sounds of gunfire and knew at once it did not originate from the front line. Instantly he knew it was the three who had found him after the Carso, the ones who had begged not to be left behind, who had pleaded to travel with him, but who then, once they had understood his great vision, had lost their stomach for the fight and attempted to stop him. He'd been a fool to welcome them into his clan at all. He knew that now.

He played with the wolf pelt under his thumb and looked across at the young Italian soldier next to him, his face scorched sooty-black from the flames and smoke, before holding up the fur and pushing it towards him.

"Take it, Pablo," he commanded, thrusting it into his eager hands. Pablo's heart raced and he trembled as he gathered the pelt cap, holding it close to him like a treasured prize. Its terrible power when worn, imbuing whoever put it on with brawn, passion and mastery over all things, had become like a drug to the young man. He had only worn the pelt a few times, but his desire to wear it, to covet it, to be its sole owner, had grown even more terrible, its draw upon him even tighter. "For too long these three have pursued us," Poré said, pointing towards the sounds of close gunfire. "For too long they have hugged our shadows and put at risk all that we are trying to achieve." His eyes narrowed on the young man. "It is time to show them how far we have come. Call the wolves," he commanded. "Call them to you. Be their master while you wear the pelt and kill Sandrine Prideux and the two who travel with her. Kill all of them! And then, return to me."

For a fleeting moment Pablo hesitated, torn by conflicting memories of past friendship with the three he had been commanded to kill, of salvation under their care from that deathly black pinnacle of hateful rock in the Karst, of camaraderie and togetherness, at least in those early days, something he had never previously known. But then the stinking magnificence of what he held in his hands reached his nose and he shivered, relishing the chance to wear it again and be bound up in its emancipating clutches.

He nodded and turned, drawing the pelt up over his head as Poré with the other followers vanished into the trees in the opposite direction, away from the gunfire and shrieks and the flicker of monstrous flames.

Moments later, Henry and Isabella heard the deathly howl rise up out of the trees beyond the church and stopped shooting.

"Oh my God," cried Henry, looking back immediately to the line of trees behind him, hoping to see Sandrine still standing there amongst the boughs and low branches. His first thought was that Sandrine herself had been tempted to change into the wolf that possessed her in times of anger and pain and fight Poré that way, exposing herself to the uncontrollable rage that the change always brought with it. But then she fell against him, behind the wall.

"Did you hear that?" she asked urgently, her eyes clear and wide.

And Henry nodded and looked across at Isabella in growing horror, knowing they were terribly under-gunned and unprepared to face this sort of enemy, three of them against Poré's horde, with barely enough silver to arm themselves.

"Wolves!" he cried, the word shredding his throat. "They have wolves!"

NINE

ŞURDEŞTI. ROMANIA.

He had lost them earlier in the day, lost them where the broad mountains passes dropped fast over crumbling black granite to shatter and surrender to grey scree and heather-covered hills, undulating and sinking like great rolling plateaus of green, broken up by valleys of fast-flowing clear streams and broad tall firs. Lost them, as he had rested and waited for his body to recover enough for him to move on. He would have prayed for help to find them, but he supposed he was beyond such things now.

Stupid.

He had lost them in the land where every field seemed full of soldiers and horses and trucks, where everything was carved up black and grey, all colour ground and burnt and blown out of the place.

Two years ago it never would have happened. He never would have lost those he was pursuing. But two years ago may as well have been a lifetime. Two years ago he was a different man to the one he was now, and though he'd done his best to deny it, to tell himself that nothing had changed, that he was still implacable, a frenzy of power and might, he had since come to accept that everything had changed. That he was no longer the unremitting, inexorable person he had been. He had been wounded, by tooth and claw, bullet, blade and curse. Wounded too many times. Every wound had its price eventually, every trauma a cost.

The hulking figure stopped and cocked his ear to the wind. Somewhere in the maelstrom of mortar-fire and falling shells, flashing and erupting all about him, he hoped he would find what he was looking for. That he would find her safe.

A German soldier appeared from the trees and the great black shadow fell on him with the speed and precision of a plunging guillotine blade. The young man barely had a chance to squeal before the life was throttled out of him and he was thrown dead into the shallow ditch which ran the length of the trees. The soldier hadn't had to die, but the figure killed him anyway, not willing to take the risk, not here, not now, so close to the German and Russian lines. So close to what he hoped would be the end of his search. Soldiers were always keen to raise alarms, especially this near to their front line during a barrage, but dead soldiers rarely did.

And the voice in his head approved.

The giant ravaged man worked the ache out of his murderous hands and pulled a bottle of vodka from a pocket, drinking deeply. The fiery spiced spirit hit his brain like a battering ram. He gritted his teeth and felt the creeping pall of dark inside him recede a little. A brief respite.

He drained the bottle and threw it into the ditch alongside the dead German, clearing his throat and raking the side of his ravaged face with dirty fingernails as he plunged into the trees. He knew these lands well. He remembered their beauty long ago before the war had come here and torn them up, breathtaking wide vistas of green, long snaking rivers, broad banks of trees rising and falling across the undulating plains sweeping down from the Carpathian Mountains at his back, their peaks hung with clouds. Now everything had been defiled and churned into grey, the front line an ugly scar running through a diseased polluted rift of poisoned blackened earth.

Most of the trees he passed were smashed, lying splintered and broken across the shell-hole covered forest floor, fallen trunks like archways beneath which he had to crouch. Rusted broken piles of equipment and torn bushes of barbed wire were strewn throughout the place, as if the wood had been a dumping ground for the German Army. In the gloom, his eyes swept the black shadowy undergrowth. For two years he had been hunting, two years trying to find her. After all those long months, he hoped his questions might finally have answers, his search bringing him here, to this small battered wood on the eastern front and the Church of the Archangels Michael and Gabriel.

A wolf howled, the sound as alluring as it was dreadful, reawakening in him a memory long driven out. Something prickled his scaly skin and he hunkered down onto his haunches, taking out his revolver and checking the silver rounds inside. Each was stamped with the Vatican's mark. His last cache of silver bullets.

All good things came to an end, eventually, he supposed. But not yet. Not quite.

As he slammed the cylinder home and cocked his weapon he caught the acrid stink that always lingered wherever Hombre Lobo, werewolves as they were better known, were to be found. The scowl on his face was replaced with a cold knowing smile. He had been right to follow them.

Moonlight teased through the sparse broken branches above, a hazy sick veil of silver catching in the rising tendrils of cordite smoke inside the wood. His heart pounded and he grimaced, searching in an inside pocket for another bottle, something to calm himself and prepare for what lay ahead. He felt his ravaged calloused skin chafe and pull against the lining of his chain mail.

Two years could never heal all wounds. Not completely. Not his. Some wounds would never heal. Some wounds would be the death of him.

A second bottle of vodka came into his hand and he broke the seal, uncorking it and swilling the strong liquor around his tongue.

Two years.

He took a second gulp, sucking the burning fiery spirit between his teeth, tasting molasses and blood. Russian shellfire burst above the trees, peppering the wood with shrapnel and flame. The sky seemed suddenly to boil with fire. The sharp bark of gunfire, louder now, came up from the valley below, just the other side of the wood, shouting and the coarse mangle of German and Russian voices knitted together, of bombs going off and the rapid angry bark of machine-guns. He stowed the bottle and took out his revolver again, and with it a silver twelve-inch blade from its sheath on his left thigh.

In all his searching, his chasing, it was easy to forget that he was caught in a world bound up in a terrible war.

An ancient wretched voice in his head taunted him, screaming obscenities, and he matched it with his own coarse retort, moments before something moved into his field of vision, something feral and lumbering and fast, something that grew huge on him in an instant. It howled as it leapt. The revolver flashed in his hand, once, twice, and the great shaggy wolf fell from the sky and turned over, dead at his feet, its great blood-red tongue lolling from between insidious teeth.

A second wolf emerged from the trees on his right, howling and spitting as it rushed him, others following close in its wake. He shot the creature through the eye and the wolf behind it twice in the neck, tumbling with the third as it came on him too quickly, gathering him up in its enormous claws. The pair brawled and rolled between standing trunks and shattered remains of the trees, blood and fur showering the matted ground. Jaws slashed and a blade flashed and then vanished in the forest, reappearing moments later glistening crimson and wet in the moonlight. It vanished again, its entire length sliding into the creature, and he kicked the wolf away, using the final round in his revolver to kill another wolf pacing towards him, three steps away.

New silver rounds were in his bloodied hand and seconds later in the cylinder of his revolver, the ruinous sounds of the eastern front all about him like a sonnet to the bloodshed, as more wolves howled and charged, all teeth and claws and animal stink. He stood tall and shot four of them dead, throwing the fifth over his shoulder. As it flew past, he thrust upwards with the blade of his knife, raking a deep trench in its belly, gushing guts and blood across the forest floor.

Two more wolves came at him and he put his two remaining rounds into the first and slammed the blade of the silver knife clean through the ear of the beast behind, its howl dying on its slavering tongue.

His breathing was hard, as if caught in a murderous stranglehold. He stood back, his back raked open, the glimmer of blood on the silver mail beneath his long coat. He fished in a pocket and took out six more rounds, slipping them smoothly into the cylinder.

Above him, it seemed as if hell was trying to break through the heavens, the night torn apart with the clamour and fury of Russian shellfire. He was drenched in the vibrant light of the inferno. He swore, never once turning his eyes to heaven in apology, and surveyed the flaming shadows of the wood, his eyes falling upon a building, tongues of fire reaching high from its burning roof, not far from where he stood. The church! They had burned another church!

Something moved in the flare and threw itself forward, and he shot it twice. Two more wolves scrambled towards him, like wasps fleeing from a shaken nest. He emptied his chamber into them, knocking the smoking cylinder open and refilling it immediately with the last of his rounds.

He snapped it shut in time to shoot dead another great wolf, aged and matted grey, emerging from the darkness of the trees, killing it instantly. Another pounced and Tacit let it come, catching it under the jaws and setting the revolver beneath its skull. His trigger finger tightened and the gun exploded, taking the wolf from its life of torment in a flash of fire and burning flesh.

He was now at the open meadow, fifteen steps away from the flaming building. Something else lingered in the depths of its rippling shadows, the glint of a gun barrel, the shuffle of feet.

Intuition kicked in and he stepped aside the very moment the rifle erupted, blasting a splintered black hole in a tree behind him. Two seconds later he was in the full glare of the church's licking tendrils of light and heat, lashing out with his fists, knocking the weapon from the hands of his assailant, sending her sprawling to the floor.

She went down and turned over as a final wolf leapt from the surrounding blackness and the man took it by the mane and turned it over, pressing the barrel of his revolver tight to its neck and pulling the trigger for a final time. The beast roared and hung still in his grip, as a shriek and then a cry of disbelief escaped from the woman.

And a name. Just a name was spoken by her.

"Tacit!" said Isabella.

"Yes."

TEN

ŞURDEŞTI. ROMANIA.

The shrieking and the whimpering of the great wolves sounded as dreadful as they were, writhing and twisting in their death throes. Centuries of life and hate ran out of them, the noise a scourge in the ears. The crackle of gunfire battered and reverberated up the hillside. Beneath it, the moans of the dying wolves and men all around the church and its clearing were like a closing sermon of death.

"Is it you?" she asked Tacit, her hands now on his torn and butchered face.

Henry and Sandrine, raked by wolf claws and blackened by fire smoke, stumbled close to observe this apparition, this man long believed dead now reappeared amongst them.

"Is it you?" Isabella asked again, but Tacit never answered.

More gunfire and cries had torn his eyes away to the new charging enemy. He swung from Isabella, appearing to all who saw him like a great caped black demon, facing the oncoming onslaught as they rushed from the tree line alone. From the darkness, full of firelight and falling embers, men, dressed only in black, charged, their shouts ragged and coarse. Compared to that moment of quiet recognition, the sound of barked commands roared like blasphemy and the adrenaline returned like a hammer blow.

His revolver barked angrily, and moments later Isabella joined his chorus with her own weapons, the running figures tumbling and spinning as the rounds bit home. He never turned his eyes to the woman he loved crouching next to him, but he knew then that she had changed, forever branded by the horrors she had seen and experienced because of him.

"Kill the others but leave Tacit!" a voice commanded from where the light of the flames failed to fall, and Tacit narrowed his gaze on the sound and ran towards it, knowing the command had made him invincible to this new enemy.

His revolver barked three times, the air thick with gunsmoke, the sounds coming from the darkness ahead full of weeping and pleading.

Tacit saw something move amongst the bodies of Inquisitors littering the floor, another fool cocking a revolver. He shot him through the head and went hunting for their leader. For seconds, maybe minutes, Tacit didn't know, he searched for him, finally finding him, the man who had barked the command from the edge of the trees. In the confusion, the Inquisitor had doubled back and managed to come up from behind the church, snatching Isabella tight around her neck, the splay of red hair falling down her breast. Something shimmered inside Tacit to see her caught, panic tightening in his throat, the sweep of yearning scything through him like a charge. Unconsciously his fingers whitened against the grip of his revolver.

"Tacit!" the black-clad Inquisitor called out to him. Tacit recognised him, one of the Inquisitors who had vanished shortly after the start of war in Europe. It seemed to Tacit that a lot of Inquisitors had mysteriously disappeared from service around the same time. Now he understood why. Now he knew where they had gone and under whose ultimate command they now fought. The Darkest Hand.

"Let her go," Tacit growled, taking a pace forward.

"If you come with me, perhaps I *will* let her go unharmed."

At once the muscles in Tacit's face hardened. "And why would I wish to go with you? Let her go now, before I kill you." He levelled his revolver at the man.

The Inquisitor snorted and set the barrel of his own gun tight against Isabella's head, pulling back a little into the entwining shadows of the trees. Tacit froze, his eyes not leaving Isabella for an instant, the pair drinking each other in.

"Our master was right," said the Inquisitor.

"Was he now?" replied Tacit, absently, not looking at the man. His eyes were set only on one thing. To look upon Isabella again after all this time made his heart swell so greatly that it felt as if it might overwhelm him.

"Find Isabella, he said," continued the Inquisitor, a broken smile flashing between his calloused lips. "Find Isabella and you'll find Tacit. He is wise, our master, beyond measure. You will see yourself, when you return with me to him."

There were tears of astonishment in Isabella's own eyes, her mouth hanging open in disbelief at what she saw, Tacit, clearly him though he was ravaged and scarred like a man returned from a lifetime of trials.

"You were dead!" she mouthed at him.

"I'm not that easy to kill," Tacit called back, a light in his face, the lines next to his eyes deepening.

"Are you listening to me?" shouted the Inquisitor, moving to his right so that he filled Tacit's view. He shook the hostage in his arm, and Tacit's eyes were drawn onto him, turning colder. The ends of his mouth contorted. "Are you listening to me, Poldek Tacit?" asked the Inquisitor.

"No," Tacit replied, his stare like a hard morning frost.

"Well you should!" the man barked back. "You're wanted."

"By whom?"

"Like I already said! Our master!"

"No master of mine," answered Tacit, shaking his head, while the voice in his head mocked him.

The Inquisitor cocked the revolver and pressed it tighter to Isabella's skull, making her cry out. The voice lacerated inside Tacit's brain, spitting venom and heresy like a poisonous curse across his mind. He let it rise up and torment him, focusing the wrath into his trigger finger.

"We've been looking for you, Tacit. For years we've been looking for you, thinking perhaps you were dead! Finally we've found you. *I've* found you! You're to come with me. You have no choice other than to do as commanded. No one has a choice before our master."

But Tacit cleared his throat.

"I'm going to kill you," he said.

The Inquisitor spat at him, pulling back Isabella's head and setting the barrel into the pale white skin beneath her jawbone.

"Whatever happens," Tacit continued, his face hardening into a mask of hate, "I'm going to kill you. But unlike this master of yours you speak of, I *am* going to give you a choice. The choice is *how* you die. If you want it quick and quiet, let Isabella go now. Let go of her, push her to one side and let me have a clear shot at you. But if you cause her any more harm, the torment you will endure at my hands will be unlike anything you've ever experienced before, beyond anything you believed was humanly possible, so terrible you'll be begging for death to come and your agony to end."

For an instant the Inquisitor hesitated, scanning the wood to see who from his unit of Inquisitors was left. He saw only Henry and Sandrine pacing slowly towards him, shutting him in, stopping any chance of escape. "Your soul is black, Poldek Tacit," he shouted, "just as we had been told!"

Tacit shrugged, inching forward. "We all stare into the Abyss at times in our lives. It's just that some of us know when to look away."

The Inquisitor snatched a brief look again for his defeated men and instantly Tacit's gun barked. Isabella shrieked and fell away as her captor snapped backwards, his face a gash of torn showering flesh, the Inquisitor of the Darkest Hand tumbling and rolling dead between the trees behind.

"Tacit!" wept Isabella, throwing herself into his wide enveloping arms. "Tacit!"

He drew her tight to him, his hands on her back and in her hair, holding her closely to him, feeling her heat, smelling her skin and sweat.

"Is it really you?" she asked.

"It's me, Isabella! It's me!" he replied, weeping as well, their mouths seeking and finding each other and melting together in a kiss no force could break. Eventually, Tacit drew himself back. "I told you, Isabella!" he said, through gritted tears of wonder and emotion, the words clawing their way out of him. "I told you that I would never leave you! I made you that promise in the Carso, that I would never leave you. That was, and still is, my promise to you, as true as my love has always been for you! I will never leave you again."

ELEVEN

THE VATICAN. VATICAN CITY.

"The dagger that you keep at your side, Bishop Basquez," whispered Cardinal Bishop Adansoni, stepping unheard and unseen behind the eager young Bishop in the arched corridor of St Peter's Basilica. There was a hint of a smile on the old Cardinal's lips. "Tell me, is it for your protection, or what Bishops now deem appropriate to hang from their vestments?" At once the snakelike man spun to face him, measuring himself against the wall, his right hand dropping surreptitiously to the leather and steel hilt at his side. "Some suggest that the times in which we live are dangerous," continued Adansoni, enjoying mocking the Bishop he so distrusted, "but are they so terrible that we must arm ourselves even in the Vatican corridors?"

"The blade is for my protection," Basquez replied, his eyes narrowing on the bowed Cardinal, the old man still clearly amused by his attempt at humour. Something boiled in the Bishop, his teeth snapped tight. "And you would be well advised to arm yourself as well, Adansoni."

"Against whom exactly?"

"Our enemies."

The Cardinal Bishop chuckled and curled his chin into his chest, a veiled attempt to conceal his laughter. "In the Vatican?" The warmth of superiority was intertwined in his words. He clicked with his tongue and turned his gaze away. He smelt cut grass, brought in through a nearby window on the warm summer breeze, and could hear a choir somewhere in the jumble of buildings beyond. He went towards it, as if transfixed, still shaking his head gently, seeking out the open window. He'd never liked the scheming Bishop, and the fact that the man had taken to arming himself made Adansoni feel even more suspicious of him. The Bishop's voice followed him, tainting the sound of reverent singing coming from the city beyond.

"*Particularly* in the Vatican," Basquez hissed precisely. "These days there are few places it seems one may go without fearing being set upon by our enemies. Only a fool would think otherwise, which is perhaps why you speak as you do?" Basquez's eyes narrowed tighter still, but now there was humour in his own sour face, the ambitious younger man rediscovering the spirit and bite for which he was well known amongst those with whom he dealt. His fingers whitened around the hilt of his weapon, as if he was steeling himself to draw out the blade.

But Adansoni answered, "You worry too much," and waved a derisory hand, continuing to wander absently and in a vague direction towards the rising sounds of the choir. He found the open window and stood at it listening, his eyes closed, the sun on his face, breathing in the generous earthy smells of late summer.

"And you would do well to worry," spat Basquez at his back.

"Are you threatening me, Bishop Basquez?" Adansoni asked, turning to him at a speed which both surprised and alarmed the young Bishop. Basquez had never realised the old man was able to move so fast for one of his age. Adansoni raised a cautioning finger at him, as a father might to an errant son. "Floors have ears and walls eyes. Careless idle talk is damaging, not to mention dangerous."

"When the dead rise from their coffins, as they did at Cardinal Bishop Korek's funeral, when fountains of St Peter's Square run red with blood, when a war rages on our very borders, when," and Basquez paused, staring, studying Adansoni hard, "Gerard-Maurice Poré, he who attempted such horror at the Mass for Peace in Paris, reveals himself to be still alive, bringing chaos and murder to monasteries of peace and contemplation in the east, I know that we are indeed living in dark days, days when only a fool would walk about the Vatican, or indeed anywhere, unarmed." As quickly as his outburst came, it dissipated, his manner, and the grip on his knife, easing. Without another word he stepped away, seemingly satisfied with himself and his outburst, Adansoni scrutinising him as he left. But a smile crept onto the old man's face, one of quiet delight at having brought the conniving Bishop to lose his composure.

"Your smile," called another voice, this time reverent and sagacious, away to Adansoni's left, from an arched passageway which led into the one on which the old Cardinal was standing. "It cheers me to see it," said Cardinal Secretary of State Casado. "There seems so little to smile about these days." The two friends greeted each other warmly and agreed to walk together for a while, once Adansoni had checked to see that Basquez had slunk away, vanished into his warren of plotting and conspiracy.

Adansoni nodded. "There is still hope in the world, reasons to remain optimistic. And after all, if we, in our hallowed worshipful halls, cannot remain full of hope, what hope is there?"

"You no doubt heard about these churches which are burning?" asked Casado, as the warm rays of sunlight touched his gown and shimmered against the pristine marbled floor of the Papal Palace.

"All along the eastern front? Yes, I have. And the one they believe is responsible."

"Poré," said Casado. "They say it is Poré."

Adansoni pursed his lips and nodded. "Yes, our friend Bishop Basquez enjoyed passing on this latest news to me moments ago."

Sun streamed into the walkway down which the two revered Cardinals were walking, their shoes clipping staccato clacks against the blood-red floor tiles, sending echoes spinning around the tall arched dome above them. Casado cleared his throat. "Of course, we knew he was still alive. We knew he was alive in Pleven a couple of years ago when we sent the squad of Inquisitors to deal with him and his so-called brigands. But then, after that, he vanished. Never heard of until the start of this year and the desecration of these churches. Churches of the Archangels. All burnt to the ground." Casado shook his head. "Just the thought of it! The heresy!"

"And we have no idea where he has been hiding all this time? What he has been plotting?"

"None! There was the rumour that he had been involved in the events at the Carso, this apparent ritual they speak of, but nothing has ever been proved."

"One must wonder why he has returned now?"

"Why indeed?"

"Surely we can spare a few Inquisitors to search for him? Poré is trouble." The man's words were spoken like a prediction.

The old Cardinal shrugged. "A rope can only be drawn so far before it snaps. Possessions, tales of dark skulking things in all corners of the world, devilry and mayhem, not to mention this terrible war, they have all played their part in diminishing the Inquisition's effectiveness. There are even some who say Inquisitors have joined with Poré himself as foot soldiers!"

Adansoni shook his head, disappointed. "So we let him carry on, burning churches and defiling our name, do we?"

Casado ran the edge of his hand back and forth across his forehead, as if reaching for an answer which did not come. "It was not always this way."

"It was not!" replied Adansoni urgently. "And our list of great Inquisitors is long! Bernardo Gui? Konrad von Marburg? Tomás de Torquemada? Inquisitor Düül?"

The names of previous Inquisitors, each of them monstrous and magnificent in memory and deed, appeared to shrink and diminish the old Cardinal Secretary of State, as if the names were wounds upon him. He grew sallow and restless at their recounting, his hand clutched to his chest. He paused in the pillared vestry at the end of the southern hall, his hand creeping to his chin, his greying watery eyes looking out over the people and flocking birds circling around St Peter's Square. "Goodness, we have done so much wrong in our time, Javier."

"We have done what needed to be done. To persevere. To triumph. Ask yourself, would any other faith not do as we have done to ensure its continuance? Are we so different from other religions who try to enforce their creed upon others? No! We are simply better prepared and better provisioned for the task."

Though he nodded in agreement, Casado, the older Cardinal, looked troubled, his mouth opening to speak words which never came. So Javier Adansoni spoke for him. "Our way has always been, and will always be, though we all wish another way might be found. It is the fate of men, I suppose, to do harm unto each other to achieve their ambitions and betterment for their people. And really, are we so very different from those nations who throw themselves at their supposed enemies on the front lines of Europe every day? They wish victory, just as we do."

"But at what price must victory come?"

"Let victory come, and then let us count its cost."

Casado considered his friend's words and hesitantly accepted the wisdom in them. He knew he had no option other than to accept them. To do so gave him no comfort, his indecision and doubt merely confounding what he had long realised. That he lacked the compulsion and stomach to remain a decisive leader of the Holy See. "I wonder where he has gone to now?" Casado asked, forcing his thoughts to other matters forever consuming him. He turned his eyes to the ground beneath his feet, to where he supposed the answer to his question lay.

"Poré?"

"No," said Casado, a shimmer bristling through him at speaking the name. "Poldek Tacit."

They had stopped walking and stood and watched the crowds and doves across St Peter's Square. The saying of Tacit's name had brought them both to silence.

It was Casado who spoke first, as if he couldn't stand the quiet any longer, as if he had to get the confession out of himself. "We wronged you, Javier," he said, allowing his gaze to wander cautiously over to the man next to him. "We were never honest with you, although I think you always knew, didn't you? Tacit, your boy, he was always suspect to most at the Holy See, always questions about where he had come from, the skills he possessed. We... we trapped him, eventually, like we trap everything we don't trust."

"I know," Adansoni said. He wished for all the world that his friend would stop his confession, stop torturing himself with his words, but Casado never did.

"It was never my wish that he was treated as he was. But there are strong voices in the Holy See, individuals who distrusted Tacit and saw opportunity in who he was, what he might be, what he might offer to us. Bishop Basquez... he is committed and sly."

"Please, my friend, you have nothing to apologise for or to explain. Whatever happened, happened."

But Casado refused to be censored. "We tortured him to see what advantage over our enemies might be gained from him. We pursued him into his body, into his mind, trying to eke out his secrets. And now… he is dead! Good God, Javier! What have we done?"

Adansoni watched him, horrified at the old man's weakness, transfixed, as if he was watching the man mutilate himself, but was unable to step in and take the blade away from him. Eventually Casado looked up, taking his hands from his face, his skin white and pink where he had pressed his fingers tight to his skull. "I wonder sometimes," he said, "if he somehow still lives." He fell silent and then smiled wanly, a half laugh on his breath. "Ignore me," he said. "I am just thinking aloud. I feel I can do so with you, one of my oldest and dearest of friends."

"Of course," replied Adansoni, bowing.

Casado searched out a stone bench on the far side of the vestry, leading with a wavering hand, and lowered himself onto it, exhaling as he did so, as if nursing an injury. Indecision dogged him once more, and exhaustion flooded in. "I don't know. Sometimes I feel as if I am too old for my place in the Holy See. Perhaps it would be better for me to retire, allow another to take my seat of office?"

"Not at all," replied Adansoni, and Casado smiled, more warmly this time.

"I am dogged, Javier, all the time by doubts and worries. There are still many in the church who cannot, and will not, forget or forgive what happened at the Mass for Peace, particularly those tied up with it."

"We will find Poré eventually," said Adansoni, taking the Secretary's words to refer to the traitorous Cardinal.

"I am speaking of Sister Isabella," he said.

"Another who has vanished also!"

"There is a suggestion amongst some that she travels with Poré. Perhaps she has information that will help us find him?"

Adansoni darkened and nodded. "If this is true, then I suppose we *must* try to find her, for if Isabella has such information, perhaps she will know where Tacit is, or lies buried? It is clear that she and he formed a… fondness for each other. Perhaps with a specific target, the Inquisition's limited resources can be better used?"

The Secretary of State considered the words before closing his eyes and acknowledging this suggestion with a gentle nod of his head. "Thank you, Javier. I can always rely on you for guidance! Let us see if any rumour of

Isabella can be found by the Inquisition. If so, perhaps we will be able to find both Poré and the final resting place of Poldek Tacit? And so make sure that death claims them both!"

TWELVE

ŞURDEŞTI. ROMANIA.

The church fell into glowing ruins, groaning and crashing to the ground, fireflies of orange and white spinning and chasing high into the night sky beneath the tumbling burning rafters. Though all gunfire had fallen silent around the crackling smouldering remains of the building, they could all still hear the rattle of war in the valley beyond, the relentless thump and battering of bombs and shells and small arms from the onslaught of Russians, a sonnet to the dead who lay still in the nearby fields, Inquisitors of the Darkest Hand, wolves and servants of those who had followed Poré.

Henry staggered against a gate post and clawed the breath into his lungs, his silhouette clipped and eroded against the flames of the church behind him. He wavered on unsteady legs, consciousness blending in and out of focus. And then he saw him.

"Oh my God!" he cried, coming forward and reaching out in a moment of wild abandonment to embrace the man who had saved them from the wolves, the man they had long thought was dead. "It's you!" Tacit fended off the attempt to hold him, shoving him away and studying Isabella, gazing at her as if she were a drink and he a burning thirst to be quenched. "We thought you were dead!" marvelled Henry.

Tacit turned his attention slowly back to the soldier.

"I'm a hard man to kill," he said.

"Clearly! You look terrible!" Henry replied, half laughing, but he thought he had never spoken a truer word in his life. For Tacit did look terrible, torn and shambling. His body appeared misshapen, lopsided, heavier on one side as if he carried an injury there, his face ravaged by wounds and tides and time, though still proud and defiant, a look that Henry remembered so well.

Tacit thought the same of Henry, filthy and bloodied from this most recent of battles against both wolves and Inquisitors. "You're hardly a picture of health."

Henry spread his arms wide, like an actor accepting plaudits. "We knew it would never be an easy path we walked. But you, where the hell have you been, Tacit? It's been two years! You fell! You fell from the Carso into the Soča River! A thousand feet!" Henry's hands were now in his hair in wonder and despair at recalling the scene. Sandrine was standing beside him, her revolvers smoking as she gazed at Tacit with grim admiration and equal amazement. Henry reached towards him again, as if to check Tacit was not an imposter. "We saw you fall! There was no way someone could have survived such a fall!"

"Then it seems that I'm not that someone."

"The last time I saw you, Tacit, you were hanging by your fingernails to that lump of rock," said Sandrine. There was warmth behind the comment, intended as a quip, but there was also the suggestion of tears in her eyes, relief snagged in her throat. "It is good to see you again! There! I've said it! It's good to see you again, Tacit, you bastard! I bet you never thought you'd hear me saying that!" Like Henry, she hesitated between coming forward and throwing her arms about him and staying back. Her indecision was born not just out of seeing Tacit's response to Henry's unappreciated attempt at greeting, but also because of how Tacit seemed, wild and feral, unhinged, even more unpredictable than she remembered. Instead she chose to do the latter, crossing her arms and looking at him incredulously. "Have you been looking for us for all this time?"

"As soon as I was able," replied Tacit, his eyes back on Isabella, devouring her. "It's good to see you again, Isabella!"

"And you, Tacit!" laughed Henry, daring to slap him across the shoulders. Tacit fended the generous greeting away.

"Keep your hands off me," he warned. "I've not come back for you and your friendship, Henry. Only for Isabella." And then something caught his attention and he seemed to change, looking more as Henry remembered him, looking beyond the soldier to the burning church. "Still no strangers to trouble, I see? Wolves? Inquisitors? Never had you down as people who would burn churches, though?"

"Poré," said Sandrine, and Tacit's demeanour darkened once again upon hearing the name of the man he hadn't seen since the Mass for Peace in Paris, three years ago. "It was Poré, and his men. He's been burning churches."

"So, that traitor's not dead? Pity. I knew I should have killed him when I had the chance."

"He was there, Tacit," said Henry, "at the Carso. At the ceremony, the summoning of the Princes of Hell. The wolves, the wolves that came into the place on the pinnacle of the Karst that night, the wolves who tore down the Priests. Did you know?" Tacit growled something indiscernible, a seething rush of hot curses, shaking his head. But Henry nodded, persistent. "It was him, him and his clan of wolves. Werewolves."

"Impossible," Tacit scowled, still shaking his head. "Couldn't have been him."

"It was," replied Isabella, taking hold of his heavy calloused hand. "We know. We followed him. We travelled with him, for a little while afterwards at least."

"Poré," said Henry, "he has found some way of drawing them to his command," and at once Tacit thought of the pelt that Poré had used in Arras. He looked out over the Inquisitors' bodies littering the field, and Henry watched his gaze, knowing that Tacit also recognised which side the dead had served. "Poré is no friend of the Darkest Hand. We owe him that much."

"And yet he burns churches?"

"And threatens much more. From what little we know, what little we have discovered."

"I don't care what you have discovered!" He looked back at the red-headed woman next to him. "I've only returned for Isabella."

Sandrine blew through her lips, looking away into the flickering shadows of dancing night and fire. "Some welcome!" she spat. "Listen to me, you oaf! Poré must be stopped! His intentions for the world, they are terrible!"

"He means to bring some catastrophe to it," said Henry. "Some devastation, some warning, from some greater power. Divine retribution, he called it. Condemnation for all those who have sinned, all those who have wronged him."

Tacit shrugged. "Sounds like his way, the arrogance of the man."

"There were hints, clues, suggestions, all of which made us wary, concerned, concerned enough to try and stop him."

A great shattering explosion, shells landing close to where they stood, made them cower and draw back a little further from the burning church and the direction of the front line.

"Pablo," continued Henry, "the boy who was to be sacrificed at the pinnacle in the Carso, the young Italian soldier who came with us, he deceived us, and Poré and his gathering left us behind. We have been following them ever since."

Tacit sneered, as if offended. "You travelled with him? With Poré?"

"For a little while, yes. We found him, after the Carso, after many months looking for him. We had nowhere else to go, no one else to trust, no other hope. And Poré, he seemed like an ally, someone who fought with us against the same foe."

"But his plans," said Sandrine, holstering the now cool revolvers, her dark hair falling across her breast, "as they were slowly revealed to us, we realised that they were as corrupt as the Darkest Hand's."

"I don't understand why you're telling me any of this?"

"Don't you care?" asked Sandrine. "Really, don't you care about Poré? About what he might be planning?"

"No."

He could see the incredulity in their faces. He wanted to laugh, laugh now that he had found Isabella, sweep her up into his arms and waltz away from them. But something glimmered in Tacit, a sliver of admiration, perhaps even respect for the pair of them who had accompanied him up the Carso, those who had continued the fight while he had recuperated and searched for his own answers. Something close to shame twisted inside him and he knew he should show them at least a little civility. "Where are you going next?"

"We don't know. We've been following Poré. But now that you're back…"

"Well, I wish you luck," said Tacit, already uninterested. "I'll accompany you as far as the nearest town."

"What's that's supposed to mean?"

Tacit's eyes were solely on Isabella. Instantly the man who was always so powerful seemed suddenly heavy and obtuse, as if labouring under his own doubts, the inkling of discomfort for what he was to reveal. "I didn't come back here for this," he said, looking about himself, at the ruination of the ground, the broken torn bodies, riddled with gunfire or raked by claws. "I didn't come back for any of this."

"But you did come back," muttered Henry, taking a step forward, the voice childlike in his throat. "You came back, Tacit, you came back!"

"I did what I needed to do," he said, looking only at Isabella again. "I did what I needed to do to find you, Isabella. All this… this fighting…"

His words failed him and he shook his head, shaking back the grim demeanour for which they all knew him. "It's over for me," he growled, his voice black as jet. "I've only come back for you, Isabella. I've come back to take you away from this." The sly wicked voice in his head ridiculed him, calling him a liar.

"You came all this way, just for Isabella?" asked Sandrine, disbelievingly.

"I told you, Isabella, that I would never leave you again. I've kept that promise." He reached out for her but she drew away from him. "What is it? What's the matter?"

"I can't go back, Poldek," she replied. "Not now. I've come too far."

"And I haven't? Isabella, you're the reason I've come here, the reason I am still alive."

"And you're the reason why I still am still alive, Poldek," and they both remembered the chamber and the gunshot from Georgi's revolver. "But Henry, Sandrine and I, we have come so far, done so much. And tell me," she continued, her voice as passionate as it was desperate, "where is there for us to go away to? Where is there that we can hope to go, Poldek, where Poré or the Darkest Hand cannot hope to reach, to escape them? If you think we can live without fear that they will never leave us alone, live without all the time wondering and fearing for what is happening, what is coming into the world, what is happening to it, then you are a fool, Poldek!"

"Is it me?" he asked her, his hands held up as if some specimen to observe. "Is it what has been done to me? Am I too terrible to look upon?"

"Don't mock me or think me a fool! I love you, Poldek, no matter what wounds you carry, inside or out, for that is why I love you. But you… you cannot simply reappear and draw me back into your arms," and Isabella half turned, waving absently towards the burning church, "because of this, because of him, because of Poré, because of what he is doing, because of the Darkest Hand, because of that," she cried, lifting her hand and turning her ear to the sounds of battle growing ever closer in the distance. "Look at that church!" she exclaimed, waving a final time towards it.

"What am I supposed to be seeing?"

"What Poré is doing!"

Tacit shrugged, but there was a crescendo of mocking voices shrieking in his head. "Poré is burning churches? So what? Churches have always burnt!"

"And every church has some purpose," cried Isabella, taking hold of his hand and yanking it as if trying to shake some sense into him. "Don't you see, Poldek? Poré, he's trying to do something, something terrible."

"All the churches he has burnt have been churches of the Archangels," added Henry.

Tacit scowled. "And does that make a difference?"

Isabella made a noise in her throat. "Poré means to do the world harm. He talked of a Tribulation, of a time when all sinners would be taken from the world, and that only those worthy would remain. He's discovered something, we do not know what, but for a small time we were party to some of his plans. They are depraved, wicked, an insult to all that is good. He might not be aligned with the Darkest Hand but his plans are as corrupt as anything they are planning. He is filled with only wickedness and malice, malice that must be stopped. Malice that we are trying to stop.

"I love you, Poldek," Isabella urged, taking both his arms in her hands, "I love you, but I'm not coming with you. I can't. Not now. I can't leave." And she let go of him and stepped back, picking up the rifle she had put to one side. "I'm sorry, but if you will not come with us, will not fight with us, then this is where we part." And the voice in her own head, the voice which had been with her ever since the Carso, cackled and spat a tirade of obscenities and then congratulated her.

Tacit walked alone, abandoned, close to where the church had burnt to charcoal and cinders, the caustic smell sharp in the air. In the glade in front of the church, the earth dashed with dark pools of dried blood and the churn of boots and claws, boxes stood, piled up or lying on their sides from where they had been knocked aside, their golden trinkets and valuables spewing out over the ground. They had not been looted, not burnt and destroyed with the rest of the building. Poré hadn't taken them for himself. He didn't covet the wealth they contained. It was the church that Poré had wanted to remove, the church and the secrets it held.

Tacit hung his head, letting the voices run wild in him, cursing and defiling with every heresy they knew. A pain throbbed suddenly in his side. His hand went to it and he felt warmth and wetness, taking it away he found his fingers bloodied. His wounds, old wounds, torn open from the recent activity, wounds proving to him, if he ever needed to remember, that life was only fleeting. He thought of all that had gone before, of his journey to this place, of Isabella.

"Okay," he called to them, "tell me everything that you know about what Poré is up to."

THIRTEEN

The Vatican. Vatican City.

The chamber in which the three Cardinals sat was spacious, with a high-arched ceiling into which fantastical and religious carvings had been worked in the dark wood. At the entrance to the chamber, Father Strettavario's pale eyes flickered over the group and the table around which they had gathered, china cups and slices of lemon cake set out on a silver tray. For a moment he watched the men and the morsels of sweet sponges, before stepping forward.

"Father Strettavario," called Adansoni, getting up slowly from his chair to greet the russet-haired Father, and at once Strettavario bowed his saggy neck to his chest and crossed the wooden floor to where they had set the table and chairs in a circle of light fed from the lattice window next to them.

"Cardinal Bishop Adansoni," the Father said, taking the man's proffered hand. "Cardinal Secretary of State Casado," he continued around the group, bowing his head to each in turn. "Cardinal Bishop Innocenti." Strettavario knew of the younger Cardinal Innocenti, even though the man did not reside in the Vatican. His seat was in Bavaria and it was the first time the Father had seen him in Vatican City in many years.

"Father Strettavario," muttered Casado, not even attempting to look up, the aged Cardinal's eyes buried in his lap and the cup he held there, its contents cold, only partially drunk. "There's no need for extended niceties, for drawn-out greetings. Why don't you bring us straight to the point you wish to raise with us and then allow us to continue with our discussions?"

"I have just received information from the Seers."

"And?" asked Casado, pointedly.

"They have news, and the news is very grave." Strettavario pursed his lips tighter so they turned white and sunk his neck even lower onto his chest, the flaccid skin around his jawline bunching tight like a tumour.

"Go on," urged Innocenti, dark-haired, but flecked with grey.

"The Antichrist," said Strettavario, expecting an immediate reaction to the naming of such a thing. When none was forthcoming, he continued, "His returning is any time now."

The youngest Cardinal cleared his throat, taking a moment to collect his thoughts. "The Seers," he said, "they have predicted such a thing before. What makes them, *you*, so sure they are correct this time? What makes you certain that this news you've brought to us should be believed?"

"The house of sight has lost its most powerful Seer," said Casado, his voice trembling as he spoke, "and with it much of the power to see. Can they still be trusted with the greatest of their kind… lost? With Sister Malpeghi gone," he continued slowly, almost grievously, as if recalling her name was almost too terrible a trial to endure, the flush of vexation now gone from his face and replaced with a drawn pallid hue. Her grievous murder had been a crime beyond comprehension, her eyes cut from their sockets as part of a satanic ritual. The cup rattled in his hands as he tried to speak and his words failed him.

But Strettavario's words did not fail him. "You have known the Seers for longer than any in the Holy See, Cardinal Bishop Casado," replied the old Father. "You know their abilities, and fallibilities. They are not always correct. Not always do they see with clarity or precision. They have been wrong before and certainly they have been hurt, hindered in their sight by the death of Sister Malpeghi. But they are not yet blind. Their sight is not ended. They still can see, can still predict." Strettavario looked at the tempting slices of cake and swallowed hungrily. "The vision they saw and sensed as one the other day told of End Times, the coming of the Apocalypse. They witnessed it together and it was as clear as it was terrible to witness, from what they have told me."

Casado went to speak but Strettavario spoke across him. "But since then, they have seen and learnt of another, a man returning in the coming weeks or months, if he is not already in the world, who will do terrible harm to it and its people and will take his place at the head of all this ruination from the heart of its flames. And nothing but darkness will flow out of him, and all light shall be wrung out of the world. Have no doubt," he pressed, his pale eyes as cold as sleet, "the Antichrist, he is returning. His moment is nigh."

"But the Seven Princes," said Innocenti in a heated rush, and Strettavario knew then that the young Cardinal was scared, despite his best efforts to hide his fears, "they never came through. They were stopped!"

"Yes, they were stopped, but this does not mean that the Lord of Darkness himself was stopped, or that he will ever stop in his plans to return, to ascend to his wicked place in the world."

"Even if the crows have departed the Vatican?" the young Cardinal asked, growing paler, turning absently to look at the windows. "Even if possessions in the city have abated?"

But the Father raised an eyebrow above his cold dead right eye. "Possessions abated?" He shook his head and turned his attention to the slice of lemon-coloured cake on the tray. "I think not. We do not need the Seers alone to tell us of the darkness that has come to the world, the dark things in the woods that our Inquisition fights against tirelessly, that fallen Inquisitors are like an iron harvest in many fields across Europe and beyond. That we are replacing their falling number with boys, not trained men."

"It has been this way before," said Casado. "The Inquisition, it rises and falls, like the tide."

"It does," replied Strettavario, his lips pursed in thought, "but unlike the tide which always returns eventually to the rocks, the Inquisition appears set on one course."

"Which is?"

"To be cast upon them! Obliteration, if the losses continue. While the Seven Princes *were* stopped, their Lord still exists to take his place upon his throne, protected by many, not least by the Darkest Hand. And they are an enticing instrument for power, particularly for those who have grown upon the foundations of war and rage and superiority by strength of arms."

"So, what are you saying? That death alone is not claiming our Inquisitors? That they are turning to the side more attuned to their skills?"

"Correct," nodded the pale-eyed Father. "To the side which appears to be winning."

"We should have killed Poré when we had the chance," growled Adansoni, leaving his chair and stalking to the window. He looked more youthful in the light of the day and with his cheeks flushed with indignation at this latest news, staring down onto the comings and goings of the Vatican City streets.

"What has Poré got to do with anything?" asked Cardinal Innocenti.

Adansoni made a sound which seemed like a growl. "The man tried to bring down the Catholic faith at the Mass for Peace! He killed a whole unit of Inquisitors in Pleven!"

"And you know what some are saying about Cardinal Poré?" asked Strettavario, testing the nails of his fingers against his thumb.

"No. What are they saying?"

"That it was *he* who stopped the Seven Princes."

"Impossible," croaked Casado, and he rattled his cup and saucer onto the tray. "Poré is the Antichrist. Clearly he is! As Cardinal Adansoni rightly said, he wished the church's downfall at the Mass for Peace. He travels with wolves. He was with wolves at Pleven, when the Inquisitors discovered him hiding there. Wickedness seeks out wickedness," said the old Cardinal. "Together it thrives."

"He must have found a way of turning them to his will," said Adansoni, as if to himself, his eyes looking out of the window directly into the sun so that they ached. "Drawing them under his control."

"Only the Antichrist is capable of doing such a thing, commanding the beasts of Hell to work for him." Casado's words were assured.

But Strettavario countered them with his own. "Those beasts of Hell, as you call them, don't forget that they are also the 'Children of our Faith'. Men and women cast down by our brethren long ago and turned into wolves. Hombre Lobo."

"How dare you, Father Strettavario!" replied Casado.

The old Father shrugged again. "An unfortunate truth, Cardinal Bishop Casado." He considered leaning forward and taking the slice of cake from the tray but thought better of it, and instead turned to stand next to Adansoni at the window. "We created them, we put them onto this earth, sent them under the ground. We must remember that they came *not* from Hell, but from our own incantations and spells."

"An incantation which has long been lost," added Cardinal Bishop Innocenti.

"So what are you suggesting, Father Strettavario?" asked Casado, ignoring the younger Cardinal.

"Merely that just because Poré travels with wolves, that he appears to have command over them, does not mean that he is born of the Devil."

"So what of the Mass for Peace? The fact he tried to destroy the church? Does that count for nothing?"

"Of course it should be considered. Do not forget that I was there, throughout the entire assessment of Poldek Tacit in Arras. That it was I who was watching as Tacit saved us in Paris, saved the church."

"It is a shame he could not save himself," mused Casado sadly, and he looked back to Adansoni briefly.

"Poré," scowled Adansoni, eager to turn the conversation back to the man they hunted and from the man he loved as a son, "he was last seen in Ukraine, burning churches?"

"Yes," said Strettavario. "For what purpose we do not know."

"We should not give up trying to find him," growled Cardinal Bishop Innocenti. "We should be able to hunt him wherever he goes. After all, we are the Catholic church. We carry our Pope's banner."

"I agree," said Casado. "No land or country should be safe for him, especially if he is the Antichrist."

"*If* he is the Antichrist," said Strettavario. "*If* he is."

"I think that is without question, Father Strettavario, old friend," said Adansoni.

"Perhaps. But we will know soon enough."

"How so?" asked Casado.

Strettavario cleared this throat, finally coming to his announcement. "The Seers. If it was the Antichrist whom they believed they felt coming into their visions that night, very soon they will confirm it."

"How do they hope to do that?" asked Adansoni. "They have a name?"

"They have been searching their visions, focusing their minds as one, to tease the true identity of the Antichrist from them."

At once all three Cardinals rounded on him, and Strettavario could see their hope and surprise flare up.

"So we might..." began Adansoni, but Strettavario spoke for him, nodding.

"Yes, we might be able to identify the Antichrist and kill him before he can take his place on that most dreadful of thrones. The Seers are searching for a name at the moment, picking through the shards of their visions. When they find it, they will reveal it."

"This is wondrous news to hear on a day I thought was only to be black!" exclaimed Innocenti. "When do they hope to have the name of the one who is the Antichrist?"

"Soon. And then we can kill whoever it is before he brings damnation to the world and so ensure that the Seers' visions of End Times fail to transpire."

FOURTEEN

ŞURDEŞTI. ROMANIA.

"The Russians," Tacit began, attending to the fire he was constructing in the low entrance to the shallow cave, nursing the small tongue of amber fire with pieces of kindling until it had grown into broader, lashing flames. "They will be pushing hard into German territory."

Though all were exhausted, Tacit had refused to let them rest until they had reached a place many miles west of the destroyed church and the onslaught playing out at the front line, a place where he felt certain the approaching Russian Army would not reach, at least not before the arrival of dawn. He had brought them all to a cave he had known and used many times when he walked this land as an Inquisitor, covered by a tumble of stones and caught in the shadow of a great elm tree, its roots growing through the walls, dry and broad enough to house them all easily.

"We had to draw back, away from the front line, or be caught in their advance," said Tacit. "The Russians, they won't care who we are if they find us, only that we're in their way. Four against an army, even I don't fancy those odds."

"We must be four miles from the front line now?" asked Henry.

"And there's a million men moving east towards us. The Kerensky Offensive they're calling it. They are bound to achieve some successes, although their gains will be short-lived. The Germans and Austro-Hungarians are too strong, too well equipped, too well entrenched. The Russians, they are being broken by revolution, mutiny, their soldiers dreaming of home, or change and hope and peace. Not that they will have it when the Red Army storms the palaces of Petrograd and the Czar and his royal family are removed." For a moment Tacit paused and winced, as if suddenly ailed by something under his clothing, before saying, "From out of this revolution even greater terror shall come. Mark my words."

He sat back from the fire and saw that Isabella was looking at him, proud but still appearing dumbfounded at his sudden return.

"So tell me then, what has Poré been up to?" he began, but Isabella shook her head.

"No, you tell us, Poldek! You tell us! What… how did you survive the fall into the Soča River? How did you… did you find us?"

He said nothing for a long time, watching the flames, feeling their warmth lick his face and hands. He felt for something at his back, a bottle, and uncorked it, going to drink before pausing and offering it to the others. Isabella laughed to see it, to see that he still carried hard liquor with him, and reached across, taking it from him and a sip from the bottle, before resting it in her lap and watching him closely. His eyes dropped from her face to the bottle and then back again, supposing the bottle would not be returning to his grasp any moment soon. He sought out another in the depths of his cloak.

"Always have enough, eh, Poldek?" she asked him wryly, taking another sip, before handing the bottle to Henry.

"Not always, as you might remember, but I try," he replied, recalling a similar conversation they had in Fampoux years before when he thought Isabella beautiful and spirited but still resisted giving in to her completely.

He drank, and Henry lowered the bottle and asked him again where he had been, how he had survived.

"If you want the truth, I don't know," Tacit replied. "Lucky, I suppose," and something malicious derided him in his head. "We fell and hit the water, Georgi and I. We fought for a while, but the current drew us apart and… I suppose he must be dead now. Drowned. Me? Half drowned myself, I managed to crawl onto a piece of drifting wreckage washed down river with us. I clung on to it and there I lay, for days, weeks, months? I don't know.

"They found me, an Austro-Hungarian battleship, I never knew its name, in the Adriatic. The river must have washed me out into the sea where I drifted until I was picked up. For weeks they confined me to the sick bay, nothing but the stink of anaesthetic and bandages and oil. The place, the smells, everything about it, it was maddening, but the crew, their care of me, saved me. I suppose I should be thankful to them for that. Had they not found me adrift in the ocean, taken me on board, then… well… who knows what might have happened?

"My wounds, grievous though they were, healed, healed well enough so that when we docked in Trieste, I could be transferred to one of the town's hospitals. But the staff there, the doctors and the nurses, they didn't want me, they didn't trust me, didn't like the look of me, not after what they found on me, my chain mail and crucifix." Tacit lay his hand to his breast, Henry supposed as a way of saying that he still wore and carried them with him.

"The hospital, they thought me cursed, a devil pulled from the oceans, a thing with no right to be alive. Perhaps they were right. No one trusted me and they were right not to, because all I thought of was how to escape from them, from their care and captivity. For I knew that I wanted to be away from them and to start looking for you. It was easy enough to slip away, once my wounds had healed sufficiently for me to begin my search.

"I returned to the Carso, to that place where we parted. It seemed to me that so little had changed there, other than the mountainside seemed even more blasted and despoiled, ruined by relentless war, the stalemate in those killing peaks still ground into the rock, neither side having made any gain, neither going east or west. Both armies chained to that terrible place of the Karst.

"I hunted for what news I could find of you. There seemed to be none, nothing I could use. And then eventually, I found word, word that you'd gone east, into Slovenia."

"We followed Poré," interrupted Henry, nodding.

"And I followed the path the best I could. There were many dead ends and many times it seemed to me that I would never find you. The only means by which I could guide myself was through the wolves I encountered in the mountains and amongst rocks in the hills and they are tricksy and sly, not good talkers, especially when, as I now know, they have been drawn to the banner and command of the man I was unknowingly trying to find, Poré.

"But eventually I did find your scent, close to Uzhok, in the Ukraine, and followed you here. There," he said, shrugging and taking a pull from his bottle, "not so strange. But I've spoken enough. Now you. Tell me, what's been going on? What's all this about Poré, about these churches?"

"He has burned seven churches now," replied Sandrine, through the crackling dancing firelight separating them, "all of them churches of the

Seven Archangels, their treasures never taken or damaged, just piled up in crates and boxes before the church is destroyed. He doesn't want their riches, he wants to destroy the buildings as if they offend him, as if he wants them wiped from the world. We caught up with him as he was torching the third church in Baku, Azerbaijan."

"You've come a long way pursuing him, then?"

"And we still have further to go," suggested Henry.

"We learnt of the other churches, Nesebar in Bulgaria and Vagharshapat in Armenia, both burnt to the ground before we found him, both churches of the Seven Archangels," said Sandrine.

"We followed him up through Georgia, into Poland, then down into the Ukraine and on to Romania," added Isabella.

"As he has travelled," Henry went on, "he has grown his legion of wolves, some of whom you met this evening, travelling always by night, resting by day. It made him difficult to follow, going as he did in the dark and going quickly. Wolves travel fast, and he was always able to stay ahead of us. Whenever we got close, he would move on even quicker, elude us. And he had spies, other wolves and followers who had flocked to his banner, people in his employ setting traps and misdirections for us. We know that Inquisitors have defected to him, to what he represents."

"It seems the world has become even more tangled than when I left it." Tacit supposed he was now caught tight in it. He cursed, privately, and wished that things were different. But they weren't, so he asked, "This Pablo you mentioned before, who is he?"

"Pablo Gilda. He was an Italian soldier, brought to the Carso and the ceremony by Priests of the Darkest Hand. Priests from Udine," replied Sandrine.

"What was his involvement with them?"

"The intended sacrifice, at the final ceremony," said Henry.

"Six-fingered," said Sandrine."

"A descendant of Gath," added Henry.

Tacit nodded. It made sense to him, whatever sense that was. The summoning of the Seven Princes required a great sacrifice and the blood from a descendant of Gath, the ancient Philistine city believed to be the home to Goliath and his kin descended from Nephelim, fallen angels walking amongst men. Identified by their six fingers on each hand, their blood, combined with that of uncountable innocents, was required to be shed upon the spot marked by a pentangle star through which the demons would come. They had tried before to summon the Princes in Pleven, Bulgaria, in the year 1877, an attempt which had apparently failed. Twenty thousand Russian and Turkish soldiers killed on that desolate field had not proved enough to draw through the great demons of Hell. In 1915 they had tried again, with even greater numbers of dead.

"Pablo, he came with us. With Poré," continued Henry, "but immediately he seemed enamoured by the man, possessed by Poré's plans. He betrayed us, revealed our doubts and plans to kill Poré. One morning they were gone."

"We've been tracking them ever since," said Sandrine, "following this line of burning churches, this most recent attack on the eastern front."

"Whatever plans he has with these churches, they must serve a purpose," muttered Tacit.

"This is the seventh church we have reached," said Isabella, nodding towards the smouldering flames, "burned to the ground before we managed to reach it, to reach whatever was inside that Poré wished not to share with anyone else."

"We have faced Poré before, but this is the first time the wolves who travel with him have been thrown into battle against us," said Henry.

"He's obviously finally grown tired of your meddling?"

"Or he has an army of wolves large enough to use as he wishes," said Sandrine.

"But the Darkest Hand, this is the first time we have encountered them too. We know nothing of what they have been doing in the last two years. We supposed that when the Seven Princes were stopped, the Darkest Hand too were stopped," said Henry.

"If only it was that simple," growled Tacit. "And Poré, what does he represent? When I knew him, he was a snivelling Cardinal."

"Revolution? Anarchy? People, whoever they are… they are tired of their old masters," said Isabella.

"At Uzhok we finally got close to him, close enough to try and stop him, but to no avail. And at Şurdeşti, well, you know the rest," said Sandrine.

"But why?" asked Tacit. "What was it that convinced you he was not to be trusted, that he had to be stopped?"

"He spoke always of retribution, the time of Tribulation, the end of one war but another coming, another even more terrible time from which a new age of peace would come. We disliked his rhetoric, and agreed to stop him in any way we could, but were then betrayed by Pablo. He revealed our plans to Poré, they escaped with the other wolves, leaving us behind," said Henry.

"These angels then," asked Sandrine. "The Seven Archangels. Who are they?"

"Michael. Gabriel. Raphael. Uriel. Camael. Jophiel. Zadkiel." The names came easily to Tacit. "The greatest of the angels."

"But why them? And why these churches?" the female half-wolf asked again.

Tacit shrugged and drank hard from the bottle, as if the liquor might unlock some instinct or insight in him from which he would pull the answer. But all he could say was, "I need more to go on. More than Seven Archangels!" And then he paused and said, "Unless…"

"Unless what?" asked Henry, sitting forward, his eyebrows arched. He recognised the keen light in Tacit's dark eyes, a look always adopted whenever the Inquisitor had discovered a vital clue. He was pleased to see it. It meant that this feral distant man, the one who seemed so remote and indifferent to all they had told him, was now snagged by its mystery.

"Poré talked of the Tribulation?"

"Yes," nodded Henry. "Is that important?"

Tacit ignored the question.

"The Tribulation. Seven Angels. Seven Seals. Seven…" Tacit waved his hand in the air in front of him, as if trying to draw the words from the ether. "Seven codes. Passwords."

"And these passwords?" asked Henry.

"It's said that each Archangel has a secret code, words only they can bear and know, carried in their own seal." Tacit climbed to his feet, more slowly than he might have done years ago, Isabella thought, and she asked him if he was okay, another question he ignored.

"And where are these seals?" asked Henry.

Tacit clicked his fingers. "In the churches."

"Which are now gone," said Sandrine.

"So now we know why Poré was burning them," growled Tacit, his hand, curled into a fist, pressed hard against the entrance to the cave mouth. "He's gathering the secret words, words he wants no one else to discover, so no one else will be able to use them."

"And these passwords, what are they? What do they mean?" asked Sandrine.

"The Seven Archangels, they are sometimes referred to as the Seven Trumpeters."

"What is that?" asked Henry.

"Angels, bearing trumpets. A sound. A seal. Seven angels, seven trumpets, seven seals." And he looked back at the three seated around the fire, waiting for one of them to understand the gravity of what he was revealing. "The Seven Seals… of Revelation. Seven angels, the Lords of Heaven, bearing seven trumpets to open the Seventh Seal."

Henry scowled. "So that is what Poré is trying to do? Open this Seventh Seal?"

"And what lies beyond the Seventh Seal?" asked Sandrine, perplexed.

"As you said," replied Tacit. "The Tribulation."

"And what is that?" asked Henry, his hands stretched wide and white in exasperation and confusion.

"The coming of the Antichrist," answered Tacit. And he bowed his head. "End Days, Henry. End Days for the world."

FIFTEEN

The Vatican. Vatican City.

Father Strettavario thought he heard the sound of bombs failing beyond the tall walls of Vatican City. He stopped and turned his ear to the pristine blue Italian sky, listening, feeling his relief like a wave when he realised he had been wrong and that war had not in fact come to his city. All he could hear were the sounds of gulls circling above him and the yammer of people in the capital beyond. Somewhere in a street a voice cried out and a heavy weight dropped to the cobbles, scattering goods, breaking crockery. The voice changed to a curse and other voices joined it. Strettavario signed the cross in the direction of the jostling arguing Italians and walked on.

The old Father bowed his head, the loose skin on his neckline gathering into a pink paunchy roll. In the midday heat he stopped with the sun on the back of his neck and shoulders and thought, his eyes gazing unseeingly at the ground. A moment's pause, a chance to take stock, away from the meetings and the chambers and the motives of others.

Much had changed in the weeks following the news that Poré was burning churches and that the Antichrist was returning, thoughts and prayers given over to preparing for End Times. It seemed that meetings now took on a more pressured and urgent edge, idle chatter giving way to addressing pressing issues quickly and with efficiency. The Inquisition, stretched as it was, seemed to have grown graver still, as if they knew they had to harden themselves against a great power and a power that was real, for it had a name. The Darkest Hand, as they were referred to by those who knew them, the Devil's servants, determined at all costs to see his return into the world and oversee his rise to power from the ruin and flames of total war engulfing the world.

Even the young inquisitional acolytes, trained too quickly and warned too little of the perils they faced in the darkening world, seemed changed, harder, fiercer, more focused on what it was they were setting out to do and witness.

The clues as to the Devil's reach were everywhere. Already too many countries had been drawn into the maelstrom of violence and hate, too eager and willing to sharpen their fangs on an enemy whom just years before they had regarded as an ally. Every corner of the globe had set its shoulder to the war effort and sent its young men and provisions to fight. And now America, the great and ever-growing power in the west, had turned from diplomacy to bombs to decide the outcome.

The Darkest Hand had reached far out across the world, and clenched.

Strettavario's unfocused eyes stared at the slabs of granite beneath his shoes and sharpened on the cracks of grey-green mortar running between each great length of stone. But where he stood he realised that the cracks between the slabs were not grey-green but stained darker. He was standing in the very place where Korek had fallen from the window above and his blood had surged out into these channels of mortar. Stepping back quickly, he peered up at the building above him, following the stonework, interlaced with searching grappling leafy climbers, upwards into the vaults.

The window out of which Korek had fallen was closed this day, but on the night of the accident it had been open. 'To allow the cool of night in after the day's heat.' Strettavario still remembered the explanation, the one he'd been given as to why the window had been open when he had casually asked the Swiss Guards cleaning up the bloody aftermath.

Strettavario had never believed for an instant that the Cardinal had fallen. Korek was many things, old, clumsy, but he wasn't frail and he certainly wasn't foolish enough to have slipped inadvertently from a window to his death. Something stirred in the Father, just as it had done at the time of the old Cardinal's death. Cardinal Berberino poisoned. Cardinal Bishop Korek pushed to his death. The heart ripped out of the Holy See. An Inquisition stretched across the globe by the Darkest Hand. A war of too many nations, growing in number and barbarity with every passing day, unleashed in the heart of Europe.

Something in the short grass a little way from the path caught Strettavario's eyes, glistening and shimmering by passing rays of sunlight, something missed after all this time. The old Father crouched and reached towards it, plucking it from the earth where it had rolled and partially submerged itself. It was a brooch, the one Korek always wore, the metal dulled from years of exposure the elements. But there was no question for Strettavario that it was Korek's.

He turned the small item in his fingers, tracing the metalwork around the jade-green stone in the centre. And as he did so, the sound of many feet running surprised him, as did the shouts of alarm which followed. He turned his head in the direction of the noise and smelt smoke. He knew that something was not right. He could see the flames on the far side of the Vatican wall, feel the heat from the courtyard into which he now ran. And he knew which building was on fire. The building which housed the Seers. The House of the Seers! It was ablaze, and every floor was engulfed in flames.

SIXTEEN

SOFIA. BULGARIA.

A thin strip of moonlight shone through a slit in the drapes across the naked bodies in the bed. Its glimmering trail reflected from the lovers' skin, the beads of sweat shining like quicksilver. Once more the silhouettes melted into one and rolled like a growing storm. Dominated by desire and longing, hands clutched and slipped against skin, nails raking eager flesh as their craving for each other devoured them. Everything they were and could be and had for so long longed to share they poured into one another, their love consummated, their bond now forever tied.

In his arms, Isabella felt tiny and unassailable, harboured in a place where she hoped she could stay for the remainder of her days. For Tacit, Isabella smelt as he believed heaven would smell, intoxicating and magnificent, everything about her as he had dared to imagine, impetuous, yearning and kind.

In the dark, their cries grew to a crescendo, untamed, before being snatched back at their height and ebbing away in a slow release. They sunk back into the sheets, coolness settling across their skin, the billion shining pinpricks of perspiration a mirror to the billion stars in the clear Bulgarian night sky above their room.

And nothingness swept in, as if death had come visiting. An end, and a new beginning.

They lay together, their arms, legs and breath intertwined, exhausted from their passion and weeks on the road. Isabella watched him, his eyes closed, the curl of damp dark hair across his forehead, and realised that the voices which had taunted her since the Carso had fallen silent. Her hands traced his scarred and lacerated body, feeling every wound, every tear in his embattled flesh.

"I've got old," growled Tacit, his voice as if dredged from a deep ocean.

"You always seemed old beyond your years," replied Isabella lightly, smiling and nestling against him.

"I thought perhaps you would not take me back," he said, "when you saw what the waters and time had done to me. I am wounded beyond what any man can usually bear."

"I still think you are quite handsome," smiled Isabella, stroking his firm body. And then, after a long while, she said, "We have both changed from who we were in Arras."

The comment stirred him back from the edge of darkness over which he was slowly slipping.

"Yes, there is an anger in you too," said Tacit, his eyes still closed, listening to the sounds from across the city, feeling the hot breezes from the Vitosha Mountain entering the room like invisible searching fingers. "An anger that was not there before. I saw it, in Uzhok. What you did to that man."

"Are you disappointed in me?"

"No."

"What did it make you think?"

"It made me think I was looking into a mirror."

"It was not me. It is not who I am."

"I know."

"But since the Carso, when I glimpsed into Hell, since I felt their eyes upon me, the heat of their domain upon my skin, sometimes it seems to me as if I am possessed by their wickedness, hear their voices in my ears, commanding me to do terrible things. That they have left their mark upon me. That I am forever damned."

Tacit understood, for he felt it too, had felt it every day since the moment he was drawn as a young man to the voices on that mountainside and lights had come about him and lifted him by their power and majesty.

"Do you still hear them?"

"No."

"I do, every day. But not now. Not with you." And he realised then that there was silence in him, no voices of wretchedness or cruel depravity, just peace. He opened his eyes and kissed the crown of her head. She smelt of lavender and soft fruit.

"Do you consider yourself damned, too?"

"I did," he replied, low, like a growl. He allowed his hand to play down the length of her delicate back to the top of her buttocks and back again, feeling the softness and smoothness of her skin, pristine and perfect, unlike his own ruined hide. "But not any more."

She turned to face him, her head propped up on her hand, her scarlet hair rushing like crimson over the sheets about them. "Of course, you know what this means, don't you?"

"What?"

"That you've failed your assessment, the one first set for you by the Holy See in Arras." Tacit chuckled darkly, making the whole bed vibrate as he did so. "It might have taken three years," she laughed, punching him lightly, "but finally you're ensnared!"

"Guilty!" he replied, pulling her close to him again. Desire flared in him, and he kissed her lips as she raised them to his. But something had snagged. "It was a trap that the Holy See set for me, Isabella. They wanted me to fail. If Poré and Monteria had succeeded in unleashing the wolf in Notre Dame, it would have been the end of me. By stopping Monteria as I did, it was the end of me anyway. Someone wanted me removed from where I might cause difficulties. Placed where I might be interrogated, analysed. But also placed on an assignment where I might fall in love. With you."

"Well, I've enjoyed analysing you, Poldek Tacit," Isabella replied, and she kissed him again, "and I think I might need to continue my interrogation of you now!" Her hand searched beneath the sheets, but he gently took hold of her hands and kissed them, smelling sweat and himself.

"What is it?"

"They fear me."

"Of course they do."

"No, they *fear me*, the Holy See, for who they think I am."

"And who are you?"

"I don't know. But the voices, the lights which confounded me and drove me on, I know the Holy See wished to discover what they were, what lay in them, and beyond them. They took me in after Paris, after the Mass for Peace, to experiment on me. To unlock these secrets. To use me and them against the coming darkness. To find a link between them and the darkness, to open up a parley with it."

He looked back up at the ceiling. The rasp of a single demonic voice had begun to grind in the recesses of his mind.

"Someone knew, or suspected, what it is that possesses me, and wished to discover more."

"But they are not here now," she soothed, and he smiled, his hand returning to the small of her back.

"No, you are right," he replied, kissing her, "they are not. But we are here." And he pushed her onto her back and covered her neck and shoulders in kisses.

"Do you believe in our faith?" she asked. "In those we served? What we did?"

Tacit searched through souvenirs of ghosts and broken weeping spirits, of demons and their shrieking possessions, of their terrible revelations and

81

his own grim assumptions of the future. "No," he replied. He looked up at her, a smile warming his features. He looked gallant and savage and handsome. "I did, once. I believed it as if it was my life's code. But now? No, things have changed. I am changed."

"What's that supposed to mean?" she asked, smiling herself, feigning a light punch in his ribs to draw out a confession. "Don't tell me you're becoming softer in your old age, Poldek Tacit?"

But he remained serious. "Everything I was ever told, everything I was ever taught, it seems to me to have been a lie. The Church has lied to me, manipulated me, ever since I was first taken into their care. They used me for their own ambitions." He breathed deeply again, as if girding himself for a brave and final admission. "No more. I refuse to play their games any more. I only ever came back to find you. They are now behind me. I cannot see or feel them any more."

She wrapped herself around him, and they rolled together, their gentle laughter turning to hot wet kisses. Their passions flared again, but then she paused and held herself against him, silent and still.

"When all this is done, Poldek, when we've found Poré –"

"*If* we ever find Poré!" said Tacit. "We have lost all sign of him and his wolves. He might be anywhere!"

"But when all this is done, do you think we will we ever find peace? Will the Holy See leave us alone? Will things be all right?"

Tacit smiled darkly, and shook his head. "Is anything ever all right?" he replied, his voice like rust. "I don't know what the future holds, bright or grim. But I know that whatever comes we might face it together and with you I am stronger."

"Perhaps we need to find an island, and maroon ourselves on it?" smiled Isabella. At once she felt him freeze.

"What is it?" she gasped. "What have I said?"

"Patmos!"

"Whatever do you mean?"

"John the Divine! Patmos! It was on that island that he was marooned by the Romans, where he received the vision of Revelation, where he wrote down the words! Of course. It's obvious, too obvious! That's where Poré is going! The Seventh Seal is on Patmos!"

SEVENTEEN

London. England.

Of all the places that Pablo had seen and experienced, London was by far the most confusing. Everywhere there seemed to be noise and people, cars and fog. And in the crowds of people meandering about as if they had nowhere to go, most of the men were invalids, missing arms or legs, walking on crutches or assisted by wives, sisters or mothers, three-legged shambling figures in overcoats, sad and diminished individuals rather than war heroes who had 'done their bit'.

Pablo had arrived in the city three days ago, armed with one suit, a suitcase, the name 'Gareth Hart' and a falsified position in the echelons of the war effort to orchestrate logistics: the accumulation of war materials, the transport of commodities to the front line, the mustering of an ever larger workforce to stoke the war's endless fires. He had come straight from Uzhok, that battle lost but enough gathered, according to Poré, for him to begin his chief role.

Everything was grey and drab in the capital, the weather and the clothes everyone was wearing. The shops he passed on the way to Pall Mall seemed to be half empty, their windows showing barren trays. Advertisements for cigarettes and encouragements to 'save for the war effort' showed smiling, colourful, determined faces, but there was little in the streets over which they loomed that resembled these generous people, ten feet tall, drawn in vibrant yellows and reds.

Pablo stood in front of the government building in Pall Mall. He swallowed, took his hands out of his pockets and straightened his suit, stepping back to let a young man and woman pass. The man tapped along the street with his cane, feeling his way, his arm tucked into his wife's. Pablo watched them, feeling something harden in his chest.

He thought of Poré, of the wolf pelt back in its owner's grip. But mostly he thought of the road upon which he found himself and the two silver six-fingered daggers he carried concealed in the depths of his case, the same ones he had carried all the way from the Carso.

He cleared his throat and crossed the road to the building, now to try to deceive not just a country but an entire world.

EIGHTEEN

The Vatican. Vatican City.

Father Strettavario stood in the shadow of the smoking ruin, his hands clenched lightly by his side. There were tears in his eyes, but they weren't tears of sadness. They were tears of rage. His eyes hadn't left the smouldering remains of the Seers' building for over half an hour. He stared and he watched and he hoped to see figures crawl from the building, but no one came out, no one alive at least from the burnt ruins. He had tried to save some of Seers inside, he and others who had rushed to the site, a few Swiss Guards, Priests, Inquisitors. They had all tried to save the women, but the flames had been too strong, the heat too intense. The building had gone up as if it had been stoked with dry tinder.

"They saw many things," said Adansoni, charred by his own endeavours to help reach the Seers, one of the many who now stood and watched from the edge of the courtyard.

"Perhaps they saw too much?" replied Strettavario. "Things someone never wanted them to see?"

"Well, they never saw this coming," said the old Cardinal, and he coughed to clear his ravaged throat.

"The doors," Strettavario muttered, and for the first time Adansoni saw something approaching sadness in the cold-eyed Father, "they'd been chained. They couldn't get out. The flames took very quickly. There must have been an accelerant. This was no accident, Javier. This was murder."

The Cardinal nodded. "I suppose there's nothing left inside?"

Strettavario turned away and stared into the cool of a dark corner of the Vatican. "No, there's nothing left inside. No more eyes to see what is coming, to see who the Antichrist is." And he looked across at his old friend. "They've put out our eyes, Javier."

PART TWO

"When the Lamb opened the seventh seal, there was silence in heaven."

REVELATION 8:1

NINETEEN

THE VATICAN. VATICAN CITY.

Father Strettavario was walking in the Vatican grounds, alone amongst the last of the late hyacinths, tulips and delphiniums, banks of darkening salmon pink, yellow, dark purple and orange flame, trapped between great seas of green lawns and weaving paths of golden-brown gravel and granite-white Indian stone, alone with his thoughts, his indecision.

The burning of the Seers, the loss of the Antichrist's name, the supposed death of Tacit, the returning of Poré, all churned in him like a poison.

His garments were stiff with embroidery and the weight of lush fabric, heavy against his squat but sturdy frame, and he sweated under their weight, under the heat of the day and the doubts in his mind. For an instant his frustration turned to wild abandon, and for a moment he wished only that he could strip himself free of the clothes and be damned, feel the cool of his sweat and the autumnal wind upon it seep into his light clothing, lift and prickle his skin like a goose's flesh. For a moment feel less bound up with formality and sacrament. Scream to the heavens. Cry out his frustration and his rage.

A gaggle of boys ran past, acolytes of the Inquisition he supposed, their steps and breath as one, with the exception of a few who laboured at the back, diffident exhausted children, and one at the front, racing ahead, leading the pack. Strettavario admired him and supposed Tacit would have been such a boy when he was younger, fit, untarnished, uncorrupted.

He paused, watching them go up the path, vanishing around a high hedge, the huff and puff of their exertions dying with them as they went. There was a smile back on his face at witnessing their youthfulness and he was pleased for it, but then his thoughts turned back to the Seers, the burnt building, the efforts he and Adansoni had made to get out those still inside, though the flames were too terrible. He could still hear the screams from inside, still hear the building as it groaned and snapped, as if it too was dying in the incalculable heat.

And in that moment he wished, as a child might wish, for all the world that Tacit was back, even though he knew that it was impossible, for Tacit was dead and nothing could ever bring him back. But he knew then that if he had a wish, if he had a divine offering from his Lord God placed in his hands, he would request that Tacit be brought back into the world and come and save them now. For Tacit would know what to do. It seemed to Strettavario that no one else knew what was required, what should be said, what should be done.

The Inquisition? It was overburdened, spread too far and too wide, fighting too many enemies across too much of the world. The Holy See? Directionless and impotent, led by a Secretary who knew himself to be exactly the same.

And this enemy that they faced, invisible and sly. This enemy, the Darkest Hand, was no longer simply at the gates of the Vatican. It was inside them. It was in the city, and it was moving at will.

He cursed, a silent blasphemy meant only for him, quiet enough he hoped that he and he alone had heard it, and walked on, his head bowed, his mouthed scrunched into a tight pink knot, his pale eyes boring into the gravel path ahead of him. Thinking.

More hurried breathing came from behind him and with it the heavy crunch of shoes upon the gravel. Without looking, the old Father stepped to one side to let the boys pass. But almost at once he realised that the breathing was singular and stopped, turning to see that it belonged to a servant, one he knew well enough by name.

"Achille!" he called generously, pleased to see the eager young man he liked so much, but his cheery demeanour changed immediately when he realised the servant's fevered look. "What is it?" he asked urgently, fearing to hear it.

"Thank goodness I've found you, Father Strettavario!" the young man cried.

"What is it?"

"Cardinal Secretary of State Casado – he's been murdered!" cried the messenger.

TWENTY

Kavala. Greece.

The dawn light punched through the broken shade of the room and stirred Henry from restless sleep. He rose from the sheets, padding across the bedroom towards the window. It had been a hot night, as it had been for as many days as he could remember, the raging late summer heat searing itself into the myriad side-streets and courtyards of the town during the day, forcing its populace to endure its intolerable afterglow throughout the long dark of night.

He lit a cigarette and looked down on the excited activity of the sea port below. There were too many ships moored in the port to count, steamers, transport vessels, battleships and frigates, belching sooty smoke from great black funnels or wedged motionless at their moorings, tied by ropes to great blocks of iron like rusted teeth hammered into the quayside. The noise from below, of soldiers going up the main streets, the melody of Greek voices mixed with the hubbub of traffic and traders, the turning of wagon wheels, the clip of horses' hooves, the chatter and chaos of children and port officials, the bark of dogs and of laughter, all of it sounded like a great cauldron of life, a world and people on the move.

A horn from one of the ships blew, rattling windows and ringing ears. Gulls leapt and circled. A brisk wind came in off the Aegean, bringing with it salt and sea air. For the first time in an age Henry Frost felt trepidation tease his gut.

From behind, Sandrine enveloped him in her arms and the sheet draped around her body, and for a long time they stood looking down on the bustle and commotion of the port.

Eventually Sandrine said, "We've come so far."

Henry stubbed out the cigarette that was now burning his fingers. "It is a shame that most of Thessalonica is burnt. We would have got a ship to Patmos far quicker from the main port there than we've be able to from here. *If* Poré has gone to Patmos."

"Tacit is certain he has gone there. Do you believe him?"

Henry kissed the top of her head and let his eyes drift back to the sea. "I believe *in* him," replied Henry, admiring the conformity and precise lines of a Russian unit marching along the promenade under the watchful gaze of their Sergeant. The last he had heard, the Bolsheviks had all but seized power in Russia, promising an end to the country's involvement in the conflict. "That should be enough. What else can we do?"

Henry took out and lit another cigarette, blowing the smoke through his nose, dragon-like. He turned to look at Sandrine, to admire her, and as he did so a weight began to gather in his throat. He knew he could never tire of looking at her. He had long hoped to look at her till his eyes went blind. He smiled, a sad smile of tenderness and fear, and, not wishing her to see his weakness, dropped his eyes to the tops of her breasts framed beneath the white sheet she held around herself.

"He's changed," he continued. "He seems even more savage, feral even. But also resigned. As if he is knows this is the end for him. His final act. Do you know what I mean?"

"I love you, Lieutenant Henry Frost," declared Sandrine unexpectedly, sweeping him up in the sheet.

Henry allowed himself to laugh and tumble sideways onto the bed with her. "*Lieutenant* Henry Frost, eh?" replied Henry. "I thought, my darling, that *Lieutenant* Henry Frost died in Fampoux?" Sandrine climbed on top of him, doing nothing to hide her nakedness beneath the sheet. "Sadly there's nothing left of him, my darling, only a memory now, a name on a register." And he smiled and pulled her down to him, kissing her.

"Not just a name. There's also your war diary," she reminded him.

Henry laughed, and for a moment worry fell away from him as he remembered the carefully and lovingly written journal and the risk he took in seeing it delivered into army hands in Arras, all of his knowledge of the war and the wolves and the wickedness of the world documented in its pages. "Goodness, yes!" he said, allowing his hands to run the length of her body, coming to rest on the fleshy outside of her thighs. "I wonder whatever happened to that thing? If it was ever read?"

"I doubt it!" replied Sandrine, reaching forward to unbutton his shirt. He objected, lightly, saying he needed to get dressed, but she ignored him, playing his limp hands away. "Probably processed and filed, gathering dust in some library somewhere, a vault containing all the other lies of this war."

She opened his shirt and asked quite suddenly, "Will they win?" With the question, the passion and discipline in her seemed for a moment to waver.

Henry smiled and shook his head, reaching up and kissing her. "No, *they* will not win. But our victory will come at a price. You know that." She shivered, despite the heat. "We know what needs to be done," he said, and he kissed her again, chasing away invisible tears on her cheeks with his fingers. "There is still so much we need to do."

He reached back with his arms, so that he was stretched out across the width of the bed, open, inviting her onto him, crucified in their tangle of sheets. But her eyes turned from him slowly to the bedside table and the black Colt revolver lying there, watching it as if for assurance. "Sandrine," he urged, seeing her doubt, "we will prevail and we will return from Patmos and from this journey. I believe it is to be."

"Then why is it that I feel that this is the end?" she asked, throwing out her arms in desperation.

"Because it is!" laughed Henry coldly. "Just as Tacit said, End Times are now upon us. We might as well enjoy the moments we have," he added, as he embraced her on the bed.

TWENTY-ONE

October 13th, 1917. Fátima. Portugal.

It had rained for days, and the red-brown dust of the Portuguese vale had turned into a ruddy paste stirred by the feet of the hundred thousand who had come with prophetic assurances and a growing rumour that the Blessed Virgin Mary would appear to all in the heavens. They had come by foot, cart, automobile, half-slipping and feeling their way down the slope at the rear of the vast bowl of mud to the viewing platforms, to join the already vast and eager crowd waiting for the vision to appear. At the rear of the basin, as far as the eye could see, people stood with hands and arms across their foreheads, shielding their eyes from the sun whenever it broke through the clouds. But for long hours nothing stirred in the heavens, save the constant patter of rain. Grumbling and disenchantment grew. The sky was as bleak as the turning mood, everything above a patchwork of tangled grey and torn sheets of black clouds, everything below damp and cold and dispirited.

"Why have we bothered coming here?" someone shouted.

"Some God!" another replied, throwing her hands in the air. "Even he has forsaken us!"

Many were preparing to leave when suddenly there was a shrieking and pointing towards the sun, which in that instant had turned translucent and begun to spin like a coin. And then the orb of shimmering light danced right and almost immediately left again, zig-zagging through the clouds as if tossed by invisible forces across the wide vista of heaven. And the crowd suddenly realised that it had stopped raining and all the puddles had dried up, as had their clothes.

"A miracle!" someone shouted.

"The heat!" someone answered, the valley intense with sudden warmth.

"We shall all be killed!" cried a third, and others took up the refrain, holding out their hands beseechingly, believing then that they had been brought here not to witness God but to be judged.

But instantly a voice called out to warn them that Hell had come into the world, and that its son and his great Lieutenant were in the world and manifest. And that a plague would follow, so terrible that ten times the number killed in the Great War would submit to it. And not even the Devil would have an answer.

TWENTY-TWO

Skala. Patmos.

The unrelenting sun seemed to suck the life out of the sea lapping limply against the boat cutting across it. The croak of a sea bird that had followed the ship for the last three hours, hoping for scraps which never came, wavered and then drifted away as the cliffs of the island grew tall before the boat.

Tacit stood close to Isabella at the prow, watching Skala fill his vision, the island broad and burnt, the town of Skala itself a scatter of white buildings thrown around the apex of the scorched and arid bay.

Everything seemed lazy and still. Even the sea, smelling of brine, appeared tired, breaking lifeless against the shore, as the boat drew through the cobalt waters towards the harbour. There were Italian soldiers on the dockside watching the boat, weary and hot, disinterested, looking out as they had for the last three months, thinking only of home and family, and the heat and cold fresh water. The heat. The incessant heat. They thought of the western alps and snow and wished themselves away from this island prison.

The ship hit the quayside's edge, a sailor called out, ropes were tied and the vessel snagged tight. Mount Kastelli stared down on them from on high in the middle of the island, the fortified monastery at its summit indelible in the late day sun.

Henry wiped the sweat from his neck and followed Tacit's eye to the summit. "Is that where we're going then?"

"No," Tacit growled, sweeping the quayside to make sure they weren't being observed by anyone he didn't like the look of. "Not all the way. To the Cave of the Apocalypse. It's halfway up."

"They called it that?" Henry chuckled, shaking his head. "I'm amazed we didn't think about coming here sooner. The answer's in the name!"

Tacit scowled and they filed off the boat. Beyond the quayside, every head turned in their direction as they went by, each person watching them intently, new visitors to the island, some of the soldiers standing to get a better view, fishermen with cigarettes clasped between their lips, muttering.

"At least it's daylight," said Tacit, turning his eyes to the sky.

"And bloody hot!" exclaimed Henry, wiping at the skin of his neck testily. "It's October and it's still bloody hot! Not sure how the infernal sun might help us?"

"Hombre Lobo," replied Tacit, surreptitiously checking his revolver, stowed in a coat pocket. "Remember, they only come out at night."

"Wolves, on Patmos?" Henry asked. "You don't honestly believe they would be here?"

"I do," nodded Tacit. "If Poré's been here, I'm sure he's left something behind for us, a little welcoming gift should we decide to follow him. Let's get up to the cave and back before it's nightfall. It's not far. And I think the sooner we can get off this island, the better."

"And how will we get off?" asked Henry, watching the boat by which they had arrived draw back into the harbour and turn for the open sea.

"We'll find a way," muttered Tacit, glancing at the harbour edge and the fishing boats lining it. Across from the quayside front a squinting scowling woman was watching them from the front veranda of her home, dressed all in black like an old crow. "And as quickly as possible. I don't like the feel of this place."

The gravel road turned right behind a line of buildings and then rose into the mountain, changing from a solid road to a narrow roughly hewn track of rubble and dust that turned their boots sandy white and kicked up into their faces under the dry heat. It seemed as if everything had been burnt out of the place by the relentless heat. Everything was dead or barely holding on to life.

Only the lizards moved, hundreds of them, across the stones and scrabbling in the rustle of scrub beside the path. A line of people, villagers mostly, stood to watch them leave before turning back to their labours.

After thirty minutes, but a hike which felt longer in the midday heat, they reached a bleached building, close to the path up the hill, squat and square like a miniature rustic fort, forged and gouged into the side of the mountainside, grey stone slabs and broad sides of rocks pushed away from it. A granite tumbling house of cards. The breathless air was full of clicking cicadas and the spiced drying swelter of the brush. Above there was still the endless blue of sky. Nothing but blue above, grey-white below and heat all about them.

Tacit toiled to reach the end of the climb, every step a labour for his ravaged body. Isabella laughed to see how he struggled, not immediately appreciating his effort, thinking him just unfit, a rare figure of mirth, at least until she spotted the body lying half in and half out of the door leading into the stone building. There was blood on the floor from where the life had been bashed out of him.

"Poré," growled Tacit, his sweaty hand falling to the handle of his revolver, "he's already been here."

"That means we're too late!" muttered Sandrine, her words like a choke.

"I don't hear thunder," replied Henry, turning his ear to the sky. "I don't see a storm?"

"And you wouldn't," replied Tacit, going forward and checking the body. The man had been hit, bludgeoned to death, the back of his head bloody, his dead skin burnt red after hours in the hot sun. "What do you want, Henry? Explosions? The voice of God breaking down the valleys?" He shook his head, looking like a teacher admonishing a failed student. "On the opening of the Seventh Seal it is said that there'll be nothing to reveal the act has been committed, nothing but silence." He looked around himself. "And I'm hearing nothing." But his words were a lie, for he was hearing voices in his head, and they were demeaning and foul, an incessant chatter of filth and horror at what Tacit had discovered.

He stood, turning his head heavenwards, as if trying to divine a reading in the endless blue, while the others realised just how silent the world had fallen. The port below was deathly quiet. If Tacit saw anything in the sky, he said nothing, instead growling and then looking down to peer through the door leading to the Cave of the Apocalypse and where the Seventh Seal was supposed to have been opened.

TWENTY-THREE

THE VATICAN. VATICAN CITY.

The Inquisition estimated that Cardinal Bishop Casado had been dead for twelve hours, but his body had already started to smell. His skin had turned grey, clinging to his bones like tightly drawn pale leather, his wide blind eyes sunk deep into dark sockets, his broken bloodied mouth hanging open in an endless silent cry.

He lay on his back on the hard wooden floor of his living quarters, a halo of dashed crimson around where he had fallen for the final time, his head twisted to one side at an angle too acute for a head to turn, a knee twisted in its joint, the fingers of a hand splayed wide, covered in blood. His own blood.

The robe he had been wearing was torn open, his battered and mis-shapen body beneath it blackened by the relentless rain of blows. Any one of them would have probably been enough to have killed the old man and yet Casado's killer had not stopped hitting him until every bone in the Cardinal's chest had been broken.

And from his heart a dagger protruded, hilt deep.

"What a mess," growled the investigating Inquisitor to Father Strettavario, who stood over the body.

The pale-eyed Priest ignored him, his head bowed in respect and lam-entation for the Cardinal, but his lips were snatched into a tight knot of suspicion. Theories skirmished across his mind. Two years ago, Cardinal Berberino of the Holy See collapsed from a supposed heart attack, taken ill straight after receiving evidence that a traitor lay at the heart of the Vatican. Just days later, Cardinal Bishop Korek fell from a Vatican window, an old man too clumsy with age and indecision to judge the distance between himself and the frame over which he had toppled. So the lies excused.

Strettavario hadn't blamed the Holy See for the lies. He hadn't even chosen to suspect that the Holy See was in any way involved in the deaths of two of its longest serving and most respected members. After all, it was enough trying to endure in a conflict engulfing every nation of Europe and beyond. The last thing the faith needed was a senior Priest going around saying that members of the council of the Holy See were being murdered. The Vatican could ill afford to encourage the rumour that mutiny, revolution and murder had taken root in the heart of its faith, and Strettavario was the last to give credence to such rumours.

But now this, especially after the fire at the House of the Seers! They had spoken of End Times. For Strettavario, it was clear that they had already arrived.

"I hate the way they stink," said the Inquisitor.

The pale-eyed Priest frowned, not in disgust at the way the Inquisitor had spoken of the deceased Secretary of State, but at the stupidity and ignorance of the comment. At once Strettavario knew the Inquisitor to be an acolyte and supposed it was a symptom of the times in which they lived, an Inquisition pushed to its limits by an enemy who seemed to be everywhere. If the young Inquisitor had had a modicum of initiative, the faintest inkling of experience, he'd have realised that no body would have begun to smell so quickly or so badly after being so recently killed. The stink had the sulphurous whiff of devilry bound up with it. That was why it smelt as it did, a clue missed entirely by the young man.

Here, amongst the indiscriminate destruction of the Cardinal Secretary of State's apartment, Strettavario knew that this wasn't just a mess. This had the appearance of the beginnings of a coup. And he recognised whose scaled hand was on the tiller.

Turning away, Strettavario looked across the wreckage of the place. Though only a slight man, bowed with age and years too many for anyone to count, it seemed that Casado had fought his attacker with every measure of effort he possessed. Either that, or his attacker had revelled in his savagery and mastery over the Cardinal Bishop, throwing him around the residence like a doll. Whatever had happened, one thing was sure: Bishop Cardinal Casado, the Secretary of State for the Holy See, had been bludgeoned horribly to death.

A man he knew well appeared at the doorway and was allowed through, his hand clenched tight to his white face, horror like a condemnation upon him.

"Good heavens!" Strettavario heard his old friend mutter, breathlessly. "Pope Benedict will need to be told," said Adansoni, as much to himself as to his friend in the room.

"Pope Benedict's in Berlin. Another peace mission."

"Someone has to try, I suppose."

"Too late for Cardinal Bishop Casado," retorted the young Inquisitor, overhearing their conversation, while Strettavario picked a picture frame up off the floor and looked at its portrait, Casado in his younger days. "Too late for everyone, it seems." The Inquisitor swore silently under his breath and immediately followed it with a quiet apology heavenward. "What a mess. You believe the rumours then, Father Strettavario?"

"And what rumours would they be?" replied Strettavario, disliking the Inquisitor more with every passing moment.

"That we're heading towards Armageddon?"

Strettavario looked about the ruination of the place. "You might think that we're already here."

Priests were coming to and fro in the corridor outside, beyond the open door with its smashed hinges. He knew that something was rotten in the heart of the Vatican, something tangible and black, could almost feel its twisting fingers writhe and seethe in the apartment.

He turned his back on his dead friend and stepped in slow circles round the room, looking at the walls, at the windows, into the corners, looking either side of the simple paper shade that still hung from the candle chandelier in the centre of the ceiling. He walked the length of the room and back, taking out his hands and running them against the walls, feeling the surface of the mortar as he walked, looking for anything, something, but what exactly he did not know.

Eventually he found himself back on the spot where he had begun his search, at the open door to the room, looking back at the open cupboards and wardrobes through which he had rooted. And then he looked back at the lightshade in the middle of the room, and something inside him shifted. He took three steps towards it, so that he stood directly under it.

"Something?" asked Adansoni.

"Nothing," Strettavario said, too quickly, waiting for his friend to look away. He trusted Adansoni, trusted him more than anyone else in the city, but something suggested to him that it was now wise to be tactful with one's thoughts, to avoid drawing the eye or attention of anyone who might wish such things suppressed. Best to say nothing for now.

Adansoni moved away, his interest drawn elsewhere; the Inquisitor's nose was buried in his file as he recorded further details of Casado's death. When he knew he was not being observed, the old Priest reached up and teased the paper shade away from the chandelier. After a brief battle it came away in his hands, and Strettavario turned it over and around, looking at each side in turn, facing away, hiding it as best he could behind his body. Something was odd about the fitting. One side of it, the outside, was quite plain, weathered and marked with age and heat from candlelight, but on the inside the paper was newer, made up of lines, lines of writing, sheets of paper on which there were words, words Strettavario knew had been written by Casado, words he hadn't intended just anyone to find.

TWENTY-FOUR

The Cave of the Apocalypse. Patmos.

The air inside the grotto was stale, the aroma of scrub and dust and the whisper of two-thousand-year-old breath. As they entered the high heat of the day was instantly gone, cut off, as if the place was a mausoleum holding unkind and desolate spirits.

"You're right," growled Tacit to Sandrine, the moment his eyes adjusted to the dark. "We are too late."

"But how can we be too late?" The dark-haired woman asked the question in a rush, as if it couldn't possibly be true.

"The seal," he said, pointing with a finger to indicate the yawning hole in the far wall, "it has been opened."

They approached the seal through a shallow pit, housed inside the cave, no more than ten feet wide and five deep, around which the rustic walls had been constructed. Well-worn stone steps led down into it, down to the supposed spot, smoothed with time, where John the Divine had received the Revelation from God and captured it in his writings. The precise spot of this enlightenment had been identified by a stone, a glassy rock of grey marble, worked by the hands and feet of pilgrims who had come and sat here, hoping to be enriched by John's blessing.

Beyond was a grey-brown wall, the far end of the cave, marked with moss and lichen and veins of minerals running through it. And a single hole, perfectly round, a small doorway bearing no lock or mechanism, a circular sliver of stone opened outwards, only blackness beyond it, blackness of the shallow empty space it had concealed for two thousand years.

"We cannot be too late!" exclaimed Henry, pushing past Tacit to see. "This?" he cried, confounded by the hidden portal. "This is the Seventh Seal?!" He almost sounded disappointed, cheated.

Tacit nodded. "The seals, the secret words taken from the Churches of the Seven Archangels, the places Poré burned, they have been spoken. The Seventh Seal, the final seal of Revelation has been opened." Henry looked again, drawn to peer more closely into the yawning black of the hole. "Go on," muttered Tacit, reaching for the entrance of the grotto, back into the light and heat of the day, no longer able to look upon the place, needing to feel the warmth of the sun after the cold of the barren cave. He felt deathly weak, frail, as if the shock of the discovery had wounded him. The voices in his head had fallen silent, perhaps they too at a loss to explain how such a thing could have happened. "You can look inside if you wish," said Tacit. "It'll be empty."

"No, I can see something in here!" called Henry, squinting into the small hole, twenty-four inches wide and the same deep, the outline of the door and hinges indiscernible against the rock. Seeing it this close, it did not surprise him that the seal had gone unnoticed for so long. It was as if the opening had been forged by the hands of God himself, precise and expertly worked into the rock. Henry finally dared to reach inside, summoning every ounce of his nerve to do so. "Boxes," he called back. "Boxes, with rusted locks, all thrown open!"

"What was in them?" asked Sandrine, looking at the man shadowing out the sun in the doorway.

Tacit shrugged, disinterested, defeated. Finally he looked back, petulant. "Vials."

"Vials?"

"The seven vials. Seven vials, one for each of the seven angels to pour out their scorn upon the world. When all Seven Seals have been opened…"

"… it will herald in End Times," Isabella continued, knowing the biblical warning.

Tacit nodded, looking hard at her. "The Apocalypse, the Great Tribulation, the coming of the Antichrist, the wiping clean of the world. A time of judgement for all. The deaths of millions." He felt Isabella shiver next to him and reached out to her, holding onto her arm to assure her things would be all right, something he did not believe for an instant. "Once the Seventh Seal has been opened, so begins the time of the Rapture, when all unworthy are destroyed, and the righteous are taken up."

"Taken up?" asked Henry. "You mean…"

"Heaven." Tacit shrugged like a man who had lost all hope and faith. "Or down to Hell."

"But what exactly is in the vials?" asked Sandrine?

Tacit looked at her harder than she ever believed a man could stare. "Pestilence. Plague. Disease. God's retribution."

"The End of the World," muttered Henry, turning back to the others, and Tacit weighed the suggestion, heavy-faced, saying nothing. But after a long time he nodded.

"Yes," he said. "God's wrath is now in the world."

TWENTY-FIVE

Skala. Patmos.

Against the bleached white lintel of the entrance to the grotto Tacit's hand tightened into a fist, his figure straightening, seeming to expand, filling the doorway, blocking out all the light. Demons' barked tongues hissed curses in his ears. He welcomed their depravity.

"Let's go!" he growled, dropping down and out into the blazing sun.

"Where are we going?" asked Isabella, following his long shadow.

"Back to the port! Back to the mainland!"

He was already on the pathway and running down it, kicking up brown stones and dust, by the time Henry and Sandrine had left the cave building, stepping past the dead figure of the man they had found, whom Isabella had moved to one side to give him at least a little dignity in death. The three ran behind Tacit, hands clutched tight to weapons and pressed to pockets to keep them from bouncing as they ran. Only Henry looked back one final time to the nondescript grey-white building out of which, if Tacit was to be believed, God's wrath had been released. He shivered despite the sun, and wondered just what was being unleashed onto the world at that very moment, what devastating terrors sent out amongst the people. And he wept to think how they, just four, could hope to do anything about it, losing his footing briefly and only then setting his sights and concentration on the treacherous tumbling path down to the small island port.

They bounced and skidded through the dust and rubble to the cluster of homesteads and goat barns at the edge of Skala, the path weaving wildly between the buildings, people turning to see the four who had gone up the mountain only a short time ago now rushing back down it.

Sailors sat fixing fishing nets or languidly attending to their boats. The Italian soldiers had long since pushed off, vanished indoors somewhere to find a little peace. An official-looking individual, in that he was wearing a shirt which had not seen a night's fishing or a day's toil under the sun, was watching from a gaggle of people halfway along the quay. Tacit went towards him, his command of the Greek language surprising Henry and the others.

"A man," he asked, the official looking both astonished and pleased to find the ravaged giant spoke his own nation's tongue, "the man who came to the island before us, who went up to the cave," Tacit continued, indicating to the mountain down which they had just run, "he took a boat? He has left Patmos?"

The man nodded, looking from Tacit to the others, his eyes lingering longer over Sandrine and Isabella, before turning back to him.

"When? How long since he left?"

The man shrugged and looked at the other fishermen gathered about him. "An hour?" he asked them. They pulled faces and suggested a little longer. "Maybe two? Not long. He left not long after your boat arrived."

Tacit could feel the eyes of Isabella and the others on him. They made the hairs on his back bristle. Poré must have seen them leave and made good his escape while they had been climbing the scorched brush hill to discover what he had already taken. He slammed his fist into a palm and looked along the line of boats moored in the harbour. There was a larger boat at the far end of the quay, a tall-masted sailing ship, thirty feet long, the only candidate for a voyage chasing an enemy across a vast open sea.

"Where did he go?"

"He went back to the mainland," replied the man, with a shrug of his arm across the glittering blue waters of the bay.

"Greece?"

"Turkey. Bodrum."

"The next boat for the mainland? For Turkey?" Tacit asked the port official urgently. "When does it leave?"

The man shrugged again. "Tomorrow?" he suggested, disinterested. "This infernal war, boats come, boats go, as of their own accord."

"That boat," said Tacit, indicating the sailing ship with a nod, "whose is it?"

The man shrugged again. "He came yesterday, with other men. They went up to Chora," and Tacit followed the man's eyes to the mountain. On its summit the main capital town of Patmos wedged itself amongst the high rocks, the whitewashed walls of its buildings scattered about the mountainside, snaking away from the grey granite walls of the monastery at its very centre like the roots of a tree.

"What does this mean?" asked Henry.

"It means we've lost him," growled Tacit. "It means Poré has got away."

"Unless we find the owner of that sailing ship?" said Isabella, "And ask him to take us?"

"Or we take it ourselves?" replied Henry, shocking himself at the suggestion, but feeling empowered and daring because of it.

"You know how to sail?" asked Tacit, cocking an eyebrow.

"A little," replied Henry, clenching and unclenching his fists in anticipation. "They taught you all manner of things at Winchester College."

But just then gunfire rattled the quayside close to where they were standing and no one gave any more thought to sailing ships or pursuing Poré, just finding cover from this sudden attack.

TWENTY-SIX

The Vatican. Vatican City.

Strettavario had left Casado's residence immediately after retrieving the notes. He was relieved to be away from it, the place filled with the sulphurous stench of devilry and death, despite being sweetened by the aroma of lavender. The scent had always been Casado's favoured smell, floral and crisp, an enlightening and uplifting fragrance whenever Strettavario caught the essence of it. Now it seemed nothing more than a sad reminder of the old man, hanging like an epitaph in the air.

Casado's notes consisted of only a few pages. With reverent care and speed, the old Father had slipped them unseen into a deep pocket, leaving immediately afterwards, not even looking at Adansoni and the young Inquisitor as he bade them farewell.

Defiance and daring shimmered inside him as he made good his escape. He knew that he had removed a clue from the scene, perhaps a significant one. He could have laughed at the ease by which he had managed it. But he didn't feel like laughing.

Despite his excitement, he waited until he was home to see what Casado had written. He locked his door, closed the shutters and hurried to his desk, where he sat down and began to read:

Being watched. If you are reading this, I pray to God that you are fighting with us, for goodness and truth, and not against us. I also know that when you read this, I will probably be dead. They have sent away my guards. They say the Inquisitors are unnecessary and needed elsewhere. But they want me dead.

I cannot leave. I am doomed. I am always watched.

For what I have discovered. For what I know about Tacit. About the Antichrist. About the darkness that grows in our city.

Don't know who to trust. I'm the most powerful man in the Vatican, after Pope Benedict, and yet I feel abandoned. It's too much. I cannot go to the Inquisition with what I have found. Most in the Vatican now seem in league with the Darkest Hand. The Holy See? Many of them seem suspicious too. Strange. As if they too have been turned, or are in the process of being turned over to the Darkest Hand. To him.

As the Seers decreed, the Antichrist is here, in the Vatican! He is looking to grow his influence and power in the Holy See, and then beyond.

Strettavario cleared his throat and looked up, tracing the fine shard of moonlight slipping through a gap in the shutters across the window. He could see fine dust spin and twist through the narrow band of light cast upon the desk. The sight was both bewitching and pointless.

He is already in a position of great power, but his ascendancy cannot be achieved until his Lieutenant is beside him.

We have all been played by the Antichrist. All along the Antichrist has claimed that Tacit had to be brought to heel. But only because the Antichrist needs Tacit, needs him close, to stand alongside him. Because the Antichrist and Tacit are bound up with each other.

TWENTY-SEVEN

SKALA. PATMOS.

It seemed to be raining metal from the sky. From one end of the long quayside gunmen had opened up their weapons without warning, raking the slipway with bullets. A heavy machine-gun was drumming somewhere amongst the crack of rifle and revolver barrels.

Tacit and the others had taken cover behind a shallow stone ledge at the back of the quay. The official hadn't been quick enough and now lay on his side on the hot bleached stone, twisting erratically. The fishermen had been more quick-witted, jumping into the water to escape the hail of lead.

"I think we've been introduced to the owner of the boat!" called Henry against the rattle and roar of gunfire.

Tacit drew out a revolver and then a second from inside the folds of his cloak, checking the rounds inside.

Henry grabbed him by the arm. "You can't seriously be thinking about taking them on?"

"And what do you suggest?" retorted Tacit, his face a scowl, his mind a maelstrom of vitriolic voices. "Make for the boats!"

"Poldek!" called Isabella, but he had cleared the wall already and was powering up the quayside in the direction of the heaviest gunfire, zig-zagging as he went. He knew he wanted to capture the machine-gun position first: the most dangerous of the weapons, it could also be the most useful to him.

Ten feet forward he took refuge behind a wall, dropping to one knee to check the way ahead. His ruined body groaned with pain. He thrust the agony to the back of his mind and let the demons in his ears holler and insult him, using their obscenities to empower and embolden himself. The machine-gunner was on a first-floor balcony just across the road, shooting down where Tacit was hidden, raking the wall over and over with heavy-calibre rounds. There was no way across the road from where he was, but a little way up it was covered and a quick dash would see him safely across.

He took it, working his way along the wall in a crouched shuffle and then springing over the track of tarmac, dust and stone and into the embracing shadows of the building opposite. A flight of stairs led up to the balcony at the rear of the house and Tacit ran up it in seconds, three steps at a time, shooting the gunner in the back before he had a chance to turn and snatching the Browning before he had even hit the floor. There were two grenades in the man's belt and Tacit grabbed them, setting them in his own belt.

Gunfire blasted the wall of the open-air terrace, showering him with debris and stone, making his ears ring. He withdrew, meeting another man on his way back down the stairs. The machine-gun kicked in his hands and the man fell back, torn open. Tacit nodded, satisfied with the weapon's calibre.

More gunfire pattered the ground and stonework around him. Tacit spun into cover and looked in the direction from where the shots had been fired. There were three men coming down the pathway towards him. He lifted the heavy gun to his shoulder and pulled the trigger, all three of them dropping to the ground, the bullets scything through them. The crack of more gunfire echoed around the port. He went towards it, relishing the opportunity for more killing.

He found it quicker than he had expected, three of them on a street corner, running to find a vantage point from which to throw their fire. He blasted two of them from the path, battering the third out of the way with the back of his hand, before dropping to his knees and killing three more lurking amongst the rocks ahead, who had been firing at Isabella and the others on the quayside. Poré's small regular army was all but lost.

The route up the hillside, out of the town, fell silent and Tacit climbed it, twenty feet further into enemy territory. He threw himself behind a tall rock, slung the machine-gun over his shoulder and took out his revolvers, reloading from the belt of bullets at his waist. He stole a brief look at the enemy, counting at least ten, hidden amongst the crags, crouched or lying on the ledge either side of the path to the Cave of the Apocalypse. Anyone trying to flee from Skala back up the mountain would be a rabbit in a trap.

Pain grew in Tacit, a stunning, shimmering agony from the depths of his thigh, clawing up his left side and into his shoulder. Old wounds returning to remind him of his mortality. It made him sweat and wince, a shuddering ache. He swallowed hard and waited for the torment to abate.

It did, and he traced a route with his eyes along the rock face to where the ground climbed to a bank opposite and level with Poré's entrenched soldiers. He might be able to launch his final attack on this last outpost from there. He charged towards it, bullets zipping and pinging in his wake, sank down behind a boulder and leaned close into the rock as bullets sparked and ricocheted against stone. The first grenade was in his hand and he primed it, watching it flare into blinding life in front of his eyes, his nostrils filling with the caustic bite of cordite. It smelt like nightmares. It smelt like coming home.

TWENTY-EIGHT

The Vatican. Vatican City.

In the gloom and quiet of his room Strettavario paused, his pale moist eyes lifting to the single flickering flame of the candle dancing in the murmur of a breeze. Something caught in him, holding him from reading on, fearful of just what he might discover in the final pages of Casado's journal. But he knew, having risked stealing the pages away, listening to the urging in his heart, that he had to discover the truth.

We always knew that a darkness possessed Tacit. It was why we captured him, tortured him, tried to unlock that which we thought was prophesied years before.

When we caught Tacit, held him deep in Toulouse Inquisitional Prison, I thought that our problems were finally over. Of course, our plan, our actions in Arras and Paris, they came at a price. Tacit captured, but only after he gunned down Cardinal Bishop Monteria from the pulpit of Notre Dame. Eleven men to restrain and subdue him! But I suppose it could have been much worse. But has it proved to be a risk worth taking?

Tacit was full of anger, a monster. What power drives this man, if he is a man? Or is he something else? That was the point wasn't it? To try to find out if we could use the dark power in him for our benefit.

From the very start of the torture it was clear we had never witnessed anything like him before. No one had. People in the prison were calling him Diablo, the Devil.

How many years had we tried to ensnare him? It seems to me as if he has always been a menace, and yet there were times when he filled me with hope. Now I have anything but hope! Such monstrous power. Long known. Long feared. Long expected.

We should have known no Inquisitional Prison could hold him. Can anything hold something of such power? No cell was too deep for one such as him.

The Seven Princes, they did not fail! Bishop Basquez always suspected! And he was proved right. Something did come through, which ever since has brought only mayhem and hate, leaving a trail of destruction, a thing of darkness and chaos, something that the Antichrist has cherished and nourished and now wishes again.

There was nothing more.

Strettavario turned the last sheet over and then turned back to the very first page. There was nothing, nothing more written, nothing more Strettavario could discern from the words. But Strettavario did have a name. He thought of the dagger sticking from Casado's heart.

Basquez.

He knew where his next step would take him.

TWENTY-NINE

SKALA. PATMOS.

Tacit turned and leaned back, launching the grenade across the broad mountain path, watching it arch and then fall amongst the stones where it clattered and tumbled harmlessly, moments before detonating, the echo of its explosion reverberating about every rock, crevice and whitewashed building in the vicinity. The eye of every soldier Tacit faced turned to the sound, the attention of every follower of Poré drawn to the flash of light and angry fire.

Tacit took his chance, bounding up the rutted stony bank to the ledge upon which the soldiers lay waiting. He dropped to one knee and fired at the ambushing troops.

The revolvers spat fire and the soldier closest to him was flung back, the next soldier along crouched on the dusty rock, shrieking and contorting into a writhing ball. A third soldier turned, cursing and panicking, training his weapon, but Tacit was too quick for him and shot him in the neck, the soldier snapping back, his hand clutched all too briefly to his torn throat before lying still. A fourth and then a fifth soldier yelped before lying motionless from Tacit's onslaught. A sixth pulled a revolver and Tacit blew a hole in the man's chest, before belting the revolvers and gathering the Browning machine-gun from around his shoulders and into his hands.

He dropped to his knee and pulled the trigger. Glistening brass rounds threaded out of the barrel like corn from a threshing machine, quicker than a blink. The head of another soldier exploded, showering those behind him with blood and bone. Another tried to stand and flee, terrified by this new assault, but Tacit's first shot took him in the leg and the second in the back of the head. Tacit counted three remaining soldiers and dispatched two of them before they were even able to train their weapons on him. The last man threw down his gun and locked his hands together in a tight white knot of fingers in front of him.

"Please!" he cried, knowing he was beaten by a man greater than any he had faced before. "Please!"

A voice began to sound in Tacit's ears, a voice he had heard for as long as he could remember, not the dereliction of demons but another voice, more ancient and wicked and enthralling, to match all the previous voices in his head. The voice beseeched Tacit to give in to him, to turn his emotion and his spirit over to him utterly. To allow himself to bask in the glory of utmost power.

"Please!" the man wept, sinking down onto his hands and knees, his head cast into the dry dust of the rock. "Please don't kill me! I have a family. I am only a soldier, like you."

Something human twisted in Tacit and he hesitated, the soldier sensing that his life was not lost for certain. He looked up beseechingly, tears and hope in his eyes, his hands clasped tight white to his chest.

"Please."

And then the ancient voice laughed and a wave of anger gushed into Tacit. He remembered the Karst and the Seven Princes and Isabella and

Georgi and the death of his parents and the path of darkness and agony it seemed he only ever walked and breathed. And the essence of humanity hardened in him and then was snuffed out as he growled, "No," before training the barrel of the gun on the man's face and pulling the trigger.

THIRTY

Skala. Patmos.

"You killed them!" muttered Henry disbelievingly, standing on the quayside wall when Tacit emerged from the growing silence of the port buildings. He had his hands up on his head, shielding the sun from his eyes. "You killed them all!"

"They deserved no better," replied Tacit, slinging the machine-gun over his shoulder and setting the revolvers in his holsters, once he had checked their cylinders were empty. He knew he was lying as he spoke, the words like a stain in his mouth, but the voice in his head, clearer now than ever, cheered his victory with a forked tongue and barbed words to match. He grimaced, feeling sick, as the adrenaline peeled off him and other demons' cackling base voices started up their cacophony of hate in his ears. He thought he might go mad with them, if he wasn't already.

There were people coming out of their homes now, appearing from cover and closed locked doors. They gathered as a steadily growing crowd at the rear of the quay, chatting quietly and gesticulating. Italian soldiers were amongst them, but none of them, despite their training and their weapons, suggested for a moment that they wished to intervene. Instead they stood and looked, pointing and waving, arguing amongst themselves, unsure as to what they should do.

"There were loads of them!" Henry stammered, as Tacit and Isabella looked at each other. "A small army!" It seemed to Tacit that Isabella observed him differently too, as if she had detected the voices which compelled and condemned him. As if she too had caught hold of their cacophony of hate. "There must have been twenty, twenty-five of them!" marvelled Henry. "You killed them all!"

108

"And you said you knew how to sail a boat," replied Tacit, walking past him and looking up into the dropped sails of the sailing ship. Something growled in his side, the returning flare of pain now that the charge of action had run out of him. He stifled a groan and turned his head away so they wouldn't see him grimace, fighting against the agonies of his wounds. A filthy-tongued voice mocked in his head. He let it. How many more fights did he have in him, he wondered, till his luck and his body gave out? Or perhaps even his soul?

Henry turned his attention to the vessel and nodded after a moment. "Yes, I suppose so. But…"

"Good, then let's go."

He stepped up the gangplank and onto the vessel, the long length of wood bowing beneath his great weight.

"Go where?" asked Isabella, following him onto the ship.

"Turkey. Bodrum."

"Do you know where that is?" she asked, half in jest, half bemused by him, by the gunfight and by the voices in her own head.

"No," replied Tacit, shaking his head. He watched Henry draw back the gangplank and Sandrine untie the ropes holding the ship to the quay-side. "But it can't be too hard to find." He shrugged and looked up at the tall mast of the ship, as a naval officer might do ahead of a great voyage, before looking back down the harbour to the slowly growing crowd of soldiers and locals stepping nearer to see these violent strangers off their island. "We simply go east until we reach land."

THIRTY-ONE

The Vatican. Vatican City.

Strettavario stood breathless in the doorway of Bishop Basquez's apartment. Eclipsed in shadow and candlelight, he tensed against the blackness beyond, his right hand raised to the lintel of the entrance, his left brushing the wooden panels of the open door. His pale eyes scoured the dark, watching, as an owl might watch for prey in the endless night, waiting for something to appear, for something to reveal itself from the darkness ahead.

But nothing did.

Instead the Priest could discern only something in the air, the faint reek of decay, flowers, stagnant water perhaps? The apartment was caught in an air of utter nothingness. Still. Silent. Strettavario was suddenly aware how, beyond the confines of the passageway, the Vatican rattled and chimed in a great confusion of noise. The sounds amazed him. All his life he had thought of the city as a haven of solitude and quiet reflection.

He had knocked three times against the closed door before testing the handle and finding it unlocked. An unattended and unlocked apartment in the Vatican was not in itself a peculiar occurrence. Few Bishops or Priests felt the need to lock their doors whenever they were away or relaxing quietly in their residences. Most would argue, untruthfully, that they had little to hide, and would happily leave their entrances unlocked, even informing their colleagues of the fact. But when it came to the secretive and sly Bishop, Strettavario knew things would always be different, the eager young Basquez with much to hide and keep from prying eyes.

Something beat in Strettavario, the tease of adrenaline brought on by a sixth sense the old Priest had long appreciated and always relied upon. He'd lived long enough to know he should listen to these cautioning voices of warning.

At the end of the corridor, where the main entrance to the Bishop's apartment stood partially ajar and faint light squeezed through, deathlessness seeped out. Trepidation clutched at Strettavario, and the Priest took a step back, but almost instantly he hesitated, his apprehension turning to something approaching anger, a disbelief that someone of his experience, after all he had seen and done, was afraid of what he might find behind a closed door, the second time he had fought against indecision and won.

His hands had already curled into balls by the time he had taken three steps down the corridor towards the open door. A cursory sweep afforded by the gap urged him on and he pushed the door open, walking in determinedly. The quarters were exactly as Strettavario had hoped them to be. Quiet, empty, and with no sign of Basquez or a struggle.

Feeling foolish and naive for his initial trepidation, he now walked briskly through the place, recognising at once that the driven Bishop had done well for himself, a fine residence, understated opulence, an eye for detail, rich fabrics and quality essentials. Leather-bound books stood wedged into book shelves, tables were leather-topped and upon them tomes of highest quality vellum were laid. Ostrich quills stood in finest Indian ink, cut crystal decanters stood on silver trays glistening with beguiling brown and amber spirits inside.

Once satisfied that there was no sign of malpractice in the entrance hall, he walked into the Bishop's private quarters. Drawers stood partially opened, partially emptied, some of their contents, cloths, stockings, hanging from the open drawers like cud dangling from a cow's mouth. The place had been ransacked, cleared of its most essential items. But not by any villain, not unless Basquez himself was a villain. The Bishop had gone. Had left his opulence and wealth, and left quickly. A man fearing for his own safety, or a murderer making good his escape while he still could? Strettavario thought of the dagger and wondered.

He stepped back through the apartment, heading for the table, adorned with papers, some arranged in careful piles, others more carelessly splayed across the work surface. Strettavario picked his way through them, looking for anything which might suggest where Basquez had gone. He'd always been a secretive man, closed, someone with no friends, few acquaintances. But he must have studied, he must have made connections in some parts of the church's hierarchy?

There was a book of names and addresses under the papers, pushed to one side. Strettavario picked it up and looked at the page which was open. There was only one name and address on the page, one belonging to Father Gregorio Mansi, and the monastery under his watch. The Abbey of Monte Cassino.

Thunder bristled suddenly on the horizon, with it flashes of light.

A storm was rolling into the city.

THIRTY-TWO

The Vatican. Vatican City.

A door banged and a figure in the shadows of the chamber, hidden save for the glint of moisture in his tired eyes, shifted.

"It's all right," he said, casting his glare over the unexpected intruder and then back to the open window of his room, waving his visitor forward with a hand that the man never saw in the darkness. "Come in, damn you, come in and shut the door. Were you followed?" The Inquisitor shook his head, and the man in the shadows did the same. "Makes no odds if you were. Makes no odds to anyone any more. Not now, not with everyone running with their hands in the air, their heads clean off their shoulders after what has befallen Casado. The council he once led has had its own head cut off. The Vatican is now directionless, rudderless. They cannot oppose me. No one can oppose me now. Not even the Pope."

He stood and walked, his silhouette murky in the darkness, bowing his head and frowning on the assembly of oddments and papers on the desk as he stepped past it and leaned on the windowsill, looking out over the dark of the city, the twinkling lights of Rome a mirror to the myriad stars above.

"I was so loved as a child," he began, unexpectedly, quite tenderly, his hand touching his heart in illustration, as if the rumour of love he once felt still resided in this blackened wicked organ. "I thought it normal that all humans were treated in such a way. It was only when I was older and the path allotted for me was realised and revealed that I understood why such care and fondness had been shown to me.

"When they first told me that the world would be my domain, that I would rule all and all would fall before me, I thought them cruel. Cruel!" He laughed, a short forced laugh. "Cruel that they should mock me like that, tell me what I supposed were such lies. Of course, I had always known that I was different from my peers, that I possessed certain talents that no one else about me seemed to share. But even I didn't have the arrogance to think that all would turn to me and that those who did not would be crushed out from the world.

"There have been so many who have gone before, so many people who have dared to take the name Antichrist, so many who have failed. And why have they failed? They thought that power and supremacy could be gained by might alone, by force of arms, by conflict. Genghis Khan, Charlemagne, Napoleon Bonaparte, they all tried to recreate the world in their own image and to rule by conflict and expansion. But even just one physical battle only brings more battles. And with every battle come the blades and arrows of enemies. And any one arrow, struck by unhappy chance, let alone skill, might be enough to kill. So it has been throughout history."

He raised a finger. "A battle of words, manipulation of minds, the control of people's opinions and ideas, the ability to turn people to your will, make them act and do for you, that is where the true Antichrist fights his battles. This whole world war, so expertly constructed, has been exactly that. And there will be other wars. This is only the beginning. When I ascend to my rightful place with my Lieutenant by my side, and turn all to ruination, this world war will seem like a skirmish compared to what is to come, with ever more terrible armies and weapons and rhetoric."

And he stopped and smiled to reminisce and to imagine.

"Poldek Tacit," the man chuckled, shaking his head slowly, "he almost ruined everything. In Sarajevo. Archduke Ferdinand. The Black Hand. He almost succeeded in stopping his assassination, the spark required to ignite the war. Father Strettavario got to him just in time. The irony of it! Both ignorant. Neither aware of what it was they were doing, achieving, of bringing to the world!

"And now Tacit has returned! I felt him! I felt his anger, his wickedness, his conflict and majesty!"

And then he stopped and looked at the man who had visited him. "Why have you come here?" he asked, as if catching hold of himself, realising that he had spoken a stream of consciousness to an audience as much as to himself.

"The Seventh Seal. It has been opened."

The face of the man darkened immediately. "So I have been led to understand. Most strange. I am at a loss. The opening of the Seventh Seal, the bringing of damnation into the world, I am sure that is my domain and my domain alone."

The Inquisitor bringing the news hesitated, confused as to how his master could already have received the news. "Tacit, he was seen commandeering a boat to the island from mainland Greece. We sent people there. The scene we discovered, there had been a terrible battle. Many dead were laid out on the quayside, covered in sheets. And the seal... it had been opened! The tomb beyond... empty!"

"Who?" the man asked. In the shadows, he seemed to seethe at the question, his whole body shaking as if on fire, his hands held in tight balls of fury. "Who was responsible for this insult then, I wonder?"

"One with the power to open the seal?" And the man then said the name that the Antichrist was already considering, the name of another who had bested him before at the Karst Plateau. "Poré!" said the messenger. "It was Gerard-Maurice Poré!"

THIRTY-THREE

Somewhere in the Aegean Sea.

Salt-water spray from the dark sea flying beneath the boat stung wounds, making skin shimmer in the sun. Boat boards and ropes creaked, the white sails straining full against their ties and the mast, as the prow of the sailing ship rose and fell over the waves. Tacit's hands were clutched tight to the rail of the boat as he looked down at the wash shooting past. Isabella observed him and crossed the deck to stand next to him, slipping her hand through the crook in his arm. She looked up and smiled as their eyes met, before they looked together to the horizon.

"I heard them, Poldek," she said, after a while. "The voices. On the island."

"I am sorry. Hell has left its mark on you."

She nodded. "Will I ever be free? Will *you* ever be free of them?"

"Yes, one day," he said.

He searched the heavens. Birds trailed the boat, white and black wings against the sky. Blue, endless blue, drifted above dark churning depths. Driving through the waves, the wind tugged at hair and clothes, fresh in the nose and lungs. Tears were teased from eyes, leaving salty trails across temples. There was a wild abandonment from the rushing air that all of them on the boat felt, being drawn along on the crest of wide waves, unfettered and untroubled, the full sails and sleek boat more powerful than any engine or locomotive. Dolphins, like sentinels, guided the boat onwards, jumping and diving at its prow.

And the four of them stared into the endless blotch of indigo ahead, watching and waiting and hoping they might catch up with Poré, already at the very least three hours ahead of them.

"Is that something there?" asked Sandrine eventually, pointing towards something indefinable in the distance.

A vague shape was on the horizon, a smudge of dark, away to their right.

"It's a ship," confirmed Isabella.

"Go towards it, Henry!" called Tacit.

Henry spun the broad wooden wheel to starboard and instantly the vessel cut knife-like through the surf, making them all reach for ropes and masts against which to steady themselves. The boat lifted and fell, speeding effortlessly across the waves.

The shape on the horizon grew larger and more distinct.

Henry set his hands tight to the handles of the wheel and imagined himself the captain of a great sailing ship of ages past, looking up into the tangle of sails. He thought it then a grand life, aboard that ship, driving it through the calm Aegean Sea, and all the doubts and darkness which had consumed him were forgotten for a little while. Shallow waves rose out of the infinite dark waters, every breaking crest like a seam of diamonds, every spray a cascade of glittering jewels beneath the pale golden sun.

They continued to gain on the shadow in the distance, the shape which became a boat and then a beautiful schooner, majestic on the water, but on a course which seemed slower than Henry's.

From the wheel of the boat, Henry identified the type of ship it was and announced it with a cry, pointing and drawing his boat straight at it.

"We're gaining!" Isabella cried.

"Is it them?" asked Sandrine.

"We'll see soon enough," growled Tacit. "Are we still going east?"

"East south-east," confirmed Henry, looking down at the compass and loving the words in his mouth, the smooth feel of the wheel in his hands, the wind in his hair. He knew he'd go away to the sea after all of this, take a boat with Sandrine and make the seas his domain.

"Even if it's not them," Tacit muttered to Isabella, "we're still going in the right direction." He willed the boat on with a urgent bend of his neck.

They were closer still now. They could all make out the different aspects of the boat, its colour, the markings on its sail, the people aboard, now pointing and gesticulating hurriedly back at the gaining ship.

Gunfire suddenly erupted from its stern, pattering the waves and troughs around the boat Henry steered.

Tacit laughed, believing for once luck was on their side, sweeping a keen knowing look across his crew and thrusting with his hand to drive Henry and the boat on. He took a bottle from his cloak and put it to his lips, guzzling deep, in that moment looking more than ever to everyone else on the boat like a ravaged sea captain from an earlier time.

Their boat sped nearer. More gunfire sprayed out from the back of the one they pursued and they all cowered for cover, bullets ripping into the boat and over it. The white tips of the waves, spreading and breaking before the prow of the boat, looked like wild horses' manes.

Closer.

The figures were now clearly visible. Tacit could make out their features, the glint of their eyes, the glimmer of sun on dull gunmetal. A machine-gun opened up and Henry took evasive action, steering away, showing their broadside to the attack.

"No!" cried Tacit, gesturing with a thrusting pointing hand. "Straight at them! Go straight at them! We need to make ourselves as small a target as possible!"

Henry winced, putting the beautiful boat in harm's way, bullets peppering the prow and starboard side, ripping up great chunks of wood from the beautiful inlaid hazel and beech veneers. He set the ship on a direct collision course towards Poré.

The front of the boat began to be torn up by the oncoming gunfire. Ropes frayed and span away, wood splintered and fell into the wake of the vessel, as if the boat was being driven onto rocks hidden beneath the dark surface of the sea.

Twenty feet away, men on Poré's boat started to run backwards and forwards across the deck, shouting and gesticulating even more wildly.

Ten feet from the boats hitting, the machine-gunner threw down his weapon and dashed to the opposite side of the ship.

"Get alongside!" cried Tacit, and Henry spun the wheel hard as the sailing ship twisted violently in the ocean, turning hard to port, more gunfire erupting, exploding and zipping about them, tearing wood and punching holes in the sails. For a moment everyone waited for the ships to hit, and then they did, the vessel Henry was steering ramming up and over the schooner, its prow driving across it, shuddering the snagged ship to a hard stop, tearing wood and twisting metal, as if it had dropped anchor and instantly been held. The sound was atrocious, the scream of ripping metal, wrenching wood.

Like a buccaneer boarding a raided ship, Tacit sprang over the side onto the schooner's deck, throwing himself into the midst of the chaos, battering at Poré's crew, sending the men onto the deck floor or over the side with his hammer-like fists. Behind him, Isabella unleashed fire with an automatic rifle, shuddering three of the sailors backwards into the water.

Sandrine landed square in her boots on the deck of the ship they had rammed, her revolver turning over. Once, twice it fired. She trained it on the man at the helm and zeroed him in her sights. Immediately he held his hands skywards, clean off the wheel, and stepped backwards, away from any means of steering the stricken vessel.

Tacit looked across the deck for more sailors. All seemed accounted for, dead, dazed or splashing about in the sea, grappling any flotsam they could reach. He ran to the helm, pushing the Captain aside and looking down to the door at the bottom of a short flight of steps that led from the wheel. He jumped down them and kicked the door off its hinges, bundling inside. A gun fired, ripping into his shoulder, the rings of his armour taking most of the impact. He roared forward, battering the gun from the man's hand and knocking him down.

The man rolled over, his hand locked to the top of the box he was protecting. Tacit picked him up in the cramped berth and threw him against the wall, battering him into the wooden wall, reaching forward and gathering the box into his own hands, turning back towards the light coming in from the open door. He stepped into it and opened the lid expectantly. Inside was an earthenware pot, covered by its own lid. Without hesitation he reached to lift it, but the man he had thrown against the side of the cabin called out to him.

"You're too late," he croaked through shattered ribs. "They've gone."

Tacit drew back his hand and turned to look down at the man over his shoulder.

"What do you mean they've gone?"

"Seven vials. There are seven of them! You've only got one of them."

"And the others?"

"To the four corners of the globe, Poldek Tacit!" sneered the man, his lips bloody. "You might have stopped me, but there are another six which have escaped. Seven vials to destroy the world, and only one is enough to complete the task." And he laughed, through the tested breath of broken bones. "The Tribulation has begun!"

"What does the box contain?" asked Isabella, stepping up to Tacit's shoulder and peering to see.

Tacit went to answer but the man spoke for him, a mocking leering tone. "The dust of ages, the dust of God's wrath!"

Tacit turned to look at him, his murderous eyes on the injured man lying in the shadow of the floor of the ship's cabin.

THIRTY-FOUR

The Vatican. Vatican City.

Strettavario pushed the door to his apartment open and waited, listening for any sounds which suggested there might be someone inside waiting for him.

When satisfied, he entered and stood in the darkness of his hallway, listening again. He could hear the clock on his mantelpiece tick, a choral voice somewhere in the courtyards below, the click of shoes in a passageway, the faint rumble of traffic and life in Rome. But nothing else. He shivered, partly from the chill of night and partly from what he knew he had been reduced to, a skulking scared visitor in his own home, timidity bound up with every step. And hated himself for it, for what he was, a scared frail old man.

He toured his apartment cautiously, turning on lights as he went. Only when he was certain that no one was lying in wait, preparing to pierce him from behind, did he fill his washbasin, sinking his hands into the cold water, bringing palmfuls of it up to his face to cool his eyes and skin, to give him a moment to ponder, think and plan. He caught sight of himself in the mirror and shuddered. He looked grey, sullen, as if he had visibly aged in the last few hours of discovery.

He felt ancient and lumpen, too old to be considering the course of action that he was, and yet adrenaline coursed in him that he hadn't felt for years too many to remember.

Beyond his open window, louder thunder rumbled across the heavens in the west, dazzling white fingers of lightning shimmering over the Tyrrhenian Sea.

His face seemed to boil in the reflection back at him, mirroring his anger and shock at the revelations, the audacity and the bravado of the crimes. The sheer wickedness of what had been unleashed upon his city.

He patted his face dry, disrobed and walked to his private quarters. He thought about Cardinal Korek, of Cardinal Berberino, of the War, of the millions dying on foreign fields, of Basquez gone, of the Antichrist, of Tacit, the Seers and their burning flesh.

The world had changed, grown colder, darker, as if a skin of innocence had been peeled from it, from people's lives and sensibilities. It hurt his heart and his head, his anger and incredulity solidifying into a bristling ball. With every stride it seemed as if the thunder on the horizon gathering towards the city was growing louder, the lightning ever brighter. His tightly clasped lips trembled with the gathering fury, his hands turning to pale fists at his sides.

Lightning flashed again across the city skyline and almost at once thunder battered around the heavens. Strettavario supposed a storm was coming in off the coastline, hitting the Vatican Square in its course.

There was a door in his bedroom he hadn't opened for over twenty years, the key to which he always carried around his neck, as if a reminder of days past when things were different for him. Without ceremony or thought, he took the key from the chain and unlocked the door.

He was doubtful as to what he was about to do. He thought of what the Holy See might think, what the Inquisition might do. He relented and pulled the door open.

Beyond hung inquisitional robes and chain mail, an array of weapons hanging on hooks. He bowed his head as if acknowledging an old friend, and took the silver-ringed shirt of mail from where it hung. He marvelled at its weight and suppleness, the way the light danced across its metalwork.

Lightning and thunder crashed together. The storm had finally arrived.

THIRTY-FIVE

The Aegean Sea. Close to the Turkish border.

Tacit had made the man watch the Captain go over the side of the boat, as a way to loosen his tongue. It worked.

He'd been tasked with taking the vial to the Middle East. There were enough stores to last them until they reached Syria. There had been seven ships, one for each of the vials. Poré had met them at the agreed location in the Aegean and they had divided up the vials and gone their separate ways: to the Middle East, Far East, Russia, Africa, Europe, South America and North America.

The man on his knees was to take his to Jerusalem. He assured them he knew nothing more, nothing about the precise destinations of the other six. Only their carriers knew them. Tacit believed what he told him and that he knew little more. Still, he locked him in the cabin for future inquisition. They'd left Poré's ship listless in the sea and, after ensuring that their own was still watertight and seaworthy, had set sail for Turkey.

"At least now we know,' Tacit mused, as they saw Turkey's shoreline draw into view with the broad bronze fingers of the setting sun. "At least we know their plan, that we're not too late to stop them."

"Six ships," lamented Sandrine. "Who knows where they are now? How can we hope to catch them when we have just one ship?"

"I'm working on that," answered Tacit.

There were more vessels in the seas around the Turkish shoreline, fishing boats, steamers, transporters and battleships. A flotilla of small ships, lightly gunned, headed towards them a mile from shore. On board were black-clad people, rifles slung over their shoulders.

"I know these people," Tacit growled. "They're like me."

"Inquisitors! You have your own navy?"

"Not all battles are fought on land. You're an Englishman, you should know that. Lower the sails," Tacit called, and the battered ship slunk to a slow crawl.

"You've seen some action," called one of the Inquisitors from the approaching boats, on seeing the vessel's bullet-ridden prow and hull. And then he froze. "I don't believe it," he growled.

"Impossible!" another Inquisitor called, his hand dropping to the grip of his revolver. "You're supposed to be dead."

"I'm back," replied Tacit.

"Sister Isabella!" the first Inquisitor shouted.

"What is it?" she replied, edging surreptitiously closer to Tacit.

"We were told to look for you. The Holy See says you might lead us to Poré."

"Sadly not," she replied.

"But we are hoping that you might be able to lead us to him," said Tacit. "Constantinople. Get word to the inquisitional headquarters there. They need to know, to get a message to –"

"We don't take orders from criminals!" another called back, his rifle pointing at Tacit. "You're a marked man!"

"Whatever I am, you need to get word to the Vatican. Tell them that the Tribulation has begun. There is little time left to stop it. Maybe we are already too late." He held up the earthenware pot he had found on board Poré's ship for all to see.

"What's that?" asked an Inquisitor.

"One of the seven vials," said Tacit. Some of the Inquisitors laughed, but most knew that Tacit was not one to joke about divine things. "Poré is taking the other six across the Aegean and Mediterranean at this very moment. That is why we need to find him. Urgently! This is the message that you must relay!"

PART THREE

"Go your ways, and pour out the vials of the wrath of God upon the earth."

REVELATION 16:1

THIRTY-SIX

ALEXANDRIA. EGYPT.

Hot breezes blew in from the drifting sands of the caravan trails east of the city, meeting cooler winds from the sea and making eddies of dust snake and rise in the squares and across the quayside. At the backs of the newly arrived passengers, the Citadel of Qaitbay shone golden-white in the scorching Egyptian sun. Ahead, the hectic scuffle and squalor of the Alexandrian markets stretched, cramped colourful streets, barking stall keepers, tempting ground spices of every colour and aroma, glistening meats and dead-eyed fish, squawking birds in cages, the heaving bustle of noise and banter, while above weathered buildings loomed over crowds squeezed into the stifling squares and alleyways. A place to lose one's self, and one's life if not careful.

Poré and his small group of men swept through the throng of noise and raillery in the place, colour and heat drenching every inch of it, minarets climbing high like sentinels above, calling out to the populace. They did not stop to look at any stall. They reached a junction buried deep in the city and turned left, plunging into another writhing narrow passageway, wishing to avoid the open square ahead, where the crowds thinned and one could walk more easily, preferring to be shadowed and hidden from the sun. At the far end, Poré stopped and looked back, studying the way they had come, to make sure they were not being followed.

123

"Our caravan is waiting for us," one of his party said urgently.

"Then let us not keep it waiting," Poré replied. "Let us go on."

The hastening scuttling assortment of cloaked and hooded men, carrying with them chests and cases strung between long poles set on their shoulders, was swallowed by the labyrinth of side-streets and cobbled squares, marked with olive and clementine trees and a fortuitously positioned water hole. The noise, bustle and close heat of the markets began to recede, crowds of market-goers and pedlars thinning so they now passed only occasional residents of the great city, many beating dust from hanging carpets, brushing debris from entrances, or lounging lazily in the sun, rogue cats stepping languidly through the heat in search of a drink or food.

Halfway down the alleyway a figure blocked their way, a cloth wrapped about his face and head. Instantly hands dropped to holsters hidden beneath cloaks, but the man came forward, pulling the wraps away to reveal his face.

"The vial bound for Jerusalem," he began.

"Pablo!" called the thin man, on realising who he was. Then his face hardened. "What about it?"

"It's been intercepted. Tacit."

Poré weighed the news and said, "It makes no odds. We are still six. We will go on."

"What about the one carrying the vial? He will reveal everything!"

"He knows nothing," replied Poré, before walking on to the junction ahead and looking down each of the alleyways running away from it in turn.

"He knows of the seven continents," Pablo called after him. "They will torture him! They will find out!"

"Let them. You forget that only one of the vials needs to get through. One is enough to ensure that nothing in the world will ever be the same again."

The gaunt man noticed that the others in his group were hovering intently, loitering with anxious glances.

"Leave us for a moment," he said to them. They objected, but the lean man interrupted them. "We will join you shortly from where the caravan is to leave, just beyond this quarter of the city. Make sure everything is ready for us. Leave nothing to chance!" He watched them go before turning back to Pablo.

"London," was all he said.

Pablo nodded, drawn to a water fountain at the junction where they were speaking. He drank and washed the dust from his face. "It is done," the young Italian said. "All the paperwork completed. Weihai, Shandong. The British transport ship will leave from there in four months. They will be expecting you, Mr Archer," he said with a knowing look.

Poré nodded. "And your other business," he asked, "the one involving Tacit. You still mean to continue with your plan?"

Pablo shook his hands dry.

"Yes, I have not carried the knives of Gath with me since the Carso out of respect. When I finally meet with him, their blades will be used as they were forged to do. Once again they will be bathed in blood."

THIRTY-SEVEN

CONSTANTINOPLE.

The inquisitional long hall smelt of hookah smoke and stale liquor. The smell had ingrained itself into the fabric of the room, giving it a timeless stink, as if all of man's debauchery and misdemeanours had been bound up in the place. Tall windows along one wall were open in an attempt to allow some air into the hall, but the warm Turkish breeze only ruffled and teased at the reeking pall of smoke. The heat was growing inside the chamber. Sweat ran down skin. They had come directly to the hall upon arriving at the city, not pausing to rest or even clean themselves after their voyage across the Aegean and their exertions across the wizened Turkish countryside via a chaotic combination of train, wagon and caravan journeys, the guides earning their nightly rations of hard liquor for driving their mounts hard and keeping connections on time.

They felt sick and unwashed, but they knew the urgency of their mission, how every passing moment wasted drew the world ever closer to calamity.

Down the very centre of the hall a table was laid, tall-backed chairs lining either side of it, a clutch of them at each end, set out in uneven arcs.

Almost every one was taken and Inquisitors sat upon them, gathered in groups, their talk low but passionate, withering looks on faces, clenched fists and jaws, spurred on by their intoxication and wild tales of battles against their many enemies. The reappearance of Poldek Tacit had invigorated them, and most talk was about the large man sitting at one end of the table, disfigured but unquestionably himself. Every now and then faces turned to scowl at him, the man believed dead, the man wanted by the Vatican. They watched him closely before turning back to their gossiping huddles and leaning in, their voices lower and ever more wary.

"They watch me with suspicion," spat Tacit, as he held court amongst the small select group of Inquisitors he had gathered, those picked from the boats which had met them out at sea, some from the caravan ride across Turkey and others chosen from the moment he had stepped into the inquisitional lodge and called a council.

"And do you blame them?" asked one of his delegation, a ruddy-faced Portuguese Inquisitor called Furtado. "You're a marked man!"

Isabella watched them, knowing their eyes were on her as often as they were on Tacit. Henry and Sandrine were seated upon a long wooden bench, observing the terrible gathering of men.

"Murderers and villains, every one of them!" hissed Sandrine to Henry, who tried to calm her with a gentle pat on her wrist. He already felt dreadfully exposed as it was, having brought a half-wolf into an inquisitional headquarters, without hearing her hiss and spit the dislike of her hosts so openly.

"You come with an unexpected bounty on your head, Poldek Tacit," another of the group warned in a heavy Russian accent. He wagged a chipped and bruised finger. "If you aren't already dead, then you should be."

"And not many will be happy to witness your return," Furtado continued. "There's plenty who would like to see you hang after what you did in the Vatican. All that killing? The death of Grand Inquisitor Düül?"

Though over two years ago now, it was not easy for anyone to forget the carnage Tacit had brought to the Trastevere Monastery and Vatican buildings in Rome. Bitterness and violence was palpable in the air, at how the wolves beneath the city had flocked to his aid, the Inquisitors' sworn enemy fighting for another of their kind.

But Tacit laughed, a drunken careless laugh, and the voices inside him laughed too. "Grand Inquisitor Düül was the biggest bastard of them all! I know of no one who would have mourned his passing."

"And there are few here who will mourn yours," replied Furtado. "You caused mayhem in the heart of our capital city, Tacit. Many of these people lost colleagues and friends that night."

"Poldek did not start the fight!" said Isabella. "He did not summon the wolves."

"But they came, regardless. And fought the Inquisition. Some say it was *he* who was responsible for bringing the wolves into Rome."

"Then what hope is there of them fighting for me, fighting against Poré, if they think so little of me?" replied Tacit, draining his tankard in a single pull and slamming it back on the table. He looked up into the Inquisitors' faces. "The heat has eroded their brains." He spoke the charge loudly enough for most to hear him, as he pushed back his chair, grating it across the stone floor, and stood, preparing to address the auditorium.

"I thought it was the place of washer-women to stare and gossip?" Grumbling and angry curses at once were thrown back. "I haven't come here for your mutterings. If any one of you finds my presence here dislikable, let me hear it now. Tell it to my face, why you distrust me as you do, why you feel I should not be here. Draw your weapon and let us have it out like real Inquisitors."

He stepped away from where he had been seated, into the wider space of the hall, drawing any fire, should it come, away from Isabella and the other Inquisitors with whom he had sat and who had shown him loyalty.

"I don't care what you have been told about me," Tacit continued. "I am not one for gossip and hearsay. Let our enemies fill your heads with nonsense and lies. I came here, from beyond the grave, as your ally and in need of you!"

"You are our enemy!" someone shouted.

"If I was your enemy you'd be dead already. I have come here, Inquisitor, for your help."

"Why should we help you?" another called back.

"Because I care for the Vatican, the place I have always served!" The voice in him cheered and mocked in equal measure. Lights danced in front of his eyes, lights only he could see.

Odams, an enormous Inquisitor, climbed heavily to his feet. He was the commander at the headquarters in Constantinople, running the establishment with iron discipline and unhinged cruelty. "Did you serve it when half of the Trastevere Monastery was destroyed?" he spat. "When Rome was overrun by wolves?"

"That was not of my doing. I did not command them or call for them."

"And why were they called? Because you're a traitor!" Odams pulled out his wide-gauge revolver, levelling it on Tacit. But Tacit did not react, instead opening his arms to allow the shot to find its mark, if the Inquisitor wished to pull the trigger.

"I care not what you have been told about me and my intentions. I come here as an ally of the Vatican, someone who wishes to protect it."

"So much of an ally of the Vatican to not have heard its news then?"

"What news?"

"That it is lost?" In the dark of the hall, Odams' words sounded ruinous and grim.

"What do you mean lost?"

"The House of the Seers is gone. Burnt down. It is nothing but ruin."

Tacit's eyes widened. The voices in him celebrated with scheming hateful yelps. "When did this happen?"

"A few weeks back. No one knows who did it, but we can think why. They were about to reveal the name of the Antichrist. For a long time we've thought that something had crept into the place and taken root," said Furtado. "We now know it to be true. We suspected this peril lay in the crypts and catacombs under the Vatican, lying in wait for a time when it could act. We now know that this terror inhabits the very halls and corridors of power in the Vatican. And this wickedness is growing."

"Your news is grievous indeed!" said Tacit. Yet none of it came as a surprise to him, as if a part of him already knew, as if he had heard it somewhere else. "That is why I have come here. To rally you to *our* cause. The world hangs on the very edge of the Abyss. The time of Tribulation is now. End Times are here. Word must be got to those we can still trust, to warn the Holy See and Cardinal Secretary of State Casado to muster all Inquisitors in this most pressing of needs."

"And how do you hope to do that then?" asked the Inquisitorial commander.

"By horses! Telegram! Send word by boat to the Vatican, if you must. There are a hundred ways by which we send messages across the network."

"But who will receive it, Poldek Tacit?"

And Tacit swallowed, sensing that he knew what Odams meant. "What of the Secretary of State?" he asked.

"Stabbed, clean through the heart."

"When?"

"Shortly after the burning of the House of the Seers."

Tacit dropped his head, his face darkening.

"Sounds like something of a coup, doesn't it?" Odams asked. "Which is why I didn't have you killed outright. I needed to know what you knew, or didn't."

"Who? Who was responsible?" Tacit asked, knowing at least the organisation which would be behind the killing.

"There are many who believe that Poré is the one responsible."

But Tacit shook his head. "It's not him," he replied, almost instantly, without thought or hesitation, and something hissed and spat in his ears.

"How can you be so sure? The man who attempted such murder at the Mass for Peace? Clearly he wishes to bring downfall to the world?" argued Furtado. "At the very least downfall of the Catholic faith."

But Tacit shook his head again. "No, there is another in the Vatican."

"The Holy See is rudderless without a Secretary of State," said Isabella.

"At least until another takes that role," replied Furtado, apprehension in his eyes.

"Yes, and whoever does take it has a direct line to the Pope," said Odams, turning his eyes onto Isabella. "*That* is the most powerful position in the Vatican, the one who guides policy, the Pope's mouthpiece."

"We are at war," said Tacit, the words like a war cry of their own.

He spread his hands, like a Priest before a congregation. "You are Inquisitors, like me. It is our duty to fight for the Vatican, against the forces of evil. That is why I am here, why I have returned!

"Gerard-Maurice Poré, once the Cardinal of Arras, has opened the Seventh Seal. He has stolen the seven vials inside, vials containing God's wrath, and he is taking them about the world to unleash his anger upon this broken world.

"Regardless of what is occurring in the Vatican, we must stop Poré. I need you to help me stop him. We are only four," he said, looking at Isabella, Henry and Sandrine.

"Unless we stop Poré, everything you have fought for will be for nothing. Do with me what you will afterwards, but until the vials are found and Poré caught, honour me with your strength of arms and might."

And as he finished speaking, the voice in his head grew like a storm, cackling and mocking him mercilessly, telling him that he was lost, whatever he did.

THIRTY-EIGHT

The Vatican. Vatican City.

A downpour was drenching the city, the first rains to have fallen in months. When they came, they came like a cataclysm, a deluge so heavy that all colour and form was washed from the place.

The severity of the storm had taken Father Strettavario by surprise, much as it had the rest of the citizens of Rome and Vatican City, and he had left his horse saddled and still stabled, and now stood at a window looking out at the water pouring down over the Pontifical Villas, unwilling to ride out in the storm, unwilling to return to his apartment.

They had buried Cardinal Bishop Casado on the Friday, after laying him out in state for all to see. Father Strettavario had not gone to see his body, covered by a white shroud, as he had imagined it would have been, or even attended the state funeral. He had thought it wiser to lie low and avoid anywhere where he supposed he could be a target. For he knew he would be one, now that he knew what he did, now that he knew there was a murderer on the loose.

He listened to the rains thundering down onto the roofs above his head and watched the rivulets and streams burgeon and surge over the paths and walkways on the other side of the glass. A vague smell of sulphur made him turn, perhaps quicker than he intended.

"Apologies, Father Strettavario," said Adansoni, bowing politely. "I didn't mean to make you jump." Strettavario shook the apology away and looked back to the pouring rain. He felt the comforting weight of his armour upon him and wondered to himself why he was suddenly so glad to be wearing it. "Were you at Casado's funeral?" asked Adansoni.

"No," replied Strettavario, "I… I was busy."

"It was well attended."

"He was well liked."

"Indeed he was." They stared out of the window together, watching the storm, until Adansoni said, "You no doubt will have heard?"

"Tacit?" asked Strettavario, and Adansoni nodded, his face impossible to read, like a mask.

"In Constantinople, commanding Inquisitors no less? The man comes back from the dead and is instantly commanding others to his will!" Now Adansoni chuckled, looking up into the falling rain.

"You must be pleased?" asked Strettavario pointedly, and the Cardinal supposed there was more behind the question than first appeared.

"I am surprised," Adansoni answered nimbly.

"We all thought him dead."

"And no doubt you will also have heard about –"

"The Seventh Seal?"

Adansoni nodded grimly. "God's wrath. The seven vials. If the news had been brought by anyone else, I would have doubted its authenticity, but because it was brought by Tacit…" His words fell silent and the noise of the rain filled the chamber.

Strettavario was aware that the old Cardinal had taken a half step away and was now examining him from a distance, his head turned to one side. "Are you planning a trip, Father Strettavario?" he asked his friend, seeming only now to notice his attire, the small pack at his feet. The pale-eyed Priest watched the lines of rain run down the window pane.

"Yes," he said, "when the storm passes."

"Where are you going?"

"Away," he replied, obtuse, not wishing to reveal much of his business, even to the friend he supposed Adansoni was. And he hated himself for it and weakened. "There's somewhere I need to go."

"Of course," answered Adansoni in a veiled tone of mockery.

"Something I need to find out."

"I hope it's nothing too… troublesome? I would have hoped that the news of Tacit's reappearance might have reduced the weight of such troubles?" Strettavario stayed silent, closed, not looking at the Cardinal, and Adansoni added, "Especially as you were one of Tacit's greatest admirers?"

"Perhaps," mused the Priest. "After you."

Adansoni acknowledged the sentiment with a nod. "Do they know who killed Casado?" he asked.

Strettavario shook his head.

"I heard that Bishop Basquez was in the frame?" Adansoni admired his nails in the pale washed-out light from the window.

"You have proof it is him?" asked Strettavario. "If so, we can have him arrested at once."

"I have no proof. And we're too late, he's left, the Vatican. Vanished." And then he said, his eyes turning harder on Strettavario, a look which made the old Priest swallow, "As you well know, Father Strettavario, after you visited his residence." Adansoni turned his gaze back to the window, his fingers drumming a beat upon the stone frame. "I've never trusted him. I'm not sure why he was ever allowed to practise as he was. The fact the man's left the Vatican unannounced, with no forwarding address, nothing in his diary, proves everything."

"He was friends with Cardinal Bishop Casado," said Strettavario, finding it strange that he was defending the man he believed might be the murderer.

"They were acquaintances. They worked together. I'm not sure Casado would necessary call him a *friend*, but they did have similar interests, particularly in the sphere of pain." Adansoni arched an eyebrow pointedly. "So, if he's not here, in the Vatican, where's he gone? Must have irked the man, to leave behind his luxuries?" The old Cardinal smiled, a forced joyless smile, his eyes remaining dull and dark. And then he said, "He will be missed," watching the whites of Strettavario's own eyes in the shared silence, looking for any sign of a reaction, anything which betrayed him. "Casado, I mean, he will be missed," he repeated, Strettavario knowing the comment was once more a test for the old Priest, to see if he gave anything away. Suspicion had polluted everything in the city, polluted councils and friendships.

The puckish work of the Devil.

"He was a good man," mused Strettavario. "He did much good, for the Holy See and the faith."

The rain, turned into deep brown puddles in the gravel, was snaking from them like shimmering brown serpents, snatching leaves and small twigs as it went. "It was a shame Pope Benedict was unable to attend."

"Berlin," said the Priest, finding that the name of the place, far away from the Vatican, left him feeling relieved. "His peace mission. He would have been here, of course, but…"

"Of course," nodded Adansoni. He turned his cold eyes up to the heavens. "I suppose you wouldn't have heard, Father Strettavario?"

"Heard, Javier?"

"The Holy See, they have offered me the position of Cardinal Secretary of State."

THIRTY-NINE

Constantinople. Turkey.

A stone minaret, like a needle pointing to heaven, threw its shadow down across the squat sandy bleached building in which Tacit and the others had gathered. His call for the Inquisition's help still resonated around the headquarters.

From the Arab tower, a different call, that of prayer to a different faith, swept across the city, devout and enthralling.

The sun, low on the horizon, seemed almost smudged out by the gristle of grey-white clouds hanging motionless in the stale sky, pattering a drizzling persistent rain upon the city.

In the room, a plate of dates sat glistening and untouched on a silver dish. The pale sun streamed through a thin shade, laced with exotic creatures and vivid seaside scenes, erected between the living area and the balcony of the apartment to give a little privacy from the populace beyond. In the very centre of the terrace, Tacit purred and growled as he looked down on the many twisting labyrinthine streets and the world burrowing through them.

And he drank, to drive out the voices, to silence their devious entreaties. At first he had thought the local spirit, shipped in through secret inquisitional lines, tasted like a weak sweet wine, a watered-down grappa to nurse those wishing to experience the fortitude of alcohol at a gentler pace. He found however that it improved after the second bottle, and with it packed a decent enough punch, not as good perhaps as some Slavic vodkas or Spanish brandies, but good enough to squeeze the Devil out of him. For now.

He filled his empty glass, the surface of which had been wrought with thin spidery webs of silver, and set the bottle down, holding up the golden liquid to study it through the miserly day's light. The Inquisition, they would be interrogating the man Tacit had captured from the ship at this very moment, the one with the first vial, trying to find out its secrets and valuable snippets which might help them find the other vials, stop End Times from being unleashed, if they were not already too late. Tacit could have done the interrogation himself, but time was tight and he knew there were Inquisitors even more adept at such things. Every hour was vital. And yet, for all the urgency, he was surprised how little he cared that they had yet to return with news. Too exhausted to care. Too worn ragged and broken. Too infected by the voices and amongst them one particular voice which had grown since Patmos, more callous and commanding than all the others, beseeching him to return.

To return to a place he knew well.

For the moment, though, he resisted, resisted through his stubborn disposition and the snag of drunkenness.

Isabella stepped onto the veranda and Tacit reached out to her, taking her hand and drawing her close. Isabella stretched her hands around him and drew herself closer still, Tacit cherishing the touch of her next to him, a shield against his nightmares.

"Thank you," he said quietly.

"For what?" smiled Isabella, accepting his light kiss and kissing him back.

"More than you'll ever know."

Henry, who had followed Isabella outside, cleared his throat from the entrance to the terrace and said, "I thought you would have wished to have spoken to this sailor of Poré's yourself, Poldek?"

Tacit kissed Isabella again, this time on her forehead, before drawing back to sit on the veranda's ledge, his silver-gilded glass nursed in his hand. Isabella took the place next to him. "There are others far better skilled in retrieving information from people than me," he replied, taking a long drink and draining it.

Henry nodded. "Is it always so insufferably warm this time of year in Constantinople?" he asked, pulling at the neck of his shirt and pouring out two more glasses of spirit from the decanter and then a third for Tacit when his empty glass was thrust towards the glistening stream of liquor. Henry turned and offered one to Sandrine, who shook her head, squishing up her nose. He offered the spare drink to Isabella, who gave him the same reply. He shrugged and put the glass back down on the bronze-coloured tray, keeping hold of his own and taking a sip. He made a face himself, suggesting the women had made the right choice in declining. "You did well," he said, "rallying the Inquisitors to your call."

"It's not my call," replied Tacit, necking his refilled drink in one and feeling another more intense wave of drunkenness churn in him. He put the glass down and took up the one that Henry had filled for Sandrine. The demons in him shrank back under the shimmer of alcohol's radiance. "It's a call for all of us because it involves all of us. I did what needed to be done. That's all."

"And so there is nothing more we can do for now?" asked Sandrine, testily. She flashed her hands in front of her. "All this waiting around, it's infuriating!"

Tacit nodded. "It is, yes, and no, there is nothing we can do. Not until we find out more about what this sailor we captured knows. Whether he knows anything about where the other vials have gone."

"But they could be anywhere!"

"Yes, they might be, which is exactly why there is no point going anywhere until we know in which direction they are going, what we're dealing with."

"We know what we are dealing with!" exclaimed Sandrine. "The end of the world!"

"We might already be too late," lamented Isabella.

"Yes, we might be, but I think not." He clutched her hand gently to reassure her.

"How do you know?" asked Henry, making to take another sip from the glass, but realising he didn't want one and putting it back on the circular tray.

"The vial, on the boat we captured, why didn't the man open the vial earlier, or when we boarded the ship, release 'God's wrath' there and then, if that's what it is?"

"How do we know they haven't already?" asked Sandrine.

"We don't, but do you see the evidence of the Rapture? Do you hear the sounds of the Apocalypse? The sailor, he was locked away in his cabin. He had plenty of time to open the vial and release its contents. But he didn't. I don't know why, but he didn't, even when I charged towards him. He thrust his hand down on top of the box as if to protect the contents, not unleash them. It makes me think, gives me hope that perhaps the vials cannot simply be opened and their contents thrown anywhere in the world. Perhaps they have to be taken to some place, each of them to a specific spot?"

Tacit shrugged at the wild suggestion and let his shoulders sag, letting the exhaustion back in. As he did so, all of them heard a knock at the door to their residence and turned as one.

"I'll go," said Isabella, and they watched her leave the veranda, following inside moments later. There were three Inquisitors on the other side of the door and Isabella stepped to one side to let them enter. Tacit came forward, meeting them in the centre of the room.

"You were right," Inquisitor Furtado said, unable to hide his relief at what they had found, despite his voice sounding brittle and hard like rusted iron. "It was a good thing you didn't throw the man you stowed in the cabin over the side of the boat like you did his colleague."

"You have news?"

Furtado nodded. "We got him to speak."

"It required taking his fingers and one of his eyes," added the Inquisitor next to him.

"You've found the others," Henry asked excitedly, "the other six vials?"

"No, but we've discovered that the vials cannot simply be opened and unleashed anywhere."

"Just as you thought!" exclaimed Isabella, relieved.

Furtado continued. "They need to be taken to a precise location, somewhere in each of the seven regions, before they are opened, in order for the power in them to manifest."

The third Inquisitor said, "The one you caught, he was heading for the Middle East. Jerusalem to be exact."

Tacit looked pleased. "And the other locations?"

But Furtado darkened and shook his head. "We don't know. The man doesn't know."

"We believe him," nodded the most haggard-looking of the three. "Trust me, I worked him hard. Clearly he didn't know anything else. He only knew about his own intended destination."

"Why Jerusalem?" asked Tacit. "Why there? Did he say?"

"No, he didn't know why. It was just where Poré commanded him to go."

"So what's so special about Jerusalem?" asked Henry. "Maybe if we discover that, we can find out the other locations?"

Tacit shook his head. "Impossible. These are secrets buried for over two thousand years. By the time we find out why Jerusalem, the other six vials will have reached their intended destinations. Our best bet is try and stop the vials from getting anywhere near the intended regions. We need to put inquisitional eyes on all ports, crossing points and border controls."

Sandrine groaned, exasperated, throwing up her hands. "Europe? North America? Asia? Are we supposed to be able to watch every route into and across them?"

"No, but we have a little time and if we act fast we can track them before they manage to spread out too far." Tacit strode to the map pinned to the far wall and pushed his finger into a point in the Aegean. "How long has it been since Patmos, since the Seventh Seal was opened?"

"Twenty-four hours," replied Henry precisely.

Tacit repeated the time and circled out an area across which the remaining six vials might have reached by boat, caravan, road and rail, in his trained opinion.

Furtado nodded in agreement at this estimation. "We can move our men out of the Middle East immediately. At least we know the vials are no longer going there. We can move them into Egypt, up along the North African coastline. And north, cordoning off the main thoroughfares into Eastern Europe."

Tacit nodded, considering the suggestion. If it pleased him, he gave no hint that it did, other than saying, "It's something. We know what we're looking for. Small groups of men. They'll be going by boat, at least to begin with, to get as far away as possible, perhaps making landfall and then on by caravan and also by rail. They'll be keeping to themselves. Avoiding all contact with authorities and locals." He looked at the loitering Inquisitors. "Put watchers on ports, train stations, custom stops, places they will need to travel through and traverse. Anyone who can be freed of duties in the Middle East, in this inquisitional safe house, let's use them."

The Inquisitors nodded.

"Good," Furtado said. He ordered the two Inquisitors who had accompanied him to get the message to the headquarters in Jerusalem at once, turning back when they had vanished from the room.

"What is it?" asked Tacit, sensing something else was coming.

"The Vatican."

"What about it? What has happened there now?"

But the Inquisitor showed a masked smile, shaking his head to reassure Tacit that no further tragedy had struck the city. "No, nothing like that. Only that they've pardoned you, the Holy See. You're no longer a wanted man."

Tacit scoffed, turning back to the map, looking idly at places where the six vials might have reached, identifying them with his fingers.

"How?" Isabella asked Furtado, appearing more generous with her appreciation of the news. "How did they come to the decision so quickly? After everything that occurred in Paris and in Rome?" She laughed as she spoke, her eyes smiling. "Tacit's only been 'alive' for a day or so."

"Adansoni," said the Inquisitor.

"What about him?" asked Tacit. His finger was held firm to the map, and something cackled in his ears.

"He's the new Cardinal Secretary of State of the Holy See. He demanded your pardon."

Tacit heard Isabella breathe something that sounded like a sigh of relief. "At least we know there's now a good man at the heart of the Vatican whom we can trust!"

"Will you go back?" Furtado asked Tacit directly.

Something shrieked and insisted in Tacit's head that he did. He shook it, strangely afraid. "No, not yet. Not until these vials are found."

"And how long will that take?" asked Sandrine, her hands on her hips.

"As long as it takes."

"And if we don't find them?" she exclaimed.

"Then there won't be any Vatican to return to."

FORTY

The Vatican. Vatican City.

A fire throbbed in the hearth, teasing ribbons of heat into the room. But the air in the chamber remained defiantly cold. Autumn had arrived, shorter cooler days, chilly evenings, frost adorning the lawns with crowns of white each morning, the pale sun turning them to baubles of dew as it climbed low in the sky. But in the chamber it seemed to Cardinal Bishop Innocenti that it was undeniably colder than anywhere else he had visited in the Vatican that morning. Unnervingly so.

The figure in the chair, the man he had come to see, stared long into the lacklustre fire, appearing unaware that he had a visitor. The young Cardinal cleared his throat and knocked again on the open door to the room, calling out Adansoni's name, only then seeming to draw the old man from his private thoughts.

"Cardinal Bishop Innocenti!" exclaimed Adansoni, after taking a moment to place the man and smiling as he did do. He stood and his shadow grew behind him, making him appear monstrous. He pointed, and the shadow of his arm reached across the length the room to drop around the younger Cardinal. "Please! Welcome!" He made a broad sweep with his hand, his palm facing upwards, to encourage the man inside.

"It is cold in here, Cardinal Bishop Adansoni," replied the young Cardinal, drawing his arms around himself as if to illustrate the point, "or shall I call you Cardinal Secretary of State? Would you like me to find someone to bolster your fire a little?" he asked, seeing how the embers glowed like dull rubies, falling to grey ash. "Or perhaps I could have a go myself?" He bustled forward, crouching to work the paltry flame, wondering what strange power it was that compelled him to please the Cardinal Secretary of State so eagerly.

"No, no," replied the older Cardinal. He raised a finger and shook his head. "It is quite sufficient for me and my means. And it is fine to refer to me as 'Cardinal Bishop', or 'Javier', for you, my friend. Please." He took a small step forward and gestured with his hand towards a chair set close to the one in which he had been sitting. Cardinal Bishop Innocenti thanked him and accepted the seat, lowering himself into it slowly, as if into a hot bath. "Summer has faded," said Adansoni, looking to the window, through the glass to the murk of dusk closing in around the city. "Soon it will be winter. Another year run its course."

"And what have we achieved?" asked Innocenti, eager and obedient, like a keen servant.

"What indeed? What hope do we have going into the following year? What do we expect 1918 to bring?"

"Peace, one hopes," said the Cardinal, smoothing the ruffles in his gown flat with the pink tips of his fingers. "If Pope Benedict is right, and then –"

"Pope Benedict is misguided!" Adansoni snapped back, like dog seizing a stolen bone. The tone and the unexpected retort, brief though it was, surprised Innocenti. Adansoni saw the Cardinal's shock and immediately looked away, seeming to have surprised himself, let alone his friend, at this reckless announcement, pursing his lips and appearing to re-examine his words. "Forgive me," he said, drawing down the folds in his cheeks to his chin. "It seems as if my promotion has loosened my tongue perhaps more than it should have done? Forgive me." His hands went to his heart. "It is that I just cannot see where the sense is in touring Europe for peace, requesting meetings with leaders, only to be granted fleeting discussions with the most junior of ambassadors. Europe does not want peace, Cardinal Innocenti. Europe is locked in a struggle, a trap out of which only they can extricate themselves."

"So what are you saying, Cardinal Secretary of State? That there is no point in us at least trying to find peace amongst the nations of the world?"

"Perhaps," shrugged Adansoni. "Or perhaps we would be wiser to extricate ourselves entirely from the conflict, show favouritism to neither side, at least until it is clear who the victor in this war will be." Innocenti looked horrified, but Adansoni continued with the point he was trying to make. "We are neutral in this war, Cardinal Bishop, and we should always be seen to be such. Liaising with either side sets a dangerous precedent. Already there are some who say we favour the Central Powers more, others the Allies. It is dangerous, for both sides now consider us meddlesome and difficult. We are at risk of being disregarded by whoever wins the war. It is not a course I condone and I will be recommending to Pope Benedict that he returns to the Vatican at the first available opportunity."

Adansoni's presence had grown combative and imperious, but immediately his demeanour changed again, his face lightening, and he asked, as he stepped to his desk, absent-mindedly arranging paperwork, "So, Cardinal Bishop Innocenti, what exactly did you come to see me about? Surely not to discuss the movements of our Pope?"

Innocenti said nothing for a moment, wrong-footed by the Cardinal Secretary of State's position on Europe's negotiations and his swerving contradictions, trying to regain his composure and remember exactly what it was he had in fact come to see Adansoni about. Eventually he remembered and said, "You will no doubt have heard the news regarding Tacit?"

"Yes. After all, I am Cardinal Secretary of State." Innocenti thought Adansoni looked and sounded unusually smug with this announcement. "I make it my business to know what is going on in my country and amongst my people. He is in Constantinople with Sister Isabella. Already he has rallied the Inquisition there to him. I think that is quite satisfactory."

Adansoni arched an eyebrow and looked over at his visitor, smiling superciliously, and at once Innocenti knew that Adansoni was changed, the title of office giving him the ring of arrogance in his manner and his words. The Cardinal Secretary put down the papers he had been picking his way through and tasted some of his coffee in the china cup on the side of his desk. It was cold, but he didn't seem to mind. "I never had any doubt that Tacit was still alive. Of course, you fear the worst, begin to believe the rumours, but Tacit is resourceful. The best we have. I knew he would be all right." As he spoke the pale dusk light from the window falling on him seemed to diminish and twist, puckering like dark shadows in his face. "Cardinal Bishop Innocenti," he said, lowering his eyes onto the man, seeing that he looked uncertain and suspicious. "You are troubled?"

"I am," replied the younger man, feeling suddenly drained, desperate. Lost.

"And what troubles you?"

"What doesn't trouble me? The war? Casado's murder? Tacit's return? Poré running amok? The seven vials?" His soft fists were tight white balls of flesh in his lap. "Javier, what horrors are being unleashed upon the world at this very moment? The Seventh Seal! You know what it means, what it means for the world?!"

Adansoni screwed up his face so he resembled a dim-witted clown at a circus performance rather than the astute head of the Holy See. "The Tribulation. End Times. The Rapture!" Each phrase he said with growing wonder. And then he scowled and looked instantly murderous and dark. "Poré! Poré!" The name was like a curse in his mouth and he thrust with his head as he spat it out, his eyes falling onto the seated man opposite him, holding him in a stare which never wavered or abated. A line of spittle seemed to drop from the edge of his lips, his face suddenly red as a furnaceman's. "I am at loss to explain it! I cannot explain it! It haunts me, Cardinal Innocenti. Maddens me! For I always believed that such an event was destined to be triggered by another far more deserving than that wretch of a man!"

FORTY-ONE

TRIPOLI. LIBYA.

Three Inquisitors sat hunched on the quayside, weighed down by their armour and the monotony of the long hours they had spent watching the port and vessels arriving and leaving. They appeared conspicuous, heavy-set, dressed in bulky thick fabrics, at odds with the weather and all those around them, workers and porters of the harbour.

Another transport ship moored up, twenty thousand tons of black steel hull, the scratch of Arabic writing at its prow, an identification number stencilled beneath in fading white. Ropes were thrown to dockside workers and the ship tied fast to rusted black bollards on the quay. Minutes turned slowly into twenty and the Inquisitors' interest waned, drifting to other ships in the port, supposing that the vessel which had arrived must be empty, moored in preparation of transporting goods *away* from the city, not bringing items and people into it.

Then, suddenly, activity stirred in the doorways of the ship's hull and people began to emerge from gangplanks, streams of passengers, soldiers, native Libyans, merchants, travellers, coming down the long wooden walkways, stumbling on tentative sea legs, reaching out for the certainty and stability of the Libyan quay stone under their feet.

The Inquisitors drew their eyes back to the crowd and watched each and every one of the passengers closely, looking for anything which might betray any of them or suggest that further inspection was required based on the brief they had received from the inquisitional communiqué. None of those leaving the ship seemed remotely interesting and hope once more faded to disregard, at least until one particular group caught the eye of the Inquisitors, as tentative in their manner as they were intriguing to look at, with their careful demeanour and their cautious scrutiny of the port ahead.

The three Inquisitors studied them intently. The men descended the gangplank and instantly slipped amongst the crowd, appearing to try to lose themselves in it. At once the behaviour seemed strange, at odds with everyone else trying to make good their departure from the ship, the quay and the swarming masses. Something about them suggested to the three Inquisitors that they were worth investigating.

Intuition. A lifetime living on it.

The Inquisitors looked at each other and nodded.

"Let's check them out," the dark-skinned one in the group said, and the others followed on his heels.

The caravan of men, four in total, were fifty feet ahead, weaving and burrowing fast through the sea of people trudging slowly and occasionally jostling along the quayside. They were dressed for long-distance travel, bound up in light sheets of white and cream to fend off the heat of the sun. Their headdresses were pulled up and across their faces, not in itself unusual, but when coupled with the sheepish quick glances they shot left and right as they walked, it was all the proof the Inquisitors needed that the men were nervous or wishing to keep something hidden from the authorities, to pass through customs untroubled.

Just then, one of the men turned to look behind, a sixth sense telling him they were being trailed, and his dark eyes fell on the Inquisitors, now only a short distance away. Without hesitation he turned back and fell to a heated urgent discussion with his fellow travellers. Seconds later they ducked and faltered, each in turn looking back to see, before suddenly running off, bursting through the crowds and the customs gates just ahead, kicking through the officials and the barricades drawn up to slow the progression of traffic out of the port.

Instantly the Inquisitors were after them, driving a wedge between the scrum of people, pushing and knocking them aside, vaulting the bemused officials and sprinting away from the long broad harbour docks and into the city, hot on the heels of Poré's men.

FORTY-TWO

Tripoli. Libya.

The men fled, the Inquisitors flying behind them, kicking up clouds of dust as their boots bit into the flagstones and gravelled paths of the city. Poré's men seemed to know the warren of alleyways and ill-kempt courtyards well, plunging into their contorted twisting depths without hesitation, without stopping for an instant to check to see if they were headed towards a dead-end.

They hurtled past crowds, gawping, bemused people, shouting and gesticulating at this racing pack, only to do the same, moments later, to the group of Inquisitors thirty paces behind.

At a crossroads, without missing a step, Poré's group divided, breaking away, each going in a different direction.

"Spilt up!" the Inquisitor with the ebony skin commanded, flashing with his hands, left and right, directing the other Inquisitors as he ran straight on. They swung out of his slipstream and he powered forward, his head down, his lungs burning. He was built like a bulldog, muscular, powerful, but only over short distances. He had a disdain for running, his preference being for fast and dirty fighting. The way ahead of him swam and, for a moment, he wondered if he might lose his prey altogether.

Back at the crossroads, the Inquisitor who had veered left got lucky. The two men he chased had miscalculated, thinking themselves deeper into the city than in fact they were. Their mistake took them to a blind alley and at the mercy of the Inquisitor who showed them none, breaking the teeth of one and the neck of the other, before rifling through their belongings but finding nothing that he was after.

The man who had swung right at the crossroads lost his nerve with the gaining Inquisitor and stopped, turning his gun on his pursuer. The Inquisitor saw the drawn weapon long before it fired, giving him time to roll clear and pull out his own, gunning the man down, two inquisitional rounds to his guts. A crowd gathered as he pushed him over onto his side and rummaged through his pockets, finding them full of pouches and papers but nothing more important.

The dark-skinned Inquisitor could hear the rasp of his breath, feel the clutch of tightness in his chest, sense the incessant ache in his heavy legs. He knew he had to stop, rest for a moment, give himself a chance to recover, or else he would collapse. He swooned, staggering forward, catching himself against the right-hand wall of the alleyway down which he was running, moments before the man he was chasing shot into the road coming up fast on his right, but too quickly for his legs and the sudden change in direction. His ankle went over on the kerb and he tumbled, his trailing foot catching in the hem of his robe, sending him sprawling headlong into the stone wall of the high-sided street. He struck the stone with a sickening crunch and groaned, turning over, going down in a heap, his scalp bloodied and torn from where his balding head had connected with the edge of the building.

With wonder and renewed effort the Inquisitor leaped forward, seizing hold of the injured man and bundling him on, away from the watching eyes of the citizens, testing doors along the street as he went, dragging him by the arm, the man half-conscious and stumbling after him. The third door he tried was unlocked and he threw it open and pushed the man inside, going in after him, slamming it shut behind them.

"What…?" The man groaned disorientated from where he had fallen onto his knees in the darkness, blinded by exhaustion, confusion, his head spinning. Stars danced and a stinging pain grew in the middle of his head. "What do you…?"

The Inquisitor's right boot connected hard full in his face and he snapped back, rolling away into the dark of the corridor into which he had been thrown. He trembled for a moment, as if in spasm, before scrabbling about the blackness, trying to find a place to hide. A strong hand took hold of the back of his neck and wrenched him to his knees, pushing him against the wall of the corridor, blood in his eyes and face.

The man squealed and tried to pull away, but the Inquisitor kicked out with the sole of his boot, breaking the man's leg. He screamed, his hands going to the shattered limb. For a moment the Inquisitor let him scrabble around the floor, clutching his fractured leg, trembling and weeping. He knew the man wouldn't try to crawl away now, giving the Inquisitor the freedom to turn his attention to the bag the man had been carrying and dropped from his grip during the assault. It was a cloth bag, a long strap thrown over a shoulder, a drawstring top, pulled tight like puckered lips. He opened it to find a square shape wrapped in greying sheets of cloth. He removed it exposing a small wooden chest. He tried the lid, found that it was unlocked, and opened it to reveal a broad flat earthenware pot held tightly inside.

The Inquisitor smiled knowingly, clasping the item to his breast like the precious thing it was.

CONSTANTINOPLE. TURKEY.

The door to Tacit's apartment burst open, Inquisitor Furtado not even bothering to knock.

"What is it?" asked Tacit.

"The second vial!" Furtado choked, trying to get his words out through his tight fevered breath.

"Found?"

"And retrieved!" he cheered, recovering slowly.

"Where?" smiled Isabella, clutching hold of Tacit.

"Tripoli. Libya. They brought it ashore on a ship, a group of them. We had men watching the port. The Inquisitors didn't like the look of them, so gave chase." There was a flash of a smile in the man's face. "The vial was being carried in a chest with them, a small wooden box. It's now being kept under lock and key at the Libyan inquisitional headquarters."

"The luck of the Gods is with us it seems!" cheered Henry.

"Remember who we pit ourselves against," warned Tacit. "And Poré's men?"

"Interrogated and disposed of. They knew nothing that could help us. There is more though," continued Furtado, accepting a drink from Isabella with thanks to quench his thirst and clear his throat. "We've received news that a consignment fitting the description of one of the vials and with it a small group of men was recently seen boarding a boat from Constanta on the Black Sea, going north to Ukraine."

"The Russian vial!" said Sandrine. "It must be!"

Tacit turned back to the map on the wall and traced a line between Constantinople, Constanta and the southern Ukrainian coast.

"We can take a boat almost immediately to Odessa," said Furtado. "And then?"

"Kiev," said Tacit, stamping the end of his finger into the place on the map. "Gateway to Russia."

FORTY-THREE

THE VATICAN. VATICAN CITY.

The very moment the rains cleared and a ribbon of blue had appeared between the clouds, Strettavario collected his horse from the stables.

Throwing his reins across its neck, re-fastening the buckles beneath the creature's belly and testing the grip upon the animal's back, he flung himself up into the saddle.

"Will you be gone for long, Father Strettavario?" the stable-hand asked the Priest. The crisp clip of the horse's hooves on the approach to the stables, where slabs of stones were interlinked with straight pathways of gravel, down which horses could be ridden alongside carriages, sounded like the hollow tick of a clock counting down.

Strettavario looked at the man he had known for most his life and asked, "Why do you wish to know, Father Tiernan?", instantly regretting his words and holding up his hand in apology. "I hope not for long," he said, putting his hand on the man's shoulder. "I hope not. There is some-one I need to speak to, south of the city, most urgently."

"I hope you find answers to what you are after."

The old Father thanked him, sitting up in the saddle. "I suspect I will find the answers," said Strettavario, pulling the reins tighter in his grip, "though perhaps not the ones I wish to find." And he turned his eyes up to the balustrades and towers of the Vatican and wondered if he would look upon them ever again, before turning the horse from the stable and driving it forward into a gallop.

FORTY-FOUR

Odessa. Ukraine.

The crackle of a gramophone in the corner of the subterranean room drew Isabella's ear long before the thin whispery music rose taunting and strained from the giant conch-shaped horn. There was a tall leafy green plant standing alongside in a brown pot, the colour of life at odds with the beige walls and thin insipid glow from the solitary light in the centre of the room.

"If they're going to Kiev they will bring the vial into Russia via Odessa or Nikolaev, twenty-five miles further along the coast," assured the Inquisitor who had shown them into the sunken chambers, standing at the bottom of the stairs and extending a hand of welcome for the visitors to join him. "It's the only way," he said, watching Tacit file past, Henry and Sandrine at the surly man's back. Other Inquisitors had come with them, a heavy-booted procession down the ten shallow steps into the depths of the Ukrainian safe house. "They won't risk going via Romania. They won't get through the eastern front. Even if Russia is mutinying, even if soldiers are deserting, that front is still holding, just, all the way to the Black Sea at Vylkove on the Romanian Ukrainian border." His words sounded like an excuse as to why they had docked and now had taken residence, food and rest in the city.

"Let's hope you're right," Tacit replied over his shoulder, from the table upon which food had been spread, laid out on broad silver platters.

"And let's hope you're right about Kiev," Henry shot back slyly.

Bottles of red wine had been arranged in neat lines at the back. Tacit took a plate from a tall stack and pushed it into Isabella's hand, before turning to the wine and plucking one bottle away along with a fat-bellied glass, dropping himself into a chair in the corner.

"We've only found two of the vials so far," cautioned a wiry Inquisitor, snatching up a chicken leg from a bowl on the table and setting it alone on his plate.

"We will find the others," assured another, stepping aside in the line to let Sandrine choose from the different dishes of colourful hearty food laid out across the oval table. "All five of them."

"One vial is just ahead of us," announced another confidently. "We have a confirmed sighting in the city."

Furtado nodded. "We will move on to Kiev in the morning. We'll explore the city. You can take the train station if you like, Poldek?"

Tacit shrugged and necked his wine, filling his goblet in the next movement, hearing the voice shriek in his head at the coming onslaught of drunkenness.

"The Russian peasants," said another of the party, spooning a great ladle of goulash onto his plate, "I hear they've started seizing land from the Russian gentry."

"Kiev is burning!" someone said.

"Russia is finished," another Inquisitor replied.

"Some say Russia is just being born," growled Tacit, necking the second glass of wine and filling his third.

"Our religion in that country is doomed."

The Inquisitor who had first welcomed them to the chamber nodded, his rough hand to his rougher chin. "They will shut their borders to us. They will throw us out. Try to ban our faith. The Bolsheviks, they don't believe in religion."

"They will have no choice," retorted Tacit, necking the third glass and feeling the demon in him drown under the first wave of inebriation.

The Inquisitor closest to him put down his tankard and nodded. "Inquisitors, we simply go underground."

"There won't be any Inquisition, there won't be anything, if we don't find these vials," said Henry, at once feeling every cold eye turn on him and instantly regretting his interruption.

The gathering fell to eating and drinking and the grumbling mutter of quiet close conversation. Eventually someone said, "It's snowing," and almost everyone looked up into the thin mean window that ran along the topmost edge of one of the walls, a vignette of light into the room and a view of the world beyond.

"Are you not eating, Sister Isabella?" asked Inquisitor Furtado, standing alongside where she perched, watching the congregation feast and talk amongst themselves.

She looked down at her empty plate and shook her head, placing it back on the pile and crossing her arms about herself. "No. I'm not hungry." She grew aware, once again, of the music, weaving between the pools of conversation, taking a moment to try to identify the tune. "I didn't think Inquisitors were partial to joyous things," she said, raising her eyes and head to the ceiling and the sounds captured there.

"Don't be deceived," said Furtado. "We are hard men, but do find enjoyment in some things." He leant closer in to her, his eyes on Tacit in the chair opposite. "As you well know."

"Meaning?"

The grim Inquisitor scoffed, suddenly appearing younger and more approachable. "Come, Sister Isabella! Don't pretend and don't feel you need to hide your affections! Your fondness for each other is not a secret." His eyes passed over to Tacit and then back again.

Isabella allowed a smile to come into her face, coy, bouncing her head in time to the music and in consideration of the Inquisitor's observation. "He came looking for me," she said quietly, "as quickly as he was able after the Carso. He is grim, troubled, a hard man, but he has a good heart."

Furtado nodded, watching Tacit from the corner of his eye, the other on Isabella. "But, of course, he sought you out only after seeking answers to his own questions."

"Seeking answers?" asked Isabella. "What do you mean?"

"Of his past."

"I don't understand."

"Surely you know? Surely he told you?"

"Told me? Told me what?"

"When he got out of the hospital in Trieste, he first went back."

"Back? Back where?"

"Home, to the Tatra Mountains in Poland."

FORTY-FIVE

CONSTANTINOPLE. TURKEY.

Tacit stood in the doorway to the bedroom, watching Isabella undress. He lingered, clumsy, but peculiarly charming in his awkwardness for one so grim and assured, caught between entering and staying back in the shadows. Isabella stood with her back to him, as she had for most of the evening, a show of modesty in the bedchamber and anger during dinner, at odds with her usual openness.

"Did you hear?" he called to her, receiving no reaction. "Kiev, the third vial. They have a confirmed sighting. It is in the city!"

Isabella laid her clothes over the end of the bed, drawing the heavy woven robe around herself, slipping her arms into it and tying it at her middle, before drawing back the covers of the bed in preparation to climb into them.

"Are you going to stand there all night or are you coming to bed?"

"Are you not going to show some pleasure at the news?" retorted Tacit, the heat in him rising, the noise of the voices doing the same.

"You seem suddenly pleased for a man who has lamented the desperation of the situation, reminding all of the fact we need to find all seven vials, a seemingly impossible task in your eyes."

"Is that what this is about? You're worried." He came forward, his arms reaching out to pull her into an embrace. "Isabella, don't be worried. Everything will be all –"

"Shut the fuck up, Tacit!" she hissed, and at once Tacit froze, as if his feet were hammered hard to the floor, his eyes wide and disbelieving. Every sense had been beaten out of him by the command, including the voices. Eventually he drew forward and muttered something inaudible, hearing Isabella heave a dismissive sigh.

"What is it?" he asked. "What's the matter?" His voice sounded ethereal in the dark, imploring in the quiet of the place. "You're cross."

"Cross!" spat Isabella, her eyes cold flinty slits.

"Angry," replied Tacit, submissive. "You've barely said a word to me all evening. What is the –"

"You lied to me, Poldek!" Isabella's voice was venomous and barbed, an explosion of anger that snarled her face and clenched her fists, rocking her where she stood. "You lied to me!"

"I never –"

"You told me you came looking for me, after the Carso."

"And I did," said Tacit, his words hardening, strength returning under the growing accusation. "I did come looking for you. Of course I came looking for you! How do you think I found you? By chance?"

"Don't mock me!"

"Well, don't be foolish," retorted Tacit, regaining some of his control.

A voice spat in Isabella's head, a voice which had been silent for so long, a vulgar shadow of past miseries, and she felt the urge to rush forward and strike him, strike the arrogant difficult man, smash him firmly in the face, feel the bite of his bones against her knuckles. Her skin prickled and sweat beaded. She let the feeling pass, instead inspecting him as a killer might a potential victim.

"Furtado."

"What about him?"

"He told me, told you that went home. After Trieste. After you left the hospital. After the Carso."

Silence swept into the chamber like a cold tide. Tacit watched her, a teetering mix of venom and sorrow, Isabella not sure if he was imagining the revelations as an insult, or as a betrayal. Seconds passed, maybe minutes. And then he said, "What of it?"

"What of it?" She took two steps towards him, sizing herself against

151

him for a fight, dragging the sleeve of her robe to her elbow. "Why didn't you tell me?"

"It wasn't important."

"Not important? Poldek, you went home! Home! Back to where you grew up! Why didn't you tell me? Why did you think it not important?"

"Like I said, it wasn't important."

"How can it not be important? The place you hadn't returned to your entire life, not since…"

Her words dropped away, and with it her anger and eyes on the man.

She turned, despite the voice in her ears jabbering and hissing, urging her to speak, to find the words to describe the horror of the mountain scene of Tacit's childhood, to cast him into that dark place. She didn't, instead pouring herself a large drink from the bottle of spirit on the sideboard and necking half of it, feeling the demons within twist and writhe against the strong liquor's fiery bite. In that moment she felt as far away from herself as she could ever recall, like a silhouette of her true self, an empty vessel propped up with drink to sustain and to embolden, to give her purpose. She felt revulsion, revulsion at herself, for the voices in her head, for what her life had become, a skulking raging existence of death and murder and misery, and she went to neck the remainder of her drink. Tacit spoke before she could, making her pause, the tumbler of liquid halfway to her lips but no further.

"I attended the scene of a murder once. Leap Castle. Ireland. It was one of the last cases I attended before Arras, before…" He let his words trail off, knowing anything more said about that assignment would be wasted breath and noise.

"Is this important, Poldek?" asked Isabella, not looking at him, her back turned, but he ignored her and kept talking.

"They were brothers, three of them, those who had been murdered, although no one knew they were brothers when the bodies were first found. They'd been so badly broken and disfigured by their attacker, hands and feet removed, faces broken in with the ends of stakes, it took me hours to identify who they were from the local community, to find out who they were and who was responsible for their deaths." He looked up into the dull light, watching cold fuddled flies spin and scuttle around it, searching for warmth to sustain them. "In their death, they had become anonymous, just as I felt I had become after I was plucked from the seas after my fall into the Soča River.

152

"But unlike the brothers, death had not seized me. I had been reborn, out of salt water and the elements, ravaged though I was. It seemed to me that I had been given another chance, another chance to live. But why? What had saved me? For what purpose had I been saved? Was I still the man I was before I had fought with Georgi and fallen all that distance in the Soča? How could I live if I did not ever know who I was?

"So I went back to where it all began, to my home, to try and find out."

Isabella was looking at him now, her eyes softer, the lines about them less deep, the glass empty in her hand, breathless. Wordless. Just staring and watching and listening to him.

"And did you find what you wanted to find?" she said eventually.

"No. Because I never got there." Both of them sagged, as if defeated. "I did try to go back, but there was something, something impalpable, something on the air, something through which I could not pass."

"I'm sorry," said Isabella, her voice hollow. "What was it? What stopped you from going back?"

"Memories," said Tacit, without hesitation. "They gave me solace. Like a shade against the unbearable sun, a drop of water on my tongue. On the road to that place, I found insight, I remembered, but I could not fully face what had gone before, who I was. I was not ready. And yet… yet I remember feeling, in the foothills of the Tatras, still miles from my home, when I could go no further, when my courage waned and my strength failed me, I remember feeling, knowing, that solace can and will be found in the most terrible of places, that solace could be found there again, despite everything which happened in that place, despite all the terrible memories. That places heal. That ghosts do eventually surrender their hate and horror in a place.

"There is something in me. Something that terrifies me, something I have always been scared of."

"You've told me of the voices, Poldek, of the lights, but if there is –"

"Something else?" He grimaced a snort of humourless air from his nose. "Oh, there's something else, yes, I am sure of it. It calls to me, it tries to command me. It wishes to possess me, overwhelm and control me entirely. It has always been this way."

"Poldek, why have you…"

But Tacit shook his head. "It is a weight I alone must carry."

"But why?" asked Isabella, coming forward and reaching out to him. "Let me help!"

"You do," he said, "in ways you do not realise."

"What must I do?" She held her hands out to him, her palms open. "What else can I do?"

"Simply that when the time comes, at the very end, promise me that you will not be afraid, whatever happens, that you will not be afraid."

FORTY-SIX

KIEV. UKRAINE.

They had left Odessa for Kiev at first light.

It seemed that every square, every street, every yard in the city was burning, the smell of revolution in the air. There were lines of well-dressed anxious-looking men and women, children clutched in arms or snatched firm by the hand, filing out of homes, half running, half shuffling along streets, going nowhere but just going, watched and sometimes pursued by even longer and deeper lines of angry haggard citizens. The boldest of these citizens carried great sticks, holding them in their air, foils to their brutal cries of downfall, and the boldest wielded them.

Shouts and cries of derision spun and crackled in the fog of burning buildings and bonfires, gesticulating spokesmen conducting insistent speeches from street corners, women wailing and rallying in passing flocks, red flags unfurled from rooftops and held aloft at the front of marching lines.

"Everywhere we go," lamented Isabella, pulling her coat across herself to keep out the Ukrainian chill and hide the revolver she carried at her belt, "there is suffering." She closed her eyes to the sights.

"This war," scowled Sandrine, "it will be our children's wicked inheritance."

Henry looked across the street from where they were walking. There was a group of men armed with cudgels beating a balled-up man on the pavement, squirming under the raining blows from their clubs. A woman and young children, perhaps his family, were crying and pleading with

154

the attackers from ten feet away. "War or revolution," he said, "their tools have always been fire and violence."

"Walk on," warned Tacit. "This is not our fight."

But revolution or not, the stationmaster at Kiev station was going to make sure that the eleven o'clock train for Moscow left on time. Standing proud in his blue-black uniform and peaked hat, the moustached man put his silver whistle to his lips and blew seconds before the six-strong party of travellers ran past him and hurried up the steps into the third from last carriage.

"All aboard!" he shouted after them, glowering at the last of the men to board the train. He strode closer towards the locomotive and the platform's edge, hurrying them inside and to make it clear that he didn't take kindly to how late they had left it.

At the top of the gun-black stairs, the man looked back down the platform from where they had come. The train groaned and shunted forward, sixty-five tons of steam engine digging hard against the rails and finding purchase, rocking Poré's Russian envoy in the doorway. The guard's eyes followed those of the man back down the platform to where he was looking.

His first thought, on seeing the two men and two women running onto the platform behind the train, was that they were revolutionary thugs, come to extract revenge on those hoping to escape the retribution of the Red Army in Kiev. The man at the front enormous and cruel in appearance, those behind him with the look of anarchy and desperation about them. Revolution might have its place in the streets of the city, but as far as the stationmaster was concerned it ended at the gates to his station.

He turned to face them, his hands held up in a command to halt, while the train shunted behind him, gathering speed with every passing second.

"Woah!" he called. "Slow down! The train has gone! You're too late," as Tacit pulled a gun from his holster and slammed the side of it hard into the stationmaster's face. Instantly a barbed voice roared with black joy in Tacit's mind, as he stepped over the unconscious body and ran on towards the rear of the train.

"Jesus Christ, Tacit!" he heard Henry shout. His feet laboured as he looked back to see if he was imagining what had just happened.

"What the hell is the matter with you?" screamed Sandrine. Tacit shuddered, half wishing to weep, half wishing to laugh, rejoice in the violence of the moment. "Since when do we beat innocent people?"

He said nothing, powering along the platform edge behind the train, feeling Isabella next to him, sensing her revulsion at what he had done. He never turned to see, but he supposed Henry and Sandrine would be staring too, their faces shocked. He wanted to turn around and tell them that this was how things were, that he was damned, fallen, lost, that he could no longer control himself, his anger, his violence that came and went without his bidding, and that he wallowed in it when it did. That equally it made him feel sickened and tormented and pathetic.

And so he ran on, after the departing train, using the riot of devil's chatter in his ear as a shield to hide the horror of his crime and their dismay at what he had done.

FORTY-SEVEN

The Mediterranean Sea. Near Algiers.

Two sailing boats were heading west into a sun cooling its fiery tendrils in the sea's horizon, a strong wind in the ship's sails. A distance of only fifty yards separated the two vessels, cutting through the waters together as one, reaching and arching over each wave in time with the other. The crew, their hard work believed done, watched the horizon ahead and the ship next to them, turning frequently to look up at the sails and the full catch of breeze in them. Good humour was amongst the sailors, hope surging like the hulls of their boats over the tide, smiles on faces.

"If this wind keeps up, we will pass Gibraltar before dawn tomorrow, Ennew. And then…?" The sailor looked across at his Captain and threw an arm across his shoulders, laughing unrestrained. "And then?!" He spread his hand out across the prow of the boat, like a man offering riches to another beyond the waves.

"We still have a long way to go, Benz," contemplated the Captain. "But this is a good start! And yes, this weather looks set fair for the next few days, at the very least."

Absently he turned his eyes to the left side of the ship, towards where the vague outline of the Algerian coast lay. There was something reassuring in its long black line of sweeping coves and headlands, as if he still had a tie to land. Benz was an experienced sailor and sea captain, having travelled back and forth across the Atlantic twenty times, running the gauntlet of German U-boats every time, but for him the sea didn't hold the fascination it held for so many who went to it, his life not bound up with it, his veins not running salty with seawater. It was something he did because he knew of nothing else to do, always privately pleased and relieved when he returned back to port.

So he admired the coastline and drank it in, knowing it would be the last time he would see it for several weeks, once they left the shelter of the Mediterranean and the shoulder of Gibraltar.

Something caught his eye, and he guided Ennew's arm, directing him to take the wheel as he stole towards the side of the ship. He squinted through the haze of water and sun. There was a vessel, matt-black, stark against the smudge of the horizon, appearing from the dark of the coastline, heading directly towards them. A great black funnel belched smoke from its central engine.

An ironside.

His telescope was in his hands and to his eye in an instant.

"What is it?" Ennew asked, drawn to his Captain's sudden interest in the horizon.

Benz said nothing for several moments, his eye never leaving the headland or the telescope trained upon it. And then suddenly he turned, exploding with the command, "Turn starboard, fifteen degrees!"

"Starboard, fifteen degrees?" cried Ennew, hesitating, only for an instant, before pulling hard on the wheel and making the ship swerve hard right, throwing sailors across the deck and into rigging. The accompanying ship to their right, keeping pace with them, noticed the sudden change in tack and did the same, dragging at their own wheel sharply to turn as well, seconds later.

"Whatever is the matter?" hollered the crew from the sister boat across the waters.

"Ironside!" cried Benz, pointing with an outstretched finger. He looked down its length to the mark growing larger on the horizon. "On our course!"

Now all the sailors on both boats could see the vessel bearing down on them and they shouted orders and ran to their posts, dragging at ropes and rigging, the tips of the waves crashing into the turning hulls.

A heavy gun exploded from the front of the ironside and the sound of a shell screaming close howled across both boats, landing thirty feet ahead of them in a great eruption of noise and spray.

"They have guns!" one of the men cried.

"So do we!" called Benz. "Get to your positions!"

"It will reach us in no time!" another cried.

"So make good your guns! Go quickly!"

The deck was a thunder of pounding feet as doors were thrown open and machine-guns produced, dragged over to emplacements all along the left-hand side of the boat.

"Pull us back!" the captain cried. "Drop the sail!" he ordered, throwing his arms towards two of the sailors on the starboard side of the boat. "Let the other boat pull ahead, so that we can both fire on the enemy at the same time. We cannot outrun them! We have to fight. Two boats are better than one! Let them go ahead. Let them go –!"

Another heavy-calibre round exploded from the barrel in the front of the ironside and landed just short of the Captain's boat, showering the deck with seawater. In reply, the machine-guns started up their angry riposte, bristling the water around the approaching boat with ferocious hot lead. The sailing ship closest to the ironside dropped its sail and instantly it slowed, the sister vessel to its right moving ahead.

The Inquisitor's gun barked for a third time, every man watching the arc of black smoking metal leave the ironside's prow, watching with growing horror and dismay as it flew true, striking the prow of the leading ship. The whole front of the boat instantly exploded in a dreadful shredding cacophony of flame, as if the shell had penetrated the vessel's weapon's store. The entire front end blew itself out of the water and the ship turned over, almost immediately beginning to go down beneath the waves. Sailors could be seen trying to leap and throw themselves from the boat before the whole thing went under, some slipping and scrabbling into the web of rigging and snagging wood, drawn down into the whirlpool its demise had caused.

"All is lost!" cried one of the crew of the first boat.

"Keep going!" cried Benz. "Hoist the sail! Hoist the sail!"

"We cannot outrun them!" Ennew cried from the wheel, as calloused hands dragged at ropes.

"They are gaining on us!" another man shouted.

"Shoot your fucking machine-gun!" the Captain barked.

The ironside fired again. This time the shell struck the rear of the sailing boat, tearing a great hole in its stern. Benz turned back to see the entire wheel and Ennew with it gone, all that remained shattered jagged wood and the deck torn open, seawater pouring in.

"We are lost!" one of the sailors cried, as the ironside drew so close they could see the faces of the Inquisitors upon it. A heavy machine-gun of their own opened up, and sailors danced backwards across the deck, some falling back into the ocean, ripped open by the firestorm.

Benz drew the vial he carried in a sack about his person out and opened its lid, staring into the grey dusty contents inside, just dust, but dust decreed by God for a frightful purpose. Seconds later, heat and fire engulfed him and he was drawn down into the swelling sea in seconds, following the vial in the other ship down into the dark depths of the Mediterranean.

FORTY-EIGHT

KIEV. UKRAINE.

On board the train, Poré's men heard the gunshot ring out, followed moments later by screams and the sounds of jostling crowds back on the platform. They looked at each other and then at the Ukrainian countryside now sweeping past.

One of train's guards appeared out of the turmoil of passengers in the aisle, some fidgeting to find their seats, others muttering and peering out of windows to see what was the commotion coming from the city they had just left, praying that the revolutionaries hadn't followed them onto the train. The guard pushed past them, murmuring to himself about revolution and the Red Army.

Back on the platform, Tacit and the others careered down it, pursuing the fast-vanishing end of the train. Moments before its rear pulled clear, the four of them leaped at the endplate and grabbed hold, hanging on as the track ran faster beneath them and Kiev shrank.

"Do you think they're onboard?" one of the men three carriages into the train asked, eyes wide. "The Inquisitors?"

"How did they find us?" asked another.

"Where do we go? Do we jump?"

The men looked at the window of the train, the near countryside now a blur. A jump from the train now might mean severe injury, maybe even death. That they didn't care about, but they did worry about losing the vial, having it slip from their grip, breaking open in the dirt, its contents lost in the wilderness.

Tacit entered the first carriage, the others behind him matching his stride. At once the guard knew them to be unsavoury types and he supposed he knew for whom they were looking.

"May I help you?" he asked. A fist was thrown into his guts and the guard lurched gasping into Tacit. The huge man caught hold of him and they embraced, as if they were long-parted friends. Tacit carried him the remainder of the way through the carriage into the passage beyond. The door to the toilet opened easily and no one saw the body of guard being stored inside.

Three carriages ahead of them, the men Tacit was pursuing looked back, trying to see if they could spot the Inquisitors coming up the train. In the assault of adrenaline and fear, the carriage seemed like a sea of staring suspicious faces, a mishmash of hats and bonnets, winter suits and capes, colours and shapes distorting and surging either side of the aisle they were trying to navigate, eyes both ahead and behind them. Luggage cases caught ankles, making them trip and snatch hold of seat rests to stop from falling forward. Disgruntled grunts and apologies weaved in and about them.

There was nowhere else for them go other than forward, forever towards the front of the train, the coal car and the locomotive.

"Keep going!" called the man from the back, clasping the vial chest in his grip beneath its rags. "Go to the end of the train." And as he spoke, he felt the reassuring tap tap of his revolver against his ribs.

Tacit swung into the third carriage and ducked down, looking along the full length of the train, through the sliding glass doors at either end. He saw them, their backs, hurrying up ahead between the rows of seats. Wordlessly, he continued his pursuit.

All of them knew that they were running out of carriages, like rats caught in a slowly tightening trap. They had had enough of their senses about them to count the compartments as they had walked through them. Five were already behind them and they knew there were just two left before they reached the front of the locomotive. At the end of the penultimate carriage the man holding the vial threw a glance back, the Inquisitors now just twenty feet away, eyes fixed firm on them, hands closed tight around what he supposed were weapons beneath their cloaks.

They ran into the final compartment, knowing every step might be their last. Halfway along a shot rang out and they threw themselves sideways, into rows of seats, sprawling across shrieking passengers, crouching as low as they could go, their hands covering their heads and then reaching for their own sidearms. About them, passengers leapt from seats at the gunshot, papers flying, their screams and cries crushed together in a great crash of noise.

"End of the line," shouted Tacit, his warning shot into the ceiling of the carriage intended to bring people's attention to him. "Everyone out," he said, as a shot struck him in the shoulder. He went down cursing, caught under a ragged wave of people fighting and tussling from their seats in a rampaging chaotic scramble out of the carriage, men, women and children bolting for the door, people falling, suitcases bursting open, clothes and hats flying.

In the chaos, the men carrying the vial to Russia crawled their way to the door at the far end of the carriage and tried the handle. Locked. They sank behind the last row of chairs, partial cover, cocking pistols, waiting for the carriage to clear and fall silent. At the same time the train began to slow imperceptibly. They stood and fired without thought, battering the entrance with their firestorm, blasting great chunks of veneered wood from the door and the carriage behind, shattering glass and making more passengers scream and roll for cover.

Their firing faltered to a clumsy halt.

The doorway stood empty.

"Are they dead?" one of them shouted.

The locomotive gave a jolt, the brakes applied harder by the brakeman, and they all rocked where they stood, the train beginning to slow even more suddenly. At once they knew the driver must have been alerted as to the chaos unfolding in the train behind him, the noise of their blitz enough to make the occupants of the engine cab realise that something must be wrong. The blur of the Ukrainian countryside decelerated, slow enough now to reveal distinguishable shapes and objects in the landscape, slowing perceptively with every passing second.

They gathered around the side-doors at the far end, throwing them open, seeing the ground fly past beneath them. Cold air and the smell of damp earth poured inside to dilute the stink of gunpowder and cordite.

"Ready to jump?" someone shouted above the roar of the wheels on the track.

He had barely finished speaking when the roof of the carriage was obliterated by gunfire, torn open by rifles and revolvers blasting down from above, shooting into the far end of the carriage and the spot where they had gathered to throw themselves from the train and make good their escape. Those not struck down leaped for cover behind chairs, two of them squawking as bullets raked and tore them.

More gunfire lashed down into the carriage like hard rain, each of Poré's Russian contingent caught in the storm and crumpling between the seats. The roof above was peppered with bullet holes and wide fractures from the intensity of the onslaught. The remaining men fired back, tumbling for the open exit from the train, one of them taking a bullet in the spine and lying still with a grunt, the second reaching the end the carriage, wide-eyed and terrified. The door swung back and he pushed it open again, only to have a revolver set in his face and the trigger pulled.

He went down in a shower of crimson.

"Clear!" Henry cried, as Sandrine and Isabella dropped through the blasted roof into the obliterated carriage.

The man struck with the bullet in his spine writhed, reaching for the wooden chest which he had dropped from his grip and now lay just out of reach. Tacit strode into the carriage, towering above him, the flat of his palm held to his bloodied and bruised shoulder.

"No," he said, standing on the man's hand, pinning his fingers to the floor.

FORTY-NINE

The Vatican. Vatican City.

There was anger and defiance in the Holy See, and it cheered Adansoni greatly to see it.

He watched friends and acquaintances, Cardinals who had lived and worked together for years, some decades, fight amongst themselves with words and accusations they would never before have dreamt of using in the Holy See's grand meeting hall.

Something wicked and diseased had infiltrated the foundations of the auditorium. Something had seeped out from the roots of the city and poisoned the minds and deeds and thoughts of those supposedly too pure ever to be corrupted or misguided by trickery and deceit, prompting them, so often calm and measured, to grow quick to anger, the valves of their tempers loosened so they flared with terrible rapidity and heat at little provocation.

Adansoni smiled and dared to imagine a time when this chaotic unkind behaviour might be considered normal in Vatican proceedings, and beyond. A world where tongues were not tightened, where private thoughts were not chained to minds, but allowed to strike free and strike hard, without sympathy and without remorse. And he knew that something had given way and corrupted in him too, and he wallowed in its wonder.

He rose a hand and held it aloft until all eyes were turned to him, and the raging angry party drew to a stumbling disorganised quiet.

"Thank you. Thank you. Your passion, your commitment does you credit. And such emotion shall be needed upon the path we walk. For these are terrible times. Our numbers are threatened, both here and abroad. Danger, it seems, is lurking on every corner. We look to each other for support, confidence, belief, hope. It is, after all, all we have, when all is said and done."

The Cardinal Secretary of State paused and looked across at the large ornate chair of the Pope standing empty. He glowered. "And yet, where is our Pope when we need him the most? Where is our figurehead? Where is *he* to answer our needs, to provide us with guidance and direction at this most pressing of times?

"I'll tell you where he is. Pope Benedict is enjoying the courtesies and hospitality of these nations at war, ridiculing and shaming them with one hand, while demanding tea and cake and brandy with the other. While all the time we, his servants, must try to steer our faith the best we can in a course correct for these most black of hours, hope to find answers to help bring an end to this terrible war!"

He scowled and shook his head, looking across the audience with a fearsome glare. He scowled, as if salt was in his mouth. "No more! We must demand that he returns to the Vatican forthwith. We must bring him back to his city and his people!"

"But the Pope will not come!" someone called.

"How so?" asked Adansoni. "You seem to forget who we are, Cardinal? We are the Holy See! If we demand that he returns to the Vatican, then he *will* return to the Vatican."

"It is not safe for him here," someone said. "The murder of Cardinal Bishop Casado…"

"It is not safe for him anywhere!" countered Adansoni, his voice growing firmer still. "Especially not in the field, where we cannot see him and protect him. Tell me, who travels with him? Well-fed and feeble Priests! He needs an Inquisition who can watch and guard him."

"But he does good work," someone squeaked, "out beyond our walls."

"How can you say such a thing, Cardinal Tavares?" Adansoni retorted. "For nearly four years he has begged for an end to this war, wasted his breath with the leaders who have replied only with laughter. He has worked for nothing! He *must* come to the Vatican to show solidarity, to us, to his people! Bring him back with force if need be," he seethed. "And if he does not return willingly, then we will drag him back."

And though many were horrified, some found nervous cheers in their throats and their palms clenched together, while Inquisitors lining the walls watched each of them closely with hands on revolvers.

FIFTY

Pompeii. Italy.

Strettavario could hear the laughter of the Inquisitors thirty feet away from the front door of the tavern, looser and louder than an Inquisitor's mirth should ever be.

The pale-eyed Priest stood in the dark of the street, feeling the weight of his mace in his right hand, watching the silhouettes of drinkers though the windows of the establishment pass to and fro, gathering in groups to talk, moving between themselves, full of good spirit and too much alcohol.

He felt the weight of the armour under his robes, reacquainting himself with how the steel rings sat against his shoulders, how they cascaded down his back. How the suit affected movement. How he had to compensate accordingly, lean into it, as if he was leaning into a wind, whenever he moved or thrust with an arm.

A figure came bustling from the doorway of the tavern, tilting like a sinking ship on the ocean, too drunk to hold himself, too drunk to stay any longer amongst his friends.

Strettavario eased back into the darker shadows of the alleyway and watched him leave, the Inquisitor stumbling left and then right as the night air struck him like a slap. The Inquisitor coughed, a guttural belly cough, which sounded deep enough to draw with it vomit. He bent over, fighting the retch out of his system, then stood and lurched on into the dark streets. Strettavario let him go, one fewer to deal with inside the place he supposed. He wondered about going into the tavern right then, about facing down the remaining Inquisitors he discovered had accompanied Basquez, finding out in which hole in the city Basquez had himself hidden. He knew they were inside the tavern. He'd counted them go in and had waited for them to drink themselves weak.

But he knew that even though drunk, drunk out of their minds, they still numbered four and there was only one of him, an old man, even if he was now once again dressed as an Inquisitor. It had been decades since he had worn the armour, years since he had been armed. He wondered if he could still handle himself as he used to when he was a younger man.

He cleared his throat, doubting that he could. He thought, quite suddenly and unexpectedly, about Tacit, and pride and shame grew in him in equal measure, at what he was attempting and his hesitation at attempting it. Without any more waiting, he strode purposefully towards the tavern, his cold pale eyes on the slit of smoky light escaping from the open doorway. With each stride he clenched and unclenched his hold on the handle of the mace, swinging it about his shoulders, measuring its weight and reach. At the door he took two final deep breaths to collect his thoughts, to steady his nerves, to remember what it felt like to hurt someone, to remember what it felt like to be hurt, to remember what freshly spilt blood smelt like, the shudder of a blow as it ran up an arm, and pushed the door open.

It took a moment for the men to realise that Strettavario was standing at their table, holding in his hands a weapon intended for use against them.

They guffawed and pulled at each other, pushing back the table covered in bottles and glasses, half fighting with themselves in their drunken fervour to get to their feet and put up a semblance of defence against this one old man. They laughed and wondered where he had found such an old uniform, for none of them thought for a minute that it belonged to him or he to the Inquisition.

Laughing and gathering clumsily to their feet, they called out to Strettavario with mock threats and accusations.

"What have you come in here for, Father?"

"Surely you would be safer in your bed?"

"What's that?" one them asked, indicating the mace Strettavario held loosely at his side. "What are you hoping to do with that, old man?"

Strettavario cleared his throat again. "Brought a little something from my past, something to make your job a little easier." He threw it onto the table, where the mace stayed, sinking into the grain of the wood, making the empty bottles rock, some of them rolling off and shattering on the hard tavern floor. One of the Inquisitors closest to the long club of metal and leather picked it up and felt its weight, looking across at his friends, smiling. Without any warning he swung it in Strettavario's direction.

The plan worked exactly as the old Father had hoped.

The swing told Strettavario everything he needed to know about them. Firstly, they were indeed drunk, too drunk to fight with purpose, clarity or precision. Secondly, they weren't Inquisitors of any repute, not expertly trained in the use of weapons. The man's wielding of the mace was wild and uncouth, not controlled and directed as it would have been had he completed his training. Their careless drunkenness had been enough to suggest this. Their clumsiness confirmed it. They were thugs, nothing more, ordinary hired hands, Inquisitors on the fringes of the Inquisition, brought in to prop up diminishing numbers in the organisation, most probably in the employ of whoever paid highest for their services.

In this case, Bishop Basquez.

The mace sailed past Strettavario and he struck out with his knuckle-dusted hand, connecting with the crown of the man's head and sinking him to his knees, making him whimper and groan and drop uselessly to the floor. The second, the largest of the Inquisitors, battered through the table to get to him. Strettavario rode his blow and came up, striking the man with an uppercut which hit harder and more forcefully than

Strettavario believed he could ever have achieved in his youth. The man choked and fell to his knees, holding onto his shattered throat.

A third backed away, briefly, before steeling himself to strike. As he did so, he tripped drunkenly over the table leg, falling at Strettavario's feet, the old man shattering his skull with the heel of his boot.

Strettavario stepped over the writhing figure to stare down at the last of them. The man was whimpering and pleading.

"Please," he called over and over. "Don't hurt me!"

"Where is Bishop Basquez?"

It didn't take long for Strettavario to get his answer. Once he had it he struck the man hard across the side of his head, knocking him unconscious.

Strettavario surveyed the carnage, acknowledging the barman briefly with a curt nod, turned and headed for where Basquez was hiding. Surprise and wonder spun inside him at what he had done, what he was doing. He snatched hold of the feeling, wild and nauseous, and subdued it, knowing full well that the real fight still lay ahead of him.

FIFTY-ONE

Valbonne. France.

The Inquisitors had watched the boat come ashore close to Antibes, seeing how the darkly dressed group of five in it stowed the rowing boat in the brush at the rear of the beach and quickly merged to join the crowds of locals enjoying a warm evening's walk along the promenade. Most observers would have lost the group moments later in the dusky dark of the French night, down one of the many side-streets or across the broad cobbled squares, full of people out drinking in the nightlife of the southern port.

But the Inquisitors pursuing the men who had come ashore from the ship anchored in the pitch of the ocean half a mile out were not like most people.

They followed from a distance, making sure they did nothing to alert the men that they were being stalked, giving them no reason to suddenly bolt or separate. There were five of them and just four Inquisitors, better odds for them to slip away into the gloom of evening darkness and for the Inquisitors to lose them, should they be encouraged to scarper and hide.

Twenty minutes on from landfall, Poré's men had crossed the main thoroughfare at the rear of the town and begun to climb into the hills above Valbonne, following goat-tracks and paths made by trekkers and shepherds, ascending into the wilds of the mountains. Now the Inquisitors pursued them with greater pace and less care as to whether or not they were spotted. While they knew that here, away from crowds and the well-lit streets, it might be easy for Poré's men to slip away, hunker down in the darkness, the land lit only by a thin moon, masking themselves in the black amongst the stunted trees and cairns, the Inquisitors knew that now, with no one else around to witness or interrupt them as they closed in for the kill, there would be no reason to hide their weapons or their murderous pursuit.

The track rose to a rocky ridge across which ran a line of limestone and stunted bushes, yellowed from what seemed an eternal summer and suffocated in the dust of the rock. Behind them, the Inquisitors stepped with quickening strides, walking four abreast, their hands resting upon the grips of the revolvers hung at their belts, their eyes trained to the backs of the men thirty feet ahead, appearing like hazy apparitions in the moonlight. Something in the dark rustled, and then immediately a howl rose from out of the night. Hearing such a sound would have shredded the nerves of even the most defiant and brave of men, the noise of a werewolf like the cry of true fear from one's darkest nightmares. But rather than turn and run, the Inquisitors merely paused and watched, their eyes tight to the black horizon, waiting for another cry to come. And it did, this one even more terrible and baleful, joining the first like a symphony of hate. And then a third joined it and a fourth, all in dreadful harmony with the others like a choir of wickedness, so loud that people far away in Antibes turned their heads towards the mountains and wondered what devilry was afoot in the peaks around the port.

"Make a circle!" ordered one of the Inquisitors, as the wolves' howling grew louder and nearer.

"Defensive circle!" the other three barked in strict reply, each of them taking their place on the corner of the square they had formed, their backs to each other, their eyes facing every angle outwards.

"Silver!" called the lead Inquisitor, and instantly bolts were worked on revolvers and shimmering shining rounds slotted into breeches.

The howls grew louder and ever more terrible, and they could now hear the slow heavy padding of taloned feet stepping towards them out of the darkness through the dust and the stones. Great slavering beasts, caught on the edge of moonlight, no longer walking on all fours, but rising up on their muscular hindquarters to spring forward, covered the thirty feet between them and the Inquisitors in just three short bounds. The great monstrous things threw themselves at the men, all teeth and claws and howls, yellow eyes narrowed in wild slits full of hate.

A heartbeat away, the four revolvers of the Inquisitors exploded and the wolves wailed, turning over and crashing to a dead halt, killed instantly by precise aim, lying still at the feet of their would-be prey.

Panting, gasping air into their urgent lungs to subdue the charge of adrenaline, the Inquisitors looked back up into the darkness from where the creatures had come, watching and listening for a second round of wolves to attack, an attack which never came. Instead they heard the running of boots and at once they set off after them, finding the men they had tailed from Antibes, the wolves having been their first and only line of defence.

The Inquisitors caught up with them and placed them in a single line, shooting all but one of them dead, killing the fifth man only when they had pulled the vial from his shaking trembling fingers and discovered that he could tell them nothing more to aid them in their search for the now one remaining vial.

FIFTY-TWO

POMPEII. ITALY.

It was as if Bishop Basquez had been lying in wait all night for Strettavario to arrive. The Bishop thrust out blindly with his blade the very moment Strettavario entered from the dark outside the first-floor seafront terrace, the attack more a child-like sweep across himself rather than anything that could have caused injury to the old Priest.

Strettavario caught Basquez's hand at the wrist and twisted it away and down, making the Bishop cry out and drop to his knees, the knife tumbling from his grasp. The Father kicked the blade away and looked down on the wincing man. He enjoyed watching the Bishop writhe helplessly in his grasp for a moment, incapacitated. Eventually he pushed him away so that Basquez fell onto his back, his hand clutched to his sprained arm, the serpentine man cursing and writhing like a demon.

"You've broken my wrist!" he wept.

"Shut up," Strettavario muttered, taking hold of the back of a chair in the chamber that had been knocked over in the fracas and turning it upright in order to sit opposite his defeated opponent. He dropped into it, feeling relief at the weight coming off his tired legs. He knew he was too old for this business, all this fighting and gallivanting. His body told him as much. And yet he felt younger than he had in years. "Get a hold of yourself, you fool!" he spat at the hissing serpentine man. He watched the Bishop cower back, still nursing his wrist, watching the Father with veiled eyes.

"So what is this?" hissed Basquez.

Strettavario produced a knuckleduster from the depths of his jacket and strapped it to his right hand, playing his fingers beneath the tight grip of the weapon, testing it as if in readiness for use. The firelight from the flames in the hearth reflected like amber strips of glistening nectar upon the points of the weapon. Strettavario looked up casually and scowled.

"Don't play dumb with me, Basquez. Cardinal Bishop Casado's dead."

"I didn't kill him!" shrieked Basquez.

Strettavario ignored him. "I know what you and Casado were doing to Poldek Tacit in the Inquisitional Prison."

The Bishop faltered, not expecting that. "I… I don't know what you mean."

The old Father gave the impression he was about to leap from the chair, making Basquez cower back, fearful of another attack. Strettavario relaxed and waved a derisory hand in his direction, crossing his legs.

"Ah! You're pathetic, like all your kind. And it seems to me that there are so many of *your kind* now that we have to contend with, people who take positions of power not to help and guide and aid, but to turn the position and the profit it affords to your own advantage, advantage over your rivals, over those you most envy, while all the time those most needy are left clutching at your boot heels as you pass them by."

Strettavario clicked with his tongue and scowled. "Something *has* corrupted our faith. Corrupted our world. Perhaps it's the war? Perhaps it's the Darkest Hand? I always remember Inquisitor Poldek Tacit telling me that he knew we were losing the fight against the Devil. Do you know how he knew?"

Basquez shook his head hurriedly, using the opportunity to look to the door and gauge whether he could reach it or not. He supposed not.

"He said he knew because of the way the demon would look at him during exorcisms, the way it always looked as if it knew it was winning. And regarding Poldek Tacit, I wondered what it was you were hoping to achieve by torturing him? What you were hoping to find?"

"I don't know what you mean," Basquez repeated, this time even more urgently.

"This is why I've come here, travelled all the way from Vatican City to find you. To find the answers which have been troubling me. It would have been so much easier if you had stayed. But something made you leave. I just wonder what that was, what it was you were so worried about?"

Basquez stuttered and Strettavario had heard enough hesitation. He launched himself from his chair and gathered the cowering Bishop into his grasp, dragging him up by the collar and thrusting him hard against the wall of the chamber. His lips were drawn back from his mouth, flashing teeth like a curse.

"You lie, too easily, Basquez. You always have done. Sly, like a snake. I should warn you that the Lord does not take kindly to that sort of behaviour, even from someone like you, a supposedly Godly man. And the Lord never had much time for serpents."

"I am Godly," Basquez whimpered, tears forming from his emotion and fear.

Strettavario loosened his grip on the man and let him fall down the wall, stepping back and observing him from a few steps away. "Good, so you will then tell me the truth, tell me what it is I need to know. What it is that so scared you about Tacit? What it is that's so terrible about him? I've read Casado's journal," and Basquez's eyes widened. "Yes, he kept a journal, his hurried notes written down before he was murdered." Strettavario held up his hand, palm open towards the Bishop. "It's all right, I don't believe it was you who killed him, Basquez. I know that now. I know by looking at you, how pathetic you are.

"But someone killed Casado. The Antichrist, or one of his henchmen, more likely, because of what he was, what he represented, what he knew.

And he knew what Tacit was, that he was connected in some way with the Antichrist. Casado knew, and so do you."

"What do you want to know?" asked the young Bishop, his tongue suddenly eager, now that he knew the accusation of murder was not to be directed at him, getting to his feet and pulling his robes back into some semblance of order.

"The prison, what were you doing to him in Toulouse Prison?"

"I don't know what…"

Strettavario roared in exasperation and threw himself forward again, threatening to take hold of Basquez, to thrust him hard back against the wall. The young Bishop shrieked, dropping to his knees, pleading. Strettavario drew back, letting him recover, feeling both invincible and pathetic at his show of power over the weak man. He looked down on him, disdain eating up his features.

"I ask you again, what were you doing to him in the prison? The papers, they revealed that you were torturing for a purpose, a purpose that went beyond punishment. You were torturing. Clearly there was a reason. Why?"

"For what he was. For what he contained," Basquez said precisely, speaking the words clearly and carefully.

"What did he contain?"

Basquez wept, shaking his head. "Casado! He knew, he knew better than anyone what Tacit was, from where he came. He wanted to use him."

"Use him? How?"

"To tap into his power. Subdue him. To try to win him over. Make him cast away his depravity, put aside his wicked intentions. And if he would not…"

"What?"

"Then win him as an ally for when this world war ran its course."

"Tacit?" asked Strettavario. "Win him as an ally? I don't understand."

"Clearly. It is a heart of darkness in which we walk, the middle of everything. Everything is corrupted, everything defiled."

"Is this why you ran, left the Vatican?"

"I thought I would be next! To be murdered!"

"Why?" growled Strettavario.

"Because of what I knew. They don't want the truth to get out. They don't want anyone to know. Not until the time is right."

"Who doesn't want anyone to know?"

172

"The Antichrist. The person at the heart of the Vatican, at the heart of this darkness! No one is safe. They've been killing anyone who gets too close, whoever finds out too much." And Basquez scowled and tried to shuffle away, but Strettavario leaned forward, putting his gauntleted hand on the wall in front of him. "You, Strettavario," Basquez spat. "I don't fancy your chances! Not after all you've done, coming here, all you've tried to find out."

"And what have I found out?"

"Since Tacit was brought into the Holy See nearly thirty years ago, they've been fascinated by him, suspicious about who he is, what he contains, what possesses him. Casado knew this, as did others in the Holy See. Of course, at first it was thought that Tacit could be used to help the Holy See and the faith by becoming an Inquisitor, but soon they realised that he was too dangerous. There were some who had a semblance of command and control over him, Adansoni and you. For some reason he respected and listened to you both. But for the majority, no one could control him. And of course always there was the prophecy of one coming from the east and committing so much terror. Soon it was felt that perhaps when he was caged, he could then be used."

Strettavario let Basquez pause for breath, but only briefly. For he knew the Bishop's tongue had been loosened and that he was close to revealing the final piece of the puzzle, the piece he so feared to hear, but which he had come all this way to discover.

FIFTY-THREE

Kiev. Ukraine.

The train driver had been persuaded to turn back to Kiev to allow Tacit and the others off. Now Tacit stood alone on the street corner in the heart of the city and listened to the whistle of the locomotive as it rattled away into the grey gloom of rural Ukraine. The others had gone inside. He watched a group of soldiers swagger up the road towards him. They looked like vagrants, their eyes flitting left and right, across the street and down side-alleys, as if they were looking for someone, anything upon which to vent their fury, drunk on their violence and might. On their arms were red bands.

They walked past Tacit, observing him closely, before stepping into the empty street and halfway across breaking into a run when they heard the sound of muffled gunfire and shouting a couple of streets away, drawn on by the anticipation of more violence.

It started to snow, a wet drenching snow.

"They still haven't found Poré," called Furtado, appearing from a door near where Tacit was standing.

"They won't now," said Tacit, thrusting his hands deep into his pockets. "It's days since Patmos. He could be anywhere."

Furtado looked sick. "We have found six vials," he said, trying to find hope where he knew there was none.

"We need all seven."

Tacit turned, following something across the grey heavens, finding himself drawn to the south-west, away towards Rome and the Vatican. There was a voice once more inside him, but it seemed changed, no longer merely condemning or maligning. Instead it soothed and begged, appealing for Tacit to come, to return to the seat of power, to stand beside the man whom he always knew he one day would call his master, no matter how far he tried to run from the calling, no matter how hard he fought against it. And while before it had spoken in a rush of words and noise, now things had changed. Now it spoke clearly to him, every word precise and vivid.

"Do you think we'll ever see it again? That we'll ever go back to the Vatican?" said Furtado.

"Oh, I have no doubt that *I* will," Tacit replied, looking at the fearful, uncertain sky. "It is now only a matter of time."

FIFTY-FOUR

SOMEWHERE IN THE GULF OF ADEN.

There was nothing graceful or beautiful about the supply ship that made its escape from Egypt. Its single rusted grey funnel pumped dirty black choking smoke like a snaking poisonous haze trailing in its wake, its hard-edged, heavily riveted hull pushing rather than gliding through the calm waters of the Gulf of Aden beneath the pallid sun. The ship's decking looked as if it hadn't been cleaned since the start of the war, peeling paint and corroded metal everywhere, a rust-like cancer eating up great swathes of the gun-black metal, which grew bearably hot during the middle of the day and would cut and rip feet whenever it was walked upon without shoes.

But this mongrel ship had borne Poré away, had slipped unchecked and unmolested from the Suez Canal and into the Gulf of Aden.

Now the vessel was in open waters and commanding its top speed of fourteen knots, the engines groaning and growling as if on the edge of collapse or explosion, the sooty black clouds from the funnel growing ever more polluted and noxious, drawing a thin putrid haze across the ship and the route by which it had come. But ahead the sun was setting on a still sea and the light from it was in Poré's eyes.

Ahead, the Arabian Sea.

Coke fires burned and a wide open sea called.

FIFTY-FIVE

Pompeii. Italy.

Basquez shivered to recollect. "It was conceived not long after the war and planned for Arras. It was there that Tacit would be captured, the assessment doomed, failure the only possible outcome for him. There was no way he could have escaped. If he'd allowed the Mass for Peace to succeed, he would have been arrested as being deemed unfit for work, failing in his duties as an Inquisitor. But because he stopped Cardinal Bishop Monteria by killing him at Notre Dame, he was arrested as a murderer.

"After the Mass for Peace he was taken to Toulouse Prison. We had him. And it was then that my work truly began, under the guidance of the Holy See. They wanted to know everything that I was doing to Tacit, every type of torture carried out by Salamanca, every tool used, blades, brands, blunt weapons, and whether any of them produced anything from him, voices, lights, power, something which could be utilised or something that could be created to communicate with or used to communicate through."

"Communicate with whom?"

"Have you not yet realised from where Tacit originates, Father Strettavario? Or are you too afraid to accept such a notion?"

The old Father hesitated and Basquez scowled, regaining a little more of his control and manner. He drew away, sitting up and watching the Priest from across the room.

"Is it not obvious? Hell, Father Strettavario, Tacit originates from Hell. After all, you already know that Tacit is Hell's Lieutenant. In the year 1877, in Pleven, Bulgaria, when the summoning of the Seven Princes of Hell was attempted before, something *did* come through."

"But the ritual failed!" cried Strettavario, drawn and pallid.

"It did, but it was known that something did manage to come through. A single demon, one of the Princes, or at least the soul of one of the Princes. The greatest of them. And it was believed that this thing found its way to Poldek Tacit.

"This war, this world war in Europe, a conflict that is going to be lost by both sides, have no doubt about that, Father Strettavario, from out of it there will be no victor, no one winner. All sides will lose, in one way or another.

"These End Times in which we are living, they call for a time when we must put aside our differences and seek parley with those we would never have dared to speak to before. And Tacit is, was, a bridge between our world and Hell."

"And who do we hope to speak with?" Basquez's face darkened at Strettavario's question and he smiled wickedly. "Don't tell me you think to speak with –"

"The Devil?" asked Basquez. "Is that really such a dreadful thing? Choose your enemies carefully, Strettavario. Has it not always been our way? We fight with those from whom we can gain favour, power, prestige. It is why we have never chosen to fight alongside those who are weak."

"But the Devil?! How long was the parley expected to last?"

"Until we had gained his trust and favour, until he trusted us enough to lower his guard, to turn his back, until we had the chance and opportunity to put the knife into him. And so, by doing so, kill the Devil, once and for all!"

"Folly!" cried Strettavario. "To attempt to befriend the Devil? Lunacy!"
Basquez shrugged, the cold arrogant smile remaining resolute in his face.
"But Tacit, if Tacit is this bridge, then who is he?"

"He is the greatest of the Princes of Hell! He is Satan!"

"What do you mean?"

"Tacit is Satan, Strettavario! Satan!" And Basquez laughed as if the
news he delivered was joyous, even though the thought of it also almost
brought him to tears. "That night, in Pleven, nearly forty years ago, it
was Satan who came through. The Dark Lord's right-hand Lieutenant,
the one chosen to protect the Antichrist, to stand by his side. For when
Satan stands next to the Antichrist, they will be unbreakable. And this is
why the Antichrist is looking to draw Tacit back to him in the Vatican,
draw him back at this very moment in time. And should he go there, with
the Pope entrapped in the city at the same time, their prisoner, at their
mercy, then believe me when I tell you that all hope will be lost. We will
be defeated, and only darkness will persevere for the remainder of days."

PART FOUR

"For the wrath of God is revealed from heaven against all ungodliness and unrighteousness."

ROMANS 1:18

FIFTY-SIX

MONDAY, OCTOBER 13TH, 1884.
THE VATICAN. VATICAN CITY.

Father Javier Adansoni wasn't alone in thinking the Vatican Chapel was darker than usual. In the close shadows of Pope Leo XIII's private chapel, a creeping presence seemed to have entombed the place, an intangible feeling, like that of malingering doubt after an ill-considered word between friends.

Skin prickled and Priests shivered beneath their thick robes as if a cold front had, without warning, swept in from the Tyrrhenian Sea and engulfed the city with the first chill of winter. All across the small chapel, Priests drew their cloaks tighter about them and shuffled surreptitiously in their seats in an attempt to find warmth. Candles flickered on trays, spirals of smoke from expired wicks rising like spirits to a heaven in the ceiling above.

But if Pope Leo XIII sensed the cold felt by the others, he gave no impression that he did, closing Mass and the holy book from which he read with steady hands and a voice as bright and clear as his spry eyes.

"May the love of God and the peace of the Lord Jesus Christ bless and console us and gently wipe every tear from our eyes," he called, a light youthfulness all about him, his face seemingly rich with pleasure and warmth.

He signed the cross in front of him and set his hands in a loose knot.

"Go in the peace of Christ," he asked of the congregation, his head turned to one side in a sign of calm resignation. For he knew only peace could assure the future, a future blessed with Christ.

"Thanks be to God," the congregation called back, and Adansoni took the opportunity to hide a yawn in the folds of his sleeve, feigning a sneeze.

Adansoni was weary, exhausted from long nights throughout September and October setting out plans for his forthcoming missionary work in Eastern Europe. He felt like a candle burnt from both ends, radiated and spirited by the opportunities being afforded to him on his first ever mission outside the Vatican, but worn close to extinction, feeling too old for one of his age. Every day he had studied the maps of the east where he knew his feet would tread, the routes he would follow, the belongings he would need to take with him, the teachings he would share with those he met. The journey did not carry any fear for him, even though he would be travelling through lands filled with Orthodox Catholics and heretics, determined at all costs to undermine his faith and his messages. He knew he had to be strong, put his faith in his Lord and prepare to face all the challenges set in his path. Above everything else, he knew he had to go. It was as if a voice in him had commanded it, clear and beseeching, calling out to him, demanding to be answered.

However, right now he desired sleep above almost everything else, to throw himself into his bed and find solace for a few hours. But like the dark voice which called to him from within to take up the missionary's way and bring *his* Lord's message out into the wilds, something had compelled him to attend the Pope's Mass this evening, a nagging hook caught firm in his lip which dragged him, exhausted and restless though he was, to the private chapel to hear Pope Leo speak.

In the thin light, Pope Leo's hair appeared white as snow, his tranquil warm features like an open embrace, as he looked out onto the faces of the congregation. Somewhere above and a little away from them, an organ flared into life with Frescobaldi's *Fiori musicali* and Pope Leo stepped out from behind his lectern, his characteristic lithe movements at odds with the oppressive air still heavy in the room. He turned his hands, held up in a sign of acceptance and greeting, approaching the small congregation of Cardinals and selected Vatican officials seated before him who had come to watch and hear him give Mass.

And then he stopped in mid-stride, his body frozen, as if the chill which everyone else felt had suddenly come upon him and caught his body in a deathly embrace. For several minutes it seemed he stood there, the blood drained from his face, leaving him sickly white, now appearing like someone on the verge of death, all life spent from him, before he fell and held himself against the altar. At first no one in the congregation did or said anything, transfixed by the strange scene playing out in front of them, a moment of insight from the Pope perhaps which no one dared interrupt. But as the minutes passed, the congregation began to rise in concern and raise their voices, some going forward to him to gather him from where he had fallen, calling out to him to revive him, trying to draw him from the ailment which had possessed him.

"Pope Leo!" one of the senior Cardinals called, placing his hands reverently about the Pope's shoulders to shake him gently from his malaise. "Pope Leo, are you quite well?"

As if charged by the touch of another man, at once the Pope's face contorted into a devilish leering sneer, his entire body twisting and gnarling like that of a stabbed serpent. He hissed and spat at all those who had come forward, a guttural snarl taking root in his throat. At once the Cardinals and Priests fell back, some casting themselves prostrate onto the floor in horror and bewilderment.

"Get back, dogs!" hissed the voice, in a savage tone never known from Pope Leo before. It seemed to have been summoned from the very foundations of Hell itself, metallic and barbed. "Get back! I can destroy your church. Destroy it in an instant."

At once the congregation cried out as one, for they knew to whom the voice belonged. But then, without warning, the Pope's face sank and any residue of wickedness dropped away from it.

"You can, can you?" Pope Leo spoke, in a voice that was his own, his features soft and worshipful. "Then go ahead. Show us if you believe you have the might."

Again, the aged Pope's face contorted and snarled itself into a foul sinister thing.

"Not yet!" he snapped, his eyes flashing, his tongue licking across his thin lips like a reptile. "But soon!"

As if fighting an inner turmoil to regain control of himself, once more the old man seized back his calm demeanour.

"Then when? How much time do we have?"

At this question his face darkened even more gravely, as the dark power seized control of him. His eyes seemed to flare in his sockets and he cast his wicked look across the gathered masses in the chapel who fell back, their hands masking cries in their mouths.

"Not long enough," he hissed, drawing back his lips and showing fanged teeth. "Within a hundred years. I will return when the world is falling into ruin and the land cast into darkness, lit only by the terrible playthings I shall put into mankind's hands. When the land is ready for my return, I shall, and terrible will be my reign."

And then, as if a fever was suddenly lifted, the old man swooned and fell. A Cardinal closest to him jumped forward and caught him in his hands, with the help of others carrying him away from the chapel to his private chamber, the Pope silent and ashen. Despite his deathly colour, his face once more showed the calm benevolence of Pope Leo XIII, all suggestion of demonic possession lifted. Behind him a procession of Cardinals followed in his wake.

All except one.

On a pew in the dark shadows, Adansoni shuddered and sunk down into his seat, his head dropping like a dead weight into trembling hands. For now he understood why the voices had spoken to him, why they had beseeched him for so long to go out into the wilds of the east and look for *him*, look for the one.

FIFTY-SEVEN

MONDAY, JANUARY 7TH, 1918. NOW.
THE VATICAN. VATICAN CITY.

From a high window, Cardinal Secretary of State Adansoni looked down on the cavalcade of automobiles and foot-servants returning through the city's gates, turning into the Vatican grounds, and smiled, a cold mocking smile of defiant self-assurance. Gravel crunched beneath solid rubber wheels and Priests called orders. Doves took flight from nearby rooftops. A murder of crows hopped close and stared from the turrets and eaves of the surrounding buildings, squawking and rasping angrily at the new arrivals.

In the corner from where Adansoni watched, a songbird, yellow as a canary and with long delicate tail feathers, sang and jumped between its perches in a cage. The Cardinal turned to the Inquisitor standing guard at the door.

"So the Pope *is* answerable to the Holy See after all?" he muttered, almost to himself. He looked back through the lead-lined window, staring down the long length of his nose, as if the new arrival was a criminal caught trying to evade justice and was now being returned to his place of incarceration. "Make sure he is taken to his quarters and locked inside. We cannot risk anything happening to him, can we, especially with such horrors occurring in the world at this present time?" A grumble of wind clawed its way out of his throat, cold amusement in himself.

In the semi-circle below, one of the Pope's loyal entourage took the venerable man's arm, assisting and guiding him up the short flight of steps into the open doors ahead.

"Look at him!" growled Adansoni. "So frail! So vulnerable! Who would have thought someone so nervous and fey could believe that *he* could command so much respect and power amongst the other rulers of the world? No wonder he has failed at every quarter. Pathetic! He has dragged himself around all of Europe for the last three years, pleading with all to put down their arms. Urging the belligerent peoples and governments to become brothers once again!" Adansoni scoffed, wiping the palms of his hands down the front of his gown, sweaty with emotion, and crossed to the cage, opening it. Dutifully, like a faithful pet, the bird hopped out and sat perched on his index finger, allowing itself to be kissed and preened by the old man. "Does he not know this is a war from which there can be no end? It will run until all has been ruined or destroyed."

The old Cardinal turned back to the Inquisitor, appearing to remember that he was not alone. "What is it?" he asked the man still standing there.

"The vials."

Almost at once, Adansoni seemed to diminish and shrink, but the shadows around him darkened. "What about them?" he asked, watching as the bird hopped between his fingers.

"Six have now been accounted for. One is still missing."

"And still it proves most peculiar." The old man shook his head, his eyes narrowing on the Pope's vanishing figure, swallowed up by the yawning gloom of the doors to the building opposite, moments before they were closed behind him. The thought lingered in the anterior of his mind.

"Peculiar, my Lord? How so?"

"The vials. The End of Times. That Poré should have attempted such a thing, to have begun the Rapture. It is not decreed for him to perform such a thing. Indeed, I am amazed that he had sufficient skill, wit or heritage to do so." Adansoni's eyes turned instantly fierce and mean, rising up to the skyline, the grey clouds shifting slowly above them, the flocks of grey and white doves, harried by ravens and crows, spinning this way and that like shoals of fish in the sea before they circled one more time and settled nervously upon rooftops warmed from below. "And yet…" His words, tentative and uncertain, trailed to silence and he bowed his head to the songbird, contemplatively, in deep thought. He stood like this for a long time, his mind turning over, considerations, explanations. How it might end. Eventually he said, "Tacit."

"What of him?"

"Send a message that he must return to the Vatican forthwith."

"Will he come?"

The question seemed to change something in the old man, the sudden flare of violence shimmering out of him from nothing. He snatched hold of the bird, tight in his fist like a trap, the creature's head and claws writhing as it pitifully tried to break free. "He will come!" rasped Adansoni, and then his voice cooled and he opened his palm, the crushed songbird, a tiny corpse of feathers, falling out onto the floor, blood and down on his palm. "If I demand it of him. And already I have, in my own manner. It is only right that he is brought back to the Vatican. It is nearly time for him to stand next to me in his rightful place. Pope Benedict has returned. So must he."

The Inquisitor nodded again. "And the vial?" he asked.

"The vial is lost. End Times have begun. The Tribulation is upon us, as surely as when the Seventh Seal was opened. It was not as expected, but our Lord moves in mysterious ways."

Adansoni narrowed his eyes on the lines of buildings and weaving pathways through the courtyards and gardens below where he stood. It seemed to the Inquisitor at the chamber's edge that his master had fallen into a trance. He hesitated between going and staying. He stayed, knowing he had not yet been sent away.

"These are dangerous times," the old man began. "Time we unleashed our vision on the Vatican, now that I am Cardinal Secretary of State. We shall forthwith present to all in the city this new direction, our new way." Steel found its way into his words.

"Increase the number of Inquisitors in the city. Send out the call to every Inquisitor to return to the Vatican at once to defend it against our enemies. Ensure that all pledge their loyalty to me. Crush any who question my authority. Those Inquisitors who refuse to return reveal their heresy and will be dealt with."

The Inquisitor nodded and turned to go, but Adansoni called him back.

"And close the doors and gates to the city."

"My Lord?" asked the Inquisitor, visibly shocked at the request.

"Shut up all citizens, Priests, Bishops, their acolytes and kin in Vatican City. Let the place become a citadel, a fortification against all our enemies in the world. Let us ensure we are prepared and able to defend our walls for when our enemies come. For they will, and we must be ready. Let all within understand our new ways."

"And those that do not?"

"If they wish to leave they may do so, but they leave by your blade and your hand, Inquisitor."

FIFTY-EIGHT

POMPEII. ITALY.

Bishop Basquez set the plate of unappetising-looking food onto the table and called for Father Strettavario to join him. The old father glanced up from the chair on which he was cleaning his revolver, snapping the cylinder shut and holding it in his lap for a moment, his liver-spotted hand placed across it. His mind was a torrent of questions and confusion, and yet he supposed he had never felt so certain or assured as he did now.

"Have you worked out who it is then?" Basquez asked, gathering a simple bowl of salad and setting it between the two places he had laid. "The one in the Vatican? The one who is the Antichrist?"

"You're the one with all the answers, Bishop," Strettavario called back, his eyes drawn to the window and the view of the glittering grey-blue sea the building afforded. Cold winds were coming off the Tyrrhenian Sea, making the waters rough and wild, waves breaking on the shoreline, the sound like hollow thunder amongst the rocks. "You tell me."

"And you're the Inquisitor, Strettavario!" retorted Basquez. "I thought they enjoyed finding out answers?"

"You still have a forked tongue in your mouth!" replied the old Priest, but there was a little more generosity in his tone. He stood, seeing the meal that the Bishop had prepared for him, and something close to appreciation stirred in him. He stepped to the table, drawing out his chair and lowering himself gently into it, feeling the rings of his armour press through his undergarments and into his skin like rows of tiny biting teeth. He took up the fork and chased a piece of meat through the gravy on his plate. Finally he said, "But yes, I suspect I know, though how I wish I was wrong."

Basquez drew out his own chair opposite and sat, clearing his throat. He pursed his lips, bouncing his head gently on his shoulders. "The one who first found Tacit?" he began, like the opening line of a chant. "He who first brought *him* into the Vatican? He who first took the young man into his care? He who attempted to keep *him* out of the Inquisition, out of their meddling corrupting clutches? He who did all he could to keep Tacit close? Who has watched Tacit at every available opportunity?"

And Strettavario's eyes fell to his lap, the hunger run out of him. "Yes," he muttered, before saying the name he had long considered but always hoped never to accuse. "Cardinal Bishop Javier Adansoni."

Basquez approved of the old man's answer, and nonchalantly shovelled a heaped fork of food into his mouth.

"How I wish it wasn't him," the Priest growled bitterly.

Basquez shrugged, suddenly dismissive, not caring, forking another mouthful between his greedy thin lips. "At every turn he has fought for Tacit. He has proven himself to be deceitful and sly." He watched Strettavario continue to push the food around his plate, as if the man wished only to make patterns in the sauce. "Is the food not to your taste, Father?"

Strettavario didn't reply. The old man was lost, lost in his darkest of thoughts, his private demons. He closed his eyes, the notions coming fast, spinning and swerving about his mind.

And then he announced, quite suddenly and unexpectedly, "I need to go." He stood, apologising as he did so, turning away to collect his belongings, determination in his face and with it a fierce demeanour, where moments before there had been defeat.

"Go where?"

"Back to the Vatican. I cannot stay here."

"And what are you hoping to do?"

"To confirm that our fears are right. Or I hope wrong." He took his pack from the floor and threw it over his shoulder, tightening it around his middle.

"Do you think that is wise? An old man, facing such an enemy on his own?" The words were fierce, but the Bishop's tone facile. He turned back to his dinner, ploughing through the stew with gusto, an eager hungry light back in his eye. The serpent had been bested, his pride dented, but his pride had begun to recover and with it his spirit. "You might look like an Inquisitor, Strettavario, but looks and ability are two different things. Do not forget where you go! Whom you will face!"

"Do you wish to come with me?"

"Mercy, no!"

"Then shut up! What choice do I have?" asked Strettavario, beating the flat of his hand against the folds in his coat. "While I have named him, I won't believe it about Javier, my friend, not until I have heard it from the man himself with my own ears. I can't believe it."

"And Tacit?" Basquez asked. "What about him? What if he is entirely possessed by Satan, the Devil's Prince of Hell, sent to protect his unholy offspring, the Antichrist? What if he really is prophesied to stand at the Antichrist's side, while he, Adansoni, puts in place his plans for the earth's ruination?"

Strettavario's answer did not come for a long while. Instead he looked at the wall of the apartment, shrunken, turned in on himself. Eventually he spoke, laboured and strained, as if he knew every one of the words to be fanciful. "Tacit, he is a good man, or at least there is goodness in him. I have known him, followed him, watched him for almost all of his adult life. All his life he has lived in conflict, troubled in himself, as if he has been at war with his spirit, as if always fighting a possession. Though he is grim and hard, there is goodness in him. I know it. The possession has not overtaken him completely."

"What if he's already with the Antichrist Adansoni? Already standing next to him, his champion and protector?"

"He isn't."

"How do you know?"

"He's in Constantinople. At the inquisitional headquarters there. Or he was until recently. My position affords me certain privileges, one being to hear the news and whereabouts of inquisitional members. He's there. That's where he is. Safe, for the time being."

"So there is still time?"

"There is," said Strettavario, weighing the comment in his face.

"And Adansoni? What about him? What are you going to do when you find out that he *is* the Antichrist?"

"I'll do what any good person would do," the old Priest said, only now looking at Basquez and skewering him with a withering glare. "I am going to kill him. I am going to kill Adansoni. I am going to kill the Antichrist."

FIFTY-NINE

Jizhou. Shandong Province. China.

Behind the gaunt deathless man, the Great Wall of China swept the vista in a broad arc of grey stone and mortar, snaking around and down the undulating valley to the edge of one's vision and beyond. About him, the huddle of men, those Poré had brought with him from Alexandria on the long voyage from the Mediterranean, stood shivering and murmuring beneath their shabby gowns and cloaks under the shroud of Chinese winter, while Poré himself, dressed in an efficient-looking suit of approved British government tailoring, conversed with the contingent of Chinese from the local village. At their head stood the village elder, decadently and colourfully gowned, a flat tasselled hat matching the vibrant silken colours upon his head. The old man looked warily down into the paperwork, ratified by Pablo and brought by Poré, with hesitation and doubt.

"And you are part of the British Legation here in China?" the Chinese official asked, looking up from the papers.

"Is there an issue?" asked Poré.

"No, but your accent." The Asian's voice was light and bewitching, like a chant.

"The French and British, we fight on the same side. Just like the Chinese."

"Of course. And we are your servants." The man held his hand to his chest and bowed stiffly, fearing for a moment that he might have offended the Frenchman with his questions and doubts as to the legitimacy of the requests brought to him from the other side of the world.

"And so you understand the needs of the war?"

"A little. Whatever we can do to assist our superiors we will."

"And you will," noted Poré, his eyes simmering in his sunken dark sockets at the perceived need to unnecessarily explain himself to this individual. The official papers supplied by Pablo and the Allied powers' reputation alone should have been enough. "We need men, men who can labour and lug. These will not be fighting men. Of that you have my assurance. These will be men to work for the armies of the western front, a great honour! To assist in the making of fortifications, the construction of buildings, the carrying and supply of materials. The British Army is a hungry beast and needs to be fed. And your men will be fed and paid. While you are our servants, we do not expect your sons to work for nothing."

"And are you sure these are the men you want?" The official turned with Poré to look back at the village. Paltry looking specimens of humankind mingled and chattered between the damp pathways and rural homesteads of the collective. He waved with a hand along the long length of the Great Wall. "There are better ones, healthier ones from other villages, further to the east, in the lower valleys, where there is more food and better conditions in which to live? We –"

"The ones here will suffice," said Poré, glancing back across the vale to where the small village was situated. "They *have* to suffice. It is decreed." Sneaking pathways weaved between bamboo huts. Half-naked children wandered between them, padding in the cold mud, stray dogs sniffing and scavenging amongst the muck and detritus. A chill wind teased cloaks and collars.

"But there are others, fitter, stronger in the villages east of here."

"These are the ones I require."

"They will suffer on the voyage."

"As would any man. It is a long way from China to the shores of Europe. But this is a great war and we all must sacrifice what we can for the greater good."

"Few will survive."

189

"Trust me when I say that I will see to it that some, as indeed as many as I am able to keep alive, will survive." He fought to keep control of his growing disdain for the man and his questions. "It is in my interests to deliver them all safely to France. And I am going with them. The British government will ensure that all those families left behind will receive due payment for donating their sons to the war effort. We do not wish to leave our allies in the Far East compromised by the toll of our requirements on them."

The official took a moment to study Poré, trying to see if he could detect any falsehood in his face. Finally he nodded and set his mark to the bottom of the paper.

"The Great Wall of China," began Poré, his demeanour at once softening, turning to admire the tall impenetrable construction of stone at his back, "it was built not only to keep enemies out, but also to keep the people in, and other things beside. Some were never meant to leave. I am giving these men a great opportunity, to leave this place and to make their mark upon the world."

"It will be a great experience for them all, I am sure," replied the village elder wistfully, bowing and handing back the papers.

"Are you a religious man, San Chui?"

"Of course!" he replied, bowing.

"And I heard a great voice from the temple saying to the seven angels, 'Go your ways, and pour out the vials of the wrath of God upon the earth.'"

"That does not sound altogether encouraging!" chimed Chui. There was the hint of a smile in his face, but suspicion in his eyes.

But Poré stood tall, tears gathering in his eyes, either from the chill wind which was now blowing more strongly through the village, as if a storm was summoning at his quotation, or from the emotion of the moment. "They were words first conceived and written down in this very valley, this very place, this spot, this earth upon which we stand. Did you know that? Words from God and of God, conceived here, in this Chinese vale? And they say the Bible was conceived and written all in the Middle East!" He spread his arms wide and smiled in a rare moment of bliss, a look that seemed alien and unnatural to him. "Come, let us feast together in celebration of what your sons go to do. And, in the morning, we shall leave to achieve it."

The man nodded and stepped away. But Poré did not follow him immediately, instead he stayed and watched him all the way down the path until the official reached the camp. When he did so, Poré turned back to the Great Wall and drew out the small wooden chest, no bigger than the size of his palm, containing the seventh and last remaining vial he had brought with him, borne all the way from Patmos. He cleared his throat in a moment of reverential thought before opening it. Instantly a surreal silence overwhelmed the valley. As one, dogs lost their bark, children fell quiet from their games and tears, and mothers, hearing the news that their sons were to leave for war in Europe, found their weeping noiseless and still.

SIXTY

CONSTANTINOPLE. TURKEY.

Tacit was in the library of the inquisitional headquarters in the city, Henry, Sandrine and Isabella at the table with him, all intent on the increasingly desperate and hopeless hunt for Poré. The chamber was dark and oppressively still, full of dust and warmth and that tired smell that always lingers around books rarely opened. There was a shallow line of windows, a foot deep, running the short length of one of the walls, out of which the cream light of the cool oncoming Turkish winter morning crept almost apologetically into the chamber.

They picked over pages from tomes piled in front of them, looking for anything which might give them a clue as to where the seventh vial could have been taken. Days had turned to months since the first six had been found. Doubts had replaced initial optimism. They knew the race had been run and most probably lost. Inquisitors had long since turned to doing what they did and enjoyed best, cracking skulls and hunting. But Tacit and the others still continued their search, as if it was a penance. And the noises in Tacit's head had turned more vengeful and insistent by the day, clamorous and precise in what they wished him to do, his true duty, to return back to the Vatican, back to his master and complete the circle. Bind the knot of their union.

He'd said nothing to the others of his silent suffering, although by the way he saw them watching occasionally from the corners of their eyes, or looking up from their conversations when he walked by, he knew they perceived a little of his silent torment. They looked both intrigued and horrified by his muttering and pained expressions, and he knew that he probably didn't need to say anything to them for them to recognise the ordeal he was enduring. Often, in Isabella's arms at night, Tacit wept quietly while she held him like a child enduring nightmares, wishing there was some way she could soothe them away as a mother could with lullabies.

No one else was in the chamber this day. No one had visited the library in the three long hours they had hunted for clues and read and pondered. So quiet and dark, the library seemed more like a mausoleum than a place of insight and reflection.

So when footsteps sounded in the corridor and began to descend hurriedly down the stone steps into the basement, all four of them looked up at once. Tacit could see from the faces of the Inquisitors who had come to find them that they had news and it was grave.

"Inquisitor Odams," Tacit acknowledged the commander at the head of the contingent, approaching the table.

"Poré," said Odams. "He's been seen close to the Chinese port of Weihaiwei, a contingent of several thousand Chinese workers with him."

"So that's it!" groaned Isabella. "The seventh vial!"

"Oh my God," muttered Sandrine. "We're too late then, aren't we?"

Tacit said nothing, his eyes turning dolefully to the great leatherbound book before him. Wordlessly he picked up the front cover and dropped it closed.

"Something else, Tacit," said Odams. "You're wanted, back at the Vatican."

"On whose orders?" asked Sandrine.

"Secretary Cardinal of State Adansoni," replied the Inquisitor, defiant, squaring himself up to the woman. "He's wanted you back for weeks now. You've ignored all previous requests."

The dark voice twisted in Tacit's ears, commanding and defying. Many times he'd been called to return back to the city, and every time he had resisted. But this time, now that Poré had won, any resistance in him faltered and he perceived the suggestion as a good one. "No," he said, in a tone which seemed not his own, "Odams is right. We should go back."

Sandrine's face hardened, her eyes narrowing. "But what about Poré?"

"We're too late," replied Tacit quickly, too quickly to appease Henry. "We need to go back, to our Lord." White noise flared in his head.

"Your Lord? What do you mean by 'your Lord', Tacit?" Henry's voice was a shout. "Sounds like nonsense to me. 'Your Lord' will wait, Poré won't!"

"All right, quieten down!" warned Odams, his hand on Henry's shoulder. Henry slapped it away and started to stand, moments before the Inquisitor's fist followed through, turning him out of his chair and onto the floor.

Isabella was the first to react, kicking back her own chair, instinct driving her hand to her gun, as the Inquisitor closest to her flashed with the back of his own hand and knocked her down.

Everything seemed obscure and remote to Tacit, the figures shades of grey, the groans and cries muffled in his ears. He was aware that he was trying to stand, knowing that he had to act, retaliate. But his body and mind laboured as if dazed, weighed down with the disorientation of his mind, the voice commanding and yet confounding him.

He felt the edge of the chair against the backs of his legs, shouts all about him, the bark of a gun and then a howl, ripping a hole through his dazzlement, dragging him back to reality, back into the room and the mêlée.

He ducked, just in time, as the wolf leaped over him and tore at Inquisitor Odams, taking the man's head and shoulders away in a single wretched bite, dousing the room in his blood.

"Get the hell out!" Tacit heard Henry shout, pushing at his shoulder, sliding him away as if he was slipping on ice. Tacit caught the smell of gunsmoke and roses, Isabella next to him.

There was a door ahead and Henry kicked it open, ushering Isabella and the labouring Tacit through it as he looked back to the wolf, Sandrine, devouring the remaining two Inquisitors and heading for the stairs.

"Oh my God, Sandrine!" he whispered to her, before turning back and sprinting away. The sound of boots thundered in the corridors above them. He knew that the whole of the Inquisition was coming for them.

SIXTY-ONE

POMPEII. ITALY.

Attilio Basquez had thrived his entire life on being alone. He had never needed or sought out human friendship, never desired the warmth of human interaction. Indeed, to him, humans were flawed, which was exactly the reason why they needed the Church to guide and direct them. Father Strettavario's visit had proved that very point, yet it was precisely the old Father's visit which had illuminated something in Basquez, an insight he had never experienced before, an understanding of what it was to have and to share and work together. And to lose.

For as long as he could remember, he'd felt desperately lonely. After Strettavario left, he'd sat looking at the wall for days, unable to leave his residence, to focus on what needed to be done. Had he done wrong in the interrogation of Tacit? Had he committed a sin by carrying out his masters' orders? Had he done wrong to flee? If so, how could he have done wrong? He had done all that was commanded of him! But all those who commanded him were now dead or corrupted under the authority of the Antichrist.

He could never return to the Vatican, not as a Bishop, and even if he did, even without the Antichrist in his place of power, how would he ever be allowed to preach knowing that his reputation would forever proceed him, the one who had run, knowing that no council organisation in the Vatican would ever accept him or listen to what he had to say after what he had done? He had fled at the first sign of trouble and revolution. His hand had been on the handle which had driven the Vatican onto the rocks courtesy of Tacit's torture.

In that moment of loneliness his mind drew to the other person who had spent so much of his life alone. He didn't trust him, he had never trusted him, despite all that Strettavario had said about him, despite all the old man believed of him and in him. But he supposed he owed him something, and in that moment supposed that this person might be the only person who could save his faith, his world, and possibly him. And perhaps Basquez was the only person who could save *him*. He pulled on the small pack he had filled hours before but had thrown into the corner in a tirade of disdain and ridicule. But now, after hours contemplating what he had possessed and had since lost, he realised that he had never had anything to lose, for he never had anything to begin with. All he had left was something to gain.

He rose, taking hold of the straps, and stepped out into the streets of Pompeii, hearing the gulls above him and the banter and happy chatter of people from the city all around him. He tightened the straps over his shoulders and went looking for Poldek Tacit.

SIXTY-TWO

CONSTANTINOPLE. TURKEY.

"What is the matter with you?" shouted Henry, pushing Tacit and Isabella into a side-room off the corridor, closing the doors and setting himself against them. "You're losing your mind, Tacit!" he barked, taking out his revolvers and clumsily threading brass rounds into their cylinders, dropping some of them onto the carpet. Something rocked in the corridor outside, shaking the door on its hinges. The close explosion and Henry's stinging accusation, seeing him prepare for battle, snapped Tacit out of his momentary torpor.

"What are you doing?" he asked. Shouts and the pounding of boots grew louder, above them and outside the room.

"What the hell do you think?" seethed Henry, snapping the revolvers shut. "I'm going to help Sandrine." He cocked them and looked from Tacit's blank ravaged face, starved of any human emotion, to Isabella. She pulled one of her own revolvers from her belt and went forward, but Tacit stopped her.

"No."

"We just can't leave her!" shouted Henry. "Sandrine's your friend!"

"She's a half-wolf!" Tacit retorted cruelly.

The comment, errant and unexpected, stunned Henry and Isabella.

"So it's like that, is it?" Henry hissed. "Good God, Poldek," he said, shaking his head. "Maybe you'll manage to find some light in that black heart of yours one day. But looking at you now, I don't hold out much hope."

He threw open the doors and thrust his way out, his revolvers leading the way.

"What the hell is the matter with you, Poldek?" said Isabella, herself powering for the door and after Henry, nothing but contempt in her eyes. "Henry's right. You've changed."

"Where are you going?" he called out after her, taking two steps but then drawing back, his great hands to his head, seized in a moment of insanity. More gunfire rattled and voices shrieked from in the building. A grotesque howl clawed its way through the chambers. All of it sounded like a churning madness to Tacit. "Isabella, we need to get out of here!" He wept to the ceiling above him, going forwards and then back again, turning circles in the room, knocking against tables, turning chairs over onto their sides, all senses lost. All except one. The voice that mocked and hissed.

The window, it cackled, and Tacit looked up at where the devilish voice had directed. *Get away via the window*. Tacit ran to it, drawing it open, just wide enough for him to squeeze through. He placed his boot onto the window ledge and began to lever himself up.

Isabella. His promise to her, to never leave her.

Leave her, the voice commanded. *She has played her part*.

But Tacit drove his hand hard into his face. "No!" he retorted, and then he was running, bounding through the doors, charging down the corridor, leaping over Inquisitors already dead in the passageway, into the library and up the stairs, never bothering to look at the remains of Commander Odams and the other Inquisitors destroyed by Sandrine, just following the sounds of gunfire, the rattle of machine-guns, the returning bark of revolvers.

"Isabella!"

He shouted her name as he reached the top of the stairs, ploughing into a group of Inquisitors who had taken up a defensive position there and who were pouring fire down upon someone trapped in a corridor beyond. He fell amongst them like a demon, his eyes flaming rubies burning bright in sockets of black, his teeth locked hard in his skull. The Inquisitors saw nothing but a great beast amongst them, some shouting for silver, thinking that it was the wolf who had returned and battered into them, such was his ferocity and hate, the speed with which his hands moved and killed.

His fists thrust like a blur, punching through skin and flesh, puncturing bodies with the speed and weight of jackhammers, his knuckles torn and bloody with his own blood and the Inquisitors'. Everything was blur, a nightmarish chaotic mist of crimson and darkness and shrieking pain. One minute there was wrestling and pleading and next there was only the heavy grunt of breath in Tacit's chest and the drip of blood from his hands.

"Isabella!" he cried, leaping on from the shattered pile of bodies he had broken and eviscerated towards the corridor upon which the Inquisitors had been directing their attack.

"You bastard!" Isabella swore, coming at him from the darkness, slapping him hard across the face.

"Isabella!" he pleaded, groping for her. "I'm sorry."

"No time! We need to find Henry!"

SIXTY-THREE

Constantinople. Turkey.

Henry was running through the winding corridors and dimly lit chambers in the building, shooting at anyone that moved, going where he thought he should go, listening the best he could for the sounds of anything that sounded like a wolf. The pendant of Francis of Assisi felt cool against his hot sweaty skin, his pulse beating hard in his neck. Two Inquisitors rolled out into the corridor ahead of him, warnings on tongues, rifles in hands. But Henry was ready and tuned, his revolvers barking before they even worked the bolts in their weapons.

He drew back momentarily into the shadows of a corner of a room and reloaded, spitting curses at his predicament and at Tacit's disloyalty and cowardice. He'd lost contact with Isabella somewhere just outside the library, lost her as the Inquisitors had pinned them down. But at least she had fought with him a little way into the building, not like *him*, not like

Tacit. The bastard, the coward and bully, had changed. Henry knew from the moment they had met again in Ukraine, his fears confirmed when Tacit had beaten the platform guard in Kiev with the flat of his revolver.

Fampoux. He remembered Fampoux, reliving the murder of the German soldiers shot by Pewter in that grubby trench.

Monsters were not only things that lurked in children's nightmares.

Anger boiled and he seized on it, slamming the cylinders to his Webley revolvers shut, catching the tail of a howl somewhere above him. He powered towards it.

The inquisitional hall of the headquarters lay at the end of the corridor down which Tacit and Isabella were running, fifty yards ahead, out of which the hammer of shouts and orders bickered. They could see a group of Inquisitors running in and out, shouting and commanding. A group turned into the passageway, oblivious to the oncoming threat.

"We need more firepower," warned Isabella. "We can't fight them all with just revolvers!"

Just then, a crescendo of noise, so loud it sounded as if the roof had been torn off, erupted from the floor above. Without hesitation, Tacit went towards it, Isabella tailing him, her eyes on the way they had come. The corridor ran to a broad set of stairs going upwards. There were two Inquisitors standing guard at the bottom, their senses alert to anything approaching. Tacit shot them dead before they even moved. He flew over their bodies and up the stairs towards the cacophony of gunfire and chaos just above, his boots biting hard on the cold stone steps. More Inquisitors were at the top, hunkered down ready.

And there were now bullets at their back too, Inquisitors flocking in from behind.

"We're trapped!" cried Isabella, but Tacit never heard her. At the top step he leaped, a great arching jump, high and long, that catapulted him into the midst of the waiting Inquisitors, his revolvers flashing as he fell amongst them, striking out with his fists the instant his boots connected back with the floor. In seconds the Inquisitors lay dead or dying.

He heaved one of the bodies up off the ground, over his head, and threw it over the rail of the stairs next to him, down onto the Inquisitors coming up the other way, swatting them like flies beneath the thrown corpse. They groaned and tried to roll themselves clear. Tacit executed them, one at a time, from the top of the stairs.

The chamber into which the stairs rose was long, with doors leading off in different directions, feeding the depths of the building. Isabella skidded to a halt next to Tacit, straining to look down the passageways. There were bodies filling one in particular, clear evidence of a recent gunfight, and they went towards it. Inquisitors, felled by tooth, claw and bullets, quivering in their final dying moments or lying still from their grievous wounds, were everywhere, piled up in sweating bloody heaps. The place smelt of iron and gunpowder.

"Henry!" Tacit called into the blackness beyond.

"Here," replied a small quiet voice from a corner.

In the near-pitch dark they went forward cautiously, prepared for anything which might try to reach out and make a grab for them, something lying unseen and in wait amongst the dead.

They found him, lying on his back, his Webley revolver held in weak fingers in his lap, a pile of brass casings scattered about him. His clothes glistened crimson in the dark light, but his face was deathly pale, the life bled out of him.

"Jesus! Henry!" cried Isabella, going to his side.

Tacit swallowed, knowing at once they were too late. He knew the signs, when death had more claim on a person than life. "You check him, I'll cover us."

There was no more gunfire in the building, no more shouts of alarm and panic, just the pounding of boots, the bark of commands. The battle, for now, was over, although what its final cost was, Tacit could not tell. He glanced back at Henry, unable to look at him for long, chastened by shame and humiliation at his earlier behaviour. He could hear that Isabella and Henry were talking, but he couldn't make out their words, didn't wish to, as she tried the best she could to staunch his wounds. He looked again, catching sight of Henry's chest ripped open by bullets, the discolouration of torn organs behind the tear of skin and uniform.

"Come here, Poldek," he heard Isabella say to him.

"I need to watch, stand guard," he replied, straining harder into the darkness to emphasise the importance of his role.

"It's important," she pressed, and he looked over, down on her and Henry, deathlessly white alongside. He dropped to next to him, his eyes on the wounds of Henry's body, unable to look him in his weak greying face.

"I'm glad you came back for me, Poldek," muttered Henry. "I'm glad you came back. Thank you, my friend."

Cruel emotion clawed at Tacit's throat. "Henry…"

"Sandrine, I couldn't find her," he continued, his breathing like a whisper. "I tried, but there were too many of them. I dealt with as many as I could. The rest I'll leave to you." He smiled a weak smile.

"We'll look for Sandrine," replied Tacit, reaching across and putting his hand onto Henry's. "We'll find her."

"Never expected to die in Constantinople, but I suppose it beats dying in a sodden trench or No Man's Land." He winced, fighting against the bite of pain from his guts, coughing weakly. "I've done my bit." The words were barely audible.

"You have, Henry," Tacit nodded, his teeth gritted, but this time against the coming tears. "You have."

Henry looked at him through his fading watery vision. "Don't let them possess you completely, Poldek. Fight them, as I know you can. As you always have done. If you find Sandrine, tell her… tell her that I love her, that I loved her from the very first moment I saw her."

"She knows," Isabella assured him, her eyes full of sorrow. "She knows, Henry, she knows."

He smiled, for the last time. "It's really been quite an incredible journey. I'm glad to have taken it with you both."

And then the breath slipped out of him for the final time.

SIXTY-FOUR

THE VATICAN. VATICAN CITY.

There was shouting coming from inside the locked chamber, fervent and angry, but conversely clipped and apologetic too, as if the individual imprisoned behind the door felt ashamed to have had to resort to behaving in such a manner. And with the shouts came a banging upon the door, beating out an unsteady chaotic rhythm with the flat of a hand.

The barked angry calls and thumping lasted for five minutes and then there was silence again for an hour, perhaps two, before the banging upon the door started again, coupled with cries of indignation, the handle being tested and then more hollow banging, and yet more shouting, calling out for aides, even a passing Priest, to come and release him.

So it had gone on for most of the day, and all the days since he had been returned here.

"Pope Benedict, he is like an eager child with good lungs," suggested Adansoni, unable to stop himself from smirking at the comment made to the Inquisitors standing guard beside him. "Certainly now I understand why the governments around the world grew tired of our Pope."

The old Cardinal turned from the locked door out of which the Pope's remonstrations were issuing and strode away, his hands held loosely in front of him, long fingers knotted. "Make sure he is fed and watered. The poor man sounds as if he is quite exhausting himself. I can't quite decide yet what to do with him, whether I need him or not. His advisers?" he asked the Inquisitor, walking beside him. "Those closest to him?"

"Disposed of," nodded the burly man. "We made sure they were made an example of, their deaths a warning to any who might have been tempted to oppose you."

"Good. It's amazing what the sight of a little violence and the sound of pleading does to the opinion of possible revolutionaries. Put out the rumour that the Pope has been driven insane. Temporarily, for now." He pointed with a finger, which he then waggled in time with the quick turning of his mind. "Perhaps permanently. I will have a think and decide which it is to be. Let us say…" And he put his finger to his lips as he walked, considering what reason might be construed to have driven the unfalteringly measured Pope to madness, "… the trials of the war. His inability to bring anything even resembling peace to all those many nations he visited, all that time he wasted. All those lives lost. Consequently he has been incarcerated, for his own good. By decree of the Holy See."

He looked pleased, before adopting a false look of sorrow. "It is sad, but this madness may well prove fatal. And that the only obvious replacement is the current Cardinal Secretary of State, especially with the support I enjoy courtesy of others in the Holy See. I am sure all Cardinals who have yet to fall under my admiration and loyalty will oblige me, should it come to that, not to mention all those who have since seen the merits of loyalty to me and what happens to those who do not comply with the correct course of action. I am sure they will come to the right decision when the time arrives."

He smiled, a smirk like that of a child who's played a trick on his friend.

"Talking of loyalty," he continued, folding his hands together and hiding them in the sleeves of his robe, "what news of the Inquisition? How has the order been received for our magnificent army of Inquisitors to return to the Vatican?"

"Slow," replied the Inquisitor, begrudgingly. "We've had a trickle of Inquisitors return as commanded, most pledging their loyalty to you. But for many in the Inquisition their allegiance still lies with the Pope."

"Which perhaps gives me the answer as to what I need to do with Pope Benedict?" Adansoni brightened. "What news of Tacit? Has he left Constantinople for the Vatican yet?"

The Inquisitor cleared his throat. "Not to our knowledge," he replied. "But…"

In a blink, the Cardinal's cold humour was replaced with the menacing scowl of displeasure. "What is it?"

"There have been… difficulties, apparently. They resisted. Sandrine Prideux…"

"The half-wolf?"

"She attacked those loyal to us, master. She gave Tacit, with Sister Isabella and the Englishman, Frost, the… the opportunity to flee."

"So where are they now?"

"Still in Constantinople, we think."

Adansoni's anger seethed, but before he could unleash it a four-man contingent of Inquisitors swept around the corner from the corridor ahead, blocking his way and tempering his spirit.

"Yes?" he snapped, violence seething through his thin veneer of control. "What is it? Why the sudden intrusion?"

"There is someone to see you, my Lord," one of them said.

"To see me? And whoever has come to see me, unrequested or invited?" he spat.

"Father Strettavario, master."

SIXTY-FIVE

Constantinople. Turkey.

Tacit closed Henry's eyes and stood, helping Isabella to her feet. They embraced, their emotions threatening to overwhelm them.

"We need to go," she said.

Tacit nodded, dragging his knuckles across his moist eyes. "Inquisitional stores. Let's restock first."

"Sandrine?"

He shook his head grimly as he listened both ways down the corridor, before letting it hang. "I'm sorry, Isabella, I don't like her chances. It's gone mighty quiet. Come on."

He kept his revolvers stowed and went on with his hands splayed wide in front of him, ready to seize anyone who stepped into their path. The chaos and noise in the building had simmered down, the tension now lessened to match the hair-string tautness in Tacit's fingers. They went slowly, checking every chamber and corridor before moving through it, hugging the shadows, listening, watching for any danger and waiting for it to pass. Only when they reached the inquisitional stores, a long thin room reached by a short flight of stairs, did Tacit unleash his savagery, subduing the two Inquisitors he found there with his bare hands.

He worked his way through the racks of weaponry, finding the Browning machine-gun they had brought from Patmos and putting it into Isabella's waiting hand. Tacit stripped the stores of anything else he thought might be of use, ammunition, a few grenades, a M1917 Colt revolver that he stowed at the small of his back. There was another door from the storeroom which they took, leading them into a warren of narrow corridors and small chambers beyond, all of them empty, all leading closer to the front entrance and escape.

"The place has been cleared out!" said Isabella.

"They're still looking for us," replied Tacit.

His words were prophetic.

The sudden deafening hammer of gunfire exploded around them and

Tacit pushed Isabella out of the hall into which they had crept and on into a brightly lit antechamber. There were windows lining the right-hand wall, looking out into the Constantinople street and the approach to the inquisitorial building. A group of Inquisitors on the gate were running in and out, unsure if they were to stand guard or go in and help. They vanished inside briefly and Tacit took the opportunity, launching himself at one of the windows, blasting through it in a shower of glass and wood. He rolled out into the road, coming up onto his feet and reaching forward to help Isabella out.

Gunfire flew in her slipstream as they raced across the street to the sandy-coloured buildings opposite and the street nestled between the houses, bullets bristling the cobbles and buildings either side.

Two steps on, the M1917 Colt revolver was in Tacit's hand.

He knew it was a weapon much praised for its precision and stopping power. The first shot took the leg off an Inquisitor below the knee, the second removed his left hand in a burst of red, skin and bone.

Isabella flew on into the narrow street, Tacit three steps behind her, high buildings looming up on either side, blocking out the winter sun, the route down which they ran appearing more like a tunnel than a street. There were cold stones beneath their boots and wind in their hair.

And bullets at their back.

The building to their left erupted in a cloud of dust and rubble as they sprang to the end of the road, where the street spilt four ways at a small square, Isabella spinning right and Tacit following, charging down the slope on the far side, a ramshackle wooden-fronted building directly ahead. They took the narrow lane to the right of it, going ten paces on before Tacit turned and fired back on his pursuers, both revolvers now in his hands, lighting up the way they had come with lead slugs, dropping the Inquisitors as the rounds tore home.

"Go on!" cried Tacit, turning back to Isabella, waving with his hand. "Go on! Go on!"

But these words were frozen on his tongue as a motorised truck pulled up at the bottom of the street and then braked, blocking any way forward.

There were Inquisitors in the vehicle's cabin and pouring down the street towards them.

"No way through!" cried Isabella, whipping the Browning rifle from her shoulders and turning back to make a final stand with Tacit.

"Get in!" cried a voice from the cabin, which they recognised at once as Inquisitor Furtado's. Tacit looked back up the way they had come, the street now full of Inquisitors. They needed no second invitation.

"Go!" he shouted, helping Isabella into the back of the vehicle with the heavy weapon, throwing himself in afterwards and pounding on the ceiling with his fist.

Something spat and revolted inside him as the truck shuddered forward into first; by second gear it was speeding away, bullets zipping and ricocheting through the truck as they vanished up the street.

The truck burst out of the western gates of Constantinople and was driven hard along the coastal road, as if all the demons of Hell were pursuing. Only after an hour did the driver finally ease back on the accelerator pedal, pulling over into the seaside town of Silivri Sahil, remote, quiet, with a safe house known to Furtado buried between narrow side-streets off the beach promenade.

Tacit threw his revolvers onto the table and himself into a chair alongside, his face buried in his hands.

From the shadows of the dingy room into which they had been brought, Inquisitor Furtado lurched. "What the hell's the matter with you two?"

"Watch your tongue, Furtado," warned Tacit. "We left our friend in that place."

"I don't care who you lost. What the hell were you playing at, starting a war in the inquisitional headquarters?" he cried, glaring at Isabella.

"It wasn't us," she retorted. "Inquisitor Odams. He seemed overly keen to return us to the Vatican."

Tacit needed a drink, to silence the mocking in his head. He jumped up, snatching a bottle from the sideboard and drank deeply, savouring the burn and twist of the strong liquor in his throat and then, moments later, in his mind.

"Sandrine Prideux," he growled, taking the bottle from his lips and looking hard at Furtado. "The wolf. Did they find her, do you know? Did they... kill her?"

Furtado shook his head, dropping his head into the palm of a hand. "No, they've found nothing... yet."

At once Tacit looked over at Isabella and they relaxed. "If they've not found a body, she must have got away! Thank God!" He took her into his arms and they held each other.

"Can one of you tell me just what is going on?" Furtado asked, looking at them with something resembling discomfort at their embrace. "There's chaos at the moment in Constantinople. Inquisitors with their spirits up, people looking for you, Tacit, saying all manner of ugly things. Seems like Rome all over again."

"It's not how it looks," said Isabella.

"You're building one hell of a reputation, Tacit, but then again, that's nothing new."

"So why come looking for me, Furtado, if you're so disagreeable?" he replied, letting Isabella go and taking up the bottle. "If you're so disapproving, so suspicious?"

"Who said I was disapproving? Suspicious? No, I trust you. You're one of the few I *do* trust, Tacit. Seems to me a lot of the Inquisition at Constantinople have… questionable allegiances." His eyes swept the room, to the other Inquisitors amongst them and back again. Tacit knew at once it was his way of trying to unite them. "Inquisitors, they like to win. And many seem to under the impression that the side that is winning is aligned with the Devil." He nodded, seeing their faces. "Victory, it might come at a cost, but some just want to taste it, however it might stick in the craw."

"So what are you saying?" asked Isabella.

"It's why I came looking for you, me and the other Inquisitors here. You know there's been a call? For all Inquisitors to return to the Vatican?"

"For what purpose?" asked Isabella.

"To defend the city."

"From what?"

"Enemies," Furtado replied, "whoever they are. And a lot have already answered the call and gone back there. Seems like Odams was answering the call, looking to take you with him."

"The Darkest Hand," added Isabella. "If rumour is true, they've infiltrated every office, every nation, every position of power! But the Vatican as well?"

The voice in Tacit flared and retched through the dizzying churn of alcohol, demanding that he should return.

"We should go back," said Tacit.

"After all that I've told you, after all that just happened, you want to go back now?"

"I agree," said Isabella. "Poldek, it's them, they're trying to fool you, in here." She put her hand up to his head.

"Look, we need find out what is going on. What else do you propose we do?" he asked. "Where else can we go? Take a boat to China? Try and find Poré? It seems to be me we have only one choice. And that is to go there. To face this evil."

"But the Vatican?" Isabella shook her head. "I don't like it. I don't like the command it has over people. Over you," she said, reaching out to him.

Fucking whore. Bitch. Ignore her.

Tacit watched Isabella, silent, his dark eyes feasting on her, and he had to battle to wrench them away. The voice rattled imploringly inside him, demanding that he return, back to the Vatican, go at once. He wondered how long he could keep up the pretence, the pretence of knowing that it was all just a matter of time, a matter of time until he did as he was bid and he went to his calling. After all, it was inevitable, just as End Times were now inevitable, now that the vial Poré had been seized had almost certainly been opened. And he wondered then, more strongly than ever, just what point there was in fighting any more? He wanted to cry out, to reveal his turmoil. A scuffle came from the entrance and drew him back into the basement, aware of fighting on the steps into the room, a bound figure being dragged in.

The captured man, scared, serpentine, tore at the ties which held, hissing and spitting like a wild animal beneath his bonds.

"We found him skulking," said the Inquisitor, pushing the man into the centre of the room with his boot and pulling away the gag which covered his mouth. "Outside. Close to the promenade, down one of the avenues."

"I wasn't skulking!" spat the man, his face partially covered by his robe which had ridden up and which he fought to pull from his features so he could see and speak clearly. "I was looking for Tacit."

"Bishop Basquez!" he exclaimed, on seeing the man's face.

"Kill me if you wish, Tacit," shrieked Basquez, clutched in the giant man's murderous hands, "but for God's sake don't go back to the Vatican!"

207

SIXTY-SIX

The Vatican. Vatican City.

Adansoni's welcoming smile to his old friend was as broad as his hands were held wide, but Strettavario noticed that the Cardinal made no effort to step towards him in greeting, instead keeping the writing desk between them.

"Welcome back, Father Strettavario!" he called lightly. "I trust your journey south proved... instructive?"

"Most," Strettavario replied precisely.

"And did you manage to find our errant Bishop?"

"I did."

"And was he forthcoming?"

"I know why he fled, if that's what you mean. I know what he discovered. What terrified him so much. What made him flee the city, the city that, despite all he is and says and does, he loves very much. The city he did not wish to leave, but felt that if he did not, his life was certainly in danger."

The comment was left hanging. Each waited for the other to speak. Neither did, and it was the pale-eyed Priest who relented first.

"Do you not have anything to say, Javier? After all, you are Cardinal Secretary of State? I have never known you to be at a loss for words."

Adansoni watched his friend keenly, his eyes watery, the bags around them heavy and clotted. Still he said nothing.

Strettavario considered the silence and moved away from the spot where he had found himself rooted during their stilted greeting, stepping over towards the fireplace and the mantelpiece above it. The fire wasn't lit, but out of habit Strettavario was drawn towards it, to stand with one arm resting against its ledge, his other brushing the smooth marble clear of specks of soot and dirt, attempting to promote a façade of calm even though his heart beat like a funeral drum and his guts writhed and twisted like tongues of flame. There was dirt on the mantelpiece, unusual in that it was there. The Vatican, especially the Cardinal Secretary of State's high quarters, was always pristine, but the whole place had become untidy, filthy even.

It seemed to Strettavario that much of the city had begun to tarnish, the halls and churches seeming less cared for. Degraded, as if it all seemed like too much effort. Corridors were marked with the prints of passing shoes, litter, blown by the cold winter winds, gathered in the flowerbeds or was strewn across pathways, a degradation which would never have been allowed to happen before.

"Things have slipped, Cardinal Secretary of State Adansoni, since I've been away?"

"You speak like you have authority here, Father?"

"I have my eyes and ears. I care about my city."

Adansoni shrugged, holding his arms out wider still, supercilious smugness engraved in the lines of his face. "We find ourselves in a war. We need to tighten our belts, make sacrifices, just like our neighbours."

"And the closing of the doors into the Vatican? The shutting of the ways into and out of the city? Is that because of the war also?"

"One must take measures. We are not exempt from the sacrifices and horrors of war. We have many enemies, Father Strettavario."

"Oh, don't worry, Cardinal Bishop Adansoni, I know that our faith has an enemy. And I know its name."

"So what was it that Bishop Basquez had discovered?" Adansoni asked, side-stepping the comment he perceived as an accusation.

Strettavario spoke like a statement of fact. "That Tacit is Satan."

Adansoni's face darkened but the smile remained with the skill of a shrewd politician. "A bold suggestion!"

"It's all very obvious really," Strettavario continued. "Tacit was born in the year 1877, the very same year, the same month, of the first attempt to draw the Seven Princes through. That ritual, it was only partially successful. There was not enough blood shed upon the place, given by the Russian and Turkish forces, armies watched over by Czar Alexander, an early convert to the Darkest Hand, and assured that a doorway into Hell would be opened by the conflict. No, it was not a large enough sacrifice to draw all Seven Princes through, but it was enough for *one* to come through, the most terrible of all the Princes of Hell. Satan. And into the body of Poldek Tacit that demon wormed himself.

"How much of this young Poldek knew I don't know, although there must've come a time, perhaps when he joined the Inquisition, or shortly before maybe, I don't know, when he began to suspect that not everything was as it should be with him. The voices. Tacit always talked of the voices.

And the lights, these empowering lights. Of course, we always knew about his power, his great strength, his indefatigability, the rage in the man. And yet he was not always this way. As a child he was gentle and kind, a beacon of decency, of hope, someone who people would go to, someone respected and admired. No, I suspect he only began to grow suspicious, became aware of the darkness that lay in him, when the Inquisition took him in and showed what it was to hate and hurt and to kill, when they turned him into the man he now is."

Adansoni applauded, a slow arrogant handclap. "And all this you have learnt from our sly traitorous Bishop, have you?" He stepped out from behind his desk, moving closer to the Priest, who instinctively backed away, taking little steps away from the Cardinal. "I am impressed. Most impressed."

"Of course, Satan is just one of the Devil's foot soldiers," Strettavario continued, manoeuvring himself to put a little more distance between himself and Adansoni. "Mischievous, destructive. But he is only that, a foot soldier. The real power, the real danger, lies in those who these foot soldiers serve. The Antichrist.

"Cardinal Bishop Berberino. Korek, Casado, they all discovered this, that the Antichrist had returned, just as Pope Leo had foretold all those years ago. They discovered the truth and they all paid the price for it. For who the Antichrist is. For what he is trying to do."

"And what is that exactly, Father Strettavario?"

"To bring about End Times."

Adansoni closed his eyes, shaking his head and making a piffling noise in his nose. "And so we come to the one who has opened the Seventh Seal, the one who has taken the vials out into the world? Poré."

Strettavario fixed him with a fierce unyielding stare. "No," he said.

"No?"

"Poré is many things, but he's not who you appear to be suggesting he is. Because I know who you are, Javier."

Adansoni's eyes flashed, shimmered with a cruelty Strettavario had never seen before in any one, let alone his friend. "And who is that?"

"*You* are the Antichrist. Pope Leo XIII, he foresaw it, foresaw you. In 1884. You were there, in the chapel that night, when the Devil visited Pope Leo and he received that vision, the vision which he revealed to all in that chamber. That was when you realised. That was when you knew the moment had come to go and look for Tacit, under the pretence of being a missionary, to find Poldek Tacit and set in motion the series of events that would bring you to the very crest of authority and command and dominion over all the world, with your Lieutenant at your side!

"Each of the Cardinals, Berberino, Korek, they knew, or supposed. They were a risk to you, your plans. The Seers, they discovered your name and were about to reveal it. Word was got to Casado, another whom you needed to murder, perhaps because of this, but I suppose he had to be got rid of anyway in order for you to take his place as Cardinal Secretary of State? Because once you assumed that role, you could begin to corrupt and control, as you are doing, all in the Vatican and beyond in the Inquisition, desecrating as you do all minds, innocent and wicked alike!"

A shadow had fallen across Adansoni's face, concealing all of his features like a shroud. But his eyes glowered from the black, pinpricks of ruby fire, precise, fixed on the old Father, lidless, unwavering and malevolent. "Goodness, you really are quite the brilliant mind yourself, aren't you, Strettavario?" he spoke coldly, easing forward from the shadow. A change had come upon Adansoni. His kindly ambassadorial features had been spoiled, churned into a devilish mask of venom, loathsome and depraved. "Any chance you could enlighten me as to the game that Poré then is playing?"

Strettavario resisted the urge to cry out. "I wouldn't call the killing of all in the world a game."

"Indeed," said Adansoni, "I have been wondering about what Poré is up to. I was hoping you might be able to tell me. After all, there can only be one false Messiah." His eyes flashed dreadfully and he opened his arms, as if to reveal his true self. "One Antichrist."

SIXTY-SEVEN

Silivri Sahil. Turkey.

Tacit sent everyone away, Isabella, Furtado and the other Inquisitors, telling them to go out onto the seafront to breathe the cool night air, to cool their feet in the surf, to find provisions. To give him time alone with Basquez.

The Bishop's shrieked proclamation about Tacit's returning to the Vatican, mirroring the same concerns as Furtado and Isabella, had startled and shifted something in him. The certainty with which the Bishop had spoken his warning had assured Tacit that it was something he was sure he did not want the others to hear, not at this moment.

"How do we know you won't kill him?" asked Furtado.

"You have my word," replied Tacit, his eyes never leaving the Bishop.

"Which means nothing in Constantinople," replied Furtado, before filing out behind Isabella.

Basquez shrank back as the giant man loomed over him, appearing even larger and more monstrous than Basquez remembered. He was ravaged and bowed, marked by the grim trials of his life, beaten up with wounds and injuries, his face scarred and torn. A murderous light hung in his eyes.

In the street outside, the sounds of his party's footsteps faded, merging with the clop and creak of a horse and its cart circling the square behind the house, the shuffle of more feet, the quiet mutter of voices.

"What are you doing here?" He pushed the Bishop back into the chair and stood over him. "Why've you come?"

"I came to find you. I had to find you. To warn you, against him. The Antichrist." Something vicious spat in Tacit's head and he was tempted to dash out the serpentine's man's brains with his bare hands. "You cannot go back to the Vatican, Tacit!" Basquez implored, seeing the heat rise in his face.

"I'll go where the hell I choose! I'll not take orders, not from the likes of you. How the hell did you find me anyway?"

"Father Strettavario."

At once Tacit's anger seemed to dissipate and his eyes narrowed to hear the man's name spoken. "Since when were you and he such good friends to share gossip and news of me?"

"He came to find me, after Casado was murdered."

"And why would he want to do that? No doubt he suspected that you had murdered the Cardinal Secretary of State? Was that it? Had he come for justice? Revenge?"

"Perhaps, at the start, yes. But he left knowing the truth, or at least what I could tell him. It's why he's gone back to the Vatican, to see if he can discover the final few pieces which are missing, to see them with his own eyes, things I have long suspected. I tried to dissuade him, but he wouldn't listen."

"What the hell are you talking about?"

"Adansoni."

The uttering of this name sucked the air out of the room and drew silence in after it.

"Don't you dare try and besmirch the character of that man," Tacit hissed, staring down his finger at the sly shifting figure. "He's worth a thousand of you, Basquez!"

"Perhaps once," nodded the Bishop, "but things have changed."

"What are you trying to suggest?"

"The Vatican is a den of corruption and darkness."

Tacit shook his head and the noise from the voices subsided a little. "This from a man whom no one trusts! Why should I now?"

"I have come here, all the way from Southern Italy, to warn you! Is that not proof enough?"

"Perhaps you came all the way here for retribution?"

"What reason would I have to wish you harm?"

Something resonated in Tacit at the words, a vague memory, a cold sliver of a dark past, Basquez's name on a paper, the Bishop's signature, the mentioning of something which sounded like Basquez's name by Inquisitor Salamanca, his jailer and torturer in the cold depths of Toulouse Inquisitional Prison. Realisation struck him and he bent down, taking hold of the arms of the chair, sealing the man in it. "You! You're the one who tortured me!"

"I only did as I was commanded to do." His voice was like a squeak and he covered his face with an arm, his eyes wide behind it, fearing a blow.

"It was you! You helped send me to Toulouse Prison, sent Salamanca to torture me! You tried to break me, tried to uncover something in me. Peel back the layers, not just of my flesh but also of what lay beneath, what lay in my soul!"

"And what does lie beneath, Tacit?" replied Basquez, once again finding his own spirit, as any cornered animal will do at the death. "Darkness? Hmm? Hell? I know, and that's why I know you cannot go back. Casado also knew as well, and now he's dead."

"I'm not scared of death!"

213

"It's not *your* death which concerns me, Tacit. It's what happens to the rest of us should you go back. Adansoni, he wants you to go back. That's what he is trying to achieve. He needs you."

"So why has Strettavario has gone back to the Vatican?"

"To face him. To try and kill him."

"Has he gone alone?" Basquez's dispassionate face gave him his reply. "Just one man, against such odds? What was he thinking?"

"He was thinking like an Inquisitor."

"Like me then? Like I must do! To go and face him!"

"But you are so much more than simply an Inquisitor, aren't you, Tacit? The lights, the voices? There is something in you, isn't there?"

Tacit bristled with spite. "And is that what you were trying to find when you tortured me?"

"Yes, a bridge, to Hell."

A noise from the door drew them both to look. "Isabella!" cried Tacit, going to her, Basquez using the opportunity to escape from the chair, his prison throughout the interrogation.

"It's all right," she replied, holding out her hands to stop Tacit from coming too close, as if she was scared of him. "It's all right," she repeated, setting them gently upon him, feeling out to him with caution, as if he might be scorching to the touch. "I… I'm not scared." Tears were in her eyes, but they were cold tears of daring as much as tears of love. "Adansoni, what does he want from Poldek?" she asked Basquez, Tacit following her gaze to the man now retreated into a corner. "Why does he need him to join him?"

"What is the Antichrist without protection, the support of his Lieutenant, his greatest Lieutenant? Satan?"

Tacit stepped towards him, measuring himself against the man. "So why have you come here to speak with me, if you think me corrupt? Think me possessed?"

"One thing I learnt about you in Toulouse is that you are not beyond salvation, that you are not wholly consumed by that which lies in you. There is still goodness in you. There is darkness in you, Tacit, but it's not utterly filled with evil, not yet. That is why you must not go back to the Vatican until you are ready. To do so will corrupt you utterly in his presence, defeat you finally and drag you to his side, forever his Lieutenant, in his employ."

"And all this you knew, years ago?"

"We suspected you, have done for years, as I'm sure you knew. Casado, Berberino, Korek, along with others in the Holy See."

"And Strettavario?"

"He suspected, but it was only when he found Casado's journal that his fears, his concerns about you, were confirmed."

"Oh my darling!" wept Isabella, taking Tacit into her arms, but only for a moment. "What do you propose we do?"

"Stay on the path you were following," answered Basquez. "Stop Poré. Leave the Vatican to Strettavario."

"But where is Poré?" asked Isabella, the question shouted to the heavens.

"He is aboard a ship destined for Nantes," replied Basquez, with certainty. "He is bringing Chinese workers. For what purpose, I don't know." Suspicion darkened Tacit's face. "I have made it my business to know the comings and goings of people and things. Just as I knew of this safe house."

"What are you going to do now?" asked Tacit.

"I'm going to follow Strettavario back to the Vatican, to do what I can to help him if I'm not too late, to do what I can to bring about the Antichrist's downfall. Perhaps that way I can redeem myself in the eyes of those I have wronged, those I have failed."

SIXTY-EIGHT

The Vatican. Vatican City.

Strettavario didn't give Adansoni the opportunity to prepare himself for an attack.

In a flash, he launched himself at the old man, fingers taut white like murderous talons, his hands stretched out in front of him, reaching for the Cardinal's thin grey neck. But it wasn't there. At super-human speed, Adansoni knocked Strettavario down.

The old Father landed on his hands and knees and prepared to attack again. Before he could, Adansoni followed through with a wide sweeping kick into Strettavario's guts, doubling the man up. Adansoni kicked him again, this time in the face with his other foot, tumbling him like a rag doll into the table, sending the chair he struck flying, blood in this mouth, teeth broken.

The prostrate man groaned, his body and mind feeling detached from the rest of him, sensing everything sink away and nausea rise. But he had enough wits to feel hands on his neck, weakly trying to lash out and remove them, open his pale eyes, delirium creeping into his mind and spinning his vision.

Adansoni was on top of him, barred teeth gritted, his hard bony hands around Strettavario's throat, the air trapped inside him. Strettavario's right hand swung down to his hip, clumsily reaching for the handle of his revolver. But his old friend effortlessly slapped the weapon from his hand and then repeated the blow, this time to Strettavario's face, beating it hard to one side, revealing the glint of coiled armour beneath the collar of his cloak. Adansoni laughed, taking hold of his shirt and tearing it away, revealing a long length of glittering armour beneath.

He laughed, a cruel cutting laugh. "Pathetic," he roared. "What are you trying to do? Play at being an Inquisitor, Strettavario?"

"I was an Inquisitor once!" Strettavario spat back, blood between his broken teeth. "And we are commanded to fight against you, the Antichrist, with all the strength we possess! And that is what I'll do."

Speaking the old vow sent new strength through Strettavario's veins. He pushed Adansoni aside, rolling up onto his knees, coming at the old Cardinal again. But as he reached him, something cold and sharp and concealed in the sleeve of Adansoni's right arm slid effortlessly through his robe, scaled armour and skin, sinking deep into the Priest's guts. The air choked in his lungs and his pale eyes turned pink, growing large in their open sockets. Breathless words were on his tongue, bloody spittle dripping from the tip of it, as he sank silent to his knees.

Adansoni stood back, admiring the eight inches of bloodied white steel he had pulled from the mortally wounded man, setting the blade onto the table next to him and wiping his hand on a cloth alongside.

"You always had a soft spot for Tacit, didn't you, Father Strettavario?" he asked, tutting with his tongue against his teeth, disapproving, the old Priest on his knees in the centre of the room, every move showing as agony in his face. "Sometimes I wondered if perhaps you could have been of more use to me in my pursuit of power, have brought about my ascension quicker. You did help, of course, many times, in Sarajevo for example, ensuring that Tacit failed to stop the assassination of Archduke

Ferdinand. You were sent there with that express job, and you succeeded. Succeeded in ensuring the war happened unabated. Exemplary! Although I suppose you never knew? Pathetic!

"You were always so fucking loyal which made you so fucking blind!" Adansoni kicked out with his right boot, turning Strettavario over so he lay on his side, the wound in his stomach torn wider, his guts and blood seeping out onto the floor through the rip in his armour and shirt. Voiceless words were on the Father's bloody lips, his breath growing shallow and frail. "Rest assured that Tacit will return to me and once he does, together we will reign together over the wasteland that will be left once this war has run its course. After all, it is our combined prophecy, me the master, he the Lieutenant, my protector."

"You cannot win, Adansoni," croaked Strettavario, summoning the words with every final effort he could muster, holding the remainder of his guts from spilling out over the floor with his fist. "You will not! Even in my death, you shall be defeated. Evil cannot endure. It cannot conquer." His voice sounded far away, distant, like the room in which he lay dying.

But the Antichrist merely laughed. "Oh I think you'll find that it does. And that I will."

He looked down on Strettavario, disdain unexpectedly hooking the side of his face. His eyes flashed, like a cat's before a kill, and he raised his foot, bringing the heel down onto the old man's face. The old Father's nose splintered and the bones behind it cracked. Adansoni lifted his boot again, driving it down hard, obliterating the bridge of Strettavario's nose, turning it to a sodden flaccid sack of crimson.

He lifted his foot once more, driving down with all the force he possessed. The front of the old man's skull collapsed, the sockets of his eyes pulverising and turning in on themselves, his pale eyeballs popping free. He kicked down for a fourth time, crushing one of the eyeballs flat, tearing through skin, cracking bone. And again, smashing through Strettavario's skull, gore flicking up around Adansoni's heel, the old Father's face now a gaping hole filled with blood and brains, his mouth horribly open in a silent final scream.

His old friend chuckled and brushed his shoe clean on the old Father's clothes.

The port ticket office rang with the clatter of heels on hard floors and stamps pounding papers. Beyond the bank of windows, the Turkish port of Izmir sat somewhere in the fug of cold sea mist. The clerk behind the ticket desk could tell that the woman who approached his station was sophisticated and alluring by the way she walked, despite hiding her face behind a colourful scarf. Protection against the cold and prying eyes. She moved with a tempestuous ease in her movements, a long graceful arm holding a single small brown suitcase.

"Good morning, madam," he said, in English.

"Good morning."

Her accent surprised and captivated him for a moment. "You are travelling alone or with your family?"

"Alone."

It seemed to the woman that he was checking behind her to make sure this was really the case.

"Is it not acceptable for a woman to travel on her own?" she asked him.

"You are French?"

"From France originally, yes."

"And what is your business in Turkey?"

"Whatever my business was, it is not my business any more. Or yours."

She unwound her headdress in the warmth, revealing her face to the ticket-seller. He hesitated on seeing her raging beauty.

"Forgive me," he said, correcting his papers in front of him, as a way of hiding his awkwardness. "It is because of the war that I need to ask these questions. I would not usually do so, but my superiors, they demand it of us."

"Of course."

"And where are you bound, madam?" he asked, coughing into his hand and drawing down the front of his suit, his authority returned, preparing to issue a ticket for the voyage.

"Rome," said Sandrine. "The Vatican."

SIXTY-NINE

VANCOUVER. CANADA.

Ten thousand miles of wide blue sky stretched above the port, only the suggestion of clouds, lace-thin and very high, in the heavens. Gulls squawked greedily as they scoured the quayside looking for discarded titbits upon which to feast, slapping this way and that across the wooden boards with their bright orange feet or cutting tight smooth circles through the pale Vancouver sun spreading its wide chalky fingers of light across the bay.

The great black transporter vessel, nameless but for a tarnished enamelled white number painted on its hull, had been at the port only for six hours, nestling deep in the dark green waters, but already its stores had been emptied of its cargo brought from the Far East.

Gerard-Maurice Poré stared at the vast sides of the ship, his eyes working from bow to stern and back again, watching every facet and nook of the boat. Amongst the crush of people on the quayside, importers, merchant sailors, port officials, porters, soldiers and government officials, he looked like any other foreigner caught up in the vortex of war, flung thousands of miles from home and wondering if and when he would ever see France again.

He could feel the feather of the sun's heat on the back of his scrawny neck, ringed by a crisp white shirt to give his presence at the port authority and sincerity. There was a chill wintry wind coming in off the ocean that made him shiver and draw his travelling overcoat tighter around his hollow frame.

"Well, everything seems to be in order, Mr Archer," called a round voice, padding up from the quayside behind him while checking the notes on the paperwork Pablo had provided clutched firm in his plump hand for a final time. The smear-haired man, his dark suit buttoned too tight at his middle, stepped alongside Poré, a boastful look swelling his paunchy features, as together they gazed out across the waters towards the vessel. "It's a magnificent ship," he continued generously, playing with an ostentatious cigar between his fingers which he occasionally threatened to smoke, but never did. "One of our best. A gem of the oceans. One hundred thousand tons. Twenty-three knots. A hold that can easily carry twelve hundred men. Already has ten thousand miles of sea travel under her prow this year alone."

The facts came quickly to the slick port official.

"It's a rusting wreck," replied Poré.

"It's quite seaworthy," the officer stuttered, the veil of assurance slipping briefly from his commanding demeanour.

"Perhaps," replied Poré. "It didn't sink on its voyage getting here."

"And on board," continued the man, beginning to perspire under the weak sun and the tone of his client, "conditions are far from uncomfortable. Your cargo, Mr Archer, it has been unloaded and all appears well, you'll be pleased to hear. The men you've brought, they seem to be in good spirits. Much laughter amongst them. Clearly they are pleased to have arrived in Canada. Not pining for home. I hate it when they pine for home. Makes a man sick to do so over a long period of time. Seen it a lot in my merchant days. You can treat a man with any wound on his body, with a disease in his system, but when the wound he carries is in his head," and the fat official tapped at his temple with a chubby manicured finger, "there is nothing that can be done to heal that. A couple of them seemed to have picked up a sneeze or two on the voyage. A runny nose here and there. A little chill from off the Bering Sea to blame, no doubt. Nothing unusual. Even at this time of year, the winds from the Bering Straight, from off the Chukchi Sea beyond, can be hostile. But otherwise, they are in the peak of fitness. Better, dare I boast, if you forgive me, than when they first stepped aboard the ship, I wager."

He took a look back over his shoulder towards the bank on the boundary of the port to the road which climbed up to the railway goods station before returning to his babbling. "But no, nothing can be done for a man who's gone sick in his head," he resumed on his previous tack, "but your fellows, they seem a sprightly bunch. Good ship you see," he insisted, turning back to the vessel and nodding knowingly. "They've been well kept on their journey. Fed and watered. We do things differently here. Take pride in our work. Everything we take under our responsibility is *our* responsibility." He nudged an insistent arm into Poré and pushed his cigar into his mouth. Around it he mumbled, "Well, shall we go up and see them?"

Without reply, and relieved to finally have the garrulous man's torrent brought to a temporary end, Poré nodded, turning his back on the harbour, and they walked along the quayside together, the waddling port officer with the bundle of customs and import papers under his left arm, his right hand working the cigar into and out of his mouth in between short puffs, his head turned up in an authoritative and supercilious manner. His experience and standing in the port ensured that he would never say anything untoward to the strangely quiet man who had brought the Chinese to Canada, but the lacquered well-fed official privately thought Mr Archer a most peculiar character. In his experience, those involved with the import and export of provisions and goods for the war effort seemed almost always open to discussion and rumour, but this man appeared most reserved, almost rudely so.

They stepped off the stone quayside and over the narrow bridge which separated the port from the city beyond.

"So you work for the British government?" asked the port official, hoping for a response he never got. "You seem to be making some headway at last with all that business, now that the Americans have come on board." He continued against the stony silence. "After the Somme and Verdun, I did wonder what it was all for, as I'm sure you did. Whether we would ever be done with the fighting, but I suppose that's the thing, you never really know with war. You just have to keep going. A war of attrition. That's what they call it, don't they?

"I meet a lot of Germans in my line of work and let me tell you, they don't have the heart for it. Surprised they ever did. Maybe at the beginning they did, when they thought it was all going to be so easy for them, before they realised that they had picked a fight with the wrong nation, underestimated the size of the task in hand. It's what I do, estimating. Have done it all my life. Well, as a port official you have to estimate. Estimate size of cargoes, size of ships, how long they will stay in port, how long they'll need to unload and refuel. It's what I do. Estimate. Perhaps the Germans should have come to me for advice before they started?" He pretended to laugh. "Although, how the Germans could have underestimated this war, I don't know. They might have an empire, but it's no empire compared to the British and French empires, not when you put them together. So, are you French working for the British government or are you British but from France?"

"Does it matter?" replied Poré.

"No," replied the man, shaking his head. "Just interested. See, it seems to me as if the Germans know that they are beat. Seems to me they are looking for a way out. Of course, they've invested so much that they're not inclined to just drop everything and surrender, but it seems to me that they must know that they are beat. All right, Russia is finished, on its knees with revolution, but now that America has come into the war, it's only a matter of time until the end arrives. And you probably can't wish for it to come too soon, can you?"

There was a long grey goods train standing in the station. Poré heard and smelt the thing half a mile from the platform, sizzling and popping, the engine turning the air sulphurous and coarse.

"So the Chinese," the rotund official continued, "they are for the front line, are they?" Poré said nothing, but the quaymaster was not so willing to give up his line of enquiry. "If you beg my pardon, they don't look much like fighting men."

"And what does a fighting man look like, pray tell?" replied Poré, in a rare moment of conversation.

"Fair point," replied the official, nodding, pleased to have drawn a response out of this stubbornly quiet man.

By now both men could hear a great noise of Chinese chatter upon the platform or from the train they were trying to board like a exodus. Poré and the official could smell them as well, the tangible reek of filthy bodies, like that given off by cattle driven into crates and sent out on a long airless voyage. The port official looked across at Poré fleetingly.

"I wondered if perhaps they should have been given the opportunity to wash before they were loaded onto the transport train?" he asked, a little sheepishly.

"That won't be necessary," replied Poré. "There is little time. We have to get on."

"Of course."

They reached the great archway leading onto the railway station and the official stopped.

"This is as far as my jurisdiction goes," he said, planting the soggy chewed end of his cigar back in his mouth and bringing his hand towards Poré.

The man took it suspiciously.

"Good luck," said the official, and squeezing Poré's hand he was surprised how much strength it possessed for a man so frail and small.

SEVENTY

The Vatican. Vatican City.

Adansoni paraded into the council chamber like a conquering king, his entourage of inquisitional guards striding behind him, and headed directly for the Pope's ostentatious chair without ceremony or hesitation. Inquisitors in his wake swept to either side of its ornate golden arms, staring muscularly out into the auditorium, like bulldogs waiting to be let loose.

"I think you may be in the wrong seat?" one of the Cardinals gathered in the circular hall suggested, indicating with a limp prod of a wilting finger the Cardinal Secretary of State's usual mundane seat alongside the elaborate golden throne on which he had set himself. "You're in Pope Benedict's chair?"

"And you have a problem with that, Cardinal Mardell?" Adansoni replied, generously.

The two Cardinals stared at each other, one dumbstruck, the other watching with vacant disdain. It seemed to everyone in the chamber that the air had turned suddenly sulphurous and cold, and that a pressure had grown in the ears. A clock ticked somewhere close by. The muffled clack and clop of the Cardinals' shoes on the passageway outside the chamber doors sounded like deadened hammers. Above them, chairs being drawn back in the hall across stone floors screeched and growled. The grumbling quiet mutter of distrusting voices grew against the backdrop of the tightening stretch of inquisitorial gloves being gripped in fists.

And then Cardinal Mardell screamed, like a madman, "Yes I do! Yes I do have a problem! You're not Pope yet!" he exclaimed, thrusting with a finger, his face seeming to boil up into a cauldron of heat and desperation. "Though I know *that* is what you desire, Adansoni! Where is Pope Benedict, Cardinal Secretary of State?" He spoke the title with venomous disdain. "Where is he? We demand to know!"

Cardinal Mardell, always known for his delicacy and forbearance, was eaten up with rage, now on his feet and stalking towards Adansoni and his legion of Inquisitors, pushing chairs and tables in his path aside, his fierce wide eyes firm on the man. "Tell us where he is, you... you devil!

Tell us! Where is he? I know he returned months ago, but we have seen neither sight nor sound of him since he came back to our city, the city whose doors you have decided to lock up!"

"Not entirely true!" retorted Adansoni, wafting an idle hand from the rich chair. "I hear Pope Benedict often, too often, as I pass the door to his residence. Banging on the door, shouting, all the time. It's enough to drive one insane. To do something foolish."

"Then he should be released! At once! This man is our figurehead!"

"He is unwell. We hold him for his own protection."

"This will not stand."

"And I suppose neither will you." Adansoni's eyes were like poisonous slits. He signalled with a casually raised finger from the armrest of his grand throne and two Darkest Hand Inquisitors stepped forward, drawing their revolvers.

"What is this?" asked Mardell, his hands extended towards Adansoni. "A coup?"

His answer was delivered by a shattering onslaught of bullets, spinning and tumbling the man backwards to the floor, the Cardinal's body twitching for a brief moment before lying distorted and still, his body bloody and torn. Gunfire ricocheted around the auditorium, monstrously loud, battering around the beams and the topmost rafters of the chamber, eventually being taken away, sucked into the fabric of the walls and roof. As the terrible violence shrank, the final breath passed from the decimated bleeding man, heard by everyone in the hall, sounding even more desperate and small after the terror moments before.

Adansoni laughed, applauding loudly, before instantly crushing any emotion from his appearance. He waved dismissively to remove the body.

"Saints preserve us!"

"I suspect they won't, Cardinal Larkins," said Adansoni. "You can go too." The remaining Inquisitors stepped forward and heaved him from his chair. "Take him outside and shoot him," Adansoni called after them. "But make sure you do so away from any witnesses. We can't have a rumour getting about that things have turned... unforeseen in the Holy See. Not quite yet, anyway." His eyes flashed with a horror never before seen in the Vatican and he turned them back on the trembling terrified congregation. Some half stood in terror, their hands clawed to their desks, their eyes disbelieving, trembling muttering mouths of silence. Others had already bolted for the doors, but found them policed on the other side by Inquisitors, who pushed them roughly back, like prisoners in holding-pens. Most however had remained seated, bloodless faces, paralysed with shock and fear.

Adansoni stood and looked down on them from the platform on which the throne was placed. "For generations you have worked for the Holy See. Unquestioning. Unflinching. Doing as the Holy See guided. Let me assure you that nothing has changed there. You continue to work for the Holy See. What has changed is the manner in which we now do things."

"It was never this way!" exclaimed Innocenti, unable to control his tongue. There was defiance in his words, but terror was in his eyes at his outburst and what it might bring him.

"Are you questioning my methods, Cardinal?"

"What has become of you, Adansoni?"

"Become of me? If anything has become of me it is that I am finally embracing what is mine, and has been decreed to me for all times."

"But this behaviour, it is most ungodly! Devilish!"

"And your question is?"

"Murdering Cardinals of the Holy See!"

"That is not a question, Innocenti. It is a statement of fact, and one that I have committed and shall commit again, if required."

"Cardinal Bishop Adansoni –"

"Cardinal Secretary of State," corrected Adansoni, raising his index finger.

"Have a care, Adansoni. There are paintings in the Vatican which are vomiting blood, Cardinal! Fountains pour with the stuff!"

"Why should that concern me?"

"Why indeed?" hissed the Cardinal. "For now I understand!"

The Secretary of State's face had turned crimson and fierce. "I don't like your rhetoric, Innocenti! I had high hopes for you, but perhaps you need to be removed as well?"

Adansoni beckoned and heavy inquisitional hands clapped on Innocenti's shoulders from behind him, snatching around his arms and dragging him from the chamber, screaming and kicking as he went.

"Is there anyone else who needs reminding whom they answer to?" Adansoni swept the chamber with a glare for any more dissension, which was not forthcoming. The colour was teasing back out of his face, liver spots and the anaemia of old age returning. "Good. The Pope is currently engaged, engaged with his madness. For now, *I* will be taking control.

The first thing that the Holy See will do is focus its efforts on finding the man called Poldek Tacit. He seems reluctant about returning to me. Every available Priest, Bishop and acolyte shall be thrown into the task of seeking him out and bringing him back to the Vatican. It seems that he is proving to be a little… unenthusiastic in joining us. But his reluctance is only a matter of time. The Inquisition, with their ever-swelling numbers, they shall remain here, an army for our fortress."

"An army against whom?" someone dared to ask.

"Our misguided enemies," replied Adansoni, assuredly. "For they are many. And I *do* expect them to come eventually."

SEVENTY-ONE

Somewhere crossing Canada.

Twenty cattle trucks were pulling through the falling snows of Canada, twenty trucks bringing Poré's promise to mainland Europe.

His promise to the world? God's wrath.

Every one of the trucks had been sealed up and locked, each one containing the Chinese workers, packed in tight, sweating and groping blindly in the darkness of the rattling, rolling cages. To hear the pens shunt and roll past through the silently still landscape, the train's clattering chug over the steel tracks, the squealing shrieks from inside the stalls, it sounded like a train of terrified pigs heading for slaughter, not of men brought to war.

On the side of each truck were brass plates stamped with three letters, pressed deep into the metal.

C.L.C.

The Chinese Labour Corps, drawn into service by commission from the British government.

When the Chinese labourers had first been funnelled inside the trucks, already disoriented and unsteady from their long voyage across the great China Sea, confused by the light and the time and the frigid climate, with no time to collect their bearings, no chance to recover their sea legs, they had cried out as one, pleading on knees, like slaves to masters, exclaiming that they needed time, just a little time to taste the fresh cold air. To heal in its cool embrace.

It was a request denied.

As they were pushed towards the waiting wagons, it wasn't that they *thought* there wasn't enough room in the trucks to hold them. It was only that, once inside the pens, they *knew* that there was simply not enough room for so many. Some disobeyed their new masters and risked family honour, fighting to break free, fleeing from the crowds, only to be hit and pushed back inside by the soldiers lining the way, bloodied and bruised, a warning to their fellow men that an even greater penalty would be exacted on any should they persist and not do as was commanded, if they didn't go quietly into the carriages and wait patiently for the train to depart.

Many still did resist, at least to begin with, pushing and shoving back at the soldiers and the ranks of workers, burrowing through the crowds, some even managing to make a run for it, only to be shot down in five paces from the platform or beaten and broken open, bloodied husks in front of the waiting lines, their foolishness made an example of so that no one else was tempted to make a run for it. After the first few were caught and killed in this way, the workers filed into the wagons like drugged cattle into their awaiting pens. And when the last one was pushed inside, Poré, who had watched proceedings impassively, his face a veil of cold, nodded, satisfied that they were ready to move on.

Doors were drawn shut across the wagons on heavy iron runners, and moments later the dull sound of the catches dropping was heard. A long shrill whistle rang the entire length of the train and the carriages ground slowly forward, grating and gripping against the slippery iced track, metal screaming on metal.

Inside each carriage was almost total darkness, filled with the jabber of high-pitched Chinese voices, panicked cries and protestations, mixed up with their stink and an immediate strange relief that the full carriages were hot with bodies, chasing away the chill of the cold Canadian winter, all of them bound so close together, the heat filling the narrow spaces.

But after four hours on the railway line, and with the heat and huddle of bodies growing slick and tighter still, any initial relief was tainted with the return of despairing cries for compassion and release. And banging, endless banging upon the carriage walls, cries and pleas heard by Poré and the other soldiers on the train, but always going unanswered as their filth and canker festered.

227

SEVENTY-TWO

HALIFAX. CANADA.

The transport train had drawn its sinuous way through the Canadian wastes for weeks, but it seemed to all on board like months, both to those imprisoned and to those who had had to listen to the awful crying of the Chinese.

"Air! Air!", those trapped inside cried, their protestations and pleas now clearly audible, as the train began its slow descent into the port on the eastern side of Canada. The pitiful sound that squeezed from the coaches was like a sludge of noise, inhuman, at odds with the pristine light and air of the world beyond those locked pens.

The wild Canadian countryside had given way to the industrialised town and port of Halifax, metal and stone, smoke and bustle, replacing the deathlessness and silence of the Canadian prairies and dramatic rise and fall of the snow-covered mountains. The train began to decelerate, grinding imperceptibly to a halt, the long lengths of carriage sliding into the waiting station.

With a final grating clamour the train shuddered to a stop, great clouds of smoke and steam twisting and hissing out of the engine, filling the station platform with its caustic stink, as if some fissure had been opened up in the ground from a deeply buried fault line. There was crying and lamenting coming out of all the carriages, the sound like that of bleating terrified sheep brought to an abattoir.

A figure stood on the platform waiting, his grey silhouette emerging from the slowly dissipating clouds of steam fizzing all about him. His young searching eyes ran the length of the carriages and back again, looking for any movement off the train, any signs of life other than the wailing and the pleading coming from the locked-up wagons. At the sound of a carriage door opening and then slamming shut, he glanced towards the front of the ruby-red locomotive and the man walking through the steam to meet him.

His tall gaunt appearance, masked by the heavy coat he wore to fend off the chill, looked even more heinous than he remembered previously in Egypt.

"Poré!" he called, going forward to shake his hand.

Poré took it, not looking at him, instead studying the grey heavens, immediately asking, "Are we ready to go on? Is the boat in harbour and prepared for us?"

"It is," replied Pablo, almost feeling the urge to laugh at the lack of greeting or hospitality shown by the man. But the smell from the carriages, now discernible through the stink of coal fire, and the baleful cries from the poor creatures inside, cut away any thoughts of humour. "All is ready," he nodded solemnly. "All is prepared for the next stage of your journey."

As if on cue, British soldiers and officials, bearing governmental marks and symbols on their suit breasts and lapels, appeared from the shadows and streamed onto the platform, the doors to the transport train thrown open. At once the true horror of what was awaiting them inside revealed itself, in sight, sound and smell, the surviving hordes of Chinese spilling out into the station like detritus from an opened drain.

A stinking fleshy wave of pestilence and disease oozed onto the platform. Some hobbled on wavering unsteady legs, shielding their eyes from the pale Canadian sun after having been entombed for so long. Others limped or half crawled out of the cells. A few dragged themselves forward on hands and knees, collapsing onto the cold stone platform, as if the chilled wet stone were some nirvana, just glad to be free of those terrible carriages.

Soldiers took hold of them and whisked them away. Behind, in the depths of the compartments, the stinking residue of those who had not survived the journey remained, crushed bodies and the waste of days penned up together in the infernal sweaty heat, covering the floor and filling up corners.

What came off the train was barely human, stinking reeking fetid things, thin and sickly, gaunt and yellowed as if jaundiced, things inhabiting nightmares rather than human beings.

"Good God!" one of the officials was heard to say, the back of his hand to his nose, stepping backwards two steps on seeing the detritus of mankind vomit out onto the platform. "This cannot be allowed!" he said.

"Keep the sentiments to yourself, Corporal," muttered a passing Captain, his face hardening against the smell.

They watched as the shambling coughing crowd was rounded up and moved away from the train and the station.

"What are we doing in this war?" the Canadian stationmaster asked, as much to himself as to Pablo standing alongside. "What have we become? These poor souls! They're like sick animals! They cannot be expected to work! Half of them won't survive the night, judging by the look of them, let alone a voyage to Europe, if that's what you're intending Mr… Mr…" He checked his notes in his hand, assembled from the papers arranged and supplied by Pablo. "Mr… Archer. At least let them rest awhile, recover from their hardships? Surely that would be agreeable for all involved?"

"No," said Poré. He shook his head, surveying the platform and town beyond it. The port of Halifax lay a short walk from the station. Carts had been drawn up outside the platform exit to take the most infirm and sick to the boat, those unable to walk down the incline to the vessel. "Round them up and get them into the port. Use the carts if need be to get them there."

"But what about the most sick?"

"Especially them! The sick must go first. Carry them onto the boat if need be."

"This cannot be right!"

"This is God's wish! This must be right!"

"Then I ask, what sort of a God is it we serve, if he condones such dreadful behaviour against our fellow man?"

Poré watched the shambling masses move out of the station. "A God who wishes for us to change our ways. And we will. Trust me. We will. All of us."

SEVENTY-THREE

MONDAY, MARCH 4TH, 1918.
CAMP FUNSTON. FORT RILEY. KANSAS. AMERICA.

There was the sound of a bugle calling American troops to action.

Across the training fields and pathways, boots pounded in strict unison, the cry of "Hut Hut" keeping time with their measured precise steps. A field in one corner of the camp was marked out with rows and rows of starched white-clothed soldiers, stretching and leaping, exercising like the apparatus of some great machine or vast ritual. Beyond the wall and hedges which masked the field, guns could be heard to fire. There was the heavy clank of a mechanised piece of machinery spluttering into and then out of life. A long line of lorries drew through a raised wooden gate and up the sweeping driveway, snaking around and pulling up into the exercise yard, tailgates dropping down and ejecting young eager men, hopping and skipping like excited dogs from the back of the trucks. They threw themselves into lines at the front of the square.

The dull ring of a hammer on iron could be heard, the relentless chatter of voices, the coo of pigeons, the brilliant cackle of laughter, the sharp remonstration of a senior officer to a junior.

Out on the sports field behind the army headquarters' main building block, a game of American football was being played. Cheers and laughter accompanied every piece of action. Good humour soared with spirits.

A team of soldiers ran by.

The year's first early rains had abated and in their place had come a beautiful dawn, long auburn fingers of light stretching from the incalculably bright horizon to every part of the complex it could reach, everything lit up in a golden light, like that of spring.

In the quiet of the library one could almost hear the fiendish scrabble of pen nibs on paper, the vexations and considerations in the minds of soldiers at study. Commanders looked at maps and memos of France. Voices were low and reverential. Coherent. In stark contrast, the barked banter of hungry men rattled in the mess hall.

Efficiency. Precision. Routine. Abundance. Belief.

The American Dream. The fort ran on it.

In the kitchens behind the main headquarters, Company cook Albert Gitchell put down his ladle and said, "Fuck this."

"What's the matter, Albe?" asked the cook next to him.

"Me," he groaned weakly. "That's the matter. I feel like I'm dying."

"What you got?"

"Flamin' cold." He staggered to one side, losing his balance momentarily, holding himself against the workbench. "I'm sick, Marv."

"What do you mean, sick?"

"Got the chills. Feel terrible. Feels like I'm gonna die. Ma' head!" He held his hands to it tight, as if fearing his skull might break open.

"How long you felt like this, Albe?"

231

"Dunno. A week or so. I've caught somethin'. Maybe I caught somethin' bad from ma' trip to Canada. I just know it. I feel terrible!"

"So you said."

"I've gotta go see the doc."

"But what about breakfast, Albe?"

"Screw breakfast. I gotta go see…" Albert staggered to the right from where he had been holding himself upright, Marv catching him as he tumbled.

"Jeez, Albert! You is sick after all! It's all right, I'll take you," he said, looping the chef's arm around his shoulders. "Like you say, breakfast can damn well wait."

SEVENTY-FOUR

The Atlantic Ocean. Approaching Europe.

The wind blowing across the deck of the transport ship that had set out from Halifax twenty days earlier was as cold and cruel as an insult between old friends. Waves, thirty feet high, came pounding against the vessel's vast black hull, one immediately after the other, lifting the huge ship, turning its prow to face the heavens moments before pulling it down into the trough beyond, as it pitched and rolled its long weary course towards Europe lying somewhere in the mishmash of black and grey clouds far beyond.

Poré and Pablo stood alone together on the deck, their hands gripped tight to the rail, riding out the frightful journey the best they could to stop themselves from being thrown down by the ship's great sawing and seething movements as it rose and fell between the waves.

"I think I see land," suggested Pablo, squinting his eyes to the far distance. "Lights? Are those lights? God, I'll be pleased to see Europe."

"As I always knew we would."

Pablo studied Poré, looking for any sign to suggest a little warmth in the comment, something to suggest that there was honesty and humanity bound up in him. After all, there hadn't been a day which had gone past while designing, formulating and then putting their plan into action when Pablo had not feared for problems rearing their heads, missed connections, fallibilities of their forged identities, and primarily the attention of the Inquisition. They had travelled under false names, but what little Pablo knew about the Inquisition was how well-drilled and wide-spread they were. He had no doubt they would have had a foothold in the British government and would undoubtedly be looking for Poré and himself there.

"Have you never been concerned, Poré?" asked Pablo, suspicion on his face and woven into his question.

"We do God's bidding. We come bringing his wrath with us. We are protected by his majesty and might. I have worried about nothing, not since the plan was first presented to us."

The words *majesty* and *might*, when compared to the poorly workers brought from China, troubled Pablo, and he faltered, turning away.

"What is it?" asked Poré, thinking him sick himself, perhaps unwell from the rolling seas.

"These poor souls we carry in this ship's hull, the Chinese workers, I don't think of them as a mirror to God's *majesty*. I don't see his *might* in them. I just see... I see torture and cruelty!"

"We are not monsters, Pablo," warned Poré, taking hold of his arm with a hand like a gripping white-taloned claw. "We come to do a great thing."

Pablo nodded, but he still could not bring himself to look at the old man next to him, the man who had so inspired and moved him when they had first met, the man who had drawn him from his path of despair after the betrayal at the Carso, feeling loss and the betrayal of all that he thought he knew and was.

"Is everything taken care of in England?" Poré asked. "Those who will be looking for us, have they been dealt with?"

"Have I failed you so far?" retorted Pablo, a rare flash of anger. "I'm sorry," he said moments later, holding up his hand as a sign of apology and begging forgiveness under Poré's fierce glare. "Yes. They will be looking for us in the wrong place. The cargo they expect to find will not be as planned or hoped for. Instead something entirely different will be waiting for them, gathered from your own disciples."

"Excellent!" Pore smiled grimly, the first sign of satisfaction Pablo had seen the bleak man show since the entire scheme had been devised. "I so hope Tacit enjoys the little treat we have left for him! I suspect it won't be enough to deter him entirely from his persistence in pursuing me, but perhaps it will confirm to him that this is a race he cannot now win. I admire him, his tenacity. But he knows that he has finally been bested, by a better man. I suspect he always knew it to be so, even back then in Paris at the very start of the war."

SEVENTY-FIVE

NANTES. FRANCE.

After weeks being rocked by boats in the Mediterranean and herded like cattle through queues and port customs, Tacit and Isabella boarded a train going north from Barcelona. Beyond, Toulouse, Limoges, Poitiers and, finally, Nantes lay on its route. It was a gunmetal-black grain transporter which smoked too much and smelt of grease and oil, taking provisions and supplies to the troops on the western front, and logistical equipment and staff to the north-western port. The station guards asked no questions and let them ride in one of the open carriages, disinterested, lacklustre in their care and manner, as if everything in the war and their life had become impossible to control and it was therefore pointless to try.

While slow-going, uncomfortable and acrid, the motion of the train on the track felt better than walking and the coal-fire stink of the locomotive engines made one less sick than the roll of the ocean.

There were frequent stops as the train pulled through the Pyrenees, passing stations full of soldiers, looking idle and bored. The train crept up and between the high sides of majestic granite peaks, slithering its way back down the other side, from lofty heights where the air smelt thinner and cleaner to deep immersive valleys, where mist hung and enclaves of trees bound everything up in green either side of the railway line.

By time the train rolled into Nantes, the air had turned polluted and thick, the landscape corrupted into the structured necessity of the French port, lines of soldiers, fevered activity, crowds of people, noise and smoke and bluster everywhere.

Tacit jumped from the gunmetal footplate of the carriage and turned to help Isabella down.

"Come on," he spoke, like a curse, "let's go and find Poré."

The great ship emerged through a heavy fog which had descended upon the French port, entombing everything. Fog lamps shone on the harbour wall and from the vessel's hull, looking like balls of frosted light, their ghostly fingers teasing through the cold winter air. All along the railings and peppered about the deck, smudged pinpricks of light emerged like ghostly will-o'-the-wisps as the transport ship picked its way up the broad river towards the harbour's edge. The choke and chatter of Nantes seemed to fall away as the vessel drew ever closer into its berth, Tacit and Isabella standing side by side watching and waiting for it to make its mooring.

"And you're sure this is the ship that came from Halifax?" Tacit asked, stroking his square jaw with his fingers.

Isabella nodded, curling and uncurling her fingers as if in expectation of the confrontation to come with those onboard.

"Yes," she said. "The ship left Halifax three weeks ago. Cargo intended for the western front. Ammunitions. Vehicles. Munitions and logistical equipment."

"And a Chinese labour force, fresh from the Weihaiwei district," Tacit added, lowering his eyes. He scowled, feasting on the desire for retribution, to strike back against their loss, the burden of sorrow they had carried since Constantinople. For Henry. "Finally, we have him."

"We might be too late to stop it," muttered Isabella.

"What is it they say about cold revenge? And after all that's been done to us, it's time to serve it up."

The vast ship, outlined by the searching pale lights across its deck, suddenly let out a mournful hoot, announcing its arrival to all in the port. The quayside filled with workers preparing to receive the vessel, porters, port officials, lackeys and quayside workers, emerging from the port's eastern end, watching the ghostly ship appear, lounging in their disinterested groups or watching absently in twos or threes for the ship to cut its engines and make ready to unload. To them yet another boat into port. Another boat to help with the war effort.

For many minutes it seemed as if the ship had run aground in the waterway, seeming to move neither forward nor away from where it sat low in the river. But then its great engines started up again and the transporter drew slowly forward, inching into position where it had been assigned a docking place at the quayside. Ropes were thrown and expertly tied to the quayside, holding the boat firmly in place.

Doors opened at the front and stern and gangplanks were teased out, lowered onto the quayside and then secured.

"Do we go on board now?" asked Isabella.

Tacit shook its head. "No," he said, "let's just wait for a while and see what happens."

They waited, the minutes passing painfully slowly. A contingent of sailors appeared at the front doorway, the Captain amongst them, trotting down the gangplank and making their way across the quay past where Tacit stood. He watched them leave, examining each one closely, checking to see if he recognised any of them, checking to see if any of them turned their eyes suspiciously towards him, something, anything to give them away. But nothing suggested to Tacit that they were anything other than ordinary sailors. Another group emerged, laughing and merry, pleased to be ashore.

A third group appeared, oily crewmen, smeared in black and grey over their discoloured overalls. Tacit muttered something and went forward from where they were standing to watch more closely, Isabella calling after him and asking where he was going. He didn't reply, instead stepping into the path of the workers and exchanging some brief words with them.

"Something's wrong," he said. "This ship, it didn't come from Canada. It came from New York. Come on," he said, looking between both walkways but seeing no more movement. "Let's go and have a look on board anyway. Just to be sure, work our way through the boat. See what we might find inside."

"I am hoping sick Chinese labourers," said Isabella, before they strode across the wet stones of quayside to the gangplank, their hands held tight to their waists and the revolvers hidden there.

SEVENTY-SIX

NANTES. FRANCE.

Silence.

The boat was utterly quiet, save for the monotonous rumble of its slowing engines dying in the ship's belly. Tacit and Isabella's footsteps sounded hollow and heavy on the steel floor, ringing out dully like slow deep hammer blows across the passageways and throughout the ship's cabins and quarters beyond. Isabella could hear Tacit grumbling and growling as they walked, the darkness and the emptiness unsettling, disconcerting. She supposed if Tacit was troubled by the darkness, then she should be too, but instead she felt only a growing sense of helplessness.

Without warning, Tacit suddenly stopped and took out his revolver.

"What is it?" she asked, immediately feeling the need to take out her own weapon.

"I don't like it," replied Tacit, lifting his nose to the air like a dog to a fresh breeze. "There's something on this ship," he said. He stood for a moment, listening and smelling, before saying, "Come on," and stepping further into the vessel's dark depths.

They walked on, more slowly now, quieter too, along corridors lit only by occasional emergency lights, making everything appear obscure and out of reach. Tacit's boots squeaked as he rolled his foot forward onto his toes to try to make as little sound as possible. Once again he stopped, holding up his hand to draw Isabella to a halt with him, in the same movement bringing his index finger to his lips. She watched his eyes rise up to the ceiling, as if he saw that something was moving above them. And then he walked on again, ever more slowly, a dead crawl, utterly silent.

She wished desperately to ask him what it was that concerned him so much, what he thought it was on the ship, but knew it was wiser to keep quiet and say nothing.

At the end of the corridor, lined only by hot-water pipes and rivets in precise lines in the steel wall, there was a flight of stairs going down into blackness. The ghostly glow of lanterns teased from the shadows at the bottom. Tacit put his ear to the stairwell and listened, before turning his eyes to Isabella and beginning to climb down into the dark. At the bottom he paused again, looking left and then right, something about the left-hand passageway intriguing him and drawing him that way. He made sure that Isabella walked behind him, his own body turned so that the revolver in his right hand faced always forward to the blackness beyond, should anything come out of it.

Tacit sensed that something wasn't right, stepping further on into the black of the ship's hull. Every sense was alive to the darkness about him, his breath like a whisper in the quiet of the place. There was no one about, no crew, no passengers, no cargo. He knew that some of the crew had departed the ship, those small groups he'd seen leaving the ship earlier. But a ship this big, he was certain that there would be more on board. There had to be. He doubted that so few could ever have piloted such a large ship themselves. And he couldn't help but think, when space for freight was at such a premium, why had such a big ship been used for so little cargo?

He was certain that either the crew or a significant cargo must still be on board, stored somewhere. The questions were where it was and just what it was.

He walked on, descending further into the bowels, his way lit by infrequent gas bulbs, orbs of urine-coloured light pooling on the metal floor and walls. It seemed that the engines in the ship had slowed almost to a stop, their noise now just a dull vibrating rumble, making the rest of the silence in the ship seem even more oppressive, almost as entombing as the dark.

At the end of the corridor there was a closed door, locked with a metal holding arm. Tacit put his ear to it and listened but could hear nothing coming from the other side. He went to pull the handle up, but something made him pause.

He thought then about whether they should go back, accept that nothing was down here. He thought of Sandrine and Henry and something raged in him, a longing, a taunting wrench of loss and anger.

The handle was tight, gripped firm by rust and condensation and the twisted metal in the ship's bowels.

"Stand back," he said, setting his entire weight and strength against it, and the handle shifted. The instant the door opened a crack, steel-black talons and monstrous red jaws snapped and slashed at the opening and a howl rang out of the chasm of dark beyond.

Wolves!

Tacit roared, taking out his gun, able to fire off just a single shot before the entire corridor was overrun by the terrible things.

PART FIVE

"You will chase your enemies and they will fall before you
by the sword."

LEVITICUS 26:7

SEVENTY-SEVEN

THE VATICAN. VATICAN CITY.

Gaulterio, the old inquisitional storekeeper, had been walking the steps
down into the crypts for fifty years, down into the bowels of the earth,
beneath the inquisitional hall, beneath the Great Library.

The overflow of his stores were kept down here in the cold expansive
dark and so he had no choice but to come down. But recently, something
else had drawn him into the endless labyrinthine corridors, the damp
unlit chambers of murk and disquiet, as if something was calling to him,
drawing him into the silence to look and see.

Things had changed in the Vatican. At first Gaulterio chose to ignore
the rumour, the murmurings that a malevolent presence had made its
home in the city. But then came the stories from in the Holy See, of
summary executions, of chaos in meetings, of a cruel undeniable malice
creeping into proceedings, of Cardinal Bishop Adansoni's brutish reign
as Secretary of State and head of the Holy See, and Gaulterio started to
find he was able to ignore no more.

For centuries the crypt had also been used as a morgue. It was a snapshot
of the wrong end of Vatican life. Ever younger Inquisitors, old Fathers,
Bishops, paunchy even in death, errant Priests the Vatican increasingly
preferred to get rid of quietly, Cardinals, oh so many more Cardinals
than usual, snatched away in a blast of violence from Inquisitors' guns.

It now seemed that the steady stream had turned into a raging torrent of the departed, most now blackened and bruised, stabbed and bloodied. It had been a concern to witness the increase in the number of dead being processed through the underworld. In fifty years he had seen the numbers rise and fall with the seasons, war and tragedy, but he had never known death in the city on this scale.

This evening Gaulterio could smell the deceased from the chamber opposite his stores, the sweet sickly reek of festering bodies in the morgue. Only one step inside and his eyes fell upon Strettavario, his face horribly smashed in, discoloured with decay. But Gaulterio still recognised his old friend at once, the familiar shape of his mouth, the paunchy hang of his chin. The old man's broken body had been tossed onto the middle of the pile of bodies in the room.

A noise squawked from his throat and the old storekeeper wrapped his fingers across his mouth to dampen the cry, a savage sound, at seeing his old friend laid out like a ruined piece of meat in front of him. Immediately the feeling of horror was replaced with another emotion, not of hate or even of anger but fear, fear of what had to come into the Vatican and what was happening in its corridors in the halls of the city he loved. And with this fear came crystal understanding as to what he had to do. He knew that everything depended upon it.

That he had to get word out to those Inquisitors still loyal, to come and overthrow with force, if necessary, the terror which had infected the city.

SEVENTY-EIGHT

NANTES. FRANCE.

Tacit's inquisitional chain mail resisted the first onslaught, the first wave of talons and teeth as they raked and bit over him, tearing his great trench coat from his back, shredding many of his clothes. But then the second wave drove into him, a whole host of foul stinking wolves devouring his body, the looped links of hammered metal, cast in the Vatican's deepest, hottest furnaces, tearing away, leaving him naked and exposed.

Jaws snapped tight onto flesh, claws ripped through his skin. He cried out, feeling his body torn apart, the greatest of torments he had ever endured.

"Isabella!" he cried, a final shout in his throat, not to call her to him but to warn her to get away, to flee if she was able.

The sound of a heavy machine answered, barking deep and loud in that steel corridor, a river of spent rounds gushing from the breech, its barrel appearing to be on fire. As it fired every round sounded like a heavy hammer on an anvil, the spent rounds like clipped.cymbal beats as they hit the ground ringing.

All around him, wolves exploded, obliterated as they bit down, as if to touch Tacit's flesh was cursed. Fur, blood and bones pulverised around and over him, as he dropped and rolled away, his whole body on fire from his wounds, his skin slick with their blood and his own. He slithered and scrambled aside, trying to escape the carnage, into a corner of the passageway, hunkered down as the Browning machine-gun kicked and spat hot silver at the wolves, tearing the clan apart.

Stars shimmered in his eyes, from shock and blood loss, and then vanished like the wolves from the corridor. Strength returned and Tacit rose, pulling his other revolver out of its holster, shredded like his clothing. His senses had been extirpated, but he detected the flash of gunfire from his left and pointed his weapons in the opposite direction, pulling the triggers at any shadows that moved.

Wolves howled and spun away from the new onslaught of silver bullets, Tacit staggering slowly forwards into their midst, blasting and hitting out at anything.

His guns were smoking hot by the time he powered through the barred door into the hold out of which the wolves had come. From the darkness beyond, pitiful howls of defeat and agony rose. He'd never seen so many wolves in one place, not even in the most remote corners of the Carpathian Mountains, where wolves gathered in their great clans, chased from civilisation by flaming torches and flaring condemnation. So many Hombre Lobo lying in wait for him and Isabella.

Isabella!

"Isabella!" he cried, spinning back up the way he had staggered. "Isabella!" He wept, slipping amongst the slick fur and blood of the dead creatures, his vision blurred and contorted, just shadows and heavy colours like a morbid abstract painting. "Isabella!" he wailed. "Where are you!"

Tears were in his blinded eyes, a lump like a stone in his throat, its weight almost too great to bear. "Isabella!"

"I'm here," her small voice called, and Tacit fell into her arms, weeping and holding onto her, smelling her, drawing her body tight to his, wet with gore and sweat.

"My love!" he cried. "I thought you were dead!"

She clutched onto him, crying as well, shuddering with relief and joy. "I'm not that easy to kill," she replied, and she laughed to repeat the very same words Tacit had spoken nearly a year ago. She put her hands to his head. "But you! I thought you were lost. They were all over you!"

"And so did I!" replied Tacit, his vision slowly returning.

"Your armour!" said Isabella, pitifully, holding the shreds of his chain mail and clothes in her hands. "And you're injured! Oh, Tacit!" she wailed, seeing the blood behind the torn armour and clothing. "Oh, Jesus, Tacit! Jesus! You're badly injured!" Blood poured out of him from deep furrows through his skin.

This time he let her tend to him, finding a place where he could sit and let her bind the grievous wounds on his body the best she could in the dark and with so little to work with.

"God, you're a mess, Poldek!" she exclaimed, shaking her head at the sodden bandages she had bound about the wounds she could see in the darkness.

"I'll live," he growled, a light coming to his face, dark mirth. "You killed a lot of wolves," he said. "I'll make an Inquisitor of you yet, Isabella!"

Tacit sat back and broke open his revolvers, threading six more silver rounds inside the cylinders of each weapon, stamped with the inquisitional mark of Turkey, snapping them shut. The dead littered the floors, the steel beneath their feet slick with their ichor. Without warning he shot something large and feral moving into the orb of light up ahead.

"It's not over," he warned. "There's still more of them, down in the hold. How's your ammunition situation?" he called over his shoulder as he climbed ungainly to his feet, moments before two more wolves ran towards them. Tacit shot them clean through the head. "They might be regrouping for another attack."

"How's your ammunition?" replied Isabella, drawing back the bolt and resetting her gun's action. Her eyes never left the gloom behind them. "I have plenty."

Tacit shot another wolf, grotesque and wilder than any he had yet

242

seen in the hull, hitting it twice in the head and once in the belly before it rolled over and lay still, its monstrous claws clattering like iron nails against the steel floor.

"I'm fine," he replied, something growling in the cortex of his mind, the chatter of devilish voices, laughing and celebrating the carnage, almost in adulation and praise. "It was a trap," he said, his face turning up into a venomous twist of hate. The voices in him continued to spit and mock. Tacit knew his folly had nearly cost him his life and that of the woman he loved. "We've walked straight into it."

"Basquez?"

"Has to be, working with Poré no doubt," nodded Tacit. "He sent us here. Stupid," he said, going to slap himself hard against the side of the face, but finding the agony of his body too great even to raise his arm to aim a blow. "We should never have believed him, not without checking first. We've travelled halfway across Europe on the word of a liar!"

Tacit looked away, back over the slaughtered wolves. His sorrow was almost overwhelming, the voices in him wallowing in the agony of it, loving the twist of agony he felt, the tease of adrenaline. Their voices danced in the churn of emotion.

"Oh Poldek!" wept Isabella. She buried her head in her hand, before sinking her face onto his bandaged crimson chest. "The horror of it!"

"Yes," nodded Tacit, and he felt a rage and a passion he hadn't felt since the time he had faced Georgi on the pinnacle of rock in the Carso. "This has to end. We need to find Poré and stop him."

Something shifted in the darkness beyond Isabella's shoulder. He raised his revolver and shot dead another wolf as it howled and scurried towards them from the passageway.

SEVENTY-NINE

PORTSMOUTH. ENGLAND.

The ship that Tacit believed was docking in Nantes drew slowly into Portsmouth harbour and headed for the quayside. Gulls circled the vessel, while tugs and other small boats filled the cold black waters around it. A berth at the port side was found and the ship eased into it, caressing all fifteen thousand tons of steel into its allotted place with reverent care and skill.

"What's on board?" the port official asked Poré, waiting for them as they left the gangplank and stepped into the customs bay, checking his disembarkment notes.

"Shouldn't you be telling me that?" Poré retorted, coughing into his scarf and wiping the spittle away.

The official scowled and took a surreptitious step back from the man. "Are you well?"

"A sea chill," replied Poré swiftly. "Nothing more. If you have any concerns regarding our cargo, ask the Captain." The gaunt man motioned towards the ship with his head.

"The Captain steers the ship," muttered the official testily, but avoiding eye contact, "you're named on the file as the importer. What's on board?"

"Something to benefit the war effort," replied Poré. He wrapped the long length of mean thin fabric around his face to hide it from the official's suspicious eyes and the biting wind swirling around the quay.

"Same could be said for all the ships that dock here." Now the official was watching him intently, clearing his throat and then checking his notes again, growling that he didn't have time for this sort of nonsense.

"Do any of us?" Poré asked, pointedly.

The official walked away, suppressing a yawn and calling out across the busy harbour to port hands to begin unloading the ship. "Supplies and workers from Canada," he shouted, with a jerk of his thumb over his shoulder. "British government approved. Get them unloaded. We've got another three ships coming in in the next four hours. I want this quayside cleared for them. Fast."

Poré's eyes dropped to Pablo and they walked on, out of harm's way.

Boxes and crates flooded out from the ship, drawn forward by teams of porters and bearers, carried on broad shoulders and pushed away on carts. Lines of soldiers muscled the goods ashore, a conveyor belt of synchronised limbs.

The Chinese workers came last, belched from the vessel, down the gangplanks in a pestilent stream, groping to the harbour, a quivering staggering line of human detritus.

"For fuck's sake!" someone was heard to say as the coughing and vomiting scrum of men gathered in a ragged crowd and strayed uncertainly about the unloading bay, going this way and that, but mainly lying down and trying to regain some strength in the cold sterile air and rest tired aching limbs, despite the bite of the winter breeze.

"Third fucking batch this week."

"None as bad looking as this lot. Someone wash those poor bastards down!" someone suggested.

"Where are they bound?" asked another.

"Collection camp, set up for them on Southsea Common," another official with a pad answered. "They can wash them down there. Get them off my bloody quayside. They're a bloody disgrace."

"The disgrace lies with the British government bringing them over in this condition in the first place," shouted a suited man, at his throat a bulbous necktie matching the handkerchief in his breast pocket, someone important if his attire was to be believed. A politician perhaps, a man of authority and position. "How can they treat people like this? Don't they know they're human beings too?"

"If they were human beings, then they're not now," someone said.

The pair of Priests at the port entrance watched the ragged men being rounded up and staggering to their feet, pushed forwards towards the rear of the harbour docks.

"What have we become, Father, eh?" one of the soldiers asked the watching Priests, as he helped push the contingent of Chinese workers through the waiting gates and into the dark of the street beyond. There were open-bed trucks lined up for the short journey to the common. "Say a prayer for us, and them," nodded the soldier with his head towards the sick workers ahead of him. "I think we'll all need one when this war is run."

The two Priests watched the crowds of men shamble past, paying special attention to the two individuals who walked with the crowds, Europeans, one tall and gaunt, bound up in a filthy scarf, the other they recognised from descriptions as an Italian seen in various government buildings going about by the name of Gareth Hart.

"Inform H.Q.," one of the Inquisitors muttered to the other next to him, "that we have them." He broke away and followed the group towards the waiting trucks, gathering a bicycle from next to the iron railings at the entrance to the harbour and pedalling after the vehicles in the direction of

Southsea and the camps of workers and goods, all of which were bound for France and the front line.

EIGHTY

The Vatican. Vatican City.

In St Peter's Square the otherwise deathly quiet was punctuated by the persistent crack of small-arms fire. Doves spun and circled around the city's rooftops, chimneys and towers, trying to avoid the lead shot, every now and then folding back their wings and plummeting to the ground where they thumped and rolled still, or writhed pathetically on shattered legs. The unit of Inquisitors kept firing into the heavens at the white and grey birds until the floor beneath their feet glistened with a carpet of brass shells and only a small number of doves remained, toiling across the grey heavens, out of the city, away from their nests to safer places to rest.

In the grounds of the city a group of gesticulating and pleading Priests was being rounded up and bullied in the direction of the Vatican buildings, their groans and protestations sounding even more alien against the serenity of the gurgling of blood-coloured water from the Eagle Fountain on the other side of the path up which the protesting Priests were being marched. In the cold shadow of the church of St Stephen of the Abyssinians they were filing past, three Inquisitors were dragging the great doors to the church shut and hammering broad heavy wooden beams to hold the entrance locked.

In the Basilica, a confusion of anarchy, desperation and disbelief had worked itself into the fabric of the chamber and the hopeless timidity of still loyal and holy Cardinals who sat and listened and prayed that what they were witnessing was some aberration, some grotesque game intended to test their faith. But if it was a game, then it was clear that they were losing.

The great doors to the city had long been closed up and locked. Where before archways had stood open, licked by bright lanterns and encouraging smiles of the Priests on both sides, now tongues of red burnt in shadowy lanterns and Inquisitors stood at every entrance and exit, hands tight to triggers and grips, eyes fixed on anyone drawing too close.

When the doors were first closed up, a stream of residents, Priests, Bishops and their Acolytes, some of the staff and residents in the city did manage to flee, telling stories of treachery and dark horror, of the Devil coming to the Vatican and making it his home. Behind this initial stream followed just a trickle of people, the last to flee the city, before every way in and out was closed. These last people to escape spoke of murders, of ritualistic killings, of monstrous Satanic acts carried out in the most holy and ordained of places, of a weeping and pleading coming from one locked room in the city, the rest of the Vatican filled with wicked laughter, and a black pall which covered the city, smothering it in its polluting fog, hiding from all the atrocities being unleashed in the place, waiting for the moment to reveal the true extent of their horrors.

Waiting for Satan's return.

EIGHTY-ONE

PORTSMOUTH. ENGLAND.

"We should have given you the chance to rest," said Isabella, watching Tacit struggle momentarily on the deck of the ship they had taken from France. "Given you a chance to recover. Your wounds…"

"We have no time to wait. We have to find Poré."

The voice buzzed in his ear again, a stream of obscenities against all he loved.

She'd found him clothes in Nantes and had helped him dress.

"You cannot keep going forever, Poldek. Eventually you have to stop and pause."

Isabella knew her words, spoken not for the first time, were as futile and hollow as they sounded to her. Redundant, just as she had felt so often at Tacit's side while they pursued Poré towards the southern coast of England. After she had bound and dressed him, Tacit had broken into the handling office at the port and scrutinised all voyages to Europe from Canada, cross-referencing against passenger names and cargoes. He'd not found Poré's name, but he'd found a ship containing a contingent of Chinese Labour Corps that had left Halifax for Nantes but had, mid-journey, changed destination, steaming instead for Portsmouth. The dates fitted, as did the cargo.

Intuition had told him that was where they had to go, to where Poré was headed.

They'd slipped silent and unseen from Nantes, telling no one about what lay dead inside, littering the lower decks and passageways of the vessel. They'd leave it to the Inquisition to cover up and explain, to hide the evidence and silence those unfortunate enough to discover the truth.

The next ship bound for Portsmouth left Nantes that afternoon. Tacit and Isabella had stowed aboard and now watched from the rail the broad western coast of the Isle of Wight sweep past on their right, as they sailed at full steam towards the English mainland and the southern port. Around them, everything appeared grey. The sea, the sky, the gulls in it, the light in Tacit's eyes. Despite all that had happened to them on the boat, and in Constantinople before, the loss of Henry and Sandrine was still the most grievous of wounds they bore. But, for all that, there was too much still to do, too much at stake to wallow in their loss and their sorrow. If they were to have any hope of finding Poré, they both needed to be decisive and focused, not errant and conquered by melancholy.

"Portsmouth?" she asked, quite without warning. "Are you sure he's gone to Portsmouth?"

Tacit nodded before shrugging dismissively, and Isabella slapped him as hard as she was able across the cheek, stinging her hand and bringing a fierce look into Tacit's face. "Buck your ideas up, Poldek!"

The voices rose to a cacophony of rage at this treatment. ⟩

"Henry's dead," Isabella said. "Accept it and move on. If we don't, if we don't find Poré, an awful lot more people will die."

The words crystallised in him, tightening his guts. He nodded, sharpened, knowing she was right, knowing why he loved her as he did, why, for now, her words had superiority over the Devil's. For now.

"Poré's travelling under a false name," he said. "Archer. He's rented a terraced flat next to the common in Southsea, if the records in the harbour logs are to be believed. That's where we go first." The voice in him disagreed, barking at him, ordering him to return to the Vatican immediately. He watched the Solent's grey waters, working a line in the wood of the rail with his nail. "One thing at a time," he said, Isabella thinking it was for her, but Tacit said it for the voice in his head.

They reached the street in Portsmouth where Poré was staying, if the shipping import notes were to be believed. The road was close to the common and just a short walk from the seafront. Tall imposing terraced buildings lined either side of it, painted matt-green and cream.

Counting numbers as they went, halfway down it Isabella stopped, saying out loud the number she had been repeating on her lips, and climbed the four stone steps to the front door. Instantly they knew that they were too late.

There was a residue of blood on the entrance tiles leading up to the front door and a broader puddle of crimson on the other side. Wide marks swept through the blood just inside from where bodies had been dragged away. Tacit and Isabella followed them to a cupboard at the rear of the deep entrance hall, tucked away behind the flight of stairs leading up to the first floor. Inside, the remains of three Inquisitors had been stacked. They had been torn apart, partially devoured, limbs and torsos piled on top of each other in a pitifully macabre attempt to hide the crime.

"They travel with wolves?" asked Isabella incredulously.

"Poré's pelt," replied Tacit. "Come on."

"Where to?"

"The common."

The broad expanse of green, set back from the seafront promenade by a road and a low wall of stone, was covered with tents, crowds of individuals of all nationalities and ranks, soldiers, officials and vast shambling units of foreign labourers, Indians, Chinese and Africans.

The official they spoke to said he recognised the description of Poré.

"Strange-looking man," the officer confirmed, nodding, looking to the sea as if the answer might lie there. "Gaunt. Haunted look about him."

"That's him."

"Had another man with him. An Italian. Young man. Dispatched from London." Isabella mouthed the name Pablo to Tacit in shock and wonder. "Came in yesterday. Government official. Part of the C.L.C."

"C.L.C.?"

"Chinese Labour Corps. Responsible for the import of Chinese workers. A ragged bunch. Stinking, disease-ridden, the lot of them. Made you sick, the stink of them." He made a disapproving noise. "Not right to treat another man like that, not even the Chinese. Look at them," he said, gesturing towards a group of Chinese workers.

"Is that them, Archer's men?" asked Isabella, with growing hope.

The man shook his head. "No, Archer's gone, and the Chinese he brought with him."

"Where is he?"

"Dover."

"Why Dover?"

"Obvious, isn't it?" asked the port official. He clutched his clipboard to his chest, fishing in a pocket for a cigarette. "They're destined for the front line. Everything that comes into Portsmouth is destined for the front line, unless it's coming back from there. And then it's almost always broken."

EIGHTY-TWO

BOULOGNE-SUR-MER. FRANCE.

As the transport ship drew into the French port, Poré stood watching bombs drop onto the town from the vessel's bridge. But the moment the crew prepared to throw ropes to the harbour, the German onslaught halted and an uneasy silence flooded into the port, the resonant thunder of battle sounding almost immediately small and indistinct, now far off in the distance, back to the front line.

A British destroyer was steaming into harbour as Poré and the Chinese workers disembarked, Poré at their head, Pablo bringing up the rear, making sure that no one fell too far behind or tried to make a run for it, even though they were all too exhausted to consider such a thing. The transport Pablo had organised to take them inland had failed to materialise and after two hours of waiting they took the decision to march out on foot. Two miles from the port they shambled past a prisoner of war camp, the drawn captured German soldiers on one side of the barbed wire a picture of health compared to the ragged Chinese workers passing down the road into the east.

"You need feeding up and a bath, Chinaman!" one of them called in perfect English. "Come this side of the wire! We have soup! And bread!"

The weary band marched on, the Germans' laughter like a curse in their ears.

They marched for four more hours, until dusk fell and the road grew dark and treacherous. Poré called them to a halt, breaking out provisions and telling them to rest. As they did so, Poré took himself a little away from the gathering, throwing himself down on the ground, like a man defeated or with a sudden urge to pray.

"Poré!" called Pablo, seeing him collapse and running to his side, but the old man pushed him away.

"I am not defeated!" he hissed. "I do not need your help!"

He looked back, up into the moon, full and very white against the night sky, holding out his arms, as if in a sign of reverence and submission.

"As I have always sought to be, I am a servant to your cause, oh Lord! A disciple, dedicated always to fight against the demons of Hell. For I am their accursed foe! Mankind, they have no true insight as to just how far the servants of evil have infiltrated into the world, just how deeply the Devil has burrowed. Just how malignant his darkness creeps. Mankind, it is blind, whereas I can see. I have always seen. It is the folly of man that he chooses to live in a world so corrupt and defiled by the Devil's hand without ever wishing to open his eyes, to observe this evil, acknowledge it and cast it out. No one wishes to acknowledge the horrors of their making that plague this earth!

"And so it is that *I* bring a plague of *our* own, *your* wrath, unto them! A damnation to the world, bearing the mark of you, Lord God, with all your magnificence and rage bound up in it. A damnation which shall check the Antichrist's ambitions in this most devastating of conflicts, a global scourge that shall decimate the Antichrist's armies and all those who contribute to the war's continuation! War shall end, and with it shall go the Antichrist's goal of world conflict!"

He stared up into the heavens, his eyes growing very wide. "I will commit this final act for you before your might and wonder claim me, your ever loyal servant."

As he finished the words, an uncontrollable coughing overcame him that he tried to catch with his hands. Finally it abated and he took his hands away, seeing they were covered in blood. He stared at the crimson on his palms.

"And I will go down in your flames of damnation."

EIGHTY-THREE

ROME. ITALY.

The tunnels beneath Rome, broad dry passageways of pumice and chalk, quarried and expanded two thousand years ago by Romans, Christians and Etruscans, were just as Sandrine remembered them from when she was last here, nearly three years ago, in every aspect except one. Something cruel and corrupt had crept into them, something malingering that hung like a curse about every turn and chamber along the way.

The rubble under her boots crunched like brittle snow as she stepped through the darkness and shivered, swapping the flaming torch she had brought to light her way from her left to her right hand and wiping the sweat from her palm down her dusty front. She lifted the flaming brand above her head and peered into the right and left passageways ahead, preferring the look of the right-hand one. She had no idea where exactly she was going, but she supposed it made no difference. Eventually she would find them, those she had come looking for.

She didn't feel fear in the dark of that place, no trepidation or concern walking in *their* domain. She was too sick with grief and loss, filled with too much anger to worry for her own safety. She thought of only one thing. Retribution, revenge for those who had taken her love. Those who had killed Henry.

She'd lost all sense of time since she had descended into this subterranean world that teemed with unspeakable terrors beneath the capital. Corridors turned into passageways, slipped into cunning chambers and then rose to broad walkways along which she could step without needing to crouch. Just then, beyond the flickering light of her torch, something ancient and foul cackled and spat. Only briefly did the dreadful sound check her step. Sandrine cleared her throat and went towards it, walking with even more purpose. In ten steps, the corridor opened out into a sea of dark, an enormous chamber spreading away below her. Her meagre amber flame reached out into it, illuminating the pallid sickly faces and forms of Hombre Lobo in front of her, wolves in human form.

"Sandrine Prideux," a rank figure at the front croaked. The fact he knew her name did not surprise Sandrine. Her coming here before and the battle in Rome was still a poignant memory for so many tormented by life in the bleak tunnels. "I am surprised you have dared to return to us. Last time you came here you brought only ruination."

"Ruination? As if your paltry existence is not already ruined?"

The man barred his teeth, a snarling blackened broken maw. "Have you come back merely to mock us?"

"Not to mock. I come to draw you together for one final fight, the greatest of battles against those who have cursed and imprisoned you in these dour catacombs."

The wolf laughed, a ravaged and diseased sound. "Sadly, Sandrine Prideux, you are too late to rally us."

"How so?" she retorted, passing the torch between her hands and taking a step forward into the cavern. "Have you decided that it is better to crawl down on your bellies, rank and fetid in your filth, than to try and rise up against your jailers?"

"Far from it!" the gaunt terrible man shouted back. At once there came the sounds of scrabbling, of taloned callused feet in the dirt, of a great gathering of bodies filing into the cavern. The stench off them was dreadful, the putrescence of a thousand years boiled into an overwhelming caustic stink. Sandrine drew back, her hand held against her nose and the wretchedness. But then intrigue and realisation overcame her and she lifted the torch higher to light more of the cavern. And she gasped, her widening eyes filling with tears. From every side-corridor, rank and bowed figures crawled, Hombre Lobo, a great army of them, innumerable, a seething sea of wicked filthy faces.

"Poré," spoke the man, "during his travels he collected together a great host of wolves, from all across the mountains east of the Carso, all of which he sent to the Vatican to join those already here. And here we have been gathering, waiting to tear the Antichrist and his false army from his throne, those who created the first incantations of excommunication, to tear away their darkness forever."

EIGHTY-FOUR

It was now a fresh easterly wind that blew in the faces of Isabella and Tacit. They had left Dover for France aboard the first boat available, a large fishing boat called 'Sark' which had been commandeered into service for the transporting of goods across the Channel.

"It's cold," said Isabella, drawing her coat tighter around herself. "It's late spring, and yet it's a cold wind blowing in from the mainland."

Tacit nodded. "This road, it has been long. Too long. But now we have a name, Archer, and we know that we're on his heels. Poré, he's just ahead of us. He won't escape us now."

"Even so, I'm scared, Poldek," said Isabella, shuddering against the cutting wind and her fears of what might lie ahead in France, "scared as to what we will find. What Poré might have done."

"I haven't dared to think," Tacit lied. "Did you hear? Back in Portsmouth?"

"Hear what?"

"People talking in the camp on Southsea Common. That something has come into the world, a disease that is striking down people. From America, to Africa, all across Europe, Russia, the Far East, people are falling sick, an illness, a mystery at the moment to doctors, something that sucks the life out of them, leaving people breathless, unable to breathe, bloodless except for their mouths and eyes, filled with blood."

Yes! Let them bleed, bleed from every orifice!

Isabella looked at him horrified, her hand to her mouth. Tacit looked back, steadying himself against the roll of the ship. "Some sort of influenza," he said. "It's spreading, with frightening speed, infecting vast swathes of the world. So now we know the manner by which God's wrath will be unleashed. And that, no matter what we do, we're too late."

254

EIGHTY-FIVE

SAINT-OMER. FRANCE.

The Chinese labourers were sick.

They had walked for three days solid, from Boulogne-sur-Mer on the coast to the town of Saint-Omer, thirty miles inland. The journey should have taken half the time, and Poré would have forced them to go quicker, but the shambling collection of men could go no faster and the main thoroughfare was also jammed with traffic, carts and vans and soldiers, going west or coming back east. The road resembled an endless conveyer belt of goods, provisions, equipment, weaponry, machinery, hardware, soldiers, horses and carts, some loaded onto transport trucks and covered by tarpaulins, mysterious lumps on the backs of wagons, other items carried on the backs of horses or men, staggering on heavy feet in the grimy churned dust of the road.

On either side, the fields acted as an overspill for the clogged detritus of the traffic, soldiers, both wounded and freshly arrived, lay out under the warm sun, and labourers, like the kind Poré had brought from China, hunkered down around fires or meandered around in groups, fighting against the cool of the northern climate, thinking of home and what lay ahead, as they tried to work some warmth into their aching joints and fought against an annoying cough they had picked up on their travels.

There was green and vibrancy during most of Poré's march east, the countryside burgeoning with life and nature's rich spring season. Hope shone in hedgerows and across the crowns of forested hills. For all the war and its toll upon the land, orchards flowered with the promise of plentiful fruit later that year, should autumn ever come. Grass in the fields had grown leafy and thick, a carpet from the earth onto which men fell and rolled and laughed and slept.

It was only as Poré and the workers drew closer to Saint-Omer that any beauty began to fester in the byways and across the vista of the land, all carved up by the war and its infernal machines, turning iridescent valleys and gently rolling hills into dirty poisoned plateaus, metal and mud replacing woods and flora.

Closer to the town, all the fields around the place had been given over to the housing and holding of the different regiments stationed in the region, teams of soldiers marching and lounging. The soldiers only ever looked too young and fresh-faced, or haggard and dirty, older than their years. Everything else was smashed and tidied away, as if the destruction had happened an age ago in the place and some semblance of order had been attempted by the armies in charge, to give a feigned sense of normality and peace despite the inescapable signs of war and destruction all around them.

Soldiers, puffing on cigarettes, watched Poré, Pablo and the ensemble of ailing workers pass by, chatting absently amongst themselves, laughter coming easily but evaporating faster, as if they were too tired to laugh with gusto or too fractured by a war which had toiled on too long to keep up the pretence of humour.

Entering the town's outskirts, Poré coughed and turned his head from the right-hand field over to his left, and then back, like a commander entering an area of danger and looking for an enemy, fearing an assault. Ahead of him, more Chinese were shuffling and lugging and building around the devastated town, a whole bastion of workers drawn into the maelstrom of the western front.

"They're for the front line," called Poré to an official bearing the marks of a logistics corps, drawing a wide exhausted arm and floating it back towards the ranks of Chinese trudging behind him, as a contingent of Sergeants and NCOs flocked around them, studying the workers as close as they dared to come before their smell grew too apparent. "Chinese Labour Force. From China, of course. Via Canada."

"Thank you," muttered the Sergeant squarely, who appeared to be in command of the situation as he took Poré's proffered paperwork. "You've come a long way, Mr…"

"Archer. William Archer. And we have."

"And you don't sound like a William." He turned over the top sheet of the wad of paper Poré had handed him, his eyes not on it, only on the sickly man in front of him. He did nothing to hide his disapproval of him, and of the men he had brought into the town.

"You clearly have never heard of William the Conqueror?"

"Consider yourself a conqueror, do you?" He laughed, falteringly. "You just don't look, or sound, like a William," the Sergeant pressed, now turning his eyes onto the paperwork.

"And you don't sound like someone who wants to win the war. Do you want the labourers or not?"

The Sergeant looked up to examine them with further disgust and shock. "Scraped the barrel with this lot, Mr Archer. Is this the best you have?"

"This is just one group. Others are coming. Other have already arrived. Look about you," said Poré, nodding towards a group of Chinese workers he saw amongst the ruins of the place. "They will all make a difference to the ending of the war."

The Sergeant made a noise in his throat and an attempt at another laugh. "Bone idle. Simpletons." He sniffed, looking up from his half-hearted attempt to read the documentation Poré had presented to him, eventually turning the paper back over on itself and holding it against his uniformed chest. "Look at them." And then Poré realised he was talking specifically about the labourers he had brought. "Can they be trusted?"

"They can wield a spade."

The Sergeant was squeezed into silence by the retort. He made a face, suggesting he'd considered the comment and accepted it. "According to your documentation, you're supposed to be travelling with another, by the name of Gareth Hart." He looked over to Pablo and squinted. "That is you, I suppose?"

Pablo acknowledged the question with a bow.

"Will you both be staying with the men?"

"Mr Hart will not," said Poré, watching Pablo with a look that, for the first time, seemed to suggest respect. "He has another errand he wishes to run, in Italy."

"What about you, Mr Archer?" asked the Sergeant. "What are your plans? If you don't mind me saying, you look dreadful."

Poré smiled, weakly. "Looks should not always be believed," he replied. "I am better than I have ever been, now I have arrived at my journey's end and my duty is done."

EIGHTY-SIX

It was the incessant slamming of rain upon the roof that made the situation even more desperate. The bristle of gunfire, a pinch of noise in the darkness, as familiar as an itch on an old healing wound, didn't concern or trouble the doctors. It was the rain, the constant pounding, hour after hour, the inane endless patter on the corrugated roof, as if the weather had nothing better to do than rain. For days it had rained, weeks it seemed to all the patients sheltered below, the ground swollen grey like the flaccid skin on a dying man, rivulets of water running everywhere, every step sodden, every step treacherous.

And added to the rain it was cold, cold and dark, like a Scottish moor or Shetland isle in winter, though this was France in the grip of spring. A damp breeze drifted through the place, teasing the stink of shit and disease around the ward. If anyone caught the sense of air, no one said anything, or at least nothing was heard above the moaning, the incessant groan and mutter, the pathetic coughing from all those housed in the clammy chill sounding as pitiful was it was painful. Nurses hurried too and fro, as efficient with their concern and faith as they were pointless with their care and their healing. Nothing they could do could heal those caught in this new deadly plague.

Doctors directed and shooed with their hands, sounding severe and resigned. Stethoscopes, like industrial jewellery, clung to their chests, snatched tight around their necks. Tired eyes surveyed the misery and morbid deathlessness of the place, hands dragged across their grey faces knowing they were hopeless and helpless to stop this growing and invisible horror lurking across every square mile of the front line, the country in which they worked, the continent they fought for, the world they inhabited.

Grey-blue skinned, bony-eyed wretches stared back from their beds, words from drawn bloodless lips spoken to invisible spirits hovering somewhere in the ether above them. In every third bed, an unmoving body lay. Some bodies were covered with blankets, drawn up over their ghastly wrenched faces. Others waited for that moment of dignity.

"Get them out. Get the healthy ones the damn hell out!" shouted a doctor suddenly, pacing down the ward and then back again, flashing with an arm. His voice sounded like a bark in the pained silence. "We need to shut this ward. Get them out!"

"What about the seriously ill patients?"

"What about them?" cried the doctor, throwing up his hands and coughing himself as he did so. The nurse and he locked wide stares and he cursed, making the nurse blush and the doctor feel even more unhinged. "They're bloody done for! We all are. Get the ones who've got a chance out! It's the least we can do for the beggars!"

"But where can they go?" replied the nurse, throwing out her hands in desperation. "All the other wards are full!"

"Yes, with flu!" The doctor coughed again, bending double as the convulsions struck him. His handkerchief came away, streaked with fine twisting lines of blood on the fabric, and he cursed and sobbed, turning away from the nurse watching him with increasing horror and pity. "Every other poor bloody hospital is done for!" he lamented. "A thousand new cases a day. We're bloody done for!" He sounded hopeless and lost, as if his words were spoken to a deaf God.

"Not just us," another nurse replied, hurrying past with a tray covered in bloodied towels. "The Germans are apparently saying the same. It's like it's some bloody plague's hit!"

The doctor spun on the nurse as she bustled by, the mutter of a sick inmate drawing his eyes.

"Plague on all our houses, hey doc?" croaked the blue-skinned soldier, as he coughed blood onto his lips and the last of his breath passed out of him.

EIGHTY-SEVEN

Laventie. France.

At Saint-Omer, an English Sergeant directed Tacit and Isabella east, towards the front line and a small town close nearby called Laventie. He assured them that a recently arrived continent of Chinese workers had been marched in that direction for building duty. A gaunt Frenchman called Archer, as sick as the workers, had arrived and left with them.

There were doves flying around the square in front of the ruined churches. They watched them as they circled the area, following them with their eyes as they landed on the broken ground in front of where they were walking, four white doves, picking at the rubble in the shadow of the shattered remains of a church.

"White doves," called Isabella in wonder, "landing in our path! Perhaps it's a sign?"

Tacit scowled. The voices and the darkness which forever tormented had now almost entirely enveloped his mind, a weight hanging heavy in him, the Devil's lodestone. But for all that his forked tongue twisted and corrupted Tacit's thoughts, he could not help but deny that there seemed to be something else on the wind, the smell of something in the air, something that suggested the end of one episode, or at least the end of its beginning.

"Four of them," mused Isabella, striding next to Tacit's shoulder, watching the birds peck at sheaves of corn and other titbits dropped amongst the stones by the soldiers and passing traffic. Something startled the doves and they took to the wing, curving up and around the square, rising high up into the ruined clock tower where they shuffled and eventually settled. "Perhaps it's a sign, Poldek? One each for us? You, me, Henry and Sandrine?"

Tacit said nothing, but he was hoping for exactly the same thing, a prayer, despite the gnawing condemnations in his ears, the prayer for an end, an end to the infernal curses.

An officer was passing close by, flanked by two soldiers. Tacit called out to him. "We're looking for someone!" he said. "A Mr Archer." The officer stopped, circling around the large ruined man and the woman who travelled with him, giving them a wide berth.

"He might be sick, frail," Isabella continued, thinking perhaps a woman's intuition might be better received, not to mention being more precise with her details. "The man unwell."

"Aren't they all, love?" replied the young officer, making both soldiers chew at their lips in worried contemplation. "Look about you." He shrugged with a nonchalant tired shoulder, making a half effort to lift his hand, before taking pity on the Father and Sister visiting the town, supposing the Mr Archer they were looking for was a friend or a colleague.

He nodded towards the part of the town behind Tacit and Isabella. "Try over at the hospital, or the church," he continued, thrusting with a thumb at the building where the doves had settled. "That's where most of the sick are being taken. But be warned, there's a lot of them."

The Church of St Vaast stood at the far end of the wasteland, the amber clay bones of its steeple rising from the shattered remains of its base, the red and cream brickwork shaped and smoothed by four years of warfare, but appearing as if its depredation had been caused by ten thousand years of the elements working and eroding the stone away. All around it was smashed devastation, a world exhausted.

Much of the roof had been blown off, the nave exposed to the greying skies above. The ingenuity of man had rigged up temporary roofing across parts that the stone roof did not cover, giving what shelter was possible from the rain and pale sun. The woven cloth sheeting and long sheets of corrugated iron hammered and slapped together whenever the wind picked up, making the roof throb and beat as if the church were some resting beast and its makeshift roof its chest, rising and falling in time to its sickly heart.

The hospital inside resembled more an abattoir than a place of peace and restoration. Maimed and bloodied bodies lay in narrow rows on fold-out beds, with just enough room to pass between each patient. The men were all bound up in dirty white cloth, speckled and spoiled with blood and filth, some burnt, others tied up like madmen so they couldn't worry their wounds even more. But above the quiet incessant weeping and moaning, there was a hacking coughing noise, as if Tacit and Isabella had walked into a ward full of victims of a mustard-gas attack.

Between the low tightly packed beds, nurses were hurrying with trays and pans, all wearing masks, covering up their noses and mouths, leaving just their eyes peering out, as if they didn't wish to be identified, as if ashamed to be seen in the place, to be in any way connected with the misery and the suffering.

Sad exhausted eyes looking out above a patch of white.

"Anything?" Tacit asked Isabella, after reconvening back at the entrance to the church's nave through which they had entered. Isabella shook her head.

"Let's go on up to the spire end," she said.

There was no way through by going on inside the church, so tightly packed in were the soldiers, what with the nurses' coming and going. They left the building, pleased to be back out in the sooty air, and walked along the outside edge, over the rubbled, churned ground, grey slabs of blasted stone lying where once had stood buildings and gravestones. There were tunnels dug into the ground all across the area, corrugated iron sheeting identifying the entrances, communication tunnels used during the worst of the fighting, now used solely to store items away from the sun.

Groups of Tommies stood around looking tired and dishevelled. Priests walked between them, hands clasped across stomachs, talking to them quietly, assuring them of the sanctity of God.

The shadow of the ruined spire fell long across the wasteland square. Without ceremony or pause, Tacit and Isabella went inside and at once their eyes fell on the man they had been pursuing for so long and for so far.

They knew it was him from the moment they saw him, the old Cardinal lying on a sheet, tiny and shrivelled like a corpse, his skin turned blue, his lips darkened red, the life almost run out of him.

EIGHTY-EIGHT

Laventie. France.

"Are you two allowed in here?"

The nurse who asked the question tried to position herself between Tacit and Isabella and the prostrate figure of Poré lying behind her.

The figure in the bed contorted, hacking and choking, both for breath and for words.

"This man is sick, Father. He needs rest."

"It's... it's... all right," croaked the figure, writhing and trembling in the soiled sheets. "It's... all right, nurse. All right..."

The woman arched an eyebrow, hesitating, examining Tacit and then Isabella, but all too briefly and making no effort to question them further, slipping away to tend to the hundreds of other sickly dying patients, too busy and exhausted to waste time negotiating visits or ejecting strangers.

"You're... you're too late..." Tacit and Isabella took a step closer, close enough to hear the wretched man croak his words, close enough to smell his fetid breath, the stink of death coming off him. "The vial… it was opened, long ago, in China. God's plague… it is in the world. Nothing can stop it. Nothing now will."

"Why, Poré?" growled Tacit. "Why have you done this thing? You've killed millions!"

The ragged skeletal man fell back on the bed, shaking his head. "No. No, I've not *killed* millions. I have *saved* millions."

"How can you say that?" spat Isabella, her eyes going thin with spite. "Look about you. These people are dying, dying because of you, because of what you've brought to the place."

"Because of the *influenza*," Poré interrupted, his voice firmer, showing he still had strength in him to fight. "The warring nations will now be impelled to put down their weapons and talk. Talk!" He coughed, a hacking pained cough that appeared to tear at his throat and lungs. He scowled, and then an exhausted peace returned to his face again. "War will end. The nations will talk. They will have no other choice. Their armies decimated, their people suffering. They *will* put down their weapons and talk."

Fucking tricksy swine! So that is it!! End Times, my gift to the world, distorted by another!

Tacit hardened at hearing Poré talk as he did. "I'll kill you this time, Poré, make no mistake about it. I won't allow you to escape like you did in Paris at the Mass for Peace."

But Poré laughed, a cruel hacking laugh, as corrupt as it was pathetic. "I'm a dead man anyway, Tacit, only hours left to live. A ragged shell." He shook his head, forcing his bloodshot eyes open and onto the man towering over him. "And you, the most ragged and corrupt of them all!" Another hacking cough consumed him, leaving him exhausted and his mouth foaming with blood. "All you have ever known it seems is hate, Poldek Tacit! And hate only fuels hate. Every one person involved in this war, from the man who commands the bombs to the woman who hammers them smooth in the factories back home, they all play their part."

Tacit tried to stand, tired of the lecture, wishing to move away from him. But Poré caught hold of his sleeve, his clutch firmer and stronger than Tacit would have believed to look at him.

"Look at you, Tacit, a dead man walking, ravaged by enemies and your own hate. It has almost overwhelmed you, Tacit, all the hate, all the anger. The voices. Their compelling cries. Almost overwhelmed you, possessed you, but not quite.

"There is a monster in you, Tacit, the shadow of a terrible demon. Satan! You know that, don't you?" He turned his eyes onto Isabella, so that she understood what he was saying, before looking back, and it seemed to both her and Tacit that Poré's manner softened. "But I know it has not consumed you utterly. Like me you were loved once, and are loved now, and perhaps that's why you have not let hate, the tempestuous Devil's taunts, consume you utterly. That you have fought. As you've always fought. Though the fight is almost at an end.

"I trust that it has not overwhelmed you completely, Poldek Tacit."

"Why do you care?" sneered Tacit.

"Because I am going to put my trust in you, Poldek Tacit, to finish what must be done."

264

PART SIX

"In peace, sons bury their fathers. In war, fathers bury their sons."

HERODOTUS

EIGHTY-NINE

LAVENTIE. FRANCE.

Poré's voice was frail, ancient, but still possessed an edge. "All I have ever done is seek peace." He fell back on the bed, seeming to pass in and out of consciousness.

But Tacit laughed. "Don't lie to me, Poré! All you have ever sought is destruction. Your path is littered with the detritus of your deeds! The Mass for Peace? Pleven? The Tribulation? What is that if not murder? The deaths of millions!"

Poldek shook his head, bloody spittle clinging to the edge of his mouth. "No, you're wrong. Perhaps there have been times when I *have* committed crimes, but when I have, I have done so only when such actions were required."

Lying dog.

Tacit's scowl remained unmoved. "It is easy to find excuses for yourself after the event. When you come to the end. Just as you have. You'll find no forgiveness from me, Poré."

The sickly man scoffed. "Look at our world, Poldek Tacit! Look at the terror of it. Look at what we have become."

"Another lecture, just like the one you gave to me in Paris? I'm tired and I've tired of you." He went to stand but Poré spoke again, in a voice both decisive and authoritative enough to make the Inquisitor listen.

"No, let me call it my eulogy. For I am dying. I have only hours to live, probably less. I have unleashed this thing on the world and it has caught me in its coil." He coughed again. There was blood on his tongue, teasing and pooling between his teeth. He snatched at his breath, clawing the air into his shredded leathery lungs. He gestured weakly with his hand. "Look out there, Tacit! See the three fronts of this war and what is beyond them. See what horrors are being committed by this conflict. What you see is merely the opening salvo once the Antichrist is unleashed. If something is not done, then we shall all fall under the wheels of his wickedness, crushed under his control and command.

"So often it felt as if I was a lone voice, one against so much darkness, so much terror. Those who fight against this madness, for that is what this war is, Tacit, a murderous madness and nothing else, these people are ridiculed and ostracised, called cowards, yellow, agents of the enemy, anarchists. For so long it has felt as if mine was a lone voice. The only ones I could draw to my banner to help to strike back against this ever-growing darkness were those beyond hope, Hombre Lobo, those cast down under the ground.

"And yet, what can just one man do against such odds? I learnt at the Mass for Peace that it was not simply enough for one man to attempt to kill a thousand in order to stop a war. Something bigger, even more unspeakable was required."

The voices in Tacit's head roiled and screamed.

Poré coughed again, more blood coming into his mouth, the raking of his lungs and throat making him wince. The blue hue of his skin seemed to darken, the veil of death growing tighter around him. "The Antichrist's hold upon so many is too strong for one man alone to act. His reach is now across the globe, armies fighting because he has infected them, making them believe that war is the only way. Nations hell-bent on the destruction of others, manufacturing more and more armaments for the completion of their plans, obliteration of their enemies, command over their rivals, control of their lands and resources. Ever bigger stockpiles of ammunition, ever larger armies, ever more terrible battles, ever more terrible weapons, ever easier ways of killing, ways of killing without even pulling a trigger, death by gas, death by suffocation, death by propaganda, ever more ingenious ways to kill and maim and ruin an enemy. To remove a whole generation of people.

"And at home, assurances of success, words sent back to loved ones that the war would be over by Christmas, controlling people by what they see, what they hear, what they read. Control, at home and on the front. People will believe lies, Poldek Tacit, if the lies are big enough. Our humanity, stripped away by the Devil and by his apparition on earth, the Antichrist and his thirst for domination through this war. Nothing able to stop him but the tiniest of things."

Poré cackled, a sickly weak sound, like the air pushing out of him for the last time. "Oh, the irony, we, the greatest of all creatures on earth, unable to resist him, and yet *he* defeated by the simplest. A virus. A flu virus!"

He coughed, blood and phlegm choking the back of his throat. "Poldek Tacit, you have seen nothing yet. God's wrath, it will end the war. My work is done. It has already begun to take hold, striking down all those of an age who can fight. The nations consumed by this war will have no choice but to end their fighting," he added with a wry smile, as his coughing overwhelmed him. "I have already done what I needed to do, far greater an achievement, far greater a vision than anything I could have achieved in Paris at the Mass for Peace. It is just a shame it has come four years too late for so many, for so much, but better now than not at all."

"How many do you expect will die, Poré?" asked Isabella.

"Many," coughed the blue-grey pallid man. "Enough. But less than will be taken by this war should it be allowed to continue. The horrors will end. Already they have given it a name, Spanish flu, perhaps after you, my dear!" he croaked with grim humour, looking at Isabella. He turned back to Tacit. "Unleashed in China from where God's wrath was perceived, brought in via Canada, spread across North America and then into Europe when the Americans brought it with them, a second wave of influenza. Its hold will be total. Millions will die. Nations will be unable to continue this senseless killing. War will end." He descended into a hacking painful choke, consuming every sinew of him. Slowly the coughs dissipated, leaving behind a heaving bag of bones the colour of slate.

When a little of his spirit and strength returned, he spoke again. "It seems to me as if we have always fought, you and I, unknowingly fighting for the same side. It is the way of things, the way of man, to fight the man he distrusts. And I did distrust you. In many ways I still do, but my time is at an end, my work done. There is only one more thing for me to do, and you, if you wish it."

"And what is that, Poré?" asked Tacit.

His hand burrowed in the folds of his cloak, drawing out the stinking wolf's pelt. "Perhaps you do not realise, but there is less that separates us than you might think, Poldek Tacit. I was an Inquisitor like you. An Inquisitor!" He laughed, a short tired cackle. "Do not think it so strange. While my time in the Inquisition was only short, a blink of the eye compared to your service, its impact upon me has lasted a lifetime. They made me understand what it felt to lose loved ones, to lose love, to learn hate, to spend one's life consumed by anger, driven on by it. But you cannot hate forever. Eventually the hate has to end. Eventually you need to drive hate from you, and with it the fear." He pushed the wolf pelt into Tacit's hands. "Take it, Poldek," he said. "Take it. Wear it. And go and kill Cardinal Bishop Adansoni. Go and kill the Antichrist."

Tacit's hand closed around the stinking hide as Poré fell back to the thin mattress. The voice in Tacit mocked, assuring him that he would never be able to do as Poré had asked him, assuring him that only one path lay ahead, and that path was already prophesied.

And Poré's eyes opened in thin slits from where he had fallen back on his bed, before he said, with his final breath, "When… when *he* finds you, do as you are bid and kill him. It is what will finally free you both."

NINETY

Etaples. France.

The soldiers had dug a great pit just a little way away from the hubbub of the regiment, patients and nursing staff, near enough so the carrying of bodies to it by an overstretched and ailing team wasn't too arduous, far enough away to keep a good distance between the living and the plague-ridden dead. It was a trench dug by twenty men, thirty feet long and ten feet wide, deep enough to pile four bodies on top of each other and a good few feet of soil on top.

"That'll suffice," remarked the Sergeant in command, only to regret his words by the end of the second day when the pit was already filled with the blue-skinned dead and another ordered to be dug alongside.

Everywhere across the famished camp was a weeping and a coughing, incoherent murmuring on rabid frothing tongues and the morbid silence

268

of death. Between the bombed-out brick buildings and erected tents, all wards were full of sickly spluttering people, feverish and blue, writhing intermittently in their beds, soiled sheets clinging to exposed skin, blood, shit and boiled grey cotton.

Everyone seemed defeated by the influenza, worn down and close to collapse, if they hadn't done so already, coughing patients in beds, soldiers slumped over their rifles hoping for a little respite from the growing chills gathering in their bodies. Exhausted-looking nurses went this way and that, going between beds to turn over a soldier or turn a sheet up over a body. The nurses barely spoke. Words could not heal here. Words couldn't help because most of the soldiers, those riddled with the plague, never heard them. But the air was full of the sounds of people when they come to the end, godless or not, weeping, feeble murmuring and prayers.

A steady stream of sweaty stumbling soldiers and porters came into the hospitals and tents, taking away bodies from the beds where they had died, carrying them out bound in their grey, red and brown stained sheets, just gathering up the corners and taking them away. Behind them, nurses then swooped, stripping down the mattresses before other bodies were put in their place.

People weren't dying. They were merely fading from life, one minute there, clinging with what little they had to life, then in the next, nothing but a breathless hush and gone.

"Sweet Mother of God!" whispered an army officer to the man opposite him, both watching the line of bodies being carried out of the hospital wards from the training square where they had lined up for bayonet practice. "They're all fucking dying in there."

"And we're fucking dying out here on the front line. Some bloody good joke someone's playing on us." The soldier rested his elbow on the muzzle of his rifle. "I only came out here for an adventure."

"Some bloody adventure."

"Rumour is it's the same in every camp hospital, every unit the length of the front line, on both sides, people falling sick. Some flu."

"They left the window open and in flew Enza," chanted a soldier next to them, standing down from his shadow fighting to join their conversation. "It's in the cities and the towns too," he added. "Right across Europe, even across the seas, apparently. America's got it bad. Australia. India. Millions they say are dying. Dropping dead in the street." He whistled. "Makes you wonder."

"Wonder what?" asked the officer.

"What it's all for, us, here, fighting, if we're getting done over by the bloody flu."

NINETY-ONE

LAVENTIE. FRANCE.

Isabella followed Tacit out of the church into the cold air. Compared to the festering stink of the makeshift hospital, the coal-dust breeze smelt like nirvana.

"So that's that then?" she asked dolefully, pushing her hands into the pockets of her coat against the wind.

She looked down at her boots, boots which had carried her across Europe and back, feeling eviscerated of sentiment, all the emotion run out of her. Dejected. She had believed that finally catching up with Poré would have brought them some sort of resolution, the tying up of loose ends. But now, here, at the end, it seemed that things were even more frayed. "We found Poré. We couldn't stop him. We're too late."

"Perhaps," replied Tacit, watching the heavens, allowing his eyes to slowly return to the clipped and disfigured buildings surrounding the square. The town looked like every other town he had passed through over the last four years, demolished by war. "Or perhaps we were never meant to stop him?"

Haha! Fickle hypocrite!

"After all we've done, all we've lost, that sounds a magnanimous admission of defeat, Poldek," said Isabella, watching Tacit out of the corner of her eye, a sly light in it.

He looked down at the wolf's pelt in his hands, massaging his fingers through the dense matted fur. The smell of it filled his nostrils, the caustic stink of animal musk and blood. It seemed to him that the more he worked at the hide, the more the smell rose off it, lingering in his senses, eating away at the voices in his head, a shield to their curses, the smell of the fur battling against the spit and hiss of the devilish sounds inside him.

"So do we go back now?" asked Isabella. "Back to the Vatican?"

Yes! Yes! Yes!

Tacit could hear the voice cheer and chant in his head, emerging through the musk of wolf stink like a screaming apparition from a heavy fog.

"'When *he* finds you, do as you are bid and kill him.' I wonder what Poré meant by that?"

"Obviously Adansoni," replied Isabella, resting against Tacit's broad side, as she pulled the boot from her foot and dropped a stone from it, "if Adansoni is who we supposed he is."

Your master, scum.

"He is," hissed Tacit, like a snatched admission, a secret he promised never to divulge.

"I never wanted to go back there, back to the Vatican, to face whatever resides in that place, but this road, it's reached its end. There seems nowhere else for us to go?"

"I agree."

"Poré's words, do they give you hope?"

"No."

Whoever spares the rod hates his son.

"They do me."

"I'm glad you have hope, for I have none any more."

"Cheery as ever, Poldek," replied Isabella, pulling her boot back on and leaning against the wall, caught in a ray of cold but bright sunshine.

"Pablo," said Tacit. "I wonder whatever happened to him? We know he was with Poré in England, that they travelled to France together?"

"Maybe he went off with the Chinese workers, maybe he's on the front line with them now? Maybe he's dead?" Isabella made each suggestion with a tone as cold as the sun. She thought of all she had done for the young man in Italy and how he had repaid her so cruelly.

Tacit shrugged, looking down the main thoroughfare towards where there was a pool of trucks parked up. He wondered whether any of them would be heading south, or back west towards the coastal ports. "But you're right. We need to go back, back to the Vatican." He considered the different routes they could take to get there and which would be the quickest. Now the desire to return back there was overwhelming. Incessant, just like the voices forever in him. And they appreciated what he was saying, that finally he was relinquishing his fight against them.

"What do you reckon?" Tacit asked. "Do we walk, or do we try and find a truck to take us to a town or city from where we can get a train onwards…"

"Let's at least try and see if we can find something that'll give us a lift some of the way," moaned Isabella. "My feet! I feel like I've walked all of Europe."

"We have, but we only have maybe one more journey left. Come on."

He stepped out from the shadows towards the waiting wagons, knowing that the gravest part of the journey now lay ahead – and the part Tacit had most feared.

NINETY-TWO

New York City. New York. America.

"Hey!" The police officer raised his baton and muscled his way over from where he had been watching the traffic and the crowds going up and down midtown towards the plaid-suited man on the sidewalk. "Did I just see you spit?" he asked, pushing back his bleached white cap over his hairline, the badge in the centre of it glinting as it caught the choking sun.

"No, sir!" replied the man, shaking his head, but the movement made his brain and vision spin and he shivered and felt a chill run the length of him. "No, sir," he replied, trying to squeeze away from the altercation and make good his escape.

"I'll split your head!" warned the officer, stepping into his path and pushing the end of his truncheon at the man's face.

"I gotta clear my throat, officer! There's no offence clearing your throat."

"You wanna believe that? I gotta go run you in now, see."

"For spitting?" The young man looked desperate and lonely.

"Damn right for spitting. Ain't you heard?"

"Heard what, sir?"

"About all this flu? You can't go spitting no more. Spitting is what pigs and hobos do, and judging by your suit, I'd say you were neither.

Or maybe you just dress up smart. But you ain't got no manners, that's for sure, boy." He looked hard at the young man, squinting. "Say, what's the matter with you anyway? You don't look so good."

"I ain't."

"You say you gotta clear your throat?"

"I sure did, officer," replied the man, dredging his fingers through his greased hair. "Like I feel I gotta do again. And my head... my head sure is pounding, sir. That, and my throat. Closing up real bad."

"What d'ya mean, closing up?"

"Exactly that. Closing up, like invisible hands is on my neck."

"Sounds like you got the flu, boy!" replied the officer, taking a step back from him quickly.

"I ain't got the flu, officer! I just gotta cold. 'Tis the coming autumn air! That's all."

"You got the flu, man. Perhaps it'd be best if I don't run you down the station after all."

"I'd mighty appreciate that, sir!"

"Best you just run on home now. You'd just spread it around the precinct house, the old flu, if I ran you in." The police officer made shapes with the end of his truncheon in the space between him and the sweating sickly man. He shooed him with the end of it. "You go on home now. Straight on home, mind. And you stay there, at your house, you hear me? You have family?"

"Just my mother."

"She sick too?"

"She's coughing. Has been for the last week or so."

"Then you damned well go home and you bolt your door and close your windows and you don't open them till you is better. You hear me?"

"I hear you, sir!" replied the man, starting off down the street.

"You get going!" the officer called after him.

"I'm going!"

"And if I see you spit again, I'll run you in faster than your feet can carry you, you hear me?"

But the man didn't. All he heard was his coughing and the word flu resonating around in his shuddering slippery mind.

NINETY-THREE

Tacit and Isabella had found a truck leaving for Arras that very evening from Laventie.

"Arras, Poldek!" said Isabella with amazement and wonder, as she drew herself into the back of the wagon and Tacit's enveloping arms.

There was also a sense of pride knotted into her words and, as they pulled into the city, close to the approach to the railway station, she paused and took a moment to remember the place where she and Tacit had first met. Where it had all begun.

The station itself was now a bombed-out ruin, but the railway line had been put back into use and was running an hourly service south to Paris. Human endurance and ingenuity. The very same which had helped them kill so many on both sides of the front line for the last four years.

"Do you remember?" she asked him, as they climbed the incline to the station and the waiting train. "Last time we were here we were running for a train to Paris!"

But Tacit shook his head, barely deciphering the words Isabella had spoken to him, his mind bound up with the torments of the voices and their enticements, almost entirely caught in the maelstrom of chaos they wove. "No," he said. "No, I don't remember."

At Paris they took a shared compartment in a sixteen-carriage train, pulled by a jet-black steam engine, spitting and hissing like a wild bull clapped in irons. Tacit fell almost immediately into an uneasy and restless sleep.

So, finally, you're returning to me then?

Tacit shuddered awake, his eyes focused on the old man sitting opposite him in the carriage, immediately bewildered and afraid.

"What are you doing here?" he cried at Adansoni, wondering how he had found them, how he had entered the carriage unheard and unseen.

Doing here? I've always been here, you fucking moron. I've always been inside you, since your mother spat you from her cunt.

Tacit wept. "Don't... don't talk about her that way!"

I'll talk about her however I want, you fucking shit. You need to remember your place, Satan. So what finally changed your mind? Losing your friend, Frost? Or the wolf-bitch, Prideux? After all, you have so few friends to lose! Or perhaps it was failing to stop Poré? The realisation that you aren't so great after all? But you will be, when you're alongside me. I'll make you great again.

He's done for us, you know? Done for us in this war. But no bother. Once you return back to the Vatican, perhaps we can use what he has started? They are End Times he's begun, after all. We can build upon his misery, find a way to lengthen the war. The Americans haven't bled enough. Plenty of young lives still to give there.

"Isa… Isabella…"

What on earth are you talking about? Isabella? Oh, Satan, no, I've dealt with Isabella.

"What? What do you mean?"

Tacit was suddenly aware of the utter silence in the carriage, the cloying smell of blood in the air. His senses were drawn to his right, to the seat next to him where Isabella had held him as he'd fallen asleep.

He looked, and at first his eyes failed to register what they were telling him. "No!" he wailed. "No!" he cried again, reaching out to the roughly hacked body, all that remained of Isabella.

"Hey," her voice soothed, and Tacit jumped, back in the train, back in the world, feeling her run her hand down the length of his arm. It was warm. "Don't worry. It was just a nightmare. Shhh. Go back to sleep." She kissed him and fell back to her own dreams.

Tacit shivered, the murmur of relief and fear peeling off him in slowly receding waves.

Night turned into day and then returned again to night, once more shadowing the carriages in black. After the initial good pace as they set out from Paris, the locomotive had fallen to a sullen jerking trundle, stopping frequently at stations where no one got on or off, but stopping all the same, as if it was expected that the train do so regardless.

After his long sleep, Tacit watched the slow roll of the French countryside trundling past with his dark hooded eyes, nothing to suggest that anything was awry beyond the compartment glass, other than the towns and villages being mostly empty, many ghost towns or occupied by women and children but rarely any men.

Gradually the train climbed into mountains and then fell, the countryside giving way to a random scattering of houses before the houses became streets and then boulevards and then broad blocks of grey and bleached white buildings. Heat teased into the carriages from opened windows, allowing the suggestion of a breeze into the train. Seagulls followed the railway line and the sight of the sea, the endless blue of the Mediterranean, filled the vision.

At Montpellier they spent days waiting for a boat to Civitavecchia in Italy to leave.

Isabella used the time to think and sleep.

Tacit used the time to let the demons slowly devour him, his mind and the last of his ability to fight them.

NINETY-FOUR

WELLINGTON. NEW ZEALAND.

The town was a living hell of rasping blue death.

To use the word *living* did a disservice to all those caught in the plague's grip, for no one was living on the island, but instead dying and dying fast, too fast for the authorities to keep up, dying from the torment dredged up from something no one had ever known before, not for over five hundred years. Not since the Black Death.

Long lines of soldiers, men sent back from the front, having done their bit or deemed too ill to serve any longer, now stood outside the hospital, bent over, cowed by sickness, clutching blankets while shivering from the fever in the persistent rain, waiting for space for them to become free. Inside, beds overflowed from wards into hallways and out onto porches.

"Look at them!" exclaimed a doctor from the front lawn, where he and his colleague had taken shelter under the broad wide branches of a willow, just five minutes away from that hell, five minutes from the stink and the suffering and the inky black putrescence filling up every patient's face. "Just look at those poor bastards, John. They go out to do a job, a brave job, a righteous job, and they come home... come home like bloody beggars. Perhaps they went out expecting to come home with a nick or two? Doesn't every soldier? But this?" He waved with his hand. "They've come home with the bloody plague!"

"Now, Sidney, I think that's a little bit strong?"

"Too strong, John? What would you call it then? It's like a bloody curse. The poor bastards can't bloody breathe." His voice was growing more desperate. "I've heard stories of some ripping out their throats to get a little air into themselves. It's all round the bloody world, John!" He began to weep. "It's around the… we're bloody doomed, John! We're bloody doomed! For God's sake, John, don't look at me!"

He turned away, hunched, letting the emotion out of himself, hacking and sobbing until pride brought the weeping to a close. He drew a sleeve across his nose, turning back. "What the bloody hell are we doing this for, hey? Tell me that, John? We're surgeons. We patch up limbs, we take off damaged ones, we reset bones. Jesus, we can even talk soldiers out of their problems. But this…" He flapped again with his hand. "We have no cure, John. There is no antidote! Nothing, anywhere in the world. And it's everywhere. It's everywhere, John. Everywhere!"

He stopped, as if exhausted by his outburst.

"Jesus, John. I'm sorry. I'm sorry. I'm just tired. Too tired."

"Sidney, please," replied the surgeon. "I understand, we're all tired."

"It's just I don't understand."

"Understand, Sidney?"

"What have we done to fall so far from God's grace, so far that he felt it only right to forsake us?"

NINETY-FIVE

The Vatican. Vatican City.

Welcome home, my son.

Tacit and Isabella stood in the quiet of Rome looking up at the dark closed walls of Vatican City, the lights beyond the impenetrable walls shrouded.

277

And they shivered.

Even during the very worst of his nightmares, when the voices assured him that when he finally came and looked on the masterpiece prepared for him, he would be cowed in wonder, Tacit always believed he would still find some solace in the knowledge that the Vatican would retain at least a small beacon of light, love and hope to him and to those of his faith. Now, as he looked at the great closed stone door, one of the entrances to the city, all shut up and grey in the dusk, he quivered and thought it the last place on the planet he wished to be. There were lights running along the top of the Vatican's wall, figures gathered in groups at its base, watching anyone foolish or brave enough to draw too close be sent away with a warning, or subdued and dragged inside.

It seemed that the city had turned from light into darkness. Hope into hate. Life into death. A prison for all the wickedness which had come into the world via the war and the Antichrist.

Look upon my works, ye mighty, and despair!

Tacit groaned and sat down, his head in his hands, fighting the raging pain within, the urgent voices willing him on. Footsteps, the sharp quick rap of shoes on cobbles from a Priest running towards them, drew him sharply out of his malaise, the man's habit hitched up around his knees, looking back over his shoulder as often as he looked ahead, glancing back at the Vatican walls from where he had escaped. His feet slapped clumsily upon the stones, too clumsily, and he went down, spinning and clattering, skin and bone connecting with paving slabs and mortar, a dull clatter, a snatched shriek, a dazed grunt, as the figure turned over and promptly sat up, nursing his grazed and bleeding forehead.

"What's the matter with you?" Tacit asked, going over to him and helping him up. "What's the rush?" But the Inquisitor's head was nothing but noise and he knew that what was tormenting him was the same that tormented the Priest, enough to make him flee from the place of its origin.

"Terrors! Terrors!" the Priest wept, half maddened, and Isabella took his hand to calm him. "The Cardinal Secretary of State!" he croaked, once his discomposure had softened and he'd regained a little more of himself again. "Possessed!" He threw his face into his hands. "Lost, lost to the forces of darkness!"

"So the rumours are true! The Vatican has fallen?"

Tacit considered Isabella's words, chewing them in his mouth, as the woman he knew he still loved, though didn't feel it then, turned her eyes back to the Vatican's walls.

"Hate to say it, but I don't rate our chances, Poldek, two against a whole city!"

Not your chances, she-dog. Bring her to me, Satan. We will rape her in the anus.

He'd heard rumours, as had Isabella as they travelled back to the city, of corruption and degradation, that malice and a cruel new rhetoric had been adopted by the Vatican. And forever he'd heard the voice in his head goad and warn as to what he would witness when he arrived. Now here, he felt adrift in a sea of his own madness and indecision, utterly bewildered by the love he felt for the woman next to him, wishing with all his heart to protect and keep her safe, while secretly crippled and absorbed by the Devil's empowering exhortations and desperation at what he could only guess was occurring in the Vatican.

He had supposed that his path would be made clear to him once he had returned to the capital of the Catholic world, once they returned back to the place of his calling. And now, secretly, he knew that it *was* clear, that he had no choice but to go to his master. Lightning flashed and thunder growled above the place. Another hard night was closing in.

Isabella stood up to watch. "Something is happening!" she called, squinting towards the noise and confusion coming from the storm above the city.

Shattered eardrums! Branded tongues! Stitched up bleeding eyes!

Next to her, Tacit winced, folding in on himself, fighting the invisible command to rise and walk to the gates. The voice was all about him, screaming in him, knowing with certainty that he had come, that he was standing just beyond the city's walls, that all he had to do was stand and walk forward towards the guards, to let them take them to his master. And after this moment, all would be complete and he would be assigned his place next to his master, and power would be all his and he would want for nought, save for bloodshed and hate, darkness and greed.

"Get down!" hissed Tacit, snapping out of his possession and reaching to pull Isabella from where she had stood to look. "They'll see you!"

"So what do we do?" she asked. "Do we just go on in and face what we must face head on?"

The voices retreated, and Tacit returned back to what he did best. He pulled both revolvers from their holsters, feeling their weight in his hands, considering an attack on the doors in front of them. He changed his mind as the last residues of devilry twisted and spun away, pushing the sidearms back in time with their disappearance. "No, let's see if there's another way in. I don't fancy our chances going this way."

He drew Isabella away from where they had been standing, knowing it was only a matter of time until the Antichrist controlled him completely.

NINETY-SIX

The Vatican. Vatican City.

Somewhere high up in the Vatican, Adansoni was singing. He possessed a baritone voice, coached from a young age, still retaining its rich vivid qualities despite the ravages of time and all that had since come to pass.

He had bathed this evening and dressed in robes of purest white mink, enjoying a glass of wine while he was being clothed and then another as he sat watching the grey shadows sound emanating up from St Peter's Square. Even in the darkness he inhabited, he could still appreciate beautiful things.

All day he had detected a change on the wind, the tease of expectation, the suggestion that something long hoped and for had finally arrived. And now, as he surveyed his domain and the twinkling lights of Rome beyond, he knew that it had.

There was the sound of gunfire, a brief shriek of panic and then a little more gunfire, a stout clipped cry and then a third burst of rifles before silence.

As the gunfire faded, ricocheting like fire crackers around the city's archways and walls, he closed his eyes and drank in the sounds and damp smells of the Vatican night, the croak and chatter of crows, the cackle of laughter, the smart march of inquisitorial boots.

And something more again.

Satan.

Adansoni had always sensed him, felt a connection with him, an understanding of emotion, of shared beliefs and expectation. And now he felt that he was close, very close, somewhere in Rome, close, but not yet close enough for him to embrace and envelop him completely.

He had felt Tacit's resistance constantly, his doubt, but with it his growing acceptance that there was only one route left open to him. The reason he had returned to the Vatican.

Adansoni knew that all of his life Tacit had himself battled possessions in his line of work as an Inquisitor, fighting for those entrapped by the Devil's seductive draw, now finding himself fighting against his slow gradual creep upon him, the entangling bonds of his promises. He knew Tacit would not give up the fight easily, Satan having picked him because he was the strongest, the quickest, unparalleled, but with such majesty came an unmatched resistance, something Adansoni had come to admire. Satan had chosen wisely.

But eventually Tacit would fail. Adansoni could sense that he was failing right now. He could feel it, smell it even, almost taste his defeat. And after all, where else did Tacit have to go, now that he had come? The man could only run so far before the prophecy caught up with him, and the Vatican was where his destiny would be finally realised.

Alongside his master, the Antichrist. And with it, Adansoni's ascension to ultimate unstoppable power.

Adansoni reached out for a small silver bell and rang it continually until an Inquisitor appeared.

"My Lord?" asked the heavy-set man.

"Pope Benedict."

"My Lord?"

"Are you slow?" Adansoni asked the Inquisitor, baring teeth. "It is time to put him to the sword."

The Inquisitor hesitated and Adansoni supposed that the guard was simple or not loyal enough. He picked up a revolver and shot him through the heart.

With the gunshot, another pair of Inquisitors came running.

"Why do you dawdle?" Adansoni spat at them, making both fierce-looking men blanch. "Why do you keep me waiting? You have your order!" He stole towards them, his fists raised, screaming his demands. "Put that dog Pope Benedict down!"

"Honoured," replied the Inquisitor, but there was still hesitancy in his manner.

"What is it?" hissed Adansoni, recognising it, his eyes as venomous as the grit of his teeth.

The Inquisitor swallowed, seeming to shrink under his master's glare and the message he was bringing. "There's something coming," he said, letting his hand wander behind him towards the corner.

"Coming?"

"From the crypts." He shivered, and for a while it seemed he might weep. "Something inside the Vatican is coming!" he cried, "with teeth and claws and rage!"

NINETY-SEVEN

The Vatican. Vatican City.

The entrance to the sewer Tacit had found to gain access to the city stank, and inside it smelt worse, as if the city's foundations were rotten and filling the tunnels and damp passages with their putrescence.

And Tacit supposed then, if he needed any further evidence, that the city was indeed rotten.

"You only ever take me to the fancy places in the world, Poldek!" muttered Isabella, placing her feet cautiously in the slippery slime of the brick walkway that ran either side of the channel of brackish slow-moving water. Small furry bodies could be seen swimming ahead, the rats occasionally climbing up onto the runoff ledges and scampering away, seeking out black holes in which to hide from these strangers.

"It's the only sure way in," replied Tacit, taking Isabella's hand and helping her cross the stream of dark-flowing waste water running straight from the Vatican's cubicles. "The only way we'll get into the city without being seen. You saw the Inquisitors on the walls to the city, the locked gates." He shook his head. "Something's changed."

"The war has changed everything."

"Which war?" retorted Tacit. The voice in his head suddenly, louder than ever, mocked him pitifully.

We haven't even begun yet, Satan. Young and old, ripped to bloody ribbons. Tears of blood!

"Once we're inside, then where do we go?"

"Adansoni," said the giant man, like an act of expiation. "Adansoni. We go straight to Adansoni."

Kiss kiss.

He paused and thrust his head down a corridor. He didn't like something about it, either the smell or the sound coming out of it, and kept walking on. "We have to find Adansoni."

Fuck you too, you bastard pig fucker.

Isabella followed him, but two paces behind, scrutinising him as they walked. Tacit felt her eyes on him and turned back to see.

"Keep up," he warned. "We need to get to Adansoni."

Yes, yes, come to me, like a whore, whore!

"So you keep saying."

"So I've said from the very beginning. I need to get to Adansoni."

"Is that what they're telling you?" asked Isabella, and when Tacit looked at her, pulling a face, feigning confusion, she added, "The voices? In here?" She held the fingertips of her right hand gently to her temple. "Is that what they're commanding you to do, Poldek?"

Tacit glowered and turned away, but Isabella snatched him by the arm, turning him to face her. Instantly the voice in him rose to a shriek and his free hand was at her throat. He threw Isabella back against the stone, hard into the wall, his fingers tightening harder still, a vice around her neck.

Yes, yes! Kill the she-bitch! Throttle the life out of her!

Isabella's eyes widened blood-red in their sockets, her pupils pinpricks, her mouth opening wide as a fish out of water, wordless, soundless, save for the pinch of a gravel-like breath from her suffocating lungs.

Squeeze the breath from her! Yes! Yes, squeeze her till her neck breaks!

Her hands were on his arms, fumbling feebly, dull fingers reaching for him to stop. Tacit could see them try, could see the last of her life pass out of her, her eyes glaze. Another wave of hate for her thudded into him and he pressed even harder at her throat. Isabella's hands went limp and fell away, her body quivering and then still, just like Mila's. Just like…

The realisation of what he was doing, the impulse of violence, struck him like a bolt and he cried out, letting go of Isabella at once, catching her as she fell.

"Isabella! Dear God!" he cried, drawing her into his arms, rocking her, shaking her back to life. "Dear God," *You'll not find him here*, "what have I done. Isabella! Isabella!" She stirred and coughed, her breath tight and strained. "Dear God, dear God, thank goodness. Thank goodness. My darling!" He said the same words, over and over, shielding her against the darkness and the cold, holding her until breath and life had returned back to her, until she could sit unaided. He wept uncontrollably, his head in his hands. "What have I become?"

Pathetic.

He was shuddering, caught in a madness. Isabella's neck felt as if she had been hung by a noose, her voice fragile and sore. She watched Tacit closely, knowing it was the madness which had devoured him temporarily, not him. She drew his hands away, holding the sides of his head so she was looking straight into his eyes, speaking calming words to him, drawing the panic and the poison out of him.

"It's all right, Poldek," she assured him, her eyes not leaving his for a moment. "It's all right. It's gone. The moment has gone."

"But I could have… if I had…"

"But you didn't. You didn't, Poldek."

He nodded, sweat beading and dripping over his eyelids, down into his eyes and across his cheeks, despite the cold and the fierce dark of the sewer.

"Yes," he replied, nodding, "yes, there's nothing now. Nothing. It's gone. Gone. Thank you, Isabella," he muttered. "Thank you. Let's go. Let's go on," he said, climbing clumsily to his feet.

As the voice in him turned once more to a vile debauched cacophony of venom, spite and ridicule, he wondered why he had lied to Isabella and wished that he had the strength to resist like the man she thought he was, the man he always wanted to be.

They reached the end of the walkway and Tacit looked up. There was a rusted square grate above them and moonlight beyond. He reached up and lifted the metal bars, grinding them from their swollen housing, drawing himself out and checking the darkened yard into which he had climbed. It was empty. Deserted, but from the heights of the building beyond came mangled and repetitive laughter, as if the Vatican had become an asylum. He reached down and proffered his hand to Isabella.

Such a gentleman.

"You've used this route before, then?" she asked him, attempting to brush the moist clinging filth of the sewer from her clothes, but deciding against it. She cursed silently, following Tacit into the shadows, watching how he walked with purpose, without thought, wondering then if she was following Tacit or again following Satan.

And then he stopped, quite suddenly.

Surprise.

In the small square ahead, beyond the arched corridor down which they were creeping, the figure of a bloodied man was hanging, nailed upside down on a wooden cross. He had been stripped naked, his stomach ripped open, his organs pulled out and left to hang over and around him like contorted jewellery of crimson flesh.

An exhibition of cruelty and warning.

They both recognised him at once, his face untouched to reveal his identity to all.

Basquez.

He didn't hear Isabella sob, he didn't even look at her. He just heard the voices fortify and coax him to admire the brutal beauty in what they had done to the traitor, what they did to all traitors, to all those who failed them.

"Come on," said Tacit. "Let's keep going."

NINETY-EIGHT

The Vatican. Vatican City.

They were inside.

Blood tricked down columns. Fresh entrails hung from hooks hammered into walls. Naked flayed bodies were roped across or strung between statues, faces smashed in with the butts of guns. Flies buzzed with the violence and malice crackling in the air. Every facet of Tacit's mind was hammering, the suggestion of slipping over into brutality hinged like a spring in his temper, just waiting to snap open. He clenched his fists so tight his palms were cut open by his nails.

The passageways and chambers were clotted up with the grubby reminder of carnage, body parts, discarded weapons, the clutter of litter from an army on the move. Something beat and heaved in the building's bowels, like the feeling that comes just before a storm is about to hit.

Everywhere Inquisitors and grim-faced Priests prowled and seethed, swearing and chanting, throwing accusations between themselves and orders to prepare to face something that was coming up from below. At once Isabella thought they meant her and Tacit and wondered how they had been discovered.

She thinks it's you for whom we prepare, arrogant swine whore.

There were thousands of Inquisitors in the Vatican, milling around, checking armour, listening attentively to orders, gathered in halls, testing their prowess in sparring matches with their peers, or watching the walls and doors of the city for anyone to come unannounced and unwanted. Their numbers and manner shocked both Tacit and Isabella. An army ready to do their master's bidding.

Holiness had turned unholy. Temperance had turn to oppression. The Vatican was ready for a war.

They reached Adansoni's apartment and private chapel, hugging the shadows and staying in the quiet corridors and back passageways in the Vatican, creeping like thieves through the lesser known and travelled paths. Blood drenched their boots and spoiled their clothes. Everywhere smelt like an abattoir.

There were three children's heads which had been ripped off and nailed in a line on the door to Adansoni's residence.

Suffer little children.

They slipped inside the Cardinal Secretary of State's residence, and at once shivered against the cold. It was bitter inside, deathly so. Though the first of autumn's tightening clutches were upon the city, winter creeping like a spectre around the edges of each day, the chamber seemed uncommonly cold, a cold store, its tendrils of ice permeating through the building. Their breath billowed in clouds and they drew their clothes tighter about them, knowing why the many bodies strung up about the ceiling by chains and cords had not started to rot and smell.

Pretty decorations. Let's hang the bitch from one of the hooks and see how long it is till she stinks.

"Shut up!" shouted Tacit, driving his hand in to his temple.

"Are you all right?" asked Isabella.

He nodded, and she snatched her fingers tighter still around the grip of her revolver, feeling the warmth spread through them. "Hello?" she called out. Nothing answered back.

"There's no one here," said Tacit.

I am otherwise engaged. For now. Revolting peasants.

Everything in the apartment was silent, like the grave.

"Where is he?" she asked. "Where's Adansoni?"

Skin prickled like plucked poultry. Isabella shivered and drew a hand into the crook of Tacit's arm. She was a aware that the curtains seemed to writhe and shimmer in the hellish candlelight. She looked closer and saw that their surface was home to a scrabbling clinging blanket of maggots, burrowing and feeding on the blood which oozed into the fabric from above.

"Dear God," she muttered, drawing back.

Wrong again.

And then she saw it, the devilish-looking statue on the table, wet with the residue of something which looked like more blood. "Good God," she said.

Will the bitch never learn?

There was a black sheet over the table, the pentagram of silver stitched in it. The same symbol dug into the earth of the cave in the Carso from which the Seven Princes had tried to drag themselves. "Then it's true?" she asked him. "All of it?"

"Was there ever any doubt?"

Of course not. You must have fucked her brains away, Satan.

The voices in his head told him he never needed to come here merely to discover it to be true. For he had always known. Always.

They searched Adansoni's apartment, Isabella's bustle and eagerness as much to work some heat into her joints as it was to make sure that the residence was empty.

Nosey.

When they knew it was, Tacit's efforts noticeably abject and tired, they returned to the main entrance hall, circling like slowly spinning dancers to a silent tune, their eyes on the walls and ceiling, coming to a halt in the very centre of the room, looking at each other.

"How did he do it?" asked Isabella. *Because I am clever and smart.* "How did he manage to get away with it? Draw so many to his banner, convince so many to serve and work for him?"

"The frailties of men's hearts," replied Tacit, sweeping the walls of the room with his eyes for any more clues. He was suddenly aware that the voice in his head had gone, that instantly he heard nothing, as if it had slipped away, vanished. The silence was like manna from heaven, a ringing gift of life. He closed his eyes and felt like weeping, such was the joy at hearing nothing but his own breathing, his own thoughts, not those of another.

"Are you all right?" asked Isabella.

"Yes!" cheered Tacit, nodding. "The voices! The voices have stopped!"

"I wonder why? Why now?"

There was a drape of black hanging across one wall, conspicuous by its morbid colour, and Tacit went towards it. "How did Adansoni get away with it?" He reached his hand up to pull it from the wall. "Power, and the promise of wielding it or at least basking in its afterglow, of being on the conquering side that wields it, it's a charm few can resist." He gathered the folds in his fingers, the fabric cold and clammy, like dead flesh. "Adansoni didn't need any tricks, didn't need any rituals to grow the Darkest Hand. Fear, ambition, greed, these are all things which reside in men's hearts, all traits which are easy to control, to turn people into the Devil's property." He took a firm grip on the black fabric and tore it down, revealing the altar behind it, lined with a cloth of black, adorned with a pentagram of silver and a larger brass statue of the Devil, glistening with darkening crimson. Beyond were more bodies, naked, strung upside down, disembowelled, some missing heads, others hands and feet, hanging like strange mouldering drying meats.

Tacit looked hard at the monstrous scene. "There can be no doubt now."

"Here, in the heart of the Vatican!" Isabella drew a shaking hand to her mouth, wishing to weep, but something hardened in her and in its place came defiance and anger. "I just can't believe how long the Darkest Hand's reach has grown. The Vatican, now a citadel of Hell?" Isabella shrieked in rage, throwing her hands in the air and stalking towards the glistening dripping statuette of the Devil, pushing it from the black sackcloth on which it sat, sending it over the side of the altar and onto the hard slate floor below. The Devil's arms and head broke off.

"The Vatican is no citadel of Hell," growled Tacit, shaking his head to chase away the demons as much as to show his intent, determination hardening in him, a final defiance, a last resistance that he supposed would be futile. "Like a soul, the city has become possessed." He looked at Isabella. "We have returned to exorcise it."

NINETY-NINE

THE VATICAN. VATICAN CITY.

A couple of paces towards the exit from Adansoni's empty residence Tacit reeled backwards, as if struck by an invisible blow. He collapsed into the fetid drape behind him on the wall, tearing it as he fell, caught by his trailing arm. It half covered him as he went down, maggots and clotted blood falling onto him.

He dragged himself free, helped by Isabella, groaning, his hands to his head.

"What is it?" cried Isabella. Her touch upon him seemed to lift whatever possession had seized him, shaking the temporary madness away.

"The voices!" he lamented, reaching out to a nearby table to steady himself. "They are back!" *Thought I had gone, Satan?* "Greater than ever!" *Fuck you I have, Devil scum.* Tacit's voice sounded small and defeated. "I don't know how much longer I can fight them."

"But you must, Poldek!"

Try. Just you try.

Tacit nodded, his face contorting into a mask of determination. "Come on," he said, standing taller and powering towards the door, "let's go."

But two more paces forwards, it sounded suddenly as if all hell had been let loose in the corridor outside. Screams, the pounding of a thousand pairs of running boots, protestations and pleading, gunfire and then panicked shouts checked their step.

Tacit stopped and held Isabella back.

And then came the howls.

He glanced across at her, and a wondering look came to their eyes, the very same which had lit them in Rome when the wolves had dragged themselves from the sewers and dark places of the city and fought the Inquisition, allowing Tacit and the others to make good their escape.

Beyond the door, an uproar was tearing through the building. It sounded to Isabella as if a cataclysm had struck and from it had poured the seething essence of chaos. When they had first come back into the Vatican, everywhere seemed full of dark foreboding silence, the shuffling menace of plotting dark voices, the wicked chattering of the Darkest Hand's incantations. But now, all of it had now been drowned out by the baleful howls of Hombre Lobo, hundreds of wolves, perhaps thousands, such was the cacophony of noise which filled the passageways and halls. Vatican City, always precise and ordered, now boiled and writhed like an angry sea, ravaged with claws and talons and the battering roar of machine-guns.

"Wolves?" shouted Isabella in amazement, pushing her ear hard to the wood of the door and listening, the prick of hope and wonder surging at her chest. "There are wolves! Wolves, everywhere in the Vatican! Who?" she asked. And Tacit believed he knew.

He smiled. "I wonder?" And he knew then why the voice had been torn away, why its attention had been drawn temporarily elsewhere.

"Sandrine?"

They had come, the vast clan of wolves gathered together by Poré and sent to the roots of the Vatican to await the order to attack. Now they had risen, with Sandrine at their head, to tear the Antichrist and his treacherous horde down from where they had seized their illicit position of power. To kill all they could find in that closed-up citadel of devilry and horror. Revenge for the centuries of excommunication and cursed isolation.

Tacit laughed, an unhinged and wild laugh – *Don't fucking mock me scum* – all the time his great weight against the door at which they listened, feeling the other side of it rocked by a sudden hammering blow. Tacit locked it with the key in the lock, setting himself back against the wooden panels, shrieks and cries the other side. Howls and the deafening bark of gunfire filled the space.

"It seems that Poré didn't save his clan just for us!" Something exploded, a grenade, and only now did Tacit draw back, pulling Isabella with him, in case an errant round struck the door and blew it from its hinges. "The ship appears to have just been a taster."

Such was the severity of the fighting, the walls and floors seemed to rock and shudder, reminding them of how the ground shook that time on the Russian front when the artillery barrage bristled the German defences, now seemingly a lifetime ago, before the seven vials, before Poré, before the Antichrist's return.

For a while they just crouched between the encroaching walls of Adansoni's quarters, listening to the fighting outside the apartment doors, the howling of the wolves, the occasional bark of gunfire, content to listen and marvel. Throughout the rampage the voice in Tacit had again diminished, its attention drawn elsewhere.

Oh, but I am still here, Satan!

"No!"

Yes! Wolves? Pah! My army of Inquisitors can more than deal with them.

"No! Leave me alone!"

Leave you alone? After you've come so far? After you've dared to trespass in my domain? Forgive us our trespasses? I think not.

"No! Please!"

Tacit fought, fought with everything he possessed, but the violence beyond the doors was now like a sonnet to him, imploring him go to it, the voice fearful and fearing in equal measure, the man he loved, perhaps had always loved, the man who'd saved him, nourished him, protected him, now requiring Tacit to do the same.

Torment rippled through Tacit, a clamour of confusion. All the time, as Isabella and he sat together, their eyes on the doors, firearms in their laps, ready to draw and shoot at anyone attempting to burst through, Tacit's mind had been raging, just like the battle beyond the doors, the voice soliciting him to stand and fight and act, growing bolder, more insistent with every passing second, every cry, every explosion.

"Isabella!" he called out without warning, his voice small and pathetic, a child lost in a crowd. "It is overwhelming me! Isabella, I am lost to it. I am lost to *him*!"

Come and be found!

Now he was shaking and weeping, his hands feeling out about himself as if he were blind, cast into utter darkness.

"Fight it, Poldek!" cried Isabella, holding onto him, trying to calm him again with her touch. "Fight it! You must fight. You must overcome, just as Poré said you must!"

"It's no good!" Tacit wept. "I fear I have run as far as I am able. My master, he calls to me and I must go. I cannot resist any longer!"

He wrestled Isabella away and ran to the doors, throwing them open, breaking the lock as he did so. At once the noise of gunfire blasted into the room, intense and everywhere, filling all corners of the residence, every nook and cranny shattered by the bark of heavy rifles and revolvers. Making the bodies swing on their nooses from the ceiling.

Yes! Come! Come to me!

"Poldek!" Isabella cried, running after him, only to be beaten back by the tempest of gunfire bristling the corridor, a river of lead and fire going both ways, no way through. "Poldek!" she cried again from the cover of the entrance to Adansoni's residence, shouting down the corridor along which he had sprinted into the intensity of battle, into the depths of the Vatican and the mêlée of fire and killing.

She cried once more. There was a firefight directly outside, Inquisitors' guns now being aimed at each other, not just at wolves, although there were wolves everywhere. She could hear them, their howling and screaming, seeing them vast and monstrous. And there were other sounds mingled amongst the howls, the returning Inquisitors' guns, louder shouts, cries of men, growing more distinct and emphatic. It seemed as if the gunfight was intensifying.

She stole a glance before retreating back inside the charnel house of the Devil. There were Inquisitors, shooting at each other! A coup? Surely not! Isabella listened, and it clearly sounded as if there was now another gunfight raging all around her, from the highest pinnacles to the deepest vaults in the bowels of the Vatican, no longer men fighting wolves but men fighting each other.

Inquisitors against Inquisitors.

With this, the firefight shrank from the corridor into which she peered, swallowed down into the city's lower levels, and she ran out, pursuing the route Tacit had taken. Almost immediately the corridor ahead of her bristled with more gunfire, making her stumble and crouch to the ground for cover. A shadow loomed over her and she looked up, trying to focus through her tears and dust.

"Poldek?" she asked hopefully.

"Sister Isabella," called back a voice she recognised after a brief hesitation, rich with a tone from lands close to her own childhood.

"Furtado!" she cried, overjoyed at seeing the man, matted with plaster and soot from gunfire, and then instantly suspicious. "What the hell are you doing here?"

He scowled, a hint of teeth between his ruddy lips. "We come here to fight and claim back the Vatican! A letter, sent by Gaulterio, calling every loyal Inquisitor to return back to the Vatican."

"Adansoni?" cried Isabella.

"Yes," nodded Furtado, "but to fight against him. And it seems Hombre Lobo have come here too!" With that he pushed Isabella to the side and aimed his revolver at an enormous slavering wolf bounding towards them. It recoiled and howled on being blasted, turning over and lying still. "Wolves who are fighting everyone! Thankfully we are many, and they have made our work easier by killing many we ourselves have come to kill!" He held up his revolver, drawing the edge of his cloak away from his hip to show the curved sheath of a long knife stowed there. "Death to the Darkest Hand!" he growled.

"Poldek!" replied Isabella, clutching hold of him, so overwhelmed she thought she might faint. "Poldek, he's gone! I've lost him! We need to find him!"

"The inquisitional hall," said Furtado. "It will be there that he has gone, where the fighting is most terrible. It is there that Adansoni was seen."

ONE HUNDRED

The Vatican. Vatican City.

Everywhere in the city rattled with the sound of fighting, gun-battles and the shrieking of dying wolves. Wherever one looked there were Priests, Inquisitors and Hombre Lobo, all of them immersed in the violence or lying prone on the stone walkways of the corridors and halls, bleeding, shaking or still. The air was full of noise and masonry dust and blood.

It had come to this. Death in the Vatican. Everything thought holy now despoiled.

A statue, two hundred years upon its plinth, toppled and fell, shattering fragments of marble across the hall, splintering into the Inquisitors wrestling each other or wolves where it fell, cutting skin and blinding eyes. A bomb was thrown and a wall exploded, blowing out windows and showering those beneath the blast in a deadly rain of colourful glass.

In many places, fires had caught hold amongst the litter and waste in the corridors and chapels, sending caustic tendrils of stinking cloying smoke up into the building, making eyes sting and lungs choke. The floor of the Vatican was littered with the spent cases of revolvers, machine-gun and rifle cartridges. Inquisitors were slipping and sliding across it, trying to find purchase as they unleashed hell on their enemy with their weapons or tried to get a thumb into the eye socket or mouth of someone in their arms.

Blood! Everywhere was awash with blood, old and freshly spilt.

Isabella ducked in time to avoid a rifle round, and sprinted alongside Inquisitor Furtado.

An Inquisitor fell into their path, Furtado snatching up his revolver to shoot him dead.

"Aster!" he shouted, recognising the man as an ally just moments before pulling the trigger. He raised the barrel of his revolver as a shot from behind rang out and Aster groaned, crumpling forward. Furtado levelled his gun again, scouring the hall and shooting dead the Darkest Hand Inquisitor responsible.

Isabella pushed him left, choosing to avoid the hall ahead in which the fighting seemed most savage, taking a corridor which curved away from it. Half a dozen steps in, two more Inquisitors came the other way.

"Friends or foe?" she asked Furtado.

"Foe," he replied, as she at once aimed her revolver and fired, killing them both.

"Where did you learn to shoot like that?"

"Good teacher." Immediately she thought of Tacit. The thought lasted as long as it took to spot a pack of wolves launching themselves at them. Isabella shot two dead through the head, Furtado the third. The fourth took him down in a pile of rending claws, turning them both over like fighting cats. They came up for breath, facing each other, and Isabella fired, the wolf shuddering and collapsing back.

"They show no allegiance to either side!" called Furtado, relief and humour in his words and his face.

"They're Hombre Lobo," replied Isabella, knocking open the cylinder to her revolver and threading more silver bullets inside. "We all are meat to them. Come on!"

At the end of the corridor they flew down a flight of steps into another chamber, swarming with scrabbling, fighting people, turned out from their places of worship and running hither and thither in panic and violence, armed with pleading hands of submission or with weapons, knuckles white, faces drawn into hideous masks of rage, their allegiance with one side or the other. From the archway beyond, streams of Inquisitors were coming from the warren beneath the vaults of the inquisitional halls, lines of hard-looking men of every nation, colour and creed, some heavily armoured, others lightly dressed, carrying with them strange and exotic weapons from lands far away. At once Isabella knew these new arrivals to be allies, and cheered and thanked them as they ran by and flooded into the main inquisitional hall, some drawing alongside the open shutters of the inquisitional stores to restock and replenish their weapons and armaments before running on into the city's heights and the battle against the Darkest Hand.

"Have you seen Poldek Tacit, down in the inquisitional hall?"

"I haven't," the man she asked replied.

An explosion rocked the far end of the chamber, Inquisitors thrown to the floor in the blast of fire and stone, groaning and rolling about the ruin, the ground covered with bodies of those caught in the flame and flying debris.

A voice rang out from the masses. "Sister Isabella!"

She span on her toes, ducking with Furtado as another bomb rocked the hall. Gaulterio appeared out of the raging torrents of Inquisitors and smoke, battling over from the broad archway to reach her, in his hands the bloody heads of hammers, mirroring the cuts to his own scalp.

"Gaulterio!" she called.

"This!" he said, lifting the clubs either side of him, pointing over the teams of Inquisitors pouring through the corridors and doorways, up from out of the city's roots, "I did all of this!" He stared at the masses, pride and grit bound up in his features, an old man once more a boy.

"Do you know where Poldek is?"

The old man shook his head. "Gone!" he spat, wrenching up the heavy head of metal. Another Inquisitor ran up screaming and Isabella shot him through the eye. "Gone, back up into the Vatican. With that bastard Cardinal Bishop Adansoni!" Part of the roof groaned and then fell in, making all of them rush back to avoid being struck by falling masonry. "He killed Father Strettavario!" cried Gaulterio, hunched over, his breath snatched in his tired old lungs. "Adansoni, he killed him! And by doing so, sealed his doom!" he added, looking around the swelling number of Inquisitors swarming into the place.

A great cry grew up from the ground beneath their feet, yet more Inquisitors arriving. At the far reaches of the hall, the Darkest Hand drew back and ran, sprinting for the Vatican's higher reaches, to set their traps and prepare to face behind their defences this new wave of Inquisitors. In the upper halls and corridors, hungry wolves prowled low and waited to feed.

ONE HUNDRED AND ONE

The Vatican. Vatican City.

The Inquisitors surged forward out of the bowels of the Vatican, up into the higher reaches, towards and into Hell. They ran on, armed with every type of weapon, every armament and device for killing offered to them in the Vatican's inquisitional stores, pouring into the lower chambers, straight into a blinding pall of smoke. The heat from the fires had grown so great that windows had shattered and paint bubbled and flaked from the walls.

"Can't see a damned thing!" one of them choked through the smouldering reek of smoke billowing off thousand-year-old tapestries. A heavy machine-gun started up somewhere in the mêlée and a line of Inquisitors toppled like ninepins, blasted bloody bits hanging off them. They slunk back, finding another way, coming up and around from another flank to where the Darkest Hand had positioned their machine-gun post, and fell upon the assassins with their axes and clubs, battering and slicing the villains until they resembled dripping hunks of meat.

"Onwards!" someone called, and as one they charged again, a terrible light in their eyes, a cry of death to the traitors in their throats.

A line of Darkest Hand Inquisitors had positioned themselves between a colonnade of statues of past saints, throwing down fire upon the surging masses. Heads exploded and faces burst open as the torrent of hot lead rained down upon them. Cordite stung eyes and burnt fingers, as grenades were primed and thrown, obliterating three of the statues and the Inquisitors around the smashed marble.

Ahead, the bulk of the Darkest Hand army slunk into murder-holes and behind barricades waiting for the Inquisitors to come, but wolves were already waiting for them.

"Kill the fucking things!" the Darkest Hand cried, loading their cartridges with silver and taking out their silver-lined blades. Barrels flashed and ears rang as the immense hulking creatures fell upon them, ripping and slashing jaws and talons tearing armour and devouring flesh. Pleading and howls knotted together, fur and skin tangled.

"Silver bomb!" someone warned, and the darkness was lit with shining light and heat, howls turned to screams and wolves to tortured writhing bodies. Inquisitors clapped bleeding hands to torn-out eyes, while Hombre Lobo turned over and over, poisoned by the shards of silver shrapnel, churning and shambling grotesquely in their death throws.

"The Inquisition!" another of the Priests shouted, looking up through shaking vision. "They are coming, up the main corridor!"

"We are the fucking Inquisition!" someone next to him shouted back. "Those who came before and will rise again! Kill the last of the fucking wolves and then kill the foolish!"

Machine-gun and rifle barrels flashed, smoking and flaming red, knives sinking deep into wolf sides, coming away slick and fetid. Hombre Lobo powered into their numbers, dashing brains from skulls, disembowelling with their monstrous claws. A cloying writhing mass of murder and hate.

Shadows gathered at the opposite end of the passageway to where the Darkest Hand had set their ambush, and in turn been ambushed by the wolves. The shadows came forward, growing into the grim faces of the Inquisition through the pall and stink of smoke. Molotov cocktails were lit and thrown, landing amongst the Darkest Hand and the wolves, bursting figures into agonising silhouettes of fire.

Up the corridors and into the broad halls the tide of Inquisitors now fought on to the death, throwing themselves into the broad ranks of the Darkest Hand turning from the last of the wolves to face this new oncoming foe. Knife points sunk into sides, limbs and torsos exploded under the ferocity of gunfire, fighting turning into a deathly scrum of gouging thumbs and stabbing blades. Eyes popped and tore from sockets, tongues were ripped out, throats grappled open, skulls crushed under repeating stamps from boots, the violence obscene and unhinged, Hell's

297

damnation flooding into the place. Everything, the Inquisitors' clothing and weapons, the walls and the floor, the ceiling above them, turned red as they fought throughout the rooms and passageways, edging always towards the summit of the Vatican and the fire blazing there high into the blackened heavens above.

A chandelier above where Isabella stood catching her breath exploded and fell. She threw herself to one side as the centrepiece of the hall came down in a cascade and crash of jewels and silver. An Inquisitor who wasn't quick enough lay trapped under it, caught beneath the ton of twisted metal and valuable stones, quivering and pleading for someone to release him. His lower half had been partially cut off by the weight of falling metal, blood welling around his oozing guts.

An Inquisitor from the Darkest Hand crouched between tall blackened columns with an assault rifle, picking off Inquisitors as they came up the passageway. Isabella caught sight of him and ran at him, firing her revolver as she went, peppering the area. One shot caught him in the throat and he stopped firing, his hands gripping at the torrent of crimson bursting from the wound, the second shot cracked him back.

She now found herself in the middle of the hall, surrounded on all sides, caught in a maelstrom of noise and clambering, tumbling bodies.

"Come here!" shouted Furtado, snatching hold of her and pushing her to one side of the hall, as another bomb exploded and bodies flew. She looked back on the apocalyptic vision, of burning walls and figures half in and half out of death wrestling for life with the last of their strength. There was vile language on the tongues of the Darkest Hand Priests and Inquisitors and burning anger in their eyes, as they tore through the ranks of charging Inquisitors, crushing and battering them, stamping them into bloody husks beneath their feet.

"The wolves!" shouted Furtado. "They've been all but crushed! Just little pockets left. But their sacrifice has not been in vain. They've torn the heart out of the Darkest Hand!"

"What about Tacit?" she replied, pushing the Inquisitor to one side and shooting dead a Priest who was taking aim at them. They scurried towards a fallen column and sunk behind it, a little cover for the moment.

"He's been seen, in the main hall above us."

"Let's go then!"

She stood, her revolvers barking at the crowd as she followed Furtado, a new wave of Inquisitors ahead of her as she ran. There was nothing but hate and killing, noise and fire, Inquisitors slaughtering Inquisitors, the last of the wolves and all sanctity.

They reached the top of a long flight of steps, a short way from St Peter's Basilica. It felt as if she had dredged herself from the drains of Hell, such was the horror of what she had run through, the killing and the torment. And yet nothing matched the savagery of hate which lay ahead, the hall filled with the worst of the fighting yet. The floor was slick with blood and the dead, bodies piled up on top of each other, wolves on top of Inquisitors, torn and dashed open and spread over the ground. The air was full of the stench of murder, humid and caustic from their exertions, thick with sulphur and iron, the stink of fear, the stench of the world's end. Guns flashed almost continuously as a group of Darkest Hand Inquisitors charged towards Furtado and Isabella, their first line cut down by an explosion of revolvers.

There was a side-door, narrow and tall, and they took it, moments before another huge explosion rocked the hall, louder than any before, as if all the store of ammunition had exploded. Furtado pushed Isabella through the doorway as the blast hit. She picked herself up and looked back. The body of Furtado lay turned over on his side, his face ashen, his right side and lower half missing, his mouth voicing noiseless words.

She ran on, weeping and pleading, the hall behind her opening up for a second time in a blaze of gunfire and flame, and she was thrown forward, picking herself up again, her back torn open, covered by plaster shot away from the wall. She clawed her way on up the stairs on her hands and knees, looking ahead as she went, a grim ascent. There was no one beyond on the winding staircase, behind her the raging sound of battle too terrible to witness, too loud to avoid, ahead the heartening echo of escape from the carnage.

The stairwell wound up forty feet, covered by bleeding bodies strewn across steps where they had been shot or brought down by stones hurled from above.

The archway at the top was just beyond and she called Tacit's name, just quietly at first, but the words growing with purpose and determination with every step closer, feeling so terribly alone and exposed in that place, hoping that by saying his name it might bring him to her, or invoke a spell for his spirit to protect her.

But instead a great surge of black Inquisitors rushed the stairwell behind her, flying up where she had climbed. She could see them, thirty steps behind her, laughing and jeering, priming their weapons to cut her down.

She flew out into the chamber beyond, a broad hall, but with no way beyond, a wall of Inquisitors now charging towards her, at her back Darkest Hand Inquisitors swelling up the stairwell. She ran on five paces, pulling out the revolver from her side and training it back to the stairs.

And then another voice above all the other noise roared from the archway. A huge man appeared, filling the archway, a light in his eye, both terrible and magnificent, trampling the already dead into the stone courtesy of his great boots. Tacit ran towards her, but not looking at her, not even appearing to see her, his grim resolve set solely on the Inquisitors behind where she stood, Inquisitors now his hated enemy. Guns rattled and flashed, bristling across the broad front of the charging Darkest Hand Priests who ran next to him, silver scales of inquisitional armour and flesh obliterating under the fresh salvo fired at them. The two lines of Inquisitors crashed into each other like waves of metal and flesh.

Isabella had cried his name as she was battered aside, trodden and turned underfoot by the hordes smashing together. Miraculously she'd reached the wall, bruised and bleeding even more terribly, her back, flayed open like a torture victim, tight to a closed door. She reached back and opened it, falling through into the blackness beyond, climbing gingerly to her feet and shouting Tacit's name again, hoping that he might hear her and be drawn from the fighting and his possession to escape into the blackness with her.

In the heat and chaos Tacit heard his name, and for a moment something hesitated in him, the hint of recognition in an otherwise utterly cowed and closed mind. But as quickly as the voice connected in his old self, it went again, dissipated like smoke before a breeze, and he turned back to the fighting, raking with his great hands into the midst of Inquisitors, sending great reams of men flying away from his blows.

She called again into the writhing fury of the monstrous tangle of bodies, and he lifted his head to the sound, now battering his way towards it, hope and hate flaring in equal measure in him. There was a figure, a woman, standing in the shadows of a door. He knew her, or at least believed he did, a dear memory from the past, a past long gone. A weight grew in his throat and chest and he felt the urge to cry out.

"Satan!" another voice shouted, from the arched entrance out of which Tacit had first emerged. The word resonated and shuddered in the great hall, the air around Adansoni who had shouted it bristling and snapping, sulphur and brimstone teasing in the acidic air. The Antichrist came forward, surrounded by his greatest generals save one, the one he had commanded. Around his heels it seemed flames and soot sprouted wherever he placed his feet, as if he had been elevated into some demonic apparition, a devil made flesh.

ONE HUNDRED AND TWO

THE VATICAN. VATICAN CITY.

Adansoni shouted again at Tacit, who drew towards him, shuffling hunched like a scolded dog towards his master. To their left, the two armies of Inquisitors fought, rocking this way and that, a malignant seething scrum of gore-drenched soldiers. "Satan, you are not yet finished! Neither is the fighting!" He pointed with a finger, commanding the man back into the carnage. "It is not time to leave the battle!"

Tacit nodded and threw himself forward, but from the doorway Isabella called out to him again.

"Poldek!" she cried. "Don't listen to him!"

The plea snagged him mid-stride, her voice a spell.

"Silence, bitch whore!" scolded Adansoni, seeking her with a stare. Now he understood why Tacit had left the battle prematurely. Tacit rocked like a mad thing, competing against the lure of her voice and the command of his master, stumbling, going down onto his knees.

A man conflicted, caught between the two he loved.

"What is this nonsense?" Adansoni demanded of him. "What are you waiting for? This is your destiny! It was given to you at your birth. You are not born of the earth, but of Hell. You have no other part to play, other than to embrace that which is laid before you. Your birthright, decreed when you were brought across forty-one years ago! There is nothing else for you. This is all you have now and all you shall know. Do not shame yourself or dare to shame me!"

He pointed with a finger to command Tacit back into battle, but instantly Isabella's voice drew both Tacit and his master to look.

"Leave him alone!"

Her voice sounded tiny in the place.

Adansoni laughed. "Sister Isabella!" He clapped his hands at his chest, cinders of light spinning from his palms like fireflies. "Your loyalty to Poldek Tacit is commendable, but misguided. You are too late! For Poldek Tacit is dead. There is only Satan now."

"The only person I see who is dead is you, Adansoni! Look about you! Look at your men. You're finished! It's over!"

He cast his eye briefly over the fighting in the hall. Though overwhelmed, he knew his forces could never be defeated with Satan in their ranks. "It's far from over, piglet whore. In fact, this only just begun. For when war comes to the Vatican, then you know that I have won and you have lost! No one will be able to resist my Lieutenant, the greatest of all the Princes of Hell! No one can harm or defeat him. Together we shall win this day and then what you see here will be only the beginning. Satan!" he shouted at Tacit, pointing towards Isabella. "Kill her and then end this battle."

Tacit turned towards Isabella, Adansoni following in his huge shadow. A great explosion rocked the hall, throwing everyone to the ground.

"Don't call him Satan! He can't be, he loves me!"

"He is Satan!" laughed the Antichrist, picking himself up behind the man he spoke about. "He is incapable of love! And he is beyond your salvation, especially as you are just one. Alone!"

"But she is not alone!" answered a voice suddenly from the shadows behind where Isabella stood. Beyond the door, shrouded in the darkness, a spiral staircase ran up from the level below. Out of this a man appeared, sooty and cut above his eye from a cruel wound, but otherwise unharmed. He stepped next to her and said again, "She is not alone!"

"Pablo!" cried Isabella.

"You!" hissed Adansoni, at once recognising the young Italian. "You who should have died on the Carso! You who ruined everything then!"

"And who will again!" He spoke with such authority and defiance that Adansoni hesitated, letting out a venomous seething curse, as if a poison had been unleashed from deep in his leathery lungs.

Isabella gathered the remains of her senses. "What? Where have you –?"

"Poré," Pablo replied, knowing what she wished to say but couldn't, watching Adansoni cautiously. "I know you doubted him –"

"I don't any more!" Isabella answered in a rush.

302

"He gave me something… real. For the first time in my life. Belief. In him. In what he to wished to change." Pablo lowered his darkening eyes on Adansoni. "In what he needed to do."

Adansoni spat at his feet, Tacit labouring between coming forward and staying where he was beside his master. Behind them, the battle raged around the hall like thunder.

"Nephelim. Fallen angels," hissed Adansoni. "You are called that for a reason! Fallen! Failed!"

"But educated well enough by *your* Darkest Hand Priests throughout my childhood to know about diplomacy, politics, organisation. Yes, *your* Priests, those who died on the Carso, trained me well in all aspects of negotiation, planning. It was not hard for me to oversee the transportation of a few thousand Chinese across the globe into Europe, to falsify documents, to adopt new personas, to ensure the spread of Spanish flu, when you've been taught deceit as I was by your kind. To bring God's wrath amongst the masses, the end of the war, the end of your plans for this conflict involving all nations!"

Adansoni shrieked, the skin of his face drawn back like a wailing phantom, showing bared diseased teeth. "I'll kill you!" he seethed, launching himself forward.

At that instant a second explosion ripped through the hall, a great crack opening up across the chamber. It expanded like a yawning black mouth, swallowing Inquisitors into the inky blackness below as it wound along, devouring them. At its edge Tacit and Adansoni threw themselves onto the floor, while the remainder of the Antichrist's henchmen wobbled on the cracked broken edge and fell backwards, down into the chasm.

The great hall had spilt in two, a vast wide abyss tearing across the length of the chamber, separating the doorway from the rest of the fighting, a small island of stone now accessible only by the winding staircase from below, trapping the four of them on it.

Adansoni snarled, glancing back to his masses on the other side of the chasm, cut off from Tacit, and now being overwhelmed by ever greater numbers of Inquisitors pouring into the chamber.

Pablo stepped in front of Isabella, a roll of cloth under his arm. "Your Inquisitors," he began, "they are lost, defeated by those who remain loyal to the faith and Pope Benedict." Adansoni spat like a wild animal, standing hunched but appearing ready to spring forward next to Tacit. "Your lies and deceit, the wickedness that beats in you, it has come full circle. It has cut you off from hope! Look at the abyss which lies between you and them!"

Anger hammered hard in the Antichrist, erupting as a roar which seemed to shake the stones from the chamber and drew many Inquisitors back from their fighting. He pulled back his black lips to reveal his bloody tear of a mouth filled with stunted black teeth and a tongue as purple as a bruise.

"You have no right to be here," commanded Pablo. "You have no jurisdiction here in this house of God. You trespass in a land consecrated by God and for God alone. You come into this place a pathetic spectral wraith, a chill sorrow upon the wind, an unwanted unkind spirit, overwhelmed and defeated by charity, goodness and godliness. You are offensive, bound up in hate, knowing nothing of love or the power contained in it. You have crept unwittingly into our world in which you will find nothing, no hope, no purchase in this place. Go back to your desolation of fire of Hell and leave this place and us in peace!"

And Adansoni laughed. "Silence! You are nothing, one man against me, the Devil's son, and Satan! You are cut off, alone, with no means to escape. I shall rip your heart from your chest and devour it before your eyes. No abyss, or fire or blackness," and he looked back briefly at the chasm behind him, "can hold me back."

"I know," retorted Pablo. "And that is why I am here."

He allowed one edge of the roll of cloth to drop, from it producing two golden knives, holding them up so that their blades glinted crimson and yellow in the firelight and the six finger-holes down each grip could be seen by them all.

Adansoni knew at once what they were, the daggers of Gath, the knives used to attempt to draw the Lieutenants of Hell back from Hell. And he supposed he knew what Pablo wished their purpose to be. He cried out, as if wounded. "Satan!" he shrieked. "Seize them!"

Trance-like, and without hesitation, Tacit came forward and snatched the knives away, pushing Pablo down as he took them.

At once, Adansoni's fear turned to mockery. He laughed, a spiteful insult of noise.

"And now all your cards are played, Pablo Gilda, failed Nephelim!" he shouted. "Give them to me," he said to Tacit, indicating the daggers.

But in Tacit, a voice, tiny and far away, a sound that had begun as a whimpering plea, was growing. The voice of Isabella, the defiance and love in it, seemed to renew and enrich the light in him, drawing him from his alias and into the chamber and the battle. He looked out across the semi-circle of stone, at Pablo and then Isabella. The voice was in him and something approaching resilience hardened. He looked from the blades to his master and said, "No, I will not serve you."

"You dare?" screamed Adansoni, his eyes boiled in his skull, his hands like claws. He threw them forward, his palms held up to Tacit. "Give them to me!" he demanded again.

"I said," growled Tacit, his teeth hardening in his skull and the madness which had entrapped him clearing, "that I will not serve you!" And he stared back in defiance, and his face was a scowl of anger, driven by a new spirit, lit by Pablo. "You tell me there is nothing else for me. You tell me that all I know is this hell, this conflict, all this murder and killing." And the voice which had grown in him sang like a symphony, and he knew to whom this new voice belonged. Not one, but two people. His mother and Mila. He threw a hand across himself, standing up from where he had been cowering. "But you tell me lies. For I have known love, have held love and been held in love, something you can never claim. You are without love, worshipped and followed purely for benefit and out of fear. But you can benefit me with nothing and I have never feared anything and especially not you."

Tacit was aware that Pablo had fallen to his knees, as if in honour and praise for him. Adansoni saw the Italian bow his head and then realised what Pablo was intending to do.

"No!" he roared, throwing himself forward to snatch the knives away, but Tacit battered him aside. The old man, for that was all he now appeared to be, stumbled and fell towards the edge of the abyss. He slipped over the side, the fingers of one hand snatching the faintest of grips on the stone.

Tacit looked back to the young man kneeling before him. And he remembered Poré's final words, spoken to him in Laventie.

"No!" cried the Antichrist, as Tacit lifted one of the daggers high above his head and brought it down on Pablo's neck.

Instantly the chamber was obliterated with blinding light that threw everyone to the floor, plucking Adansoni away from the edge and hurling him down into the darkness below.

ONE HUNDRED AND THREE

The Vatican. Vatican City.

From the blinding light, darkness fell. For an age it seemed as if there was no more light in the place, as if the entire world had died.

Then lights sparked and shimmered into life.

Tacit was lying unmoving on the edge of the abyss, the pool of blood from Pablo's decapitated neck trickling across the stone and seeping into his clothes. Isabella had been thrown down in a pile of stones, the remains of the doorway. She picked herself up from the debris, her hand to a heavily bleeding eye, and hobbled over to him, dropping to his side. She pulled him up into her arms, his body heavy and limp, his skin seared and flaking around where he had struck Pablo the final fatal blow.

She stroked the hair from his eyes and kissed his ravaged scarred temple. "Oh, Poldek," she wept.

"Isabella," he growled after a long time, his hot breath on her exposed skin, his voice laboured.

"I am here," she cried, turning his head so that she could look into his eyes. In them there was light and peace. She shuddered, trembling as she said his name, her hands on his face, in his hair, drawing back to look at him, before pulling herself to him again.

"Isabella!" he said, and he smiled and lay his head back, exhausted.

He pulled her into his strong arms. They kissed, sinking into one another, the warmth from their bodies intertwining. From across the ravine of broken stones and the collapsed hall, Inquisitors were shouting to them. "Tacit! Sister Isabella!" They knew the battle was over. It had been from the moment Tacit cut Pablo's head from his shoulders with one of the knives of Gath, severing Satan's link between this world and Hell, and sending his spirit hurtling back to the underworld in the sulphurous flash of light. With it, the loyalty and hope of the Darkest Hand Inquisitors had wavered and fallen away. Sounds of approaching boots grew on the staircase leading to their crumbled doorway and circle of stone.

"Sweet Mother of God!" one of the Inquisitors cried, on seeing Pablo's decapitated body.

"Make sure he is buried with honours," warned Tacit.

"Pope Benedict?" asked Isabella.

"Safe," assured the Inquisitor, immediately. "Unharmed. Half starved, but alive."

"And the wolves?" asked Tacit.

"Most have been dealt with. Killed. Only a few have retreated, down into the crypts below the Vatican."

Tacit and Isabella looked at each other, hoping.

"It's over, Poldek!" she said, leaning forward and kissing him as he lay on the edge of the chasm. And she laughed through her tears. "It's over! It's finished! The battle for the Vatican is ended. The Darkest Hand are defeated!"

And he smiled, pain showing in his face, and tried to sit up, but she told him to rest and held him as he spoke.

"Adansoni." He looked up at the Inquisitor. "Have you found his body? He fell, down there." He glanced to his right at the trails of smoke coming up from below.

The Inquisitor shook his head. "No, we have not found him, but we will."

Tacit turned over onto his hands and knees and tried to stand. His whole body felt broken, but he refused to be defeated, not now, not after everything that had gone before. He looked up into the faces of the Inquisitors across the divide, grim and choked with soot, but proud and victorious. There were smoking spiralling trails of spinning embers and ashes coming up from the abyss.

He turned to survey the ruins. Everything was burnt up and shattered by bullet holes and bombs. Across the snaking smog, something caught his attention, movement at the far end of the hall. For some reason Tacit was drawn to it, to peer harder, at a woman dressed in a long gown which covered her shoulders and draped along the ground.

Instantly, he wished to raise his hand to her, to acknowledge her. Instead he stood and watched, a smile gradually growing on his features. And Sandrine watched him back, long enough for her to know she had been observed, before she drew the hood up over her head and filed silently from the chamber.

Tacit turned to look at Isabella next to him, still smiling and holding out his hand for her to take.

"So let us go home, Isabella," he said.

"Home?" she replied, smiling to see his happiness. "But where is home, Poldek?"

"The Tatra Mountains," he replied, catching a tear with his fingertips that rolled down Isabella's cheek upon hearing him say the name. "Let us go home and live."

They kissed, all sounds from the residue of battle falling away from them, before they turned for the spiral stairs and away from that island of stone.

At the bottom of the abyss below, something in the shadows stirred amongst the rubble of broken boulders and rocks, something ancient and wicked. It rose, slowly, like a spirit from the grave, and then slipped away before any mortal eye could see it.

PART SEVEN

"Every new beginning comes from some other beginning's end."

SENECA

ONE HUNDRED AND FOUR

TUESDAY, OCTOBER 29TH, 1918. BERLIN. GERMANY.

The daylight streaming through the tall lace-lined windows of the main debating hall was grey as smoke. Prince Maximilian watched the Quartermaster General loiter on the circular carpet in the centre of the room, his eyes dropping to the man's boots and seeing they were dirty, their soles clotted with mud. "Well?" he scowled.

"Well what, Maximilian?" replied Wilhelm Groener testily, taking his eyes from the papers he was reading and turning them onto the proud-looking moustached man.

"For fuck's sake man! You know what, damn you, Groener! President Wilson's letter!"

"Maximilian!" replied Groener, staggered at the outburst. "Really, is there any need for such language?"

"Stop treating us all like fucking imbeciles, Groener! We've been treated like fucking imbeciles by the German Army for too long! We're all sick of it. You hear me? Sick of it! The German people have had enough. We're on the verge of revolution. In some places, it's already broken out! If we don't act now, we're finished, done for. Do you understand?" Sweat beaded across his broad high forehead, darkening the thin strands of hair laced over his head. He waited for his demeanour to cool. "There's no other option. Wilhelm II, he *has* to abdicate. If it assures us of a way to end this war, it's the only way."

"But abdication!" cried Groener, the Quartermaster General of the German Army, the ruffle of hair above his top lip twitching. "It all sounds so… cowardly! Can we not send him to the front to sacrifice himself in a hero's death at a final charge? At least allow us a little honour at the end?"

Prince Maximilian turned away, digging his hands deep into the pockets of his dark suit. He shook his head, his chin bunched into the tight collar of his shirt. "No. No more fighting, no more sacrifices, no more gallant last stands or charges, Wilhelm! All is lost. Lost, damn it. Lost. We're all sick of all this fighting. Surely you must be too?"

"You do know what that means, don't you, Maximilian? Military collapse? Socialist revolution? Do you want what happened in Russia to happen here?"

The Prince shrugged as the dull clank of a train being fitted to trucks sounded somewhere in the city below. "We already have riots, communists pacing the streets, looking for any opportunity they can! Every day it seems as if we'll fall closer into revolution, anarchy likelier with every day that goes by. An armistice is the only way to avoid it. To ensure it doesn't happen here as it happened in Petrograd."

Groener made a noise in his throat, a sound lodged somewhere between frustration and defeat. "We have an army that still wants to fight!"

But Maximilian shook his head, pursing up his lips. "We have an army on its knees, crushed, annihilated, running, running for their borders. The French and British are on their heels! Our sailors are mutinying!"

"Lies!"

"No, they are not bloody lies, Wilhelm!" he shouted, spinning to face the paunchy square-faced man, making him step back, fearing an assault. "In Wilhelmshaven, at this very moment, we have a bloody mutiny on our hands!" The Prince's hands were fists.

"Mutiny? What do you mean, mutiny?"

"They've had enough." He sunk into himself, exhausted, and turned back to the window to look down on the quiet grey streets of the city. "We've all had enough." He coughed, at first to clear his throat, to tease away a tickle from it, but the cough came again, intensifying, turning into a series of hacking splutters and chokes that drove him to hold onto the sideboard till they had passed. "This flu, this damn flu," he cursed.

"You're ill."

"It won't kill me," replied Maximilian, cleaning his mouth with his handkerchief. "Not yet. Not till this is done." He straightened up and walked to his desk. "I'm going to write, going to write to the Princes of Germany, right now, this instant, asking them to approve the abdication of the Emperor Wilhelm II. Matthias Erzberger can then begin negotiations with the Allies."

"Good God," replied Groener, stepping to the desk behind him, his hand to his heart. "So this is really the end then? Defeated?"

"This flu," the Prince repeated, picking up his pen and beginning to scratch across the paper, "if it wasn't for the flaming flu then perhaps we'd have more fight. But it's done for all of us." He wrote a little more and then paused, feeling his friend's eyes on him from the shadows opposite. "It's time to end this war."

ONE HUNDRED AND FIVE

KRAKOW. PRAGUE.

If Tacit remembered the small monastery nestled amongst the pines and birch on the hillside, greying white against the backdrop of autumnal browns and flames, he never said anything to Isabella. There was a stony path which turned off from the wider track up which many horses had ridden, judging by the hoof prints in the mud, and Tacit led Isabella that way, his eyes on the sleet-coloured building at the far end. Birds chased and circled around the tiled roof, drenched in pale autumn sun, and from somewhere in the woods behind the monastery came the sound of a woodpecker digging for grubs in the trunks of trees.

The last time he'd been here was with *him*, Adansoni, just a boy of twelve, ripped from the heart of his family, confused, afraid, unaware and unprepared for the road ahead of him.

He never understood why he'd been brought here by Adansoni, though he'd often wondered. Was it to gloat? Was it to look for answers? Or was to search for a final chance of redemption, a chance which Adansoni never took?

Whatever the reason Tacit had come here twenty-nine years ago, he knew he had to return. The closing of one circle.

The beginning of another.

Puddles had pooled in the divots and trenches cut by feet and horses' hooves along the muddy path and thin brittle skins of ice had formed on many of them, crackling and splashing cold water onto Isabella's and Tacit's boots, seeping between their toes. Isabella chuckled and groaned as she walked, noticing how quiet Tacit had fallen.

"Are you all right?" she asked, as the front door to the monastery opened and a group of sisters filed out, standing waiting for them where the path reached the stone step up to the entrance, their hands linked lightly in front of them.

"Poldek Tacit," one of them called, and then turned her eyes over to Isabella. "Sister Isabella."

"You know us?"

"Of course," the nun said. "We have been waiting for you, especially you, Poldek. Sister Angelina, she is inside, waiting for you."

"She's still alive then?" asked Tacit.

"Of course, she could not die, not without seeing you one final time."

They followed the entourage of Sisters inside the small monastery and pursued them down cold stone corridors, through halls and past chapels, the route through the building suggesting the place was far bigger than it appeared from outside, as if it wound into the hillside. Eventually they reached a door and the nuns, other than the one who had spoken to them on the threshold, stood to one side to allow her to rap quietly against the wood. She opened the door to reveal a dimly lit bedchamber. The room smelt of dust and damp. A tiny woman, shrunk by years, sat on a chair, a blanket drawn up around her to keep out the chill. The shutters were closed and while the sun touched the outside walls of the monastery, inside the dark room it was cold as a crypt.

They drew closer, and at first Tacit thought the woman was asleep, but then she opened her eyes and smiled.

"Poldek," she said, with a voice of genteel grace. She smiled. "It is good to see you again," she said, fragile as glass.

"And you," replied Tacit, and she laughed, a quiet but generous laugh.

"I doubt you even remember me, Poldek, after all you have seen and done, the people you have met, the places you have visited. You have

312

lived a lifetime many times over, Poldek. You have achieved so many things, some good, some not so, but always you have done as you were commanded, and for that you cannot be too grievously judged. For you were fooled, as we all were fooled." She shook her head, closing her eyes as she did so, as if astonished to think of all the time past and the speed by which it had flown. "You were so young when they brought you here. Now look at you! A man of middle years!"

"In that time I've done so many terrible things," answered Tacit, and the old Sister considered his words.

"Yes, but I warned them, when you were brought to me. I warned them they would do best to dispose of you, to have you sent to a sanatorium. They should have allowed you to heal, never set you on the path that they did so quickly after all that had happened to you. I warned them, more than just once, but there you go. They would not listen."

"Perhaps it would have been better if they had sent me to the sanatorium."

"Yes, it would have been better," replied Angelina. "But you were never destined for the sanatorium, were you, Poldek? You were never destined to be caged. When *he* brought you here, *he* spoke of a prophecy, that you were the *one*, the one who would unite the world, and in whose wake would be left death and destruction."

"I do not feel I have united the world. It seems to me have I torn it apart."

"No," she replied forcefully. "You *have* united the world. Perhaps unknowingly, but from out of a world of darkness, you have saved it. You have fought and you have eventually overcome."

"Not quite."

"Then you mean to find the one who first brought you into the world of darkness, do you? The one who brought you out of that dark place and placed you into the world of supposed light? The one who set you on your path and guided and directed you?"

"Yes, I do."

"He fooled us, Poldek. He fooled us all. No one ever considered his intentions were ill, his master directing him from below, not above. No one knew." Her sad watery eyes hardened. "Do you know where you will find him?"

"I am going home, where he will be expecting to find me."

And she reached out and put her hand in his, tiny in his giant fist.

"I was wrong about you, Poldek Tacit," she said, squeezing his calloused muscular fingers.

ONE HUNDRED AND SIX

The dawn forest was silent, void of all noise amongst the trees. Even the birdsong was hushed, an eerie stillness in the place, as if all life had been blown out of it. As if the world was exhausted.

But to stand and listen, one could detect there was still life, and death, in it, the occasional whine of a shell, the bristle of gunfire in the distance. But for all that, an end of sorts had come, the end of one age, the beginning of another.

The sound of motorcars suddenly churned up the quiet, rumbling along the rutted gravelled track through the wood. The vehicles drew into a clearing, a short way from where the forest was dissected by a railway line, upon which stood a single train carriage. The men in the motorcars could see that there were figures inside the train, as well as a delegation gathered around the bottom of the iron steps leading up into it. Everyone was suited in military fatigues, proudly presented, sharply dressed.

In the back of the leading car Major General Detlof von Winterfeldt of the German Army checked his wristwatch and saw that it was a minute after five o'clock in the morning.

"They are eager," he said, watching the group of officers and commanders staring back, muttering quietly among themselves as they did so. "To think that it has come to this," he said.

"We should not keep them waiting," replied Count Alfred von Oberndorff of the foreign ministry, leaning forward and tapping on the connecting glass between the back of the car and the driver and his aide in the front.

"And so we have no pride now either?" asked von Winterfeldt. "We must dance to their tune now, must we? Fall prostrate before them, like conquered dogs? Hurry along? Not keep them waiting, our new masters?"

"No one is hurrying," retorted the Count. "But we're here so we may as well get it bloody over and done with, General. We've lost. We have no further grounds upon which to negotiate!"

"Come on then," said Captain Ernst Vanselow, opening his door to the car. "Let us do what we must."

They stepped towards the collection of five officers, French and British Marshals, Captains and Admirals waiting for them at the base of the train, a scattering of accompanying soldiers close by. The faces that watched them were proud and reverential, duty bound, showing no hint of boastfulness. They met and stood opposite each other, two paces apart, hands thrust deep and firm into pockets, no suggestion either side would proffer a more generous greeting.

"Good morning," Marshal of France Ferdinand Foch said.

"Good morning," replied the Germans.

"Shall we go in and sign?" asked the only man not dressed in military fatigues, Matthias Erzberger.

"One moment please!" called a photographer, appearing from the wings. "A photograph, perhaps?"

"Must we?" asked Major General Detlof von Winterfeldt.

"For posterity," assured the photographer, setting up his camera.

"Exactly why I regret."

The camera flashed, and the delegation shook stars from their eyes before turning and climbing into the train.

There was a table, quite plain, set next to the veiled window, onto which the cold dawn light fell. Four chairs were on the window side, upon which sat Rear-Admiral George Hope, First Sea Lord Admiral Sir Rosslyn Wemyss, and the French representatives, General Maxime Weygand and Marshal Ferdinand Foch, whose carriage it was. Just two chairs were drawn up opposite for the Germans, in which Matthias Erzberger and Count Alfred von Oberndorff sat, Major General Detlof von Winterfeldt and Captain Ernst Vanselow standing behind as witnesses.

Foch turned the book setting out the terms of the Armistice towards Erzberger and he drew it towards him, reading through the details he knew already.

A couple of soldiers looked up at the windows from outside the carriage.

"Here we are then," one said to the other.

"Here we are," the other replied. "Do you think that any of them were… you know…" His words trailed off.

"Any of them were what?" asked the first soldier, studying him closely.

"The Vatican," he replied, his words uncertain, as if trying to reach for something he couldn't bring himself to admit.

"What about the Vatican?" asked the soldier.

"Order," he said, clearing his throat. "I hear that order and peace have returned there. After all that took place there."

"I don't know what you're talking about," replied the soldier, not looking at him, "but if there is peace in the Vatican then that's that, I suppose?"

They fell back to watching the windows as Erzberger nodded.

"Yes, everything looks correct," Erzberger said, looking up briefly from the terms in the document and taking up his pen. "I will now sign on behalf of the German Empire and peoples."

"Four years of war," lamented Rear-Admiral Hope.

"For what?" retorted Foch, his eyes hard on his counterpart.

"I cannot believe *he* failed us," someone said.

But no one replied, or perhaps no one knew what he meant.

ONE HUNDRED AND SEVEN

The Tatra Mountains. Poland.

Tacit looked down into the pool at the bottom of the tumble of rocks. He remembered fishing in it when he was a child, sitting on its edge, looking down into its murky depths, skewering fish with his pointed stick. And he knew it was here, on this very spot, that he first killed someone, the Slav who had come at him, one who had invaded his home, one who had set in motion the events in a single moment, all those years ago.

When Tacit was just twelve years old.

The pool had since dried up. All that remained now was a puddle of dark water at its very centre. Like his memories of the place, dried up and forgotten. He looked into all that was left of the water and felt something stir and twist in him, closing his eyes and feeling his emotions lurch, a wave of helplessness and sorrow rise up.

"Are you all right?" asked Isabella, reaching out to him and taking his arm.

He nodded, waiting for the melancholy to pass, opening his eyes, turning them from the dried-up pool at the base of the rocky climb to the tumbled-down ruin. "Yes I am," he replied, dropping his hand to hers and holding it firmly. "Come on. Let's go on up."

They took the steps slowly, careful not to slip amongst the shards of broken flint and rubble which littered the place, cracked by time and the elements. Last time he had gone this way, Tacit had sprinted up the stones two at a time, urgently reaching for the house and the monstrous sounds coming from within. Now he was returning as a man, changed in every aspect he could think of, bowed but reborn, a lifetime away from what he had been, the monster they had made him.

The ruined house grew on them. Time had not been unkind, and the building, though tilting precariously to its right over the cliff face, appeared mostly intact and weatherproof. Birds had made nests in the eaves and roof. The smell from the place was of dust and dry rot.

Their feet touched the gravel of the approach in front of the house. A sickness was gathering inside Tacit with every step he took towards it, the gnawing pain of fear and trepidation as to what he might find, at what he might discover.

The door to the building hung a little ajar, its top hinge broken clean off so that it leaned, the bottom of it snagged against the floor of the porch. They reached the short line of steps leading up from the gravel to the front porch and Tacit froze as if unable to go on, as if something, some memory, meant he was unable to go any further.

"What is it?" asked Isabella.

But Tacit did not hear her. Instead he was looking at a spot on the porch and reliving the memory, of the man, the knife in his hand and then its blade sinking hilt-deep into his assailant's groin. He closed his eyes against the vision and tried to bring his breathing under some semblance of control.

"Nothing," he said at length, setting his foot on the first step. The stair groaned beneath his weight. "Just ghosts of the past." His mind was a confusion of thought, tormenting and cruel, of when he had been last here, of when he had gone this way before, when he had flown across the gravel and up the wooden steps to protect his family. To stab and shoot and kill. Back then, he'd felt nothing but fear and trepidation. All the years between then and now, after all Tacit had seen and done, and he still felt fear and trepidation. Like a man approaching the gallows.

Had he really changed so little in all that time?

The house was empty, deserted. Dust and the scourge of years covered everything. But, despite the ruin, it seemed as if everything remained untouched as it had been left twenty-nine years ago, the sideboard, the turned-over chairs, the table over which his mother... Tacit snatched his face away from looking at the accursed piece of furniture and stared down the length of the porch and then up into Isabella's face. In that moment he had forgotten she was there and was relieved to see her. The place smelt ancient, old and damp, utterly silent. Even the birds in the roof above had fallen quiet.

"No one home," said Isabella, feeling she had to say something to break the silence.

Tacit couldn't help but stop his eyes from falling to the spot where his father had been killed, a dagger in his back, and where he had gathered up his revolver and killed the last of the Slavs who had attacked his family. The corridor beyond was exactly as he remembered it, leading through into the heart of the house, bedrooms either side. Memories of his childhood rushed back to him, of coming this way a thousand times before, sprinting from the living room to his room and back again, to gather his toys and his belongings for long days playing in the mountains, always running, always hurrying, always laughing. Light feet and a lighter heart. At the door to his old bedroom he paused, gathering the frayed strands of his confidence and pushing the door open. A grimy layer of dust and mould covered everything, his desk, his chair, his bed. The door fought against the years of filth that had covered the floor.

"Reminds me of your accommodation in Arras," said Isabella lightly, "the room where you interrogated the chorister down the barrel of your gun!"

But Tacit looked at her blankly and shook his head. "I'm sorry, Isabella. I don't remember. There's so much that I don't remember. But I remember my parents. Their love, their guidance over me. As if they knew what I was, as if they always feared for me and wished to protect me. Feared what I might become. And what I did become."

He moved towards the bed and dropped to his knees, laying his hand on the cold dusty mottled sheets, holding it there as trying to decipher the years of memories contained in the bed through his fingers.

He drew the covers back, sending a pall of dust into the air, making Isabella cough.

"What are you looking for?" she said, waving away at the clouds in front of her.

"I don't know. I just…"

He said no more, turning to the cupboards in his room and beginning to search through them, everything spoiled with age and damp. There were toys and books inside them, everything a young boy would have loved, and Isabella knew then that Tacit was correct when he said that he had been loved. Cherished.

His hunt fruitless, Tacit looked back at his bed.

"What on earth are you hoping to find?" Isabella asked, as he gripped one corner of the bed and lifted it from where its frame stood. The base came easily away and Tacit heaved it to one side, filling the room with yet more dust and the noise of splintering wood. He stood back and examined the floor beneath it. "Nothing," she said. "There's nothing there. Just bare floorboards."

But Tacit shook his head, refusing to be beaten. He dropped to his knees, shuffling forward, pounding lightly with his hands as he did. The sound changed, growing deeper the further he went.

"Is there… a hidden space under there?"

"Stand back," Tacit warned. Seconds later he raised his foot high and drove his heel back down onto the floor around where the wood sounded most hollow. Two boards cracked and lifted. He raised his boot for a second time and drove it down again, his leg vanishing up to the knee. He lifted it out and dropped down, taking hold of the shattered ends of boards and ripping them clear, working at those either side until he'd made a hole big enough for them to both peer into.

They both stared down. At first there seemed to be only blackness. But as their eyes grew accustomed to the dark they could see that beyond was a shallow cavity in which, adorning the floor and secreted into the walls, was a glittering carpet of religious icons and holy symbols. Though tarnished with time, everything that they could see was dull gold and jew-elled. There were crucifixes, paintings of Christ and of Mary Magdalene, bottles containing long since evaporated liquids, boxes encrusted with the gems and rare metals.

"My family," said Tacit, his voice cracking with emotion and realisa-tion, "they did this for me. They must have feared for me, suspected that

319

something untoward surrounded me, that something wished to possess me. All these icons and symbols, laid out beneath where I slept, always there to protect me, always there, unknown for all my childhood, to keep some darkness away from me."

"But what did they fear?" asked Isabella, who had dropped down next to him and was looking at the treasure with disbelief and wonder.

"That I would become what I *did* become." He looked at Isabella like a man bereft of all hope. "And I knew too, knew what I was at risk of becoming, what I *did* become, what I was. Just like my parents knew, that a wickedness possessed me. Perhaps I've always known? Perhaps that's why you and I came together, not through chance but perhaps someone intended us to meet, as if they knew." And then he exhaled, as if a great weight had been taken from his shoulders. "I love you," he said, and he was smiling and his eyes were wide and dark.

"I know," replied Isabella, her hands flat on the front of his shirt. "Life will no longer be so black, Poldek. Not as dark as Hell. I know how dark it can be, for I have glimpsed into it. I have seen the horrors it contains. For a long time I too heard their voices, was cursed by their malevolence."

"Do you still hear them?" he asked.

She kissed him, taking his head in her hands, and then drew back, looking into his eyes, moving the curl of black from them. And she could see the cold in them had abated, and they were warm and wide. "No," she said. "Do you?"

"Not now," replied Tacit. "Not here. Not since then. Not since Pablo."

"Just like the war, it is over." Isabella kissed him.

"I can never go back to them," he said, between kisses. "Back to the church. Back to the Inquisition."

"I know," replied Isabella.

They looked at each other for a long time, staring into the depths of each others' eyes. If they searched for doubts or falsehoods in them, they found none.

Only the sound from the room beyond, a noise at the front door, broke them apart. Tacit eased himself carefully away from Isabella and stood, pacing towards the corridor and peering into the room from where the sound had come. For a moment he stood and watched, and then he drew the door wide.

"Adansoni," he said to the figure hidden from Isabella behind the door.

"Poldek," replied the aged figure, smiling coldly. "I expected to find you here. Welcome home," he said, with a cruel slit of humour on his face.

ONE HUNDRED AND EIGHT

The Tatra Mountains. Poland.

"Well, aren't you going to invite me inside your house, Poldek?" asked Adansoni, arching one of his bushy greying eyebrows and holding out his arms, like a father to a son.

"It appears that you're already inside," replied Tacit, watching the old man carefully.

Adansoni smiled and moved to the table in the front room, pulling out a chair and sitting on it. He hesitated, a theatrical air about his manner, and looked across the table to the chairs beyond, before turning back to Tacit in a torpid attempt to pretend he only then realised the significance of where he had chosen to sit.

"Goodness!" he exclaimed, holding his liver-spotted hands to his face. "It was here, right here on this table, wasn't it, Poldek? Here that they raped her?" He smiled, running the flat of his calloused hand over the surface of the wood, and then crouched to smell it. He sniffed deep before sitting up and pointing to the chairs, still turned over and broken from the mêlée long ago. "And there, it was there that she died, and that I found you, clinging tight to her cold dead body? I am right, aren't I?" he mocked, chuckling like a fool. Tacit stared back at him darkly. Adansoni clicked with his tongue and chortled a little more, shaking his head. "Goodness me, Poldek, you have come a long way since then, haven't you? Achieved so much, done so much! One wonders if anyone else has ever achieved such a level of wickedness and cruelty in the world as you?"

"I know of someone," growled Tacit, but the old Cardinal ignored him.

"Imagine what your life could have been like if I had never found you, if I had never rescued you from the Tatra Mountains?" He blew through his lips. "Imagine what the world could be like if you'd been left to rot in this place, just like your mother and father were left to rot?" He tilted his head so he looked at Tacit through his brows. "We never buried them, Poldek, your parents. We left them to rot in here, amongst the waste. I suppose the rats enjoyed them although..." He looked around the room for a moment. "Although it looks as if all sign of them has gone? No skeletons, no bones." He pressed his hand to his face, pretending to think. "I suppose perhaps the wolves must have got in and taken them away? But then again, you'd know all about wolves, wouldn't you, Poldek?"

"It's over, Adansoni," said Tacit, his tone and words measured, seemingly unflustered by the old man's taunts, though inside his spirit twisted like a poison. So many times before, Tacit would have heard the voices in him goading, been deafened by their accusations and curses, lashed out condemned and empowered by their taunting power. But now he heard nothing, nothing but his own words and the silence from the mountains. "It's finished. You have failed."

"Failed?" Adansoni laughed lightly and cocked his head from side to side, before walking his fingers up and down the table for a short while. "Perhaps, for now, yes, but nothing ever really ends. They tried before, in 1877. They tried with *you*. They will try again. In ten, twenty, maybe thirty years? You are not unique. You are not alone in the talents you had, or should I say, *could* have had. We are legion. There is no end to our battle, or our determination."

"Perhaps," replied Tacit, "but at least you won't be around to see it."

"Oh? And how so, Poldek?"

"You're an old man. Time is against you!"

"Are you so sure?" And the old man stood, and it seemed as if an energy and a strength crackled out of him. He appeared taller than the bowed figure who had first arrived at the house. And conversely Tacit seemed to shrink back from him, aware that the old man now towered over him, as if their command of the room had been switched. "You were foolish, Poldek," said Adansoni, pushing the table to one side effortlessly and stalking towards him. "You had the opportunity to serve the Lord of Darkness, access the greatest power in this world! Instead, you chose to cast him aside. A foolish choice, for whereas before you were mighty, now you are weak."

Adansoni made a dart for him and Tacit jumped back, barking at Isabella over his shoulder to get away. There was a feeling in the space between them as if invisible waves of magnetism were rippling off the old man, seizing hold of Tacit and drawing him closer. Tacit could feel them, seeming to slow his movements, bog him down deeper with every step he took.

Adansoni raised his hands high above his head and then turned them over so that his palms pointed heavenwards, as if to catch a blessing from the God who had long condemned him and cast him out. He tensed the ends of his fingers and the door to the room behind Tacit slammed shut, locking the Inquisitor in the corridor with his former master.

"Nowhere to run, Poldek," Adansoni muttered, curling a hand into a fist. Like lightning he threw it forward, striking Tacit hard on the side of the head. He rocked into the door and collapsed, his mind spinning, stars circling. It felt as if he'd been struck by a hammer, all senses shattered and broken, utterly disorientated. He felt hands on his collar and the next minute he was being dragged from the ground and thrown back into the door that Adansoni, moments before, had slammed shut with unseen powers. To Tacit it felt like being dashed into a solid brick wall. All the air gushed out of him and he trembled, blood on his face and hair, streaking down his right side where old wounds had opened up from the force of the impact.

"How the tables have turned, eh, Poldek?" smirked Adansoni, picking the Inquisitor up effortlessly and pinning him hard against the wall, a hand tight across his throat. "How you always liked to deal out the punishments, the torture, how you revelled in the power, didn't you? How you liked to be in control? The mastery? And how I watched you with pride, perhaps envy even? You could have had it all, Poldek, and more! Could have embraced who you were, what you were, what you possessed. Together we could have been unstoppable. But, at the end, you were weak, as you've always been. And all of that is now gone." He struck Tacit again, hard across the face, and the Inquisitor felt blood dampen his forehead, drenching his eyebrows and flowing into his eyes. "You were always weak, weak because of your parents, those who thought they could save you, could change you, could bring you up to be good and true and honourable. Pathetic!"

Something grew in Tacit again, a defiance and a rage he had always known, but which had evaporated out of him since his own exorcism by Pablo. He allowed it to expand and burgeon, encouraging it on with memories of the past, losses and loves, deceit and the lies he had been told, festering in his arm and fist, before he lashed out, putting every inch of his power into his blow.

Adansoni knocked the punch harmlessly aside and returned his own into Tacit's midriff. The giant wounded man went down, groaning, the Cardinal dragging him up off the floor before he had an opportunity to rest or gather his breath. There was now a beating on the other side of the door, Isabella striking against it with every ounce of her might, crying out for Tacit. Adansoni smiled and flung Tacit back into the door, sending him splintering through it, knocking Isabella backwards as he tumbled over and on top of her, covered by shattered panels of wood. Groggily Tacit tried to get up, Isabella squirming under him, trying to rise and pull herself clear. Eventually she did, pulling Tacit, senseless, up onto his knees.

Adansoni scowled and whipped with a hand through the broken doorway, catching her under the chin and cracking her backwards. She vaulted over and into the far corner, unmoving.

"Bastard!" roared Tacit, flinging himself at the old Priest, of whom he had so often thought as a father. He caught Adansoni in the armpits and charged with him through the house, crashing him against doors and walls as he ran, carrying him like a battering ram into the main room, throwing him into the table. Adansoni caught himself against the table and twisted, taking hold of Tacit and instead spinning him across it, bowling the giant man into the chairs on the other side, tumbling them away like pins before a bowling ball.

Tacit whimpered and tried to get up, snagged and knotted amongst the chair legs and seats. Adansoni stood over him and his face hardened to crippling anger.

"And so it ends," he cried, before reaching forward to dash the last of the life out of the snagged broken man.

The wolf's howl sounded as if it had been wrenched from the worst tortures of Hell. At once, Adansoni whipped around in horror from where he had been stooped over Tacit, his bloody fists hanging over the Inquisitor's beaten body. The wolf howled again, this time even more loathsome and cruel, monstrous in every sense. The sound was coming from the room beyond the smashed door, the room in which Isabella had been beaten unconscious.

Adansoni rose and stepped back, walking three steps towards it. If he had arrived at the tumbled-down house a cowed old man, now he stood tall and straight, his shoulders broad. Tacit's blood teased down the long lengths of his fingers, collecting in points at his nails and dripping onto the floor.

"Isa… Isabella," he heard Tacit mutter.

Adansoni scowled and crouched down a little, watching the hole in the door.

With the pitiful calling of her name, the wolf howled again, and its shadow fell through the broken pane of the door, moments before the hulking monstrous thing emerged into the corridor. Adansoni crouched lower still, his feet wide, his arms outstretched like a wrestler about to fight. The great wolf's head appeared at the doorway and narrowed its eyes on him. They shimmered black and yellow, and another vengeful howl escaped from its slavering jaws, as it too watched and seethed, its black-taloned claws raking the ground, its eyes mustard in the darkening light of the place, a sickening fury gathering in them.

And then, suddenly, without warning, it leapt, howling and roaring, as it crashed towards the old Cardinal. The great wolf thundered into him and they rolled and tumbled across the room, smashing the table and chairs from their path. The wolf's claws were ripping and slashing at the man beneath it, its jaws snapping and tearing. There was blood in its mouth and on Adansoni, but still he was fighting with a ferocity and venom no earthly man possessed, shuddering the creature with his pummelling fists, a blow to the chin, another to the chest. Bones cracked and shattered, skin ruptured and tore under the severity of the onslaught the Antichrist threw upon the beast.

He got a thumb in one of the wolf's eyes and pressed down hard, making the wolf howl in pain and writhe in Adansoni's grip, trying to pull free. The Antichrist pressed harder, his bloodied torn face breaking into a smile as his thumb slipped deeper and the wolf's attempts to escape became more frantic, claws raking Adansoni, more desperate than ever to spring clear.

Eventually the wolf found purchase against the Antichrist and the ground, and flung itself away, its eye closed and balled with dark blood. Instantly Adansoni was back at the creature, battering left and right, his hands like clubs, spinning the wolf and then throwing himself forward to strangle the creature from behind. And the wolf shrieked and yammered like a mad thing, the air slowly choking out of it, everything spinning and descending into a growing blight of darkness and stars.

Adansoni was laughing now as he throttled the last of the air out of the beast. Though his plans lay in tatters, he could rebuild, return, restore the Darkest Hand, come back again and cast the world into another war, another chance to set himself on his dark throne, find another worthier host for Satan, one who wouldn't fail him, and send the whole world back into an even more terrible conflict.

The wolf slackened in his grasp and, feeling it weaken, he dropped a hand to his belt, drawing out a jagged silver knife, holding it high above his head, its cruel edge glinting against the light. He spat heresies and curses, tightening the muscles all down his arm to drive the long blade into the creature slumping at his feet.

But, at that moment, something snatched his wrist and held his death blow fast. Adansoni turned to see what had grabbed him.

"No," warned Tacit, shaking his head. Adansoni snatched his hand free, pulling it back to pummel Tacit directly in the face, a final killing blow. But as he did so, something snapped down hard from behind him and bit his clenched fist and arm clean off at the elbow. He shrieked and looked down at the bloodied stump, only to see the wolf launch itself once more at him, taking his head and biting it off in a single snap.

Instantly a blistering dark light and heat seemed to come from decapitated man, and the wolf and Tacit fell back, their arms held in front of their eyes, shielding themselves from the intense heat and light which had come into the room. Tacit rolled away, turning onto his side, trying to shield his body from the explosion of power, flames erupting from Adansoni's broken body, their tongues of fire reaching towards Tacit like snapping snake-heads of amber and red.

Adansoni was caught in a firestorm of flame and light, staggering left and right around the room, his hand held up to where his head had been before it had been ripped from his shoulders, the torn burning figure like something dredged from the deepest voids of Hell.

And then he stopped moving, and his hand dropped stock-still to his side, as if the life had been struck out of him. At first Adansoni didn't move, every inch of him burning with a white and blue fire, like a statue of ages past set alight, his clothes burnt off him, now nothing but peeling flesh and vibrant white light. And then, at first slowly, but then faster, his body began to crumble in on itself, as if he was made of sand and great winds were blowing his body into oblivion.

His body slunk back and turned in on itself, his spine suddenly removed, tumbling slowly into his dissolving vanishing body. And Tacit saw that the flames were not from a fire at all but were made up of spirits, of ghostly forms, gathering shrill in the room. And Tacit knew to whom the spirits belonged, because he saw their faces, some he recognised, amongst them his mother and father.

He looked across at the wolf who also watched the final moments of Adansoni and then looked at Tacit, before the old Cardinal fell shuddering and crumbling into dust and nothingness. All that remained were ashes and dust where Cardinal Bishop Adansoni had stood.

Tacit stared back at the spot for a long while, until the flakes of the old Cardinal's obliterated body were tugged by a sudden cool breeze which had crept into the room and carried them away through an open window. Suddenly his mind returned to Isabella and he looked over at her. The creature watched him from a corner, monstrous and huge, its claws matted with blood and ragged torn sheets of Adansoni's clothes, its long jaws glistening crimson with the Cardinal's blood and wounds of its own.

"Isabella!" called Tacit, crawling forward towards the beast, ignoring the pain racking his body. Cramp and agony ran up his side and he staggered onto his knees, exhausted and bowed, fighting with every ounce of strength to force himself back to his feet. "Isabella!" He roared the words, his hands tightening into fists. "Isabella!" He took a pace towards the wolf, the beast watching him behind sly wild yellow eyes.

And then it moved, drawing a taloned hand up to the nape of its neck, wrenching at the tufted fur at the top of its spine. The pelt of hair came away and at once the wolf changed, withering and diminishing, its coarse hair dissipating and vanishing to cream white skin, the coarse long limbs of the beast shrinking and fizzing back to delicate perfection, the snout and razored maw blending back to the beauty that was Isabella. A plunge of red fell about her naked shoulders as she fell onto her knees, panting as if in the throes of early labour.

"Isabella!" cried Tacit, dropping down next to her and bundling her into his arms. They clung to each other, tight in their clutches, listening to each other's breathing.

"Tacit?" he heard her mutter, and Tacit answered, saying he was with her.

"Is it now finally…?"

"Over?" He smoothed her red hair from her face and kissed her forehead. "Yes, it is over now. Thanks to you."

"Not me," Isabella smiled, weakly. "Poré!" She shook the pelt in her weak fingers. "Adansoni?"

"Gone." There were tears in Tacit's eyes, tears of joy, relief and wonder. He shook his head. "Eaten up by the flames of Hell. Devoured by them and snatched back down into their depths."

And she smiled, finding that to do so shot pain across the rear of her scalp and then her body. "And so it really is now over?"

"It's over," replied Tacit.

"I was not afraid," she said to him, and he smiled, knowing why she said it, what she meant, drawing her close and kissing her.

EPILOGUE

A light knock on the door to Lieutenant Colonel John Key's office drew his eyes from the latest communications from the western front to the dark side of the room. Night had fallen and the officer, engrossed as he was with the report in front of him, hadn't even realised it. Blackness was trying to squeeze between the shade over his window, street lamps glowing ghostly in the cobbled lane outside. Night had closed in hard, winter close behind it. Somewhere a whistle blew, reminding Key of an assault he had commanded years ago.

But now laughter followed it, and then a dog's bark.

Interrupted from his studies, he realised then just how cold he was and he stood, announcing, "Come," to whoever it was who had come visiting.

"Captain Saunders," he called cheerily from behind the desk, stepping out from it on seeing the younger officer, shuffling towards the dull tired embers in the fireplace.

"Lieutenant Colonel Key!" Saunders called back, accepting the senior officer's proffered hand on his way to stoke the fire.

"Good to see you, son," said Key, dropping to his knee and thrusting the end of the poker back and forth into the fire.

"And you, sir! Please let me do that for you!"

"Not at all, Captain." He poured on coal and poked at the embers again, standing when a broad amber flame had caught in its belly. "The day I can't kneel down and fix my own fire is the time to call time." He slapped his hands clean and brushed them on his knees. "What brings you to my door, then?"

"Thought you could do with the company?" replied the blond young officer. "Hadn't seen you leave and thought you might be still working. Didn't mean to disturb but thought you might like the company?"

"Damn pleased you did, Saunders!" the senior officer chortled back, waggling a finger. "Going cross-eyed at my desk! A little drink, perhaps? Something to wet your whistle? Keep out the chill?" He was at the drinks' cabinet with a decanter of whisky in his hand the instant the younger man had accepted the offer, pouring two decent measures into the thick-cut glasses and offering one to the Captain.

"How's the peace holding on the front, sir?" asked Saunders, toasting his senior officer lightly and sipping cautiously at the fiery liquor.

"It's holding," replied Key, stepping back to his desk and dropping into his chair, picking back through the report absently. "Looks like we've all had enough of the fighting."

"Shame, in many ways," suggested the young man.

"In what way, Captain?"

"In that we had old Hun on the run. Another three months we'd have chased him all the way back to Berlin's walls."

Key considered the notion. "I wouldn't worry too much, Saunders. We have the victory."

"We have an armistice, sir," corrected Saunders, "if you'll pardon me, sir. We haven't won the war."

The Lieutenant Colonel chuckled, the way an uncle might at a nephew who had pleased him. "Ah, the enthusiasm of youth," he smiled. "Don't worry, Captain, we've given the Hun a good bloody nose, and taught him a lesson he won't forget in a while." He looked up and studied his visitor closely, suspecting there might be more to the visit. "Is there something I should be aware of, something up with the men?"

"No! No, not at all. It's only that I think most of them would have liked to have finished the job, sir, but…"

"It was out of the question, what with the armistice and this bloody Spanish flu doing the rounds."

"Problems?"

"No end of them. Nasty business. Claiming a lot of men. Mainly men of fighting age too, by the looks of things. Who would have thought it? I don't mind telling you, Captain, but it's a right bloody mess, the whole shebang. Has had a big effect on recruitment. We can't recruit men quick enough to replace those dropping dead with it."

"Bad business, sir."

"As bad as it gets. All across America, Europe, Africa, the Middle East. Great swathes of Russia. India's had it terrible." He shook his head and

330

took another sip of his whisky. "Of course, there's always some scallywag saying it's a blessing, something to have halted the killing, the war. Suppose that's one way of looking at it."

"Not sure the men would agree with you there, sir," smiled Saunders gently, passing the brown notepad he'd brought with him between his hands. It was only then that the Lieutenant Colonel spotted it.

"What have you got there then, Saunders? Something you've brought for me?"

"I'm not sure exactly what it is, sir," replied the young officer, "so yes, I thought you might like to take a look." He handed it over the desk to the Lieutenant Colonel. It was a tall hazel-coloured book, an army diary. Key read the unit's name on its front.

"Crikey, haven't seen one of these diaries in a while. The British Expeditionary Force, eh?" He opened the front cover and leafed casually through the pages, stopping a short way in and turning back to the beginning, before flicking more quickly through the book and finding that most pages were empty. "What's this then, Captain?" he asked, turning it over to look at the unit name on the front. "An early volume? Unfinished?"

Captain Saunders cleared his throat. "It's the unit diary from the company who took Fampoux in 1914."

"1914, eh? Seems like a lifetime ago in this bloody war, doesn't it?" He shook his head and looked up. "Hang on, did you say Fampoux? 1914?"

"Yes sir. It's the unit which went missing, sir. Close to Arras. We believed they'd been lost when the town was overrun. The diary gone with them too. But..." He cleared his throat again and nodded towards the brown book in his commanding officer's hand. "Well, if you read that, towards the end of it, sir, you'll find it casts some light on maybe just what happened to them."

"Who was the unit's diarist?" he asked.

"Lieutenant Henry Frost, sir," replied the Captain. "Vanished with the rest of the unit in the village. Bloody shame, by all accounts. A good officer. Good soldier too. It was believed he was lost with the rest of the men when the Germans attacked."

"But you don't think that any more?" asked Key.

"Not any more. Not according to that."

Saunders fell silent and watched as Key read, the lines on the Lieutenant Colonel's forehead deepening with every revelation contained in the words.

"What's all this about then, Captain? Werewolves?! What's all this fancy? It reads like a Penny Dreadful. Occult nonsense? Clearly the ramblings of a man who had lost his mind?"

"Not at all, sir. Not according to those who knew him, reports of his service history. He was highly thought of, as an officer and a man by all accounts, both by his men and by high command. 2nd Durham Light Infantry. A good soldier. A good officer. A good man. Not the sort easily given over to the offences of the mind."

"But this," scoffed the Lieutenant Colonel, throwing the diary down on his desk, "this is all make-believe!"

"Are you a Godly man, Lieutenant Colonel Key?" asked Saunders.

"What the devil is that supposed to mean, Captain? Of course I am!"

"Catholic myself, for my sins," replied Saunders. "I showed the diary to my parish priest."

"And what did he say?"

"He told me to throw the book away. To say he was horrified in what I had in my possession would be an understatement. Which is why I thought I should bring it to you." He cleared his throat. "It seems that Frost was well versed with the most revealing of facts, all about men being turned into murderous killing machines, an army of monsters."

"I see," said Key, arching an eyebrow, a light in his eye, "monsters we are lest monster we become, eh, Saunders?"

"Something like that, sir. The findings could prove most… enlightening."

The senior officer nodded, setting his hand upon the diary as if realising the treasure it might prove to be.

"Thank you, Captain." He coughed to clear his throat, letting the heat out of his face and manner. "Well done for bringing it to my attention."

"Not at all." He drained the remains of his drink. "And now, if there's nothing else, I will bid you goodnight, sir."

"Yes, goodnight," replied the Lieutenant Colonel, climbing to his feet to see the young officer out. He watched Saunders leave, shutting the door behind him, and crossed to the window, looking down on the gaslit street. He chuckled.

'The fancies of the young!' he thought. 'An army of monsters? Whatever next?' He heard his door open.

"What is it this time, Captain?" he asked, turning to see. "Something you've forgotten?"

Key's cry sounded like an apology before it was struck from his throat and he went down in a torrent of his own blood, his neck broken roughly open. The figure stepped back, stowing the dripping dagger and lifting the diary from the table. It flicked its way briefly through the pages, reacquainting itself with an old treasured manuscript, before stowing it in the depths of its robe and vanishing back into the shadows.

ACKNOWLEDGEMENTS

Thank you to my parents John and Janet Richardson, my grandfather Fred Clarkson and his wife Denise, my sister Vicky and niece Georgia, my mother-in-law Brigid, and sister-in-law Katie. Special thanks to my brother-in-law Maurice East who has accompanied me on this journey almost every day, entertaining and guiding me in equal measure with plotline suggestions and considerations.

A big thank you to all who have encouraged me throughout; everyone in Farley, particularly Carl Groth, Tom Davies, Robin Pitkin and Neil Barnes, the Salisbury Writing Circle, Tom Bromley, Russell Mardell, Dave Key, Leigh Barnard, Peter Liney, Cal Moriarty, Gary 'John' Hart, Dereck Burgess, James Fry, Rebecca Clifton, graphic artist Warwick Fraser-Coombe, Solman Farsi, Carol Hayes, Jamie Gilman and Martin Ollivere at Our Own Thing, Jon Phillips at Muen and Paul Clifton at Paul Clifton Photography, and my proof-readers who gave me the belief and determination to keep going; Paul Malone, Joanna Pitkin-Parsons, Rob Swan and Maurice East. Thank you to fellow Duckworth housemate Ed Davey for good humour and wisdom along the way. And thank you to all my friends, family and fans of my writing, near and far, who have encouraged and appreciated what I've tried to produce with The Darkest Hand trilogy. Your kind words have meant a lot.

Ben Clark at LAW deserves a huge amount of credit for helping me reach the end with our combined sanity just about in one piece. I apologise profusely for all the rewrites I put you through, Ben!

Thank you to my editor at Duckworth, Gesche Ipsen, for picking up the baton so admirably and bringing Tacit home. Both he and I appreciate all your efforts very much. Also, thanks to my publisher in the US, Overlook Press, particularly Chelsea Cutchens and Lauren Roberts.

Last, but most certainly not least, heartfelt thanks and love to Linnie, Sam and Will, who have sacrificed and given much in order for me to achieve my dream. I will always appreciate it, and you, very much.

NOTES

World War One was responsible for the deaths of 10,000,000 soldiers and 7,000,000 civilians and achieved no tangible benefits to mankind other than in the science of medicine. It resulted in the annihilation of an entire generation of young men, bankrupted nations, broke up countries, reshaped the contours of European countries, began the slow and ever steady decline in western religion and laid the foundations of resentment, distrust and hatred that eventually dragged the world into a second world war.

Out of the arrogant and warped ambitions of one arm of the same royal family, Kaiser Wilhelm II of Germany, George V of Great Britain and Czar Nicholas II of Russia, all grandsons of Queen Victoria, all of whom controlled vast swathes of the world, all of whom eyed each cousin with growing suspicion and jealousy, all of whom, through industrialisation and mass production, were delivered the most monstrous killing machines ever known to man and the yearning desire to test them and their might against their kin, utter carnage was wrought, a first world war, the largest and most terrible of conflicts in the history of mankind. A vision of Hell.

And yet, in the end, it was the smallest of terrors, a flu virus, which eventually conspired to bring the conflict to a close, as if a divine blight had been sent by a higher power, to subdue and eventually stop the fighting on all fronts. Whatever the chaotic flawed ambitions of the old rulers of Europe, it was influenza which eventually checked them, and from the flames of revolution from people persecuted by their leaders' greed, countries, empires and old allegiances broke up. The old world order was demolished. From it a new one grew.

National Geographic, Stanford University and A+E History Network, with their theories and extensive studies on the origination and spread of Spanish flu, have all proved invaluable in the planning and writing of this novel. And as ever, H.P. Willmott's *World War I*, Peter Englund's mesmerising *The Beauty and the Sorrow*, David Stevenson's *1914–1918* and Peter Hart's *The Great War* were never far from my reach.